Book 9

In Plain Sight

Shawn Lamb

Allon Books

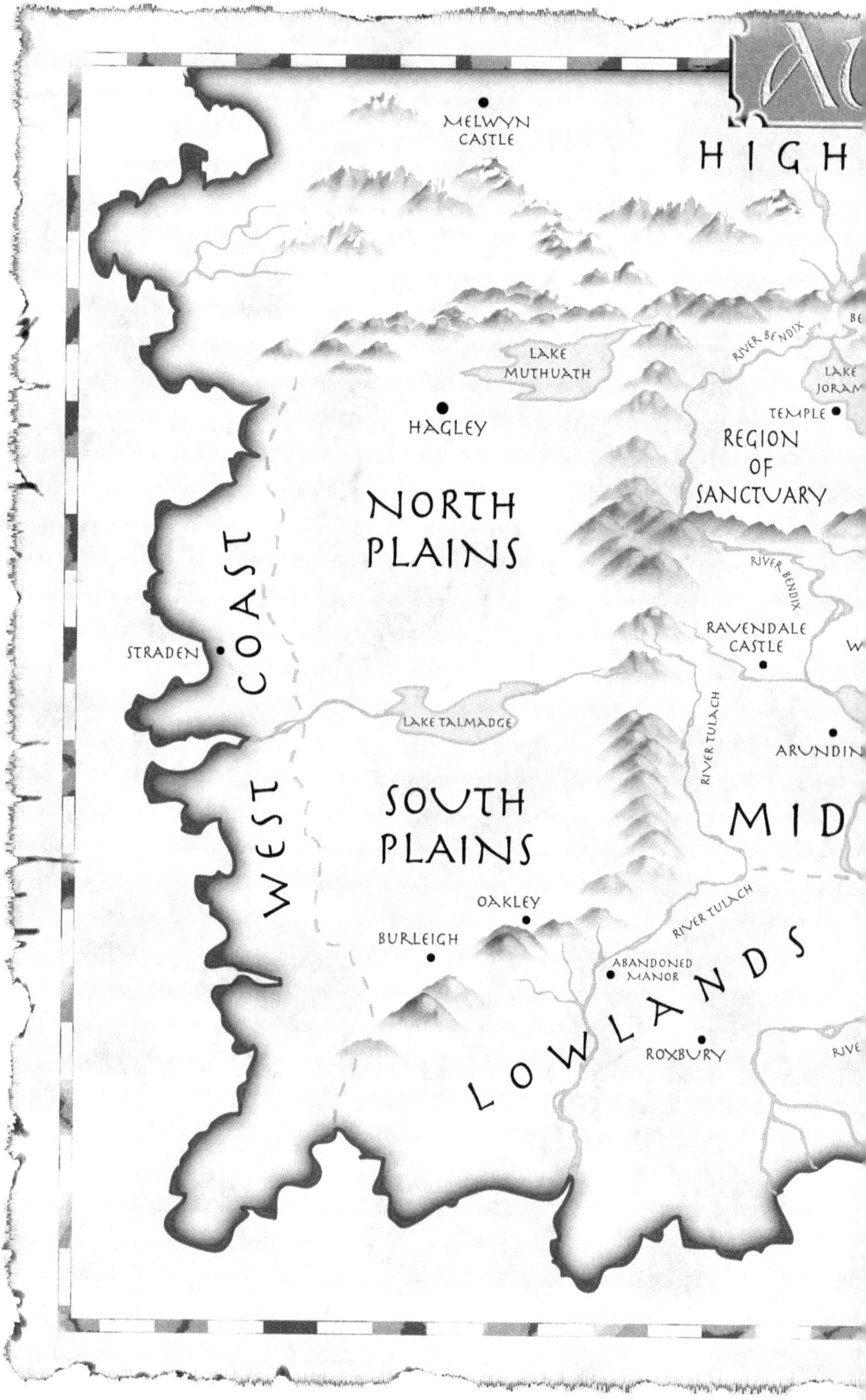
HIGH
MELWYN CASTLE
LAKE MUTHUATH
HAGLEY
RIVER BENDIX
TEMPLE
REGION OF SANCTUARY
NORTH PLAINS
RIVER BENDIX
RAVENDALE CASTLE
STRADEN
WEST COAST
LAKE TALMADGE
RIVER TULACH
SOUTH PLAINS
MID
OAKLEY
BURLEIGH
RIVER TULACH
ABANDONED MANOR
LOWLANDS
ROXBURY

ALLON ~ BOOK 9 ~ IN PLAIN SIGHT by Shawn Lamb
Published by Allon Books
209 Hickory Way Court
Antioch, Tennessee 37013
www.allonbooks.com

Cover design by Robert Lamb

International Standard Book Number: 978-0-9891029-5-7

Other Books by Shawn Lamb

Young Adult Fantasy Fiction
ALLON ~ BOOK 1
Published by Creation House, a division of Charisma Media

Published by Allon Books

ALLON ~ BOOK 2 ~ INSURRECTION
ALLON ~ BOOK 3 ~ HEIR APPARENT
ALLON ~ BOOK 4 ~ A QUESTION OF SOVEREIGNTY
ALLON ~ BOOK 5 ~ GAUNTLET
ALLON ~ BOOK 6 ~ DILEMMA
ALLON ~ BOOK 7 ~ DANGEROUS DECEPTION
ALLON ~ BOOK 8 ~ DIVIDED
PARENT STUDY GUIDE FOR ALLON ~ BOOKS 1-4
THE ACTIVITY BOOK OF ALLON

For Young Readers – ages 8-10
Allon ~ The King's Children series
NECIE AND THE APPLES
TRISTINE'S DORGIRITH ADVENTURE
NIGEL'S BROKEN PROMISE

Historical Fiction
GLENCOE
THE HUGUENOT SWORD

The Royal Family

King Tyrone
Queen Tristine
Prince Nigel, Tristine's brother, the King's Champion
Princess Mirit, wife of Prince Nigel, the Queen's Champion
Princess Necie, Tristine's younger sister, wife of Lord Angus
Prince Titus, son of Tyrone and Tristine – age 18
Prince Fraser, son of Tyrone and Tristine – age 16
Prince Eli, son of Tyrone and Tristine – age 14

Others

Sir Chad of the North Plains
Lady Valery
Count Ellis of the Meadowlands
Angus, Duke of Allon

South Plains

Count Wess
Doctor Lester
Vivian – Lester's sister
Donovan – Lester's youngest son
Squire Morley
Preston – Morley's oldest son
Reilly – Morley's youngest son
Deputy March
Sheriff Spaulding

GUARDIANS

Captain Kell – Commander of the Guardians of Jor'el
Armus – Guardian of Allon
Avatar, Commander of the Elite Jor'ellian Guards
Vidar, an archer
Virgil, a warrior
Egan, Overseer of Prince Titus
Kendrick, Overseer of Prince Fraser
Ridge, a ranger, Trio Leader of the South Plains
Wren

IMMORTALS

Locan
Fitch, a shape-shifter

Chapter 1

THE EARLY SPRING SUN GLISTENED OFF THE COOL MORNING MIST rising from the ground in the Southern Forest. Kell and his fellow Guardians: Armus, Avatar, Wren, Vidar, Egan, Skylar and Kendrick stood nearby watching the mortals partake of breakfast before returning to Waldron. The first hunt of the season had been successful. Vidar and Wren were archers, the rest warriors. Egan, Kendrick and Skylar served as overseers of the royal princes. Egan watched over Titus; Kendrick for Fraser and Skylar for Eli. All members of the royal family had Overseers during the early years of their lives. Armus performed the duty as Overseer to Tristine before becoming Guardian advisor to Tyrone and her after their coronation as king and queen. Avatar looked out for Nigel. Now, as Commander of the Elite Jor'ellian Guards, he and Nigel served together in defense of the kingdom

Upon King Ellis' death, Kell was released from his earthly duty as Guardian advisor to the king and recalled to the heavenlies. Only under dire circumstances did he return. Such a situation happened last fall when civil war erupted, making his participation paramount in keeping the country from being destroyed.

Before Kell's arrival, the Council of Twelve became divided. Some supported Ellan, who was once crowned queen after an unsuccessful coup against her father King Ellis years earlier. Others remained loyal to King Tyrone and Queen Tristine. The ensuing battle caused the most destruction and bloodshed on Allonian soil Kell witnessed since the Great Battle, when Dagar led a revolt of Guardians and mortals against Jor'el. Even after more than two thousand years, the machinations of mortals never ceased to amaze and disturb him.

True, Ellan was second born compared to Tristine being third in line. However, Ellan's hatred made her join forces with Hueil in a second attempt to seize the throne. An Original in the Guardian hierarchy, Hueil acted as scribe and liaison between Jor'el and the mortal priests. Kell believed Hueil vanquished during the Great Battle, only to be discovered centuries later posing as the supreme god of Tunlund. Tyrone defeated the clever scribe, which resulted in Hueil's capture. Kell hoped imprisonment in the nether dimension would keep Hueil bound forever. Escape was something he never anticipated, while the speed at which Hueil and Ellan moved against Tyrone and Tristine caught everyone off guard.

Kell's gaze lingered on Tyrone, who ruled Allon for the past eleven years. Tyrone proposed the hunt in an effort to relax and refocus from the aftermath of war. His unusual height of six feet eight inches by standard measure and light grey eyes were bold statements of the Guardian half of his heritage. His mortal side kept him from reaching the average Guardian height of seven feet tall. It also dulled the heavenly gleam in his unique colored eyes. This gleam is what gave the Guardian eyes their brightness and keen perception. However, Tyrone possessed uncanny insight for a mortal.

Tyrone's three sons, Titus, Fraser, and Eli, ranged in age of eighteen, sixteen and fourteen from oldest to youngest. The strong family resemblance proved boldly evident. Titus favored Tyrone in feature, only with dark brown hair and mortal color blue eyes compared to Tyrone's black hair and grey eyes. Being the eldest, Titus was also the tallest of the brothers at six feet-four inches, still four inches shorter than their father. Fraser and Eli both had shades of brown hair and brown eyes. As the youngest, Eli stood only at six feet. Nigel, Chad, Angus and Ellis joined them on the hunt.

Kell met the now twenty-seven-year-old Chad when the mortal was a lad of eight years old, and began serving as Nigel's squire. Chad worked his way through the ranks of the Jor'ellians to being knighted and given his position as lord of the North Plains. Nineteen-year-old Ellis was Titus' best friend and soon-to-be brother-in-law. He bore no relation to the late king, after whom he was named. He even looked different having brown hair and blue eyes. As a reward for saving the life of Tyrone's youngest daughter, bravery in battle and unwavering loyalty and friendship to Titus, Ellis earned the title of count and lordship of the Meadowlands. He newly married Lady Valery, a royal ward.

At hearing Nigel speak, Kell's attention turned to the former heir. Nigel's life took several dramatic turns. At sixteen he survived an assassination attempt by a Guardian traitor named Morrell. At the time, his survival was unknown. Not until five years later did Kell and Armus discover a crippled beggar wandering Allon in fear and shame. Nigel became healed when Jor'el granted a request from Avatar to rectify the evil injury done by a fellow Guardian. Yet instead of reclaiming his birthright, Nigel yielded to Tyrone, as the Great King foretold in Prophecy. Nigel acted with a grace and fortitude Kell found refreshing from a mortal.

Alas, Ellan's second coup forced Nigel do what he didn't years earlier: accept the crown when Tyrone abdicated in favor of him as the rightful heir. They hoped Ellan would yield to her older brother. She did not. Bent on revenge, she and Hueil gathered their forces and met Nigel and his army. The total combatants on both sides numbered over two hundred thousand.

Although the battle lasted a single day, it ended in tragedy and grief. Among the Council members supporting Ellan, two died in battle, two executed for treason, and one exiled. One member killed in battle, Lord

Bosley, and the one exile, Count Erasmus, showed their true support for the royal family by secretly sabotaging the artillery to lessen the effect of Ellan and Hueil's attack. On the verge of a second defeat, Hueil killed Ellan before being vanquished by Avatar.

After the victory, Nigel yielded the crown back to Tyrone. With vacancies on the Council filled, everyone set about restoring order to Allon. Thus it surprised Kell to remain in the physical realm after his assignment. True, the cornerstone for the rebuilding of Jor'el's Palace would be laid next month during the celebration week of Prince Titus' wedding to Lady Jillian. With Guardian help, the actual construction would take about a decade. Mortals could not complete such a massive and glorious structure in so short a time. He anticipated helping with the transition of power from the mortals back to Guardian rule after the Palace was complete. Yet his was not to question, rather do as Jor'el commanded, which for the time being, was to remain in physical form.

Hearty laughter came from Angus. At age thirty-five, he filled out in size with broad shoulders and chest. If not for sporting a beard he would appear younger than his years. Angus and Tyrone were in high humor this morning, with Ellis serving as their primary objective for jocularity.

"I suppose Valery will be happy when you return," said Tyrone with a teasing wink at the young lord.

Ellis blushed and took a drink of cider.

"I'm surprised the newlywed could tear himself away after only six weeks. Necie and I didn't leave Garwood for almost three months," said Angus.

"And now have six children," continued Tyrone in merry wit.

Being married men, Chad, Angus and Nigel laughed. Titus, Eli and Fraser snickered. Ellis' embarrassed flush deepened in color and he took another drink. Titus poked him in a humorous gesture, causing Ellis to spill some cider.

"Now look what you did. This hunting suit was a wedding gift from Valery."

"Somehow I don't think she'll notice," said Angus, laughing.

"Valery thought my coming would be a good idea," said Ellis in an attempt to banter back.

"Probably so she could get some rest," said Tyrone.

Nigel had difficulty containing his laughter and tried to wave Tyrone and Angus off. "Enough! The poor lad is ill equipped to handle you both."

Tyrone stood and handed his cup to Armus. He clapped Ellis on the shoulder to guide him to his feet. "Ellis knows we jest."

"Indeed, Sire. It is part of my lot in life to be sport for royals." He rolled his eyes at Titus.

Tyrone laughed. "You learn fast. But we only tease those we care about."

"I know. After recent events, I happily and willingly accept any and all sport than even entertain the thought of falling under royal wrath."

"I can't image anything from you to cause that." At Tyrone's statement, he noticed Nigel's pricked gaze shift to Angus, so he reverted back to teasing Ellis. "Now, the quicker we leave, the quicker you can get back your bride. She should be well rested by now."

Angus laughed. "Face it, you can't win," he said to Ellis while passing the young man to head for the horses.

Tyrone stopped Nigel from mounting his horse to speak privately. "Do you think of Erasmus or Bosley?"

"Both. I couldn't imagine them doing anything to incur *royal wrath*, but they did."

"Bosley saved your life and Erasmus is content in exile." Nigel didn't reply, so Tyrone continued. "This trip has succeeded in alleviating the tension. Don't negate it. Neither Bosley nor Erasmus wouldn't want that."

"Or Mirit," said Angus. He joined them unnoticed. He led his horse while Titus, Ellis, Fraser and Eli stood a few paces behind him. All held the reins to their horses.

Nigel flashed a grin of warning at Angus. "Don't start with me by using my wife. I'm more adept than the boy, and well armed with personal ammunition."

"All duds." Angus widely smiled and mounted.

For Nigel's sake, Titus stifled his great amusement yet explained the joke to a perplexed Ellis. "He and Mirit have no children."

Tyrone raised his arms in mock surrender and backed away when Nigel's irate glare found him.

At the exchange among the mortals, Kell shook his head in disapproval. Avatar and Armus tried very hard not to laugh out loud at Nigel's thwarting.

When all were ready for departure, the Guardians took the lead with Wren and Vidar a few paces in front of Kell, Armus and Avatar. Tyrone and the others followed the lead Guardians. Servants manning the wagon came next, followed by the soldiers then Egan, Skylar and Kendrick in the rear.

"I think everyone would appreciate the most direct route home, Wren," quipped Avatar.

"You think I would lead them astray?" she bantered in return.

"Isn't that what females do?"

To continue the exchange, she turned about to face him, yet kept walking backwards. "Mortal females maybe. Isn't that right, Armus? After all, didn't Tristine lead you on some merry chases?"

Armus joined in the humor. "One chase led straight to Tyrone."

"And you haven't had a moment's peace since they married."

"No, I haven't moment's peace since she was born. Nor you with Nigel," he added at hearing Avatar laugh.

"He's calmed down since marrying Mirit."

"Right. If you say so." Armus smiled and winked at Wren.

"Love will do that to you," said Avatar.

"Or send you in circles. Like it did Kell," said Wren. She turned forward and did not seeing the captain's annoyed reaction.

"What?" demanded Kell, only to be ignored when Avatar continued in humor.

"Vidar also."

This time Vidar turned around and continued to walk backwards to speak to Kell. "They mean Shannan."

"I know! I wasn't in love with Shannan."

Armus laughed, much to Kell's chagrin. "Parental love, and don't deny it. Vidar doesn't. I admit the same for Tristine, Mahon for Necie, and Avatar for Nigel."

"*Err,*" began Avatar in sarcastic dispute. "With Nigel I couldn't decide whether to rebuke him like a son or throttle him like a pesky little brother."

"That's beside the point. A Guardian Overseer can't help but feel some emotional connection with their charge."

Kell scowled at the exchange. "In our position we're supposed to be above such feelings and maintain a calm objective view to better serve the mortals."

Armus looked askew at Kell. "Oh, really? You've been able to do that?"

"As captain, it is my duty."

"You fooled me, especially when Shannan was in danger. I thought you'd take on Dagar and his forces single-handed."

"Or when you ordered me to destroy Morrell for killing her," added Vidar.

"You both sound as bad as the mortals," chided Kell.

"Kell, despite our station and duty, we can't deny there are times we are affected by our feelings," said Avatar.

"I'm not denying them. I just control them better when they flare up."

Wren snorted a loud contrary laugh, which made Vidar turn and whisper a private word of warning. She wasn't private in her response. "I thought we moved beyond such male arrogance after what happened with the Sorens. Next he'll say all females are emotional."

"If he does, will you shoot him?" quipped Avatar.

Exasperated, Kell rebuked them. "This isn't about arrogance or denial, it's about duty and controlling one's emotions and not acting fickle like mortals."

"Any louder and they will hear you." Armus made a discrete nod back toward Tyrone and the others. "Then try explaining your *unfeeling* reasoning to them."

All conversation stopped when Vidar and Wren whipped out their crossbows, alert and ready. Kell moved beside Vidar. Armus and Avatar flanked Wren, reaching to draw their swords.

"Danger. About two miles north by northwest," said Vidar.

"Animal or being?" asked Kell.

Bright copper eyes narrowed as Vidar stared in the direction he indicated. "Hard to tell precisely at this distance."

Kell tapped Vidar's shoulder. "Take the lead. Armus with me. Wren, Avatar, stay with the king."

"Where are they going?" Avatar heard Tyrone call, so he dropped back to speak to the king.

On foot, the Guardians covered distances faster than any horse. Vidar slowed their pace after a mile. He stopped behind several trees on the edge of a large meadow and motioned for Kell and Armus to halt. The warriors heeded, yet remained primed for action, hands on their swords.

"Animal," he whispered.

"Do you see it? I don't," said Armus, also keeping his voice low.

"No, but the presence is very strong."

"I'm assuming it's unnatural," said Kell.

"Ay, and dangerous." Vidar checked his crossbow so Kell and Armus drew they swords. Using a hand signal, Vidar sent them to either flank then continued on a direct course into the meadow.

Deliberate and cautious, Kell moved through the trees while keeping Vidar in sight. The archer maintained a parallel course close to the trees rimming the meadow. Kell couldn't see Armus on the far side of the meadow, but knew Armus mirrored his movement. Being an animal of unnatural origin, Vidar would deal with it while he and Armus helped to corral it and serve as back up if needed.

The eerie yet familiar howling sounded as if they were surrounded.

"Madah-dune!" shouted Kell in angry warning.

He heard the firing of a crossbow come from the meadow. Four madah-dune charged Vidar. The creatures stood nine feet tall on two legs with the body of a man completely covered in fur. Their heads were wolves with snarling, drooling fangs, and large hands with sharp claws. They wielded large spiked clubs.

Kell just reached the edge of the trees in his rush to help Vidar when a spiked club sliced across the back of his shoulder, tearing his uniform and cutting deep into flesh. He went sprawling to the ground in pain. He couldn't stay down at hearing snarling and growling. He scrambled to his knees in anticipation of another attack and managed to use his sword to block the club aimed at his head. The force of the blow knocked his sword away. He dove under the club to avoid being struck. Ignoring the pain of injury, he rolled away from another third attack only to end up smacking his wounded back against a tree.

A massive claw seized him by the collar and lifted him off feet. He came face-to-face with a salivating creature. Kell pulled his dagger from its sheath and thrust it into the creature. In reaction to being wounded, it slammed him into the tree, causing intense pain from his wound. A second slamming into the tree knocked the wind from him, and he struck the back of his head. Dazed and unable to catch his breath, he dangled at the creature's mercy. Holding Kell in both arms, it lifted him over its head and slammed him to the ground, where Kell smashed the right side of his head against a fallen log. He lay unconscious and unmoving.

The creature jerked the dagger from its body and raised the blade to strike down at Kell. A rising war cry caught its attention just before Armus' sword plunged through it from behind and out the chest, killing it. Satisfied at seeing beast was dead, Armus turned toward Kell, determined to learn the extent of injury. To his utter shock and horror, Kell vanished in grey light.

"No!" he exclaimed. He stepped forward and stopped when he felt something under his foot. Moving it revealed Kell's sword. Not far from the sword lay Kell's medallion.

Stunned to in the core, Armus clumsily reached down to pick them up. He stumbled to his knees and used his hand to catch himself and regain his balance. Befuddled, he stared at the medallion and sword trying to comprehend that his captain and friend of over two thousand years was vanquished. He snatched up the medallion and let out a tremendous cry of grief.

Vidar rushed over. He came to an abrupt halt at seeing Armus held Kell's medallion and the sword lay on the ground. He winced at realizing the reason for Armus' anguish. "Oh, no," he murmured.

"Vidar! What happened?" called Tyrone. He and the others arrived. Avatar and Wren were in the lead with Egan, Kendrick and Skylar behind the mortals.

Vidar's position blocked their view of Armus, who remained on his knees. The archer forced a reply. "I fear the unthinkable, Sire." Vidar's woeful, sympathetic gaze shifted to Avatar, making the warrior speak in guarded anticipation.

"You mean the return of the madah-dune? We saw two dead ones back there."

"No, much worse." Vidar's grip on Armus' shoulder made the warrior stand. Armus now held Kell's sword and medallion. His features were grief-stricken in turning and meeting Avatar's gaze.

Avatar clenched his fists to contain his emotions, as every muscle and sinew went rigid and his face grew pale with distress.

Shocked, Wren appeared on the verge of swooning. Egan, Kendrick and Skylar watched in speechless disbelief.

"Kell?" Nigel could barely speak.

Vidar nodded. "Eight creatures laid an ambush. All are dead."

Armus snarled, and lethal chestnut eyes stared at the offending creature he slew in an attempt to aid Kell.

"What do we do without Kell?" asked Titus.

In sober uncertainty, Tyrone shook his head. "I don't know."

"I must speak to Jor'el." Armus' voice contained no emotion. Without waiting for a reply, he moved a short distance from the group and vanished in the white light of dimension travel.

"Shouldn't you go with him?" Egan asked Vidar.

"I don't know if he can tolerate any company. Maybe Avatar."

"No, this is devastating news," began Tyrone. "Until all is settled, I want Vidar to deal with the Trio Leaders and Avatar to place the Jor'ellians on alert."

Avatar didn't react or reply to either Vidar or Tyrone. His silver eyes narrowed in regard of the dead creature. His knuckles turned white from the vise grip and veins showed on his forehead and neck from the effort to contain his emotions.

"I'll take care of the Jor'ellians, Sire. Avatar should remain for when Armus returns," said Chad.

"Very well."

Chad turned his horse and galloped off.

"Should I go with him, Uncle?" Fraser asked Nigel.

"No. We must be present when your mother and aunts learn of this."

"To Waldron at all speed." Tyrone nodded to Wren. She took several deep breaths to gather her emotions and wipe the tears from her eyes before taking the lead.

Rather than follow the others, Nigel moved his horse beside Avatar. He touched the Guardian's shoulder to get his marked attention from the creature. Avatar barely looked at him, but it didn't take much to see the deep anger and hurt in the silver eyes. "Words are not sufficient to express my sorrow. We are going to need you and Armus like never before."

Without responding, Avatar turned from the creature and they left.

18

Four days later, the group returned to Waldron. The enormous splendor and strength of the castle dominated the plain surrounded by forest and gently rolling countryside. A manicured driveway led to an elaborate oak and wrought iron gate flanked by two impressive gatehouses. From the gatehouses stretched fifteen-foot high walls, ending in massive square corner turrets at each intersection. Past the main gate lay the Grand Courtyard of white marble cobblestone with a cascading fountain in the center. The family's private quarters were located in the back building across from the gallery way.

They gathered in the family salon. So stunned by the news, Tristine couldn't cry or utter a word. She knew Kell all her life; from his service as the King's Champion and royal advisor to her father until this latest hunt. Although he never gave up his position as Jor'el's Captain, to her and the others, he became a dear family friend. Feeling weak-kneed, she sat and looked at the floor in an effort to comprehend the devastating news. Eli tried to offer support and sympathy, but she ignored him.

On the sofa, Angus held a weeping Necie. As the youngest, she was the more sensitive and tender-hearted of the siblings.

Mirit regarded Nigel in utter disbelief. She mirrored her husband in service as the Queen's Champion, thus wore clothes befitting her station, a cross between the feminine and masculine.

"Kell?" she repeated her question, and again he solemnly nodded. "It's almost inconceivable such a thing could happen to Jor'el's captain."

"But it has."

Tears swelled as reality sunk in. "Who will take his place?"

"We won't know until Armus returns."

"Armus," said Tristine, fearful and distraught.

"He is whole and unharmed, Mother," said Eli.

A flash of white light appeared in the room, placing everyone on edge. The Guardians stiffened, ready for defensive action. From the fading light, Armus appeared. Tristine rushed to him and started sobbing. For a moment no one spoke, all knowing their special bond.

He held her and let her cry for several moments before speaking in an attempt to sound encouraging. "This is a difficult time, but we will get through it."

"Really?" She searched his face for reassurance and only found pain.

"We've done so in the past, we will do so now."

"You don't sound confident."

A small plaintive smile appeared. "I trust in Jor'el that we will."

"Speaking of, what did he say?" asked Tyrone.

Armus took a deep steady breath and answered. "There is a reason, though he wouldn't elaborate."

"Will you become captain now?" asked Mahon, a blond and boyishly good-looking Guardian warrior.

Tristine gripped Armus' hand in anticipation of his answer. He gave her reassuring smile and replied, "No, I'm still second-in-command and will remain royal advisor. Until further notice we are without a captain."

"Those don't sound like satisfactory answers," said Nigel.

"It was all I could get. Inquire any more and I will trespass upon the Almighty's patience."

"As if you didn't press him for an answer about Kell's demise," groused Avatar, low enough he thought not to be heard. He received a warning jab from Wren and she motioned to Armus. Her action and Armus' stern glare made him nod in regret and apologize. "Sorry."

"I think we are all a bit touchy right now," said Tyrone.

"Ay. However," began Nigel in cautious warning, "there is more here than Kell's death. Those creatures didn't lay a trap by themselves."

"The Dark Way, of course!" snapped Tristine, her emotions raw. "Nothing else could kill Kell."

"Steady, little one," said Armus, using his personal endearment for her since birth.

She shook her head in befuddlement. "I thought those creatures were killed months ago along with Hueil and his forces."

Avatar flashed a cautious side-glance to Armus before speaking. "Not all, Majesty. We believe Locan and Fitch survived."

The statement riled Tyrone. "Why wasn't I told this, Commander?"

The question and Tyrone invoking his rank caught Avatar by surprise. "I thought Kell told you, Sire. He informed the Trio Leaders to be on the alert for signs of them. Ridge was promoted to Trio Leader of the South Plains because of his familiarity with Fitch and Locan."

Armus took up the explanation. "Kell didn't want to cause the royal family any more upset than was necessary. Since the battle, there were no indications of the Dark Way. He would have said so otherwise."

"No sign until now," chided Tyrone.

Nigel intervened to allay the tension between Armus and Tyrone by asking, "Will this affect the rebuilding of Jor'el's palace?"

"Jor'el didn't say. Fitch and Locan turned since the Great Battle, but Hueil was the last remaining rebel."

"The wedding is next month, and the plan is to lay the cornerstone as part of the celebration. Hopefully that's time enough to root them out."

"Jor'el will not be thwarted," said Avatar.

"The reports of trouble appears confined to the South Plains," said Tyrone.

"Wess admitted to having problems?" asked Nigel with surprise.

"Ridge probably told the king," said Wren.

"No. I surmised that from the monthly reports," said Tyrone.

"Perhaps I should visit the South Plains and see how Wess is doing, along with letting him know about Kell," said Nigel.

"I'll go with you," said Armus.

"I thought you said you will remain here?" asked Tristine.

"I'm second-in-command of the Guardians. If Locan and Fitch are on the loose and involved, it is my duty to administer Jor'el's justice, for Kell, for all."

"Don't worry. I'll make certain they stay out of too much trouble," said Mirit.

"*We* will," said Avatar.

"You'll need a hunter to track a shape shifter," said Wren.

Tyrone cleared his throat loud enough to get attention. "Are you all forgetting someone?"

"With all due respect, Sire, neither Avatar nor I need your permission to deal with Guardian matters," said Armus.

"True, but I want to get to the bottom of this just as much as any of you."

"You're going too?" asked Tristine with incredulity.

"No. I'm sending Fraser and Ellis with Nigel."

"And Valery. She is my squire," said Mirit.

"With such a large retinue Wess will know this isn't a social call," said Nigel.

"I don't want to take any chances! It's already been too costly," refuted Tyrone. "Avatar, fetch Chad. Wren, get Valery."

"Father, I—" began Titus.

"No! As heir, your place is here to lead if things should worsen. As second son, it is Fraser's responsibility to defend."

"And me? What are my responsibilities, sir?" asked Eli with disappointment.

Tyrone clapped his youngest son's shoulder and softened his temper. "To use your gift of encouragement to make sure we keep our faith."

"Doesn't seem like much help."

"Oh, but it is," said Tristine. "You know how much Necie, Jillian and I relied on you at the Fortress during the coup."

"It gave me peace of mind knowing you were there," said Tyrone.

"Really?" asked Eli, surprised.

"Ay. Each of you have areas of strengthen and responsibility. Used wisely and together, the security of Allon is almost guaranteed. Without such bolstering of encouragement and faith, leading and defending would be nearly impossible."

"How do you think your father, Angus and I have been successful all these years?" asked Nigel. "More than once, Angus has provided a voice of calm and reason."

Angus took up the explanation. "I don't consider the times I stayed here a demotion or of less importance, not in defense and protection of our family and Allon."

Eli grinned. "I understand, Uncle. Although sometime I would like to defend."

"Those times will come. You don't need to seek them out."

"Now," began Tyrone to Nigel. "As soon as all are assembled, you can leave."

Chapter 2

H E BEGAN TO STIR; UNEASY AT FIRST THEN MORE DETERMINED to wake. By the coolness and partial dampness beneath, he reckoned he lay on the ground. Opening his eyes, confirmed he was outside behind some bushes. Judging by the grayish light, chirping sounds and dew, he judged the time to be early.

"Morning?" he murmured in disturbed confusion. What about Armus and Vidar? The king and the others? He sat up then groaned at feeling pain and dizziness. He touched the right side of his head and flinched. He discovered blood on his fingers. If he were so injured as to remain unconscious until morning, Armus and Vidar could also be hurt—or worse.

"Armus?" he called. He pushed himself to his feet and stumbled out from behind the bushes onto a road. He came face-to-face with a female. Startled, she screamed and stepped back in surprise. "I'm sorry, miss. I didn't mean to frighten you."

Speechless, she clenched the basket of fresh picked plants and flowers she carried. She wore a full-length cloak against the morning chill. She did a quick survey of him and whirled about. "You're naked!"

"What?" He glanced at himself and sure enough, he wore no clothes. He stepped back behind the bush to look for his uniform.

She snatched a glance over her shoulder. "Don't just stand there, put something on!"

"I don't see my clothes. I must have lost them."

"How can you lose your clothes?"

"I don't know. I was fully dressed," he said confused, his voice strained and eyes blinking at the pain in his head.

She dared a more concerted glance at him, but only enough to see his face and noticed his head wound. "You're hurt." She put down her basket, took off her cloak and held it out to him while avoiding looking at him. "Here, put this on."

"I don't think it will fit me," he said with a chuckle. He put the cloak on. To his surprise, what reached to her ankles came to his mid-calf, only about a six-inch difference in height.

She turned to face him. "I think it covers you well enough."

His quizzical look went from how reasonably well the cloak fit him to her. She stood average height for a mortal female with brown hair and hazel eyes, pleasant mature features, perhaps in her mid-forties. How could her cloak fit him well enough to cover his nakedness so completely? There were slits for the passage of arms for keeping the cloak close. He used one hand to measure their height difference. Indeed, there was only around six inches gap in height, not two feet or more.

She curiously regarded him. "Are you all right?"

"I'm not sure. How tall am I?"

She began to smile in making an assessment then stopped at seeing his painful confusion. "Perhaps six feet by standard measure, why?"

"My face, hair and eyes? What do they look like?"

She shrugged while continuing to her observation. "Aside from the head injury, you're very good looking with black hair and hazel eyes, perhaps a bit more yellow in them then I've seen before, ... don't you remember what you look like?"

"I'm not sure I remember much of anything clearly."

"Do you remember your name?"

He began to speak, but found he couldn't, though he knew his name was Kell.

"You don't remember that either?"

"No, I do. K ..." he tried to force himself to speak only it came out, "K ... l ... v-v-v," he growled in frustration at not being able to speak his name.

She mistook his feeble attempt at pronunciation. "Kelvin?"

He scowled in weary resignation. "Ay, Kelvin will do."

"Must be your head wound." She took his arm. "My brother is a doctor, he'll treat you." She picked up her basket and they began walking in the direction she originally headed. "I suppose you don't remember how you came to be injured?"

"I was attacked."

"There are reports of highwayman and robbers here lately. You are fortunate all they took were your clothes and left you alive."

He surveyed the landscape as they walked. This was not where he, Armus and Vidar had been. "Where are we?"

"About two miles from Burleigh."

"In the South Plains?" he asked in surprise. "What day is it?"

"Midweek, why?"

"It can't be," he muttered. He flinched in pain and blinked his eyes.

"Easy. Your head wound is clouding your mind. My brother will help you recover."

"Ay," sighed Kell. He rubbed his eyes then focused on her. "What is your name?"

"Vivian. My brother is Sir Lester. He's a retired army physician."

"Of General Wess' command."

"Do you know him? Are you a soldier?"

"In manner of speaking."

"Then my brother should remember you and make it easier to aid your memory."

He snorted a contrary chuckle. "Somehow I don't think so."

She wryly smiled. "The last battle ended six months ago, you couldn't have changed that much."

Kell grimaced in pain and touched his head.

"Can you make it the house? Or should I fetch my brother?"

"No, I think I can walk two miles."

"Only one mile, we live outside the town."

Silence fell, and Kell tried to get his bearings while searching his memory for what happened. By the direction they walked and the

26

surroundings, he knew they headed toward the town of Burleigh and the castle bearing its name. Burleigh Castle sat situated near the lower foothills of the Grand Stanton Mountain Range. The mountains ran from the highest peaks in the northern Highlands, through the Region of Sanctuary and created the border of the North and South Plains with Midessex, ending in foothills before sharply turning to the west and separating the South Plains from the Lowlands.

The castle architects created a stair step plateau upon which to build using the foothills as the southern wall. They carved a tributary from the foothills to create a moat as the rear defense, ending in small reservoirs at the steep burrows that flanked the castle. The burrowed ten-foot walls enclosed the remaining three sides. Being built from local stone quarried in the foothills, the castle weathered to muted gold and tan variegations. The city of Burleigh was self-contained and partitioned into sections to protect its twenty thousand citizens in the event of attack.

All this Kell knew well, only how did he get here? One moment he was fighting *madah-dune* in the Southern Forest on Friday; the next he wakes up naked in the South Plains at Midweek, and apparently looking more mortal than Guardian. How? Had he been unconscious four days? Why? Unfortunately, with his head foggy from injury, what images he recalled were disjointed.

"We're here." She tugged on his arm to steer him off the road and onto the pathway to the house since in his distraction he kept walking.

He surveyed the house, hoping for something to jar any recent memory of how he came to the South Plains. It was a nice, well-kept modest size home of brick, mortar and wood. The dwelling suited the station and income of a knighted physician, yet nothing immediately familiar to jog his memory.

"Why does your brother live outside the city?"

"Country folk need doctors also. Besides, it would be too troublesome to deal with the nightwatch after the gates are closed if someone needs help. This way people from the city and the country have free access to medical treatment." Once inside the front door, she paused in the foyer. "Lester!" she called and waited for an answer.

"In the study!" came the response from the back of the house.

"Come to the infirmary. I have a patient for you."

She guided Kell through a room to the left of the foyer and into the smaller adjacent room. A table stood in the middle of the room with a tall chair beside it. Two side-tables lined the walls with one having a cupboard over it. Instruments of medical practice lay neatly arranged on the side-tables.

"Sit on the examination table. Only be careful the cloak doesn't open." She indicated the table in the center of the room. "Lester should be here momentarily."

Kell did as instructed and squirmed to get comfortable while making certain the cloak remained closed. It surprised him to find his feet dangled a couple of inches off the floor.

"What have we here?" Lester stood in the threshold. He appeared about ten years old than his sister with similar features and coloring. He was clean-shaven, and carried a book with a pair of spectacles resting on his nose. His reading must have been interrupted.

"Lester, this is Kelvin. I found him on the road, naked and injured."

He smirked. "I thought your cloak looked a little odd on him." He placed the book and spectacles aside to examine Kell's head injury. "Nasty blow. How did it happen?"

"He can't remember much," said Vivian

"I'm not surprised." Lester held up two fingers in front of Kell's face. "How many fingers am I holding up?"

"Two."

Lester put down one finger but kept his hand up. "Using just your eyes, follow my finger." He moved to the right and Kell's eyes followed, then to the left; Kell's eyes again following. "Good. Have you any other injuries?"

"I don't know, although I'm very sore."

"Hard to tell with the cloak. You appear to me my size. Viv, fetch some of my clothes while I examine him further." She left and Lester continued speaking to Kell. "Let's take this off and see."

Kell grimaced and gingerly withdrew his arms from the slits. Lester removed the cloak to reveal Kell's well-defined torso and arms. For modesty's sake, he left the cloak lying across Kell's lap.

"You're certainly a strong one," he said. After examining Kell's torso for broken or cracked ribs, he moved behind the table. There were several large, nasty bruises, abrasions and a long cut across the upper

28

back and shoulder blades. Kell cringed and hissed in pain at the examination. "I can see why you're sore. More than likely, they struck from behind first and when you turned around, cold-cocked you."

"Come to think of it, I was knocked to my knees. Everything else is a blur." Kell flinched and hissed louder when Lester continued the examination of his head.

"Judging by the force of these blows, it is by Jor'el's grace you survived. Along with the fact the wounds are days old."

"How can you tell?"

"Dried blood, scabbing and the discoloration of the bruising." He moved to the side-table with the cupboard to fetch salve and bandages.

The madah-dune injured him on Friday, but had he suffered further injury since? "Your sister said something about highwaymen and robbers in the area."

"Ay. Since the war, the province has been unsettled. Were you carrying any valuables?"

"No. Hasn't Count Wess tried to restore order?"

"Oh, ay. Unfortunately, after enduring Gareth for so long, a few malcontents decided to take advantage." While Lester dressed the wounds, Kell repeatedly winced. "The salve should help with some of the topical pain. I'll mix you something to relax and help the soreness."

The door opened and a young man of twenty years of age entered. He carried some folded clothes. "Pappy, Aunt Viv said to bring these to you."

"Put them on that side-table and prepare the sick bed. We'll have a patient for a few days."

"Aunt Viv is already doing so."

Lester grinned. "Fetch some food. You are hungry, aren't you?" he asked Kell.

Kell's brows furrowed at the question. "Come to think of it, I am very hungry."

Lester's grin increased and when his son moved to leave, said, "Donovan, not too much. Despite hunger, medicine and rest is more important for the immediate."

"Ay, Pappy."

Kell cocked a confident smile. "I'll be fine in a couple of days."

Lester laughed and wiped the salve off his hands to deal with the bandage. "Try two to three weeks."

"I heal fast."

"You're blessed to be alive. Asking for healing so fast is rather presumptuous. Raise your arms so I get around your torso."

Kell held his breath when the pain grew intense. He made no comment or complaint, and didn't relax until Lester finished.

"You're hurt worse than you want to admit."

"I think you're right. It's been a long time since I felt this bad."

As Lester prepared a tonic, Kell tried to understand what happened. Pain and fatigue of injury prevented him from any deep consideration. Lester handed him a cup and he sniffed the contents. "What is it?"

"Brandy wine with poppy and wortweed for the pain. You're fortunate Viv picked fresh wortweed this morning. I used the last of the fresh plants yesterday. It's more potent fresh than dry."

Kell took a breath between each swallow. He paused due to the pain of movement rather than the taste of the tonic. When finished, he gave the cup back to Lester.

"Can you dress yourself?"

"The breeches, ay, but I might need help with the shirt."

Lester put down the cup before picking up the breeches to hand to Kell. "Don't worry about the shirt right now. When you're ready, I'll help you to bed."

Sitting on the table, Kell put his legs through the pants then carefully stood and finished pulling on the breeches.

"Some slippers." Lester put them on the floor so Kell could step into them. After he did so, Lester helped him to an adjacent room.

Vivian stood beside a turned down bed. She came to help support a wobbling Kell. Together she and Lester eased Kell into bed. He lay on his side, the back of his shoulders too painful.

"You should feel the effects of the tonic shortly. We'll look in on you in a few hours," said Lester.

"Thank you."

Kell waited a few moments after Lester and Vivian left before slowly and painfully rising and moving to the foot of the bed. He assumed the Guardian meditative position on the floor. He needed answers and his mind too fuzzy to think clearly on his own. Taking several deep breaths, he closed his eyes and tried to stretch out his senses toward Jor'el. To his surprise, he felt intense pain in his head and all went black.

Kell heard a distant voice and someone shook his shoulder. Several times the voice spoke and each time the shake became more insistent. Finally he woke up. His vision hazy at first, then the faces of Vivian and Donovan came into focus. Both looked concerned.

"Are you all right?" she asked.

"I think so."

"Why are you on the floor?" asked Donovan.

It took a moment for Kell to recall he got out of bed to perform his usual meditation. "I guess I passed out." They helped him sit up.

"You didn't have to get out of bed. We could have gotten whatever you needed. All you had to do was call," she said.

"I didn't need anything. I was meditating."

"By sitting on the floor?" asked Donovan.

"That's how Guard ... how it's done," he was forced to correct his wording in mid-sentence.

"You tried to mediate like a Guardian? Why? Is it different than normal prayer?" she asked.

Kell regarded her in consideration of the question. "I suppose not." When his gaze passed from them, he noticed the brighter light. "What time is it?"

"Two o'clock. We came to look in on you."

The answer disturbed Kell. "I've been asleep that long?"

"Ay, and you obviously need more rest, so let's get you back in bed." She took hold of one arm to help Donovan draw Kell to his feet.

When standing, Kell frowned in surprise at feeling strange bodily sensations.

"Is something wrong? Pain perhaps?" she asked.

"Err ... no," he said sheepishly. "Where is your privy?"

She flashed a smile. "At the end of the hall. Donovan will help you."

"I can make it," said Kell. After taking two steps, he swayed.

Donovan caught Kell's arm. "Head wounds often interfere with balance."

Kell made no further argument and let Donovan escort him to the privy. "I'll wait outside the door," he said.

Kell went inside. Using the privy to relieve bodily functions was one thing, but nausea and retching proved so unsettling he poured water into a basin to splash on his face for recovery. Feeling better from the water, he found himself staring in the mirror at a decidedly mortal face. His hair remained black and the shape of his face and features similar, but in the eyes the familiarity ended. No longer were they the striking brilliant gold, rather a mortal hazel with a touch more yellow. The eyes definitely lacked the Guardian spark.

He lifted his right hand and spoke in the Ancient, *"A'lasadh"* and snapped his fingers. Nothing happened! He repeated the word for *light* and snapped again, and with the same negative result. Disconcerted, he again stared at his face in the mirror.

"No, this can't be. I can't be mortal. This must be a dream." He glanced to the ceiling. "Jor'el, tell me this is a dream," he pleaded. Receiving no reply, he looked into the mirror again. "Why? Did I do something wrong? What reason could there be?" he murmured under his breath, disconcerted and confused.

"Kelvin? Are you all right?" Donovan asked through the door. "Do you need some help?"

Staring at the reflection, Kell shook his head in befuddlement. "I don't think you can help me." He whimpered in pain and held his head.

Donovan entered. "You should be back in bed."

Kell allowed Donovan to take him back to bed.

Vivian remained in the room. "Are you feeling better?"

"Not really." Kell got into bed and gingerly lay on his side. "I thought I would be fine in a couple of days, now I'm not sure."

She pulled the blankets up over him. "However long it takes, let us help you, and don't get out of bed by yourself until Lester says you are able."

"Ay." Kell started to close his eyes when he heard male voices speaking in private tones. Lester stood in the threshold beside a very familiar person. "Wess!"

A good-looking man of fifty-six, Wess' dark hair began turning gray at the temples. Curiosity filled his dark eyes in turning toward the bed. "I'm normally not spoken to in such a familiar manner by a stranger."

Kell struggled to sit up so Vivian helped him. "Don't you recognize me?"

"Should I?"

"He told Vivian he is a soldier and knows me," said Lester.

"His name is Kelvin," she said.

Wess approached the bed to study Kell's face. "There is a familiarity. Then again, I've met many soldiers during my years of service. What campaigns have you served in?"

"All the ones you have."

"Name them and maybe I'll remember you."

"Bays Hill, Tunlund, the Soren invasion, Princess Ellan's first coup and most recently against Hueil."

Wess regarded Kell, close and with scrutiny. "Your name is Kelvin?"

Vivian grew frustrated and chided him. "Can't you see he needs rest to recover? I'm surprised you let him interrogate a patient," she mildly scolded Lester.

"I wasn't interrogating," said Wess with a wry snicker.

"You're a soldier. How else do you ask questions if not interrogating?"

"And you're an incorrigible woman, but a wonderful nurse," he added with a toothy grin when she scowled at him.

"*Shoo*, both of you!" She waved them to the door then tried to get Kell to lie back down. "Pay them no mind and go back to sleep."

"I've been in bed most of the day," groused Kell. He tried to remain sitting up, only her efforts proved insistent and he didn't have the strength to resist.

"I'll wake you when supper is ready." She pulled the covers over him.

"Will Wess still be here?"

"I don't know. Why?"

Kell fought against sleep to answer. "I need to speak to him."

"That can wait."

"Ay," he murmured and closed his eyes.

Wess and Lester were in the hall when Vivian emerged from the sick room. "Did he say anything more than his name to give a clue to his identity?" Wess asked her.

"No."

"He wasn't wearing a uniform of his regiment?"

Lester chuckled. "He wasn't wearing any clothes. She found him naked. Brought him to the infirmary wearing her cloak."

Vivian grew offended and embarrassed when Wess laughed. "You make it sound like something indecent happened!" she scolded Lester, "Well, it didn't!" then to both of them, "Blast you for saying so and blast you for laughing." She walked off in a huff.

"You can be cruel to your sister."

"It was more your laughing than what I said." Lester led Wess to a private office.

"I've been laughing at your humor since we were boys. She should know you are the instigator."

Lester smiled. After closing the door he suddenly grew pale, winced in pain and reached to rub his eyes.

"Are you all right?"

He waved off Wess. "Just tired and a bit of a headache."

"You've been working too hard. Sit down."

Lester almost fell into the chair at his desk, yet spoke in dispute. "Me? What about you? You're the new lord. I'm just your physician friend."

Wess grinned. "Very well. There hasn't been a moment's peace since we arrived." His tone and expression turned to frustration. "I thought I had things under control until this Kelvin incident."

"Maybe I shouldn't have told you." He grimaced in pain and blinked.

"No, you did right. I'm sorry it took me so long to get over here." He watched Lester deal with his pain. "I think Kelvin isn't the only one who needs to rest."

"I'll take care of my headache. You need to send word to the king for help. Whoever they are, they're becoming brazen to attack soldiers, and one as strong as him."

Wess nodded with consideration. "I'll do some more investigating on the way back to Burleigh. If what I find warrants it, I'll send for help."

Lester regarded Wess in stern annoyance. "In the meantime, Vivian makes daily trips between here and town for medicine, personal supplies and sometimes to visit you at the castle. Although Jor'el knows why, since you take her safety lightly."

"That's not true," began Wess in rebuff, yet contained his temper since Lester was out of sorts. "Every time she visits, I escort her home."

"Ay," he groused. "I'm just concerned. I've tried to convince her to take Donovan or Howey along, only she's so stubborn."

Wess wryly grinned. "You're scolding me about her safety?" Lester appeared on the verge of fainting so he moved beside the chair in support. "This is more than a headache. It's the illness, isn't it?"

Lester swallowed back his sickness to nod. "Ay."

Wess pursued his lips in regret. "I hoped asking you to move here for your retirement would not be so taxing on your health."

"Like taking command of the province would be easier on you than remaining in uniform as the king's general?" He quickly apologized at seeing Wess' wounded scowl. "I'm sorry. The pain sometimes makes me surly."

"Well, if surliness is a symptom, you've been ill since we met."

Lester's laughter was not too merry and he closed his eyes in discomfort.

"You want me to fetch Vivian or Donovan?"

He shook his head, his eyes still closed. "It's passing. I'll be fine." His eyes opened when the clock on the mantel struck two-thirty in the afternoon. "Will you stay for supper? Viv would be cross if you don't."

"She'll be cross if I do." Wess smiled and shook his head. "Thank you, no. If I'm to investigate, I need to do so before it gets dark. I'll come by in a couple of days to tell you what I learn, and speak to Kelvin again."

On this way out, Wess made a detour to find Donovan. The young man sat in the small lab where Lester mixed his medicines. He wrote in what appeared to be a journal while looking at various beakers and jars on the table in front of him. "Donovan."

"My lord." He put down the pen to give Wess his attention.

"Lester had another spell just now."

"He needs his medicine." He began to rise when Wess stopped him.

"Tell me truly, how serious have the spells become?"

"What did he say?"

"Nothing, he avoided the subject again. This is the eighth time in the past two months that I've witness a spell. I don't recall them this frequent or painful."

Donovan nodded. "Ay, the episodes are increasing in frequency and intensity."

"I hoped retirement would help him to relax and lessen the spells."

"Retirement or work is inconsequential. It's only a matter of time."

Wess to note of the discomposure and asked, "Time until what?"

Donovan looked directly at him to reply. "He loses his sight completely."

The answer first stunned Wess then annoyed him. "Blast him for being so stubborn and not telling me!"

Donovan took hold of Wess' arm and spoke in a low, private voice. "He doesn't even want Aunt Viv to know the extent. It's enough what she's given up for us. He doesn't want her to continue caring for a blind man the rest of her life."

"That won't happen. He will get the care his needs, I promise."

Donovan grinned at the offer. "I appreciate your friendship and concern for him, my lord. Arrangements have been made. After Heather and I are wed, I'll take over the surgery. Although it will be hard to keep the story from Aunt Viv by then."

Wess smiled with encouragement. "Together we'll see they want for nothing."

Donovan steadily regarded him. "I hope you mean that, sir. Not only about my father, but Aunt Viv also. She deserves some happiness, and not from a surgery."

"I do. Now, give him the medicine. I must be on my way." He accompanied Donovan into the hall and watched the young man head for Lester's study.

For a brief moment, he hesitated in leaving, wondering about staying for supper. Lester and Donovan's reference to Vivian were not lost upon him. Since moving to the South Plains at his request, they saw each other on a daily basis. True, they met years ago when Lester and Vivian moved to Waldron so Lester could study medicine with Doctor Charlton. Recently he sensed their relationship changing. What exactly that meant, he wasn't sure, though others hinted toward the romantic. Perhaps at one time there was hope for them, but now?

"Good day, my lord."

The voice of Lester's manservant broke Wess' pondering. Howey was an amiable fellow of middle years with an infectious smile and Wess couldn't help but grin.

"Howey. How are you and Drusilla getting on here?"

"Well, my lord. If you're staying for supper I'll tell Dru to set another plate."

"No. I need to be off."

Howey's winsome smile grew. "Dru made her famous venison stew and Mistress Vivian her excellent bread pudding."

"Oooh, very tempting, Howey. Yet I see by the sunlight I don't have long for investigation before dark."

"The ladies will be disappointed."

"Tell them I'll make it up to them." Wess began to leave.

"If you say so, my lord," said Howey with some skepticism.

"Tell Vivian to mark my words," insisted Wess before exiting by the front door.

Chapter 3

THE FOLLOWING MORNING, KELL SAT IN A CHAIR AT THE WINDOW watching the sunrise. He woke an hour earlier. Though stiff and sore, he managed to get out of bed. Being immortal, Guardians healed quickly in physical form, taking only a few hours for minor injuries to a couple of days for the more serious ones. The last time he spent so long recovering from wounds happened during Ellan's first coup attempt when he ran afoul of four Shadow Warriors. They seriously wounded him with a stygian arrow and captured him in a cage made of spurean metal, the two elements capable of killing or rendering a Guardian helpless. The blood loss combined with the life draining power of the metals brought him to the brink of death. If not for the timely rescue by Armus, Tristine and Tyrone he would have died. He spent four days under Tyrone's care.

Along with being a blacksmith, Tyrone possessed knowledge of the healing arts. Still, it was more than that since only care from a fellow Guardian would help to heal from such wounds. The fact Tyrone's medical assistance kept him from ceasing to exist raised Kell's curiosity of how a mortal could heal a Guardian?

During his recovery, he learned of Tyrone's half-mortal, half-Guardian parentage. Aside from Dagar's progeny, this has not happened before. Prophecy foretold of a Great King, who would be of such a heritage as to bring Guardians and mortals together like never before. Tyrone fulfilled Prophecy. At the time, Kell had answers for what happened, but not so in his present situation.

Over and over again he pondered what events he remembered. Nothing seemed to explain how he came to be in the South Plains and why he was now a mortal. He knew his own identity, yet unable to speak his name. He even faltered when mentioning Guardian mediation and fainted when he attempted to meditate. He tried praying like the mortals, which he discovered wasn't really different from the Guardian way.

However, just like the unusual restraint in speaking about his former station, he felt a void between himself and Jor'el he never experienced before. As captain he had immediate and constant access to the Almighty. Not now. Did something hinder him or was this a common experience among the mortals? Many times he heard them express frustration regarding prayer and not sensing Jor'el's presence. Was it due to a supernatural barrier or something within the mortals preventing direct, open and honest communication? He may not sense Jor'el like he once did, but he knew the Almighty was there.

He couldn't recall much of what happened after the attack or find a reason for his present condition. He had to believe the answers would come in time. Still, when the answers came, what would he do? Usually he knew his task and some idea of what was required. Now he didn't know either. Everything was a complete mystery.

He yawned. Aside from the times of injury, fatigue wasn't something he experienced and grew antsy at being incapacitated for so long. He also tried to ignore the grumbling of his stomach. He took food last night and that should be sufficient. Although he ate and drank while interacting with mortals, partaking of constant nourishment was unnecessary for Guardians. He often teased Armus about acquiring the skill of cooking, yet at the moment he wouldn't mind something to eat.

The hunger pains persisted and grew annoying. In his former state he only had to speak and food would appear, or almost anything else he needed. Each Guardian was created fully equipped with powers and special skills needed for their status. All spoke the Ancient and could do minor miracles, as the mortals called them. Being captain, he was the mightiest. In mortal form, he could speak the Ancient yet possessed no powers.

He flinched in discomfort at feeling pain and soreness from head to toe. He touched the bandage on his head to readjust it. In doing so, he again felt his face. At first the skin didn't feel any different, then he felt something prickly on his chin and cheeks.

Whiskers? I've never shaved before. Small wonder Wess didn't recognize me. Then again, Wess is mortal and can't sense the immortal, he thought. "What am I saying? I am now mortal," he lowly groused. "How? I'm still me in knowledge and spirit."

"Kelvin?"

Hearing a voice startled him from his pondering. Vivian arrived and carried a tray with a bowl, tankard, bandages and a jar.

"What are you doing? I told you to stay in bed and send for us if you needed anything."

"I was tired of lying in bed and I didn't want to disturb you. You've all been so kind already."

"Nonsense." She placed the tray on a nearby table. "You are our patient." She pulled up another chair beside him, took the bowl and spoon from the tray and sat. "I hope you're hungry. I sweetened the porridge with extra honey."

When she went to feed him, Kell balked. "I can feed myself."

"Very well. Let me see." She handed him the bowl and spoon.

Kell scooped up a spoonful of porridge. He grimaced when lifting the spoon to his mouth, the movement painful to his shoulder and upper back. Vivian skeptically watched so he tried lowering his head to meet the spoon part way from the bowl to his mouth. More pain in his neck and shoulders made him stop.

"That's enough." She took the bowl and spoon from him. "No more argument."

He gingerly sat back and she proceeded to feed him the porridge. "This is embarrassing," he groused after the first spoonful.

"Why? You need help."

"Because I'm the one accustomed to giving help not receiving it."

"That is a soldier's pride talking. I've seen it before with the wounded." She continued to feed him while speaking, her voice growing sober. "Even the dying ones still wanted to help their comrades."

At a hint of despondency in her speech, he asked, "Are you a widow?" He knew the answer; the question was more for conversation. Revealing what he knew already caused suspicion, thus he decided to be more discriminating.

"No," she said with a short ironic laugh. "I never married. I speak from experience of watching and helping my brother."

Kell studied her in his pretended role. "Ah, now I recall seeing you at the last battle. Only with your hair covered by a kerchief and your face smudged."

She grinned and continued to feed him. "You're being generous. It's dirty, bloody and messy work in a field hospital. One hardly looks their best, and I wasn't there to make an impression. Some cider?"

Kell swallowed the last spoonful of porridge and nodded. She placed the bowl aside, picked up the cup and placed the cup to his mouth to help him drink. He moved his hands to hold the cup. Her hands steadied it while he drank. Upon finishing, he still held the cup with her hands in his hands. A strange sensation overcame him when their eyes met. She flashed an awkward smile, and removed the cup and her hands from his grasp.

She avoided further direct eye contact to ask, "Any more porridge?"

"Eh, no, I think I'm fine." He tried to catch her eye again.

She rose and put the cup on the tray with the bowl. "I need to change your bandage. Sit on the bed."

"Bed, right." Kell pushed himself out of the chair and made his way back to the bed where he began to get under the covers.

"No, silly," she said and chuckled. "Sit on the edge, so I can get around your torso. I can't do so in a chair."

Once he sat in position, she undid the bandage, gentle and mindful of his wounds. He held his breath to endure the more intense pain, then relaxed when she finished. Free from the confines of the bandage he tried to move his arms, neck and shoulder.

She fetched the jar of salve. "Easy. The wounds are just forming scabs."

"It feels good to move unrestrained."

41

"I'm sure it does." She gazed up and down at his muscular torso. She blushed when he smiled and moved around to the other side of the bed to tend to his back. "I'll try not to hurt you when applying the salve."

Startled, he hissed and straightened. "That's cold!"

"Cold is good for easing pain. Haven't you ever put a cold compress on a bad bruise or strained muscle?"

"I never strained a muscle."

She stopped in surprise to again survey his impressive physique. "Never? Then how did you get so ... strong if not from hard training and conditioning?"

He started to answer, but paused to consider his reply. Being created in physical perfection wasn't a believable answer. "As you say, training. I guess I was fortunate to avoid such problems."

"Indeed," she said with a hint of admiration. She finished putting on the salve, wiped her hands on her apron, closed the jar and fetched fresh bandages. She returned to wrap the bandage on his wound, and tripped over his foot. He caught her to keep her from falling sideways. She heard him grunt in pain. "I hope I didn't hurt you?"

A gallant grin appeared when their eyes met. "You were the one falling."

"Well, isn't this cozy? Do you usually cuddle up to a patient?"

Wess' arrival surprised Kell and Vivian. Wess wore a guarded, if somewhat wry expression. Donovan and Ridge accompanied him. Ridge, a Guardian ranger and new Trio Leader of the South Plains, stood as tall as a warrior at seven and a half feet. This was unusual since most non-warrior castes only reached seven feet tall. He had a slender build, red hair, thin beard and light golden eyes. He wore the uniform of his station and armed with a dagger at his right hip and quarterstaff slung across his back.

"Ridge!" said Kell.

The ranger looked curiously at him, and did not reply.

Quick and awkward, Vivian removed herself from Kell's arms. "I started to bandage him when I tripped. He caught me, that's all."

Wess' skeptical glance found Kell where it lingered for a moment. "Is that so?"

"Ay."

"He can't do anything in his condition," she insisted.

"He looks pretty strong and fit to me." Wess glanced up and down at Kell.

She grew flustered. "Finish him." She thrust out the bandage to Donovan. The young man tried not to laugh when taking over the task. She grabbed the tray. "I hope you don't tax him by your interrogation," she snipped at Wess and left.

"You can comfort him if I do!" he called after her.

Donovan laughed under his breath.

Kell looked askew to Wess. "I don't recall you being so harsh in banter with a woman before."

Wess crossed to the bed; his face and voice firm. "You speak to me in an easy, familiar manner like we know each other, yet I can't place you."

"I'm sorry you can't remember. However, I have known you most of your life."

"Now you go too far! You can't be more than thirty years old."

"What can I say to convince you?"

"Tell me how you came to be injured for neither Ridge nor I can find evidence of foul play or ambush."

Kell moved his arms so Donovan could secure the bandage. "I wish I knew. I've been trying to remember since yesterday."

"Yet you claim to know me. How is that possible?"

"It could be the head wound affecting his short term memory, my lord," said Donovan.

Wess looked to Ridge for consensus.

"It is possible. I've heard Eldric speak of it," said the ranger.

"Do you remember how you came to the South Plains?" asked Wess.

Kell shook his head and gently rotated a sore shoulder. "The last thing I remember was hunting in the Southern Forest."

"It would take at least ten days to get here. And you can't remember anything during that time?"

Kell's brows grew level in thought and he soon became disconcerted. "No." This time when Wess looked at Ridge, Kell followed the glance. A mortal may not recognize him, but surely one of his own kind could. He boldly met Ridge's steady golden gaze. The color intensity told of the ranger's concentration. Alas, Kell saw no hint of recognition and he fought displaying disappointment. Still, Ridge spoke favorably.

"He is telling the truth, my lord."

Thoughtful, Wess pursed his lips and his eyes narrowed on Kell. "Very well. Rest and recover. And don't presume any further, either upon my good graces or Vivian!" He turned on his heels and left.

Ridge gave Kell a long considering glance. For a moment, Kell became hopeful. Again, to his disappointment, the ranger left without any acknowledgement. If Ridge didn't sense him, his essence is either gone or being masked. Perhaps by the strange restraint he felt each time he tried to speak his real name or anything related to his Guardian past.

"Do you need anything?" asked Donovan.

The question drew Kell from his dreary consideration. "No. Thank you," he answered with distraction.

"Rest until luncheon. Aunt Viv will have a good meal ready for you." Donovan moved to help Kell lay back on the bed.

"Is Wess always so brash toward Vivian?"

Donovan chuckled. "They've always acted that way with each other. He and father have known each other since they were boys."

"I don't recall him treating his sisters in such a harsh and possessive manner. Nor his wife."

"I wouldn't say that to Wess if I were you." Lester entered. He looked and sounded stern.

"Of course not. I saw his pain when Glenda and Cassie died. Then Bosley and Garrick."

Lester's eyes never left Kell, as he waved for Donovan to leave. "Shut the door," he said. When the door closed, he moved a chair beside the bed, sat and spoke in a firm, uncompromising tone. "Why have you made advances toward my sister and disparaging remarks about my friend while in my care?"

Kell was taken back. "I made no advances. She tripped and fell. I caught her."

"And Wess?"

"I told you, I know him. I asked a question since I found his behavior toward Vivian unusual."

Lester scowled, eyes intense on Kell. "You made no advances toward her?"

Kell sighed, feeling some pain in his head. "No."

"This argument isn't helping your recovery." Lester leaned forward in the chair to check the bandage on Kell's head. Once satisfied to the integrity of the bandage, he continued speaking in firm manner. "I expect better from now on. Proper behavior befitting a patient and well-disciplined soldier."

Kell stiffened and returned Lester's fixed expression. "You shall have it."

With a curt nod, Lester left the room.

In the kitchen, Ridge stood near the rear door. Vivian and Drusilla finished placing breakfast on the table. Donovan washed his hands at the pump sink. Wess sat at the table drinking tea with his breakfast.

Lester entered. "Well, I don't think he will give us any more trouble. I made it clear his behavior was unwelcomed and unwarranted."

Vivian set a loaf of brown bread on a cutting board on the table. "Oh, Lester, you didn't! I told you both nothing happened." She picked up a knife to slice the bread.

"Hearing my sister was found in the arms of a patient isn't exactly proper behavior." He sat at the table and began to help himself to breakfast

"I wasn't in his arms! I tripped and he caught me to keep me from falling."

Lester looked to Wess, who shrugged and kept eating.

Annoyed, she waved the knife at Wess. "What did you tell him?"

"What I saw." He snatched the knife from her hand by the hilt and put it on the table.

She picked up the knife to continue slicing. "You saw nothing improper."

"Wess and I are protecting your honor," said Lester.

"My honor!" she made a scoffing remark. "I've been around the army long enough to know what a woman's honor means to a soldier."

"I beg your pardon?" said Wess in a wry challenging manner.

She scowled in frustration. "I don't mean you specifically, just in general."

"I *am* a *general*."

She grew flustered and clenched the bread. "Why must you always twist my words when you know what I mean?" She crushed the loaf. Overcome with annoyance, she grunted and stormed out the rear door.

"I think you upset her," said Lester dryly.

Wess chuckled and left the kitchen to find Vivian. She grabbed a pail of feed and headed for the chicken coop. She noticed his arrival and pretended to ignore him and tossed feed to the chickens.

"I'm sorry I upset you," he said.

She didn't answer and continued the feeding.

"It was a startling sight."

She sighed in exasperation. "I told you it was an accident and nothing happened. How many times must I repeat myself for you to believe me?"

"I do believe you."

She stopped feeding the chickens to confront him. "Then why tell Lester so he scolds a patient and we quarrel?"

The questioned stymied him and he shrugged. "Sometimes I don't react well to the unexpected."

"And because of that, you don't accept the reason."

"I suppose you're right."

"I am." She left the coop area, put down the pail and took him by the hand to lead him to a nearby bench to sit. "There is something else you must hear. Lester won't tell you for fear of hurting you, but it is for your own good."

"Put that way, do I want to know?"

She tried to contain her vexation at his sarcasm. "That is a symptom of the problem, your constant banter and deflection of anything serious. In fact," she paused watching him begin to squirm, "it has grown worse since Bosley's death."

Pricked, Wess made as if to rise, and she stopped him.

"Please! Hear me, as a friend. We are friends, aren't we?" she probed, and by his expression she knew the answer.

"Of course we are."

"I realize how difficult these past three years have been for you. First losing Glenda then Cassie, Bosley and Garrick. But you're stronger than that, Wess. I've seen it. I know it."

He scowled to the contrary. "Then you know more than I. For with each death, I lost a part of myself. Glenda and I had our problems, especially concerning Karly's marriage, which she didn't want. It turned out well. I knew it would. Eric is an excellent husband and she is happy. I rated mediocre in the area of husband."

"You did well in providing for Glenda."

"Providing *what*—was a frequent matter of debate between us. Material, ay; other things—" his voice trailed off.

She sighed in an attempt to maintain her exasperation at his continuing sour mood. "It is natural for you to express remorse. She was your wife."

He shook his head. "She never understood or accepted my duty. To her, the army was an anathema, a curse. So everything that came with it proved a source of contention."

Vivian appeared a bit confused. "You were a soldier when she married—" she stopped when he sent her a pointed sideways glance. "Oh! She only married for your position and title." He turned aside, to which she quickly took hold of his arm. "Wess, that is in the past. You can't let grief, bitterness and regret rule you for rest of your life."

His cocked a plaintive smile and he patted her hand. "I appreciate what you're saying, and I've come to accept the strained relationship between us for what it was. Still, it doesn't ease the emotions at the loss of the others."

"Because you make it difficult by not seeing the good around you. You just said that despite Glenda's objections, Karly is happily married to a good man. They have blessed you with a grandson, and another child on the way. Dylan restored honor to his father's name and assumed Bosley's place on the Council. You told Lester and me how proud Cassie would be of Ellis for his service to Prince Titus, marriage to a royal ward and given lordship of Midessex. You too received a great reward for your loyalty and service with the South Plains. Granted these things cannot replace loved ones, but don't overlook them, for they are blessings from Jor'el."

He kissed her hand. "Thank you for the reminder, dear friend."

She smile grew tender. "I hope the reminder will become a remedy."

He wryly grinned. "I may need a few more doses to feel the effects."

Her smile grew teasing and warm. "Come by any time and I'll be happy to administer the proper dose."

He laughed, more from relief than humor. "Indeed I will." He stood. "In the meantime, I have business."

She tried to maintain her temper. "You're not going to speak to Kelvin again, are you?"

"No, though his situation is puzzling. He was brutally beaten, only I've found no evidence any attack occurred in the area."

She rose and took his hand to head back to the house. "I'm confident you will find the answer in time."

"Until I do, take Donovan or Howey as escort when you leave the farm for any reason."

"You sound like my brother and nephew."

He stepped in front her, his hands on her shoulders to her look directly at him. "Because you don't see the danger around you," he quoted, mimicking her tone. "We are concerned for your safety. Have an escort."

She gave him a challenging smirk. "Is that an order, General?"

"If your can prescribe me a remedy, I can give you an order."

"Ay, sir." She made a short salute then laughed. "Now, as you have business, I have chores." He released her and she went back to the house.

Lester stepped from the threshold to allow her to enter. He raised his cup in salute to Wess. "Appears you had better luck in convincing her than Donovan or I."

"You just have to know how to talk to her."

Lester almost choked on his drink for laughing.

Wess motioned to him. "Walk me to my horse. Ridge."

The ranger followed them to the front of house where Wess' horse was tethered to a hitching post. Untying the reins, Wess noticed Ridge's regard of the house.

"Is there a problem? Kelvin perhaps?"

The ranger's gaze lingered a moment on the house before turning to Wess. "He spoke the truth, yet there is a strange familiarity about him that defies my perception."

"Is that good or bad?" asked Lester.

"Since he is truthful, I can only assume good."

"You don't sound convinced."

"I'm baffled. I never encountered such a sense from a mortal before. However, I don't believe he poses a threat."

"There are other threats around," said Lester to Wess. "You haven't found evidence concerning Kelvin's attack, so when are you going to send for help?"

Wess mounted before replying. "I'm not sure yet."

Lester seized the horse's bridle. "Wess, you told me you'd make the decision this morning. Something is stirring beneath the surface. It's only a matter of time before a power keg blows. Don't be foolhardy or prideful and wait until it's too late."

"I didn't come here for a tongue lashing from the both of you!" When Lester continued to stare at him, stubborn and inflexible, Wess said, "There are still a few hours left to the morning to make my decision." He pulled on the reins to turn the horse's head, which forced Lester to release the bridle.

"Come back to tell me when you do!" he shouted after Wess.

Kell was surprised when Donovan woke him for luncheon. He didn't expect to fall back to sleep. In fact, all he did was sleep, eat and consider his situation. Except for sitting at the window, a few trips to the privy were the only times out of bed. He was grateful the nausea and retching had not happened again. Still, each time he saw his reflection in the privy mirror, it sharply drove home the point of being mortal.

Little conversation passed between him and Donovan. He wasn't in the mood for idle talk. Besides, being fed by Vivian was different than by Donovan. The only reason he could think of why she didn't come is she felt he acted inappropriately. True, when holding her hand and meeting her gaze, he felt a strange, warm sensation he never experienced before. How did that become an advance?

"You must have been hungry," said Donovan.

The comment made Kell look at the cleaned plate. "Did I eat too much?"

"No. Aunt Viv knows the right portions to prepare for a patient."

"She's a good cook."

Donovan laughed and rose to gather the tray. "Not many patients say so. I'll be sure to tell her *you* did."

"Does she fix different food for the family and patients?"

"No, she prepares the same food, except in special cases of dietary restrictions."

"Wait. Before you leave, I'd like help to sit in the chair for a while." He moved to the edge of the bed. "A change of position," he added at seeing Donovan's hesitation.

The young man put down the tray and helped Kell to the chair. He then adjusted pillows to accommodate Kell's back. "Will that do?"

"Ay. Thank you."

Donovan left and Kell stared out the window. Seeing the earlier sunrise, he reckoned the room faced toward the northeast. Continue in that direction for six days and one would reach Waldron. Four days further lay Garwood. Had ten days really passed? No, it is four days from Friday to Midweek not ten even if one counts forward. All the same, a good number of days passed since the hunt. His distress grew when Ridge didn't recognize him or at least gave no hint he sensed a fellow Guardian in spirit. A horrible thought struck him. With so much time passed and now being mortal, he may be thought of as *dead!*

"That is why Ridge didn't recognize me. To the Guardians I'm dead!" he murmured in despair. Deeply disturbed at the possible reality, he stood. Unsteady, he swayed and caught the windowsill to keep from falling. He stared out the window and up to the sky. "Oh, Jor'el, no! Don't let Armus, Avatar, Vidar and the others believe I'm dead!"

"Kelvin, what are you doing?" Vivian entered and grew concerned by his stricken pallor. "You look awful. Let me take you back to bed."

"No!" He stumbled in moving from her and sat hard in the chair. "Not my wounds. I just realized people I care about believe I'm ... "

"Believe you are dead?" she finished at seeing his great discomposure.

He nodded, as the frightful words stuck in his throat.

"Where can we send word to reassure them?"

He vehemently shook his head. "You can't!"

"There must be a way."

"No, there's not!" he clamored.

She knelt beside him. "Once you are well you can return to your family."

"That's not possible. This!" he motioned to himself, his passion raising to a fever pitch, "isn't possible, but is reality!"

"What are you talking about? Your wounds?"

"No!" He bolted to his feet. "Me! I'm not myself any more." She rose, gazing at him in befuddlement, which made him more impassioned. "I can't make you understand, though I wish I could. I wish I could make someone understand!" The furor of desperate emotions taxed his weakened condition. He collapsed into the chair barely conscious.

"Donovan! Lester!" she shouted.

They rushed in. "By the heavenlies, what happened?" asked Lester.

"He became overly excited and needs a tonic. Donovan, help me get him into bed," she said to Lester, who left.

When they got Kell into bed, he regained consciousness.

Lester returned with cup. "Drink this." He held it to Kell's lips.

Once finished drinking, Kell groaned in exhaustion and lay back on the pillow.

"You mustn't get yourself upset or you'll hamper your recovery."

Too tired to reply, Kell closed his eyes.

Lester drew her aside to ask. "What upset him?"

"He became frightened at the thought of his loved ones believing he is dead. I tried to reassure him that we could send word, only he insists there is no way to contact them."

Lester tossed a considering glance to the bed. Kell slept. "Wess said the last thing he remembered was being in the Southern Forest. I'll ask Wess to send someone to investigate and try to contact his family."

"In the meantime, I'll stay with him."

"I made the tonic stronger. He won't wake until tomorrow morning."

"Still, I'll remain in case he does wake up."

"I'll have Howey bring you a cushioned, a pillow and blanket."

Chapter 4

THE NEXT FOUR DAYS, KELL PLAYED A MODEL PATIENT, QUIET and cooperative. When Vivian, Lester, or Donovan tried to engage him in conversation, he answered in short polite sentences. He had too much to consider and try to understand to deal with idle chatter. Besides, they couldn't provide the answers he needed. When well enough, he would undertake his own investigation.

Becoming mortal and dealing with his new form proved annoying. Fearing his friends and compatriots believed him dead brought almost a futility to the change. Vivian tried to reassure him about his *family*. That was not a word he originally used to describe his fellow Guardians. Now, taking time to consider, they were his family. All were created by the heavenly ruler and endowed with the same desire to serve and protect, only with different functions, powers and abilities. Despite the hierarchy and chain of command, their personalities and relating to each other could be considered *family-like*.

Armus and Avatar were the closest to him with Armus as his counterpart and second-in-command from the beginning. Avatar started as apprentice to both then became Kell's aide. Together they formed the High Trio over all Guardians. He experienced the deepest pain and fear imagining their grief on his behalf. In mortal family terms …

Brothers, he thought. *Armus and I counterparts—twins to mortals, and Avatar ... the pesky little brother, like he called Nigel.* He smiled at the last thought. However, he dare not dwell too long on them or risk being overcome with emotion again.

Without him as captain, how will this affect the rebuilding of Jor'el's Palace? Will he play a part in it? To have come this far since his creation and not be included in the restoration and reestablishing of Guardian rule brought another stab of pain to this heart and spirit.

There must be a reason! His mind screamed in vexation. What would he do if he couldn't find any answers? If there was no clear explanation of why or how he became mortal? How could he live a mortal life when being accustomed to immortality?

For over two thousand years he observed, served and interacted with mortals. He believed he understood their fickle nature. Reality, made him rethink his assessment. The different bodily functions were a nuisance. He grew accustomed to eating at regular intervals while sleeping wasn't too dissimilar from meditation. Staying in bed for so long frustrated him and he didn't really like using the privy, mostly for seeing his reflection and being reminded of his altered appearance. Not to mention shaving for the first time, or rather allowing Donovan to put a sharp blade to his face. He had been clean-shaven from the beginning. Few male Guardians, like Avatar, had facial hair. Only they never shaved, having been created that way.

Judging by physical looks, most reckoned him to be age thirty according to mortal years. Since Allonians tended to live from one hundred to one hundred and ten years, how would he spend his days in a shortened mortal existence? How is it done? And what about the strange, warm and impulsive sensation he experiences every time Vivian drew near? Is that mortal love? He knew about love and saw it manifested in various ways. In fact, he experienced feelings for Queen Shannan, the Daughter of Allon and mother of Nigel and his sisters. He didn't deny it. After all he was present at her birth, watched her grow up, helped her and Ellis defeat Dagar, crowned her queen, witnessed the birth of her children and mourned her death. He attributed those feelings to parental love, not emotional or romantic. Or was it?

The sensation toward Vivian felt similar. Jor'el forbade the sharing of such love and relationships between mortals and Guardians. Dagar proved Guardians capable of mating with mortal females. He only did so to create progeny in his fight against Jor'el, not due to love. Tyrone's conception by Altari, a Shadow Warrior, happened by force during the relentless attempt to stop Shannan and Ellis. Those were the only exceptions.

Upon all these things he pondered during his waking hours. At night, dreams of shared adventures with comrades over the centuries became twisted with thoughts of his present situation. This proved another unusual aspect to his new existence since Guardians never dreamt. A few times he woke during the night, weeping due to the heartbreaking dreams. On very few occasions, did he experience such sorrow as to weep. The last time he shed tears came when rescued from Shadow Warriors and profoundly relieved at seeing Armus alive. Of course, he attributed it to his greatly weakened physical condition, almost to point of death. Normally he had command of his emotions. With his world dramatically changed, he wasn't certain how to feel or even what to think.

As became his habit each morning, he rose before sunrise and sat in front of the window, staring at the distant horizon deep in consideration. After five days, he no longer required the head bandage while the bandage around his torso grew smaller. He wore a shirt, however loose and not tucked into the breeches. Last night's dream increased his yearning for answers and to be among his own kind or at least recognized.

"Jor'el, please tell me the reason and perhaps I can accept why you did this," he prayed yet stopped at hearing someone entered. He didn't turn until Vivian spoke.

"Well, this is one time I'm glad to see you up. Before leaving to tend a patient, Lester said you should begin moving about to build up your strength. I came to bring you to the kitchen for luncheon."

"Luncheon? The morning is gone already?"

She laughed. "I assumed being at the window you witnessed the change in light."

Kell noticed the sun passed its apex. "I guess I was too preoccupied to notice."

"What of your appetite? Did the preoccupation curb it?" she teased, to which he grinned.

"No, a meal sounds good." He stood. After nine days, four in the field and five in their care, he wasn't so stiff. He did experience an initial ache, which lessened upon movement.

Reaching the threshold, she took hold of his arm and the warm sensation returned. He smiled. Her return smile was modest. They didn't speak until he sat at the kitchen table and she fetched the food.

"I prepared extra since your appetite is greatly improved."

He chuckled with slight embarrassment. "I don't mean to eat so much."

"You need nourishment to recover." She set the plate of food in front of him. "Enjoy."

"I do enjoy your cooking."

They heard laughter. Wess stood in the threshold. Vivian smirked at him. "I suppose I need to feed you too."

He returned her smirk and fetched a cup to pour tea from pot on the side of the stove. "I wouldn't want to deprive your patient of such fine cooking," he said in obvious sarcasm.

"I wouldn't mind sharing, my lord."

Wess shook his head, took a drink and sat at the table opposite Kell. "I ate before leaving Burleigh." He surveyed Kell. "You look much improved from last time."

"I am. Thanks to Mistress Vivian, Doctor Lester and Donovan."

Wess drank more tea and regarded Kell from the rim of the cup. "Thought of anything which might give a clue of what happened to you?"

Kell shook his head, his mouth full. "I've tried," he said after swallowing.

"I've sent a few of my men to the Southern Forest to try and locate your family to tell them you're alive."

Surprised, Kell paused in eating. "You did what?"

Vivian approached and touched Kell's shoulder to get his attention. "I told Lester how you were overcome because of fretting about them. He asked Wess to find them and reassume them concerning your well-being."

The warm sensation returned at her touch. He smiled and took hold of her hand. "Thank you, only I'm afraid that is not possible." Hearing Wess' rough clearing of his throat brought Kell's attention back to him.

The features were stern and Wess glanced at Vivian. Kell grew awkward and released her hand. "I'm grateful to all of you, my lord, but it truly is not possible to tell them."

"We'll see." Wess took another drink and continued to watch Kell.

The sense of awkwardness became joined with embarrassment so Kell resumed eating.

Vivian frowned at Wess with warning and shook her head at him. He grinned. She relaxed and moved to check the food on the stove. Wess caught sight of Kell in his observation of them. Instead of making a comment, he asked a question.

"Whereabouts in the Southern Forest do they live? That may help to locate them."

"They're not confined to one particular place."

"Ah, hunters and woodsmen."

"In a manner of speaking."

Vivian spoke to Wess. "If you promise not to interrogate him too severely, I'll leave to tend to my chores."

"I promise to behave," he replied with a friendly smile.

Her returned smile filled with affection. Different than the polite smile she gave him earlier. Kell smiled when her glance passed to him before she exited the rear door.

Again Wess made a disapproving grunt and leaned across the table. Kell recognized the familiar harsh, scolding expression he'd seen from the formidable general when reprimanding a soldier.

"You were told to stop the advances."

"Not an advance, I was thanking her. Why are you so possessive and defensive?"

"None of your concern. You are simply a patient."

The answer didn't satisfy Kell and he continued by looking directly at Wess to press the point. All Guardians did so when dealing with mortals to probe and prompt. "Donovan said you and Lester have known each other since boyhood, and you have always treated Vivian with contempt. Why?"

Offended, Wess stiffened. "Contempt? You are too bold to pretend to you know what you're talking about. Contempt, bah!"

"What else do you call snippy retorts and sarcastic exchanges with such a fine and compassionate woman?"

Wess bolted up, making the chair tip sideways from the sudden movement. The reaction brought Kell to his feet. He struck a nerve and Wess fought to control his temper.

In a strained voice, Wess said, "When next I call, you better be recovered enough to leave. Or as Jor'el is my witness, speak so boldly again about Vivian and my sword will give you new wounds!"

"You care for Vivian."

Wess' jowls flexed. He stormed out the back door, slamming it closed.

Kell sat to ponder the exchange and again being accused of making advances. Why? He believed he was expressing gratitude, nothing more. Others took it for something else. *What others? Both times it was Wess. Lester scolded me on Wess' behalf.*

He stared at the door. Normally he pursued a mortal to continue the conversation until the mortal saw his fault, error, or reason. Wess didn't react the normal way mortals did when a Guardian evoke the probing glance, agreeable or thoughtful.

I'm not Guardian anymore so I can't deal with them in the same manner. He then voiced his frustration. "How does a mortal male deal with another mortal male who is obviously infatuated with a mortal female, yet misinterprets every movement and statement of the other male?"

The quandary didn't have an immediate answer, so after a moment's pondering he went back finishing his lunch.

Outside in the small barn, Wess found Vivian milking the family cow.

"If you came to see Lester, he went to call upon Widow Purdy. Her rheumatism is acting up fiercely. He should be back by suppertime."

Wess grinned and leaned on the stall. "I came to look in on you and your patient."

Skeptical, she stopped milking to confront him. "For a social call or reconnaissance?"

"Social."

"By the way you looked at me inside?"

"Social to you, reconnaissance with him."

She went back to milking. "Ridge told Lester that Kelvin is no threat."

"Maybe. I still haven't learned what happened to him or why. Nor have you heeded my advice and taken an escort."

She paused and glanced up at him. "I can't stop my life to wait for an escort. Besides," she continued at seeing his reproving scowl, "you haven't come by for your daily dose of remedy per my instructions. Why should I follow your orders, General?"

"Oh, so we're going to pull rank on each other?"

"No." She chuckled and stood, holding a full pail of milk. "I just wish you would take my advice, for your own good."

He drew her from the stall to continue speaking. "And I wish the same about you taking my advice, for your own safety."

She smiled. "I guess we both need to do a better at taking advice." She held the pail up for him. "Pour it in the barrel to sour overnight for cheese." After he finished, she took the pail back. "I'll have an escort next time, I promise."

"And when your patient is gone, I'll come by for more remedy."

She rolled her eyes. "Wess, he's not a threat!"

"I have work to do. Tell Lester I stopped by."

She walked him to his horse and waved as he rode off.

Kell joined her. "I hope I didn't make him too angry."

"He's simply concerned."

"He's developed a funny way of showing it. Not like in the past."

"Part of his concern is what happened to you. Speaking of, you should go back inside." She took his arm intent on steering him back to the house.

"No, I'd like some fresh air. It's been days since I've been outside."

"Only for a little while."

"Agreed. What chores are you doing?"

"Oh no, you're not going to help me."

"No, sit and watch." He flashed a toothy grin.

She snorted a laugh and returned to the barn. He followed. "I was milking to make cheese and butter." She sat on the stool and placed the pail back below the udders and resumed milking. After a moment, she saw his curious interest. "You appear deep in thought."

"No. I realized I never paid attention to someone milking a cow before."

She laughed. "It's not hard. Here, have a seat and try."

He shook his head with a short uncertain chuckle. "I don't think so."

"There's no need to be afraid. She won't kick or bite. Now, come." She took his arm and drew him over. He sat on the stool. "Gently place your hand on her and squeeze."

He started to do as instructed, then balked and stopped. "No."

"A strong soldier like you afraid of milking a cow?"

He smirked at the teasing challenge and began mimicking her motion. To his surprise and delight, he was milking a cow. "This isn't hard." The cow loudly mooed, briefly startling him.

"Oh, Babs, behave," she scolded the cow and lightly slapped its rump. "Pay her no mind," she said to him.

He stood. "All the same, I don't want to upset her."

Suddenly chickens squawked wildly and a dog barked. Before they knew the reason why, a large mangy dog with a chicken in its mouth ran into the barn. Another dog followed and nipped at its heels.

"Ari! Stop," said Vivian to the second dog.

Too late! Ari cornered the mongrel and they began fighting. She took a broom to intervene and only made matters worse. Babs became upset. The cow tried to back out of the stall to escape the dogs. When the tether stopped Babs, the cow bucked and kicked in an attempt to get free.

"Kelvin! Stop Babs."

He dodged flying hooves in his attempt to calm the cow. Several of Babs' kicks impacted the stall supports and began to weaken them. Kell avoided falling pieces of debris and heard Vivian cry out. She became knocked down and trampled when the dogs fought their way out of the corner and into the yard. He moved to help her just as Babs' latest kick dislodged one of the support beams. It crashed down beside them along with debris. Kell lifted Vivian in his arms, yet had difficulty due to his injuries. More falling lumber called for urgency. With a grunt of determination, he carried her from the barn before part of it collapsed.

"Babs!" Vivian motioned for Kell to put her down. He almost dropped her and glad she landed on her feet.

She scrambled to the barn. Through the debris, Babs remained standing. Collapsed lumber blocked the entrance to the barn. Vivian tried to move the fallen timber. It wouldn't budge. Kell came to help. However, after lifting Vivian he knew he didn't have the strength he once did. He may appear strong, but Guardian strength was far superior to mortal strength. All the same, he braced his left shoulder against the beam to push. With considerable effort, the beam started to move then finally fell aside to allow passage into the barn. Laboring for breath and in pain, he backed way and sat on the ground.

Vivian fetched Babs from the barn. She tethered the cow to a nearby post then knelt beside Kell. He looked weary and distressed.

"Are you hurt again?"

He shook his head muttering, "I have no strength!"

"You're still recovering."

Seeing her injured, he stopped her from examining his bandages. "You're hurt."

"A few scrapes and bruises, nothing serious."

The warm sensation at seeing her injured turned into anxious regret. "I'm sorry I couldn't stop the collapse."

"There was nothing you could do. Now, let me check you wounds."

When she examined his forehead, Kell gave into the overwhelming impulse. He did what he witnessed countless mortal males do, kissed her on the lips. It felt tantalizing and exhilarating.

Stunned and briefly speechless, she drew back. "I don't think you meant to do that," she stammered in forced words.

"I did."

"No, it's just a reaction brought on by danger, not a true feeling," she said, trying to contain her fluster.

"I've felt this way since we first met." He went to kiss her again and she tried to force herself from him. He wouldn't let her go, he couldn't.

"No, Kelvin. You're confusing gratitude with affection."

"You're wrong," he insisted, despite the deep hurt at her rebuff.

"Kelvin, let me go."

"Vivian!" Lester and Donovan rushed over. Lester removed Vivian from Kell's grasp. "What happened?"

Uncertainty of what to say or do, Kell remained silent.

Vivian straightened her clothes in an effort to gather her emotions to answer. "One of the strays got to the chickens and Ari chased it into the barn. They started fighting and Babs got so frightened she kicked down part of her stall and the ceiling fell. Kelvin carried me out then moved the fallen lumber so I could get Babs."

Lester made quick examination of Vivian's minor cuts and scraps. "You don't look too bad."

"I'm not. I was tending to Kelvin when you arrived," she said, making an awkward gesture at Kell.

Lester didn't appear convinced. "You and Donovan check on Babs and the damage. I'll take Kelvin back to the house." He pulled Kell to his feet. Nothing was said until they reached the sick room and Kell sat on the edge of the bed. "How are your wounds?"

"Sore, but I'll be fine. You should tend to Vivian."

"Not until I know your intentions towards her."

Kell hesitated in answering, as Vivian's words echoed in his ears, *you're confusing gratitude with affection.* He acted on impulse. Something he normally didn't do, yet prompted by intense, overwhelming feelings, closely followed by deep distress at her rebuff.

"Well?" demanded Lester.

"I don't know," said Kell in befuddlement.

"Oh? You just kiss every woman you come across?"

"No, it wasn't like that! She's the first female I ever kissed."

"You expect me to believe a man as handsome and strong as you, has never kissed a woman? Be serious!"

"Upon my word."

They stared at each other. Lester appeared skeptical, and Kell wished for his Guardian perception to help convince him. It didn't work earlier on Wess, thus it surprised him when Lester spoke.

"Very well, I believe you. I also warn you—I will be watching." Suddenly, he grew pale and reached for a nearby chair to keep from collapsing.

Kell moved to support Lester and help him sit. "What's wrong?"

"Nothing. It's passing."

"No. This is the second time I've seen you nearly swoon."

Lester took a breath of recovery and let out a long, relieved sigh. "I contracted a disease some years ago that flares up now and again."

"The contagion from Tunlund."

Lester became curious. "How did you know?"

"I was in Tunlund also. I remember you and several dozen others became gravely ill with a local contagion en route home. Eldric thought it came from the native water used to re-supply before sailing. He ordered it dumped overboard."

"Ay," said Lester, studying Kell. "Priscilla refilled the barrels with fresh water. There is a familiarity to you, yet I can't recall our meeting." He grimaced and closed his eyes, appearing to swallow back some sickness.

"I'll fetch Vivian."

"No!" His eyes snapped opened and he seized Kell's arm. "She doesn't know. At least not the extent."

"Extent?"

"It grows worse. In time I will lose my eyesight. By then I hope and pray she will finally have a life of her own and not care for a blind man."

Kell observed Lester's despondency with sympathy. "You're her brother. Of course she would care for you."

"You don't understand. She's been doing that for years!" He closed his eyes when his voice cracked.

Perplexed, Kell asked, "You scorn her love and care?"

"No! I feel guilty." He frowned before continuing to explain. "You probably noticed the age difference between us. Our mother died when Viv was born, our father five years later. I was fifteen and she was five. Since no relatives lived close by, it fell to me to raise her. I got work with a wealthy farmer, who provided a small shed for housing. That first winter, one of his cousins, a royal army doctor by the name of Charlton, came to visit. He stayed until spring, tending to the local folk and establishing a clinic. He believed I possessed medical aptitude and took me on as his apprentice. We moved from the farm to his house and infirmary near Waldron Castle."

"That's how you learned your trade."

"Ay. Since Charlton was attached to then General Iain, I took his place as army doctor upon retirement."

"Why did Vivian never marry?"

Lester grew sober. "Charlton helped me convince her to marry a fine man, a farrier by trade. Unfortunately, my wife died a month before the wedding, leaving me alone with three young boys. The eldest was only four and the youngest, Donovan, still an infant."

Since Lester had difficulty speaking of the past, Kell surmised what he already knew. "Vivian chose not to marry and helped you raise the boys."

"Ay. Along with Meredith's death, my profession took me away from home for extended periods with the army. Vivian didn't want her nephews going up without parents like we did. Now the boys are grown. The two eldest married and settled, while Donovan will wed at harvest." He fought to contain his emotion. "It is time my sister had a life of her own!"

"So you keep the extent of your illness a secret."

Weary, Lester nodded. "I try. Arrangements have been made for Heather, Donovan's intended, to move here after the wedding and he'll take over the surgery. I've prayed for Jor'el to bring someone for Vivian before I'm totally capacitated."

Kell balked in surprised concern. "You think I'm that person?"

Lester's baffled expression mirrored Kell. "I'm not sure what to believe," his voice lowered and he leaned closer to speak privately. "I thought Wess. I hoped for him, then you showed up and now I'm confused."

"Wess?"

"*Shhh!* Not so loud. We have known each other since I became attached to Charlton and are good friends. When Iain died, I continued under Wess' command. In fact, he requested my help in establishing his administration here in the South Plain, which is why I retired."

Kell tried to consider the possibility of being used as an answer to prayer, and in a most unusual and unexpected manner. Why in the guise of a mortal when he could serve just as well in his original state?

"Pappy."

Donovan's voice drew Kell from his pondering and Lester to his feet. The young man showed no sign of realizing the topic of conversation he interrupted.

"All is well with Babs. How are you feeling?" Donovan asked Kell.

"Sore, but no further harm done. Right?" he asked Lester.

"Ay, considering the fallen lumber. You should rest *in here* for the remainder of the day." He gave Kell a prompting look.

"Ay. I can use it."

After the door shut on their departure, Kell sat in the chair by the window. He stared at his hands and arms. The whole incident proved disconcerting in a number of ways. Not only was he severely reduced in strength, he acted on a strange, overwhelming impulse and kissed a female. Granted the kiss produced a pleasurable sensation, however the impetuous action surprised him. More puzzling is the deep prick in his heart at her rebuff. Such strong conflicting and driving emotions proved disturbing. He witnessed mortal men act rashly in the name of 'love' but *...Why did I do it again when she withdrew? I acted like I couldn't help myself ...*

He recoiled at the thought of not being in control of his emotions and falling victim to what Guardians considered the capricious fickleness of romantic mortal love. In fact, mortal weaknesses and deficiencies often caused questions and debates among Guardians. They tried to offer mortals counsel, advice and intervention with a dose of sympathy only without clear understanding or empathy for such compelling emotions. The area of romantic love provided the most baffling situations.

What about Vivian made him act impulsively or feel pain at her reaction? She was kind, compassionate and caring. He met many mortals over the centuries fitting that description. Many with courage, fortitude and faith added, only none save Shannan for whom he felt so strong an attachment.

Is there something about Vivian's appearance? He never considered himself a judge of mortal beauty or looks. Guardians never fussed about their clothes and hair or were concerned with outward appearances. Compared to mortals, they were unmarred in feature and physically perfect. The heart of a mortal was of more heavenly concern than outward appearance. So what were the criteria for their attraction? Thus far his time as a mortal showed him the complexities of interaction between them more keenly then he ever experienced as a Guardian.

He turned at hearing the door opened. Vivian entered and she carried a cup. Outwardly, he tried to quell any emotion of his pondering from being displayed on his features. Inwardly, he experienced a knot of apprehension mingled with pleasure at seeing her. She kept her eyes veiled from meeting his gaze and spoke in a benign tone.

"Lester fixed you a tonic."

"I don't want to sleep."

"To help take away the soreness, not strong enough to make you sleep." When she held the cup out, he took it.

Before drinking he spoke, a bit awkward at first. "Vivian—mistress," he corrected himself. "I'm sorry if I acted inappropriately."

She smiled, small and kind, still not meeting his gaze. "I apologize if I gave you a wrong impression that made you act. I could never share feelings for a patient."

The heart pain struck Kell again only now this wasn't an immediate reaction on her part, rather an outright rejection. Before he wondered what about Vivian attracted him, now he wondered what about him repulsed her. He couldn't keep the pricked hurt from being seen.

"Kelvin, I'm sorry. I didn't mean to hurt you."

He tried to maintain his temper when replying yet sarcasm crept into his voice. "Any patient, or just me since Wess views me as a threat?"

She focused a sharp eye on him as her temper flared. "You do Wess an injustice by bringing him into this."

"Oh? Then why do you and he grow defensive about the other rather than acknowledge you share feelings? And why place me in the middle?"

"You kissed me! If anything you inserted yourself." She grew agitated and frustrated. "Oh, men are all blind. You mistake kindness for affection and Wess can't see past grief ... *grr!*" She began to leave and came to an abrupt stop short of the door.

Lester appeared in the threshold along with another man. Her vexation turned to apprehension upon sight of the man. He stood half a head taller than Lester, about fifteen years younger with ash blond hair and beard. By the way he carried himself, manner of dress and armed with a sword and dagger, he appeared some kind of soldier or official. Vivian gave a cautious acknowledgement to the man before leaving.

"Kelvin, this is Sheriff Spaulding of Burleigh," said Lester, escorting Spaulding further into the room.

"Sheriff." Kell began to rise.

"Don't trouble yourself," said Spaulding. He moved in front of Kell and took a seat on the window still.

Upon closer inspection, Kell reckoned the sheriff to be near the same mortal age people guessed for him. Spaulding had blue eyes, darker than any mortal Kell could recall, yet definitely of mortal hue.

"Doctor Lester and Count Wess have told me about your unfortunate incident. I came to speak to you myself."

Kell shrugged. He never took his eyes off Spaulding. "I don't know what more I can say since I told them all I remember."

"Neither of them have been scouring the countryside like I have. Which is why it took me so long to come see you." Spaulding did his own inspection of Kell, though they carried on the conversation in a casual manner. "Have you ever been to Oakley?"

Kell briefly thought. "I can't recall that I have. Why?"

"I'll ask the questions," said Spaulding. For first time, his eyes narrowed and his features grew a touch hostile. "What about Hawthorn?"

"No." Kell grew suspicious of Spaulding and his questions.

"You claim not to remember, so it is possible?"

This was more a statement than a question so Kell replied in a deliberate manner. "It is possible, however doubtful."

"I'll be the judge of that."

"Sheriff, is this interrogation necessary? I thought you … " began Lester in protest. He stopped upon receiving a withering glare from Spaulding, one of undisputed authority brooking no question or objection.

"I'll decide what is necessary and to what extent, Doctor."

Lester shied away, a sympathetic eye finding Kell.

Even in mortal form, Kell would not accept bullying or intimidation. He placed the cup on windowsill and stood to confront Spaulding. "I told you all I know. There is no need to abuse Doctor Lester."

Spaulding stood, and placed a hand on the hilt of his sword to keep it steady. He leveled a glare of warning at Kell. "If he is harboring a fugitive then he has broken the law and falls under my jurisdiction."

"Fugitive?" stammered Lester.

He spoke how Kell felt, surprise. "I'm not a fugitive. I'm a victim."

"Of highway brigands or by the hand of your partners in crime?"

"Sheriff, what are talking about? You suspect Kelvin of being a criminal?"

Spaulding ignored Lester and drew close to Kell, nearly toe-to-toe. "We caught a gang of thieves in Hawthorn and linked them to a crime spree of thievery between Hawthorn and Oakley. Unfortunately, three managed to escape when being transported to the provincial prison and are reported in the area."

The comment of possibly being a criminal and Spaulding's move toward him, made Kell go rigid with resolution. He returned Spaulding's stare and tone. "You think I'm one of them. You're wrong."

"We'll see. My men are digging up the area where you were discovered. If they find stolen items … " He didn't finish his sentence, the implication self-evident.

"They won't find anything!"

"All the same. You are not to leave Burleigh until I say so. If you do, it won't go well for the doctor." Spaulding marched from the room.

The moment Spaulding left Vivian hurried in. "You don't believe him do you?" she asked Lester.

"I'm not sure what to believe."

"I'm not a criminal," Kell staunchly refuted. "I may not remember much of how I came to be here, but I *know* I'm not a thief."

In cautious concern, Lester regarded Kell. "I want to believe you, only uncertain if I can take that chance."

"Wess won't let Spaulding wrongly accuse a friend. Nor do I take threats lightly."

"You can't leave," she said to Kell, then to Lester. "He can't leave."

"I'm not going to put you at risk."

Lester shook his head in dispute. "It is as you said, Wess won't take Spaulding throwing about accusations against me. However, for the time being, you must stay here, both to continue your recovery and for everyone's safety."

She saw the cup on the windowsill where Kell placed it to confront Spaulding. "You haven't finished your tonic. You should do so to rest."

"No tonics. I must keep a clear mind and be ready."

"Try to get some sleep. Spaulding won't be back unless he finds something. I need to send word to Wess." Lester left.

"Do as he says. I'll come by later." Vivian hastened after Lester.

Kell scowled and sat at the window. "This is getting complicated."

Vivian caught Lester in the hall. "Don't tell Wess what happened, because nothing—happened," she quickly and awkwardly explained.

"You call a kiss nothing?"

"No! Kelvin confused gratitude for affection under dire circumstances. I apologized for giving him the wrong impression."

"Apologize? It wasn't your fault." He continued to his office.

She followed. "Lester, please, this isn't about Kelvin. I just got Wess to agree to accept daily doses of remedy. This news could negate that."

"Remedy? What are talking about? Is he ill and hasn't told me?"

"No, no, not physical. I mean his brooding since Bosley's death. You expressed concern about his withdrawing."

Stunned, Lester paused in reaching his desk. "You told him that?"

"I told him what you would not because you fear hurting him. He needs to know how his behavior is affecting others."

He pursed his lips in consideration. "He accepted what you said?"

"He acknowledged how difficult it's been, and grateful I said something. That's when he agreed he needs more doses of reality to come around." She grew fretful. "If you tell him what you *think* you saw, it could hinder his progress."

He sat at the desk. Thoughtful eyes shifted between Vivian and some unseen spot during his consideration. At her determined, prompting expression, he finally spoke. "I can't just ignore it. Wess is bound to notice the fallen barn."

"Of course you can tell him about at the barn, and thanks to Kelvin neither I nor Babs suffered serious injury."

"Just omit the kiss," he snickered to her chagrin.

"Ay."

"Donovan may have seen it also."

"I'll deal with Donovan."

He reached for her. She came about the desk and took his hand. Looking her squarely in the eye he said, "Tell me truly, that nothing transpired between you two."

She knelt, squeezed his hand and softly smiled. "I swear my concern for him is only as a patient."

He touched her cheek and smiled. "I believe you." He leaned closer and whispered, "I won't tell Wess."

Grateful, she kissed his cheek. He responded by hugging her. She felt the embrace tighten and he winced, making her concerned. "Lester?" When he released her she retained hold on his arms.

68

"A headache," he said, nonchalant.

She studied his face. "You haven't slept much and look pale. Are you certain it's just a headache?"

"Ay."

"You wouldn't be keeping something more serious from me, would you?"

"It's been hectic since we moved her." He forestalled her further questioning by saying, " Tell Donovan to bring me a remedy and then I need him to deliver a note to Wess." He gave her a gentle nudge. "Go. I'll be all right, you'll see."

"You promise to retire early tonight?"

"I promise. Now tell Donovan while I compose a carefully worded letter," he said with growing smile.

Chapτer 5

THE SUNSET IN THE FOOTHILLS AROUND OAKLEY MADE IT DARK inside a shack nestled on a plateau halfway up a slope. A solitary lantern on a table gave off the only light. At the table with his feet up sat Locan, a former Guardian warrior. His wore a thin beard, which matched his auburn hair. His yellow eyes looked more bored than relaxed.

Six months earlier he, a fellow warrior by the name of Mannix and a shape-shifter named Fitch helped in the attempted coup against Tyrone. Mannix became vanquished in battle while he and Fitch escaped. Since then, they become fugitives from their former comrades for turning against Jor'el. Maintaining his existence, forced him to hide with only occasional forays into the open, thus his boredom. He didn't stir when the door opened and Spaulding entered.

"About time," he groused.

"An interesting development occurred and may be used to our advantage."

"Oh?" Locan's feet came off the table and he sat upright when Spaulding took a seat opposite him. "I thought you were doing a good job impersonating the sheriff and keeping the general off balance and running in circles."

"I am. I can stay in this form as long as those mortal fools keep the real Spaulding alive," said Fitch.

"So there is more than one flaw to your disguise. Starting with being unable to control the *madah-dune*. Now we are forced to rely on mortal thieves to keep from being discovered."

"I did what I could to control them by using tricks I learned in the Cave!"

Locan didn't accept the rebuttal. "Since they managed to kill Kell, the Guardians have gone on heightened alert. Ridge is now Trio Leader of the South Plains and helping the general."

"What? When did this happen?"

"I discovered it while you were away."

Fitch/Spaulding tried to minimize the news. "Kell ordered the Trio Leaders to be on the lookout for us after the failed coup, so dealing with Ridge shouldn't be too difficult."

Locan leaned on the table and looked incredulously at Fitch/Spaulding. "Ridge's skills will be enhanced by his promotion, but this goes beyond the Trio Leaders. Do you seriously think Armus will sit by and not act to avenge Kell's death? That Avatar won't order the Jor'ellian Guards to scour the countryside for those responsible? Every Guardian will be ready to hunt us down!"

Fitch/Spaulding tilted his head with satisfaction. "This development may prove even more useful than I originally thought."

"How so?"

"A stranger arrived in the province with no memory of how he got here or what happened to him. I can use him to cause more havoc and do so with anonymity."

"I thought you were doing so well as Spaulding, while I'm basking in luxurious accommodations." Locan gestured by spreading his arms wide.

He ignored the sarcasm. "By shedding this shell of recognizable authority, I can freely move about. Isn't that the point? To cause as much trouble as we can before we're discovered and sent to eternal oblivion?"

"Ay," snorted Locan in annoyance.

"Wait." Fitch/Spaulding stood and looked about the shack. He opened the doors to the two other rooms. "Where are the mortals and Spaulding?"

"Relax, they're all safe."

"You're supposed to be guarding them, you idiot!"

Locan bolted to his feet and reached for his sword. "I'm a warrior, vassal worm, so mind your tongue! Or better yet, change into your true form so I can enjoy the silence of your inability to speak and not endure vain babble."

"At least lack of speech doesn't translate into lack of brains."

Before Fitch/Spaulding could react, Locan drew his sword, pinned the shape-shifter against the wall and pressed the blade against his throat. "Shall I cut out your mortal vocal chorals like Dagar did to still your Guardian voice?"

"Only if you want to cut your survival chances in half."

Locan slammed Fitch/Spaulding against the wall before releasing him. "What good is such an existence?"

"You should have thought of that before following Mannix into betrayal."

"He was my Trio Mate, friend and comrade! What of your motive? Losing your voice? That could have been restored if you rededicated yourself to Jor'el."

Fitch/Spaulding snarled in painful anger. "Try being abandoned by your comrades and trapped for hundreds of years with the creatures of *infrinn*, then maybe you'll understand. Enough of this! Using Kelvin, I can free us both to work."

Locan shrugged and resumed his seat at the table. "Perhaps. How do you propose to do it?"

He joined Locan at the table. "When I, or rather Spaulding," he said with a sly grin and motioned to his appearance, "interviewed him at Lester's infirmary, I told him about the gang of thieves running loose in the area and my suspicions of him."

"You mentioned the Hawthorn and Oakley connection, no doubt," said Locan with a hint of understanding.

"Ay. Since the real Spaulding has a ruthless and hardnosed reputation, I made certain he wouldn't leave Burleigh or the doctor would suffer the consequences for harboring a fugitive. It's well known how Spaulding dislikes the meddling doctor."

Locan frowned in dispute. "It's dangerous threatening the general's friend while trying to keep him guessing."

"The reverse actually. Last thing the good Doctor Lester wants is to cause the general any difficulty, so I believe he'll keep an eye on his patient. Meanwhile, we'll use Kelvin's identity to throw suspicion from our activities onto him."

"How will you assume his identity since you must make contact in your original form to initiate the first change? You can't just walk in as Spaulding, become Fitch and walk out as Kelvin."

"We'll find a way to draw him from the doctor's farm."

"You just said you, Spaulding, warned him about leaving."

"About leaving Burleigh. He can walk from one place to another."

"I suppose I have to do the dirty work again in capturing him."

"No, I'll take care of it. You continue to keep the fools out of sight until we need them again."

"What about your recent visit to the farm? Can Ridge sense your presence?"

Fitch/Spaulding shook his head. "When fully immersed in a mortal's persona, only the most skilled and elite Guardians can sense me. However, in helping the general, he could search the area around Oakley and those fools better be careful."

Locan expression grew lethal. "That ranger so much as shows his face around here, I will act and there will be nothing you can do to stop me."

"If he shows up, I won't stop you. Until then, I'll see what I can do with Kelvin."

"This hiding better end soon. I can't tolerate inactivity and being a nanny to incompetent mortals much longer."

"Patience, my warrior friend. Once this is over, we can leave the province for a place of your choosing." Fitch/Spaulding left.

Kell never tolerated threats, and after his encounter with Spaulding he tried to remain vigilant. For a Guardian staying awake for days wasn't difficult. Even during times of meditation a Guardian never lost consciousness. They remained alert and ready for action at the slightest sound or sense of danger. For a mortal going without sleep or some form of rest for a single day proved hard. He thought he managed to do so until he woke with a start when Donovan brought breakfast. He thanked the young man. Despite not being interested in eating, the gnawing of his stomach demanded nourishment.

This mortal frame can be irksome at times. He picked at the food.

His mind continued to replay all the events he remembered, only now in response to Spaulding's visit. He knew the towns of Oakley and Hawthorn by name. He knew most of the cities, towns and settlements in Allon while serving in his capacity as Captain of the Guardians. He was also familiar with the reports of trouble and disturbances Tyrone received since the fail coup attempt. Troubled seemed concentrated in the South Plains, and the reason was easy to assume—a change in mortal leadership.

Everyone viewed it as a test of Wess' abilities. No one at Waldron or on the Council felt the slightest bit of concern. Long ago, Wess proved his capabilities and mettle. Still, Kell thought to bolster Wess' effort by assigning Ridge as the new Trio Leader of the South Plains. This was not a reflection on Elwood's management, rather Ridge's knowledge of Locan and Fitch.

The current problem showed he couldn't simply ask Ridge or Wess about the progress of any efforts to quell the trouble. People already took exception to his personal familiarity of them and about various situations. He had to harness and utilize his knowledge in such a way as to not make anyone suspicious. But could he wait to hear from Spaulding about any discovery? He felt confident nothing would be found to link him to thievery. Waiting was more the issue, as it raised more questions about why Jor'el transformed him into a mortal.

Times of reflection and consideration were interspersed with prayers requesting insight and guidance. Thus far, he received no answer, yet there had to be reasons.

Thirty minutes later, Lester, Donovan and Vivian appeared. The men were dressed for travel. She came to collect the tray and saw the food only half-eaten.

"Are you not feeling well?" she asked.

He gave her a reassuring grin. "No, I'm fine, just not hungry. Although, I do enjoy your cooking."

Donovan and Lester tried not to show amusement.

Vivian smiled at Kell. She took the tray and tossed a triumphant smirk to her brother and nephew while passing out of the room.

"She doesn't cook that bad. I've tasted worse," said Kell.

"Ay, when my father tries cooking." Donovan laughed.

"It helps you to look forward to savoring Heather's good cooking after you're married," quipped Lester.

Kell chuckled at the humor then commented upon their appearance. "Going out?"

"We have several patients to call upon and won't be back until supper time. Can I trust you to stay here?" replied Lester.

"Of course."

"And act appropriately?" he stressed.

"Ay."

Lester nodded. "Good day." He and Donovan left.

Giving his word to remain was frustrating. Considering Spaulding's warning, he had to take it slow for the sake of others. He felt better, and wanted to start his own investigation with questions that could be answered. He decided to leave the sick room and head for the kitchen, not due to hunger, rather to interview Lester's servants.

Drusilla and Howey were a friendly couple and had served Lester for twenty years. Kell saw them on a daily basis at Waldron and exchanged polite conversation. Drusilla proved talkative about almost anything, but became evasive and a bit defensive when asked about Lester, Vivian and Donovan. Not wanting to press her, Kell left to find her husband.

Howey worked to repair the barn and replied a bit gruff considering his usually easy-going nature. He said Lester informed him and Drusilla of the sheriff's suspicions. Kell couldn't find fault with their behavior and lack of information. Good, loyal servants usually acted protective of their masters and mistresses. Then again, not having lived in the area very long they provided little information to aid his investigation.

Kell noticed Vivian leave the chicken coop carrying a basket of eggs and head for the kitchen door. He followed, intent on speaking to her. When he entered the kitchen, she set the basket on the table and took off her apron.

"How are the chickens today?"

"Well. A successful day's laying, despite losing one." She hung the apron on a hook near the door, took a bonnet off another hook and put it on her head. "They should bring a good price in town."

"You're going to town now?"

"Ay. The eggs are fresh and the larder is low on flour and oatmeal." She placed a towel over the eggs then went to the door and looked out toward the barn. Howey continued the repairs while off in the distance storm clouds grew. "I hope he finishes by this afternoon. Babs won't like getting wet again. She was stingy with milk this morning in protest."

"I can help him finish it."

"No, don't strain yourself."

"What about the rain?"

She grabbed a cloak off another hook. "What do you think cloaks and bonnets are for? Besides, we must restock to eat." She fetched the basket and headed down the hall toward to the front door. Kell followed. Before leaving, she spoke. "If Lester gets back before I do, tell him not to worry I'll stop at the castle."

"There's something to worry about?" asked Kell.

She waved off his question and departed.

He took note of the dark, distant sky. He went back through the house, and out the kitchen door to the barn. "Need help?"

Howey tossed him a guarded glance before motioning at tools. "Can you handle any of those, or just a sword?"

"What I can't handle I make up for in strength."

Howey nodded, so together, he and Kell worked on repairs. Even with growing gray clouds threatening rain, the work proved hot and dirty. Kell began sweating, something else he didn't do as a Guardian. He stripped off the doublet and shirt Lester lent him. He no longer wore the torso bandage and the scabs were almost gone with the healing bruises still visible. Drusilla brought hearty sandwiches and cider for lunch. They sat on a bench in the shade of the yard's large oak tree to eat.

Wess arrived and reined his horse. "Finally doing something useful, I see," he said with a snicker.

"Thought I should earn my keep and help allay the sheriff's suspicions."

Wess dismounted. His face grew stern in response. "For my friend's sake, those suspicions better be groundless."

"They are."

"Doctor Lester is making calls, my lord. Donovan went with him. Mistress Vivian is inside," said Howey.

"No, she left for town," said Kell.

"What?" Wess' hot glare went from Kell to Howey.

The servant voiced his surprise. "I didn't know, my lord! I would not let her go alone, per your instructions and the doctor's. Why didn't you tell me?" he scolded Kell.

"I didn't know anything was wrong."

Wess accosted Kell. "Are you a complete idiot? You're nearly killed by thugs and yet let a woman travel alone? What kind of man are you? How long ago did she leave?"

Kell bolted to his feet and fought his temper to reply. "A couple of hours, and I wouldn't have let her go alone if I knew."

"You're supposed to stay here!"

"She is planning on going to the castle to call upon you. Though I can't see why since you treat her with indifference. What kind of man are you?"

Wess visibly trembled with rage. His glance at the discoloration still on Kell's forehead kept him from striking out. He vaulted into the saddle, jerked his horse around and sent it into a gallop.

"You're lucky he didn't kill you," chided Howey. "I'll finish the barn alone." He marched off.

Kell took several deep breaths to calm down. He wondered whether to follow Wess and help find Vivian. He may not like the way Wess spoke, however, he had not thought about Vivian's safety. True, he determined to stay and not place them in danger of the sheriff, but hadn't thought much beyond that. Another mortal flaw, when as captain he thought of all options.

Enough of this foolishness! Mortal or Guardian, get a hold of yourself and do what you created to do, serve and protect. He snatched the shirt and doublet to dress and leave to find Vivian. At the front of the house, he met another rider, and one in uniform.

"Are you the one called Kelvin?"

"I am."

"Sheriff Spaulding wants to see you—immediately."

"What about?"

"I don't ask questions, I just follow orders. So should you, if you don't want to make him angry. Boar's Head Tavern at the edge of town. He's waiting." He left.

Kell considered heading back to get a horse from Howey then remembered Lester only had two horses and both being used. He also thought about fetching a sword. No, it would be better to appear unarmed and no threat.

Once more the mortal frame proved inferior to the Guardian state. He couldn't cover the distance at the speed he was accustomed to running. The town of Burleigh was a mile from Lester's farm, and he wanted to finish the interview quickly and start searching for Vivian.

The castle lay beyond the town, accessible by either going through town or taking the castle road circumventing the town. Taking the circling route added time and distance yet more direct than dealing with the townspeople or navigating traffic. Being the seat of the South Plains, commerce was constant. Almost every person and shipment passed through Burleigh from the coastal town of Geary to other destinations.

Fortunately, the Boar's Head Inn stood on the same side of town on the road leading to Lester's farm. At the inn, Kell discovered Spaulding left for the castle and gave directions for him to take the castle road and avoid going through town. Running a mile proved different than running the two-mile road circumventing the town. Thickets, hedgerows and rock walls lined the road. Woods separated pastures and fields of crops from the road. Traffic on the hemmed-in road left very little room to maneuver. The fell, heavy, which added to the difficulty of the journey.

Kell tried to dodge a loaded wagon and tripped into a thicket at one of the more overgrown portions of the road. He picked the remnants of the thicket off, wincing at several thorn pricks.

"Help!" called a female voice from behind the thicket.

"Is someone there?"

"Help, please."

Careful of the thorns, Kell pushed through the thicket. The pelting rain made it hard to see. He suffered a few more scratches on his hands from thorns. After fifty yards, he stopped in a small clearing ringed by trees and dense underbrush. "Where are you?"

"Here!" the voice came from across the clearing.

By the time Kell pushed through more underbrush into a second clearing, he ventured a hundred yards off the road. A frightened girl dashed past him and headed toward the road.

"Wait! I thought you needed—" Someone tripped him. He rolled over onto his back in time to see a hand grab his face. He seized the hand and wrestled to get free. The hold proved strong and persistent. He kicked at the person and made contact. The hand slipped off. He saw the person's face and momentarily startled before recognizing—"Fitch!"

The shape-shifter's balked at hearing his name.

Their eyes met, and Kell experienced a surge of power not felt since becoming mortal. The surge reached his eyes. In a voice of full authority he said, "That's right, traitor, look at me. I am Kell!"

Fitch gaped in dreadful surprise. He broke free of Kell's hold, tearing the collar of Kell's doublet in his attempt to get away. Kell tried to stop Fitch. Alas, the surge of power allowing him to speak with his former authority, didn't translate into strength against the shape-shifter. Fitch vanished in the flash of dimension travel.

The sudden power drained away as quickly as it came and he felt queasy. For a moment he considered the situation, baffled that for an instant he could declare his identity. Why? Not until he spoke did Fitch recognize him, so it couldn't be because he knew his identity beforehand.

"No, he tried to shape-shift to take Kelvin's place only he couldn't because I still have my Guardian essence. I was able to identity myself because I came face-to-face with evil. Now he knows who I am—" his head snapped around toward the road. "The girl!"

He hurried through the thicket, ignoring the thorns tugging at his clothes and scraping the flesh of his hands. Fitch probably forced her to serve as bait and wouldn't leave a witness. Reaching the road, Kell paused, his breathing hard, more in anxious anticipation than exertion. He looked up and down the road for any sign of her.

"Get out of the way!" shouted an irate wagon driver.

The voice jolted him back to reality in time to avoid being trampled. He got splattered by more mud and wiped it off his chin. Fortunately the rain stopped. With no sign of the girl and unable to track Fitch without his Guardian ability, he continued to the castle. Although not in a presentable state, he didn't dare keep Spaulding waiting.

While walking, he considered the encounter with Fitch. What was the shape-shifter doing in Burleigh? Was Locan with him? He reviewed all the events since arriving in the South Plains, yet nothing seemed to answer the question of why Fitch was in town and tried to shape-shift into Kelvin. The call of the watch made him realize he reached the castle.

The large enclosed courtyard could hold the smaller surrounding population of farmers and craftsmen for protection from an attack if necessary. The main house was divided into four equal sides of gabled portions all ending in rounded battlements surrounding an inter courtyard. A groom led the horse away and Wess headed for the main door.

"General."

"Kelvin? What are you doing here?"

"Sheriff Spaulding wanted to see me. I initially went to the inn, where he left instructions for me to report to him here."

"I'm not aware of any meeting. And what happened to you?"

Kell searched for a quick excuse. "A wagon nearly ran me down."

Wess flashed a wry smile. "The road can be hazardous on foot." He motioned to the front door. "Let's see if Spaulding is here."

Inside, Cameron hurried to meet Wess. "You have visitors, General."

"So I was told." Wess cast a smirk at Kell. "The drawing room?" He made his way down the hall, tossing his hat into a chair and pulling off the gloves as he went.

They didn't see an individual they expected. No Spaulding, while Vivian was not alone. Ridge, Nigel, Mirit, Fraser, Ellis, Valery, Chad and the Guardians Armus, Vidar, Wren, Avatar, Kendrick and Virgil also waited. Beside Valery stood a wolf by the name of Cody. Being Mirit's squire, Valery wore a Jor'ellian cadet uniform, her strawberry blonde hair styled in a similar fashion to Mirit, a long braid pinned up to form a crown like shape.

"Nigel!" said Wess in pleasant surprise.

Kell stopped in his tracks, stupefied by Wess' speech and sight of the unexpected. Nigel and Mirit wore their uniform as the King and Queen's Champion. With so large an entourage, he realized this wasn't a social call. His mind reeled at the possibilities, and if it related to him or something else happened. Whatever the reason, it was difficult in his present state to see the mortals he served and cared for. The presence of his fellow Guardians proved almost too much, especially Armus and Avatar. None showed any sign of recognizing him. He shied and looked down to compose himself.

Nigel smiled. "Wess. You obviously weren't expecting us."

"No, but welcome. All of you." He moved to pull a bell cord and saw Cameron standing the threshold, waiting. "We have guests."

Cameron smiled. "Refreshment should be here shortly, General. The rooms are being prepared."

Grateful, Wess patted his aide's shoulder. "Thank you, Cameron."

"Of course, General." Cameron held his smile, bowed and withdrew.

"We didn't mean to startle you," said Nigel.

"Unexpected. I was out on a rather hurried errand." He tossed a look to Vivian then back to Nigel.

"Why did you bring Kelvin here? And looking so miserable. What mischief did you get him into?" asked Vivian.

Wess chuckled at her accusation. "I'm not responsible for how he looks. A wagon nearly ran him over on his way here at Spaulding's summons, not mine."

"What does Spaulding want with you?" she asked.

Kell shrugged, still recovering and wondering if he could even form words.

"Probably something to do with the investigation of Kelvin's mysterious attack."

"I thought you said a wagon nearly ran him over." Nigel motioned to Kell.

"No, Highness, the wagon is unrelated," said Kell, the words forced. At least he had voice to speak.

"You know who he is?" asked Wess.

Kell flushed at the miscue. "Everyone knows, at least soldiers know the prince, the Champion," he fumbled over his words in identifying Nigel by royal rank and his official Jor'ellian status as *Champion*.

"I still don't recognize you, despite you knowing me and the prince."

"Master Kelvin is a soldier," Vivian explained to Nigel. "He became injured in an apparent ambush by brigands. As a result, he doesn't remember how he came to be in the South Plains from the Southern Forest."

"The Southern Forest?" asked Nigel with interest. "When was this?"

"Approximately ten days ago. I've been helping the count investigate the matter. So far we've turned up nothing," said Ridge.

"About the same time as the attack," said Armus.

Ridge nodded, his expression sober. "It's probably unrelated."

"Another attack?" asked Wess.

"You haven't told him?" Armus asked the ranger.

"No chance. Or more rightly, I'm still trying to comprehend it. Hard to imagine the incidents are connected."

Kell clenched his fists against the rising tide of emotions listening to what he feared. He avoided looking at anyone until he felt a wet nose against his right hand. Cody sniffed him. The wolf inspected every new person who came into any room with Valery present. Cody protected her from the Dark Way when she fled her father to warn Tyrone of Ellan and Hueil. Since then, Cody remained with her and became a familiar sight at court, thus the wolf knew him. Kell might have looked different, but if Fitch couldn't shape-shift because he still possessed his Guardian essence, maybe Cody could sense that. Cody nudged his hand, so Kell petted the wolf's head.

"You're not afraid?" asked Fraser.

"Why should I be? He doesn't frighten everyone here and is friendly, so I assume he's tame."

"He's hardly tame," said Valery. "He was testing you. Judging by his reaction, you passed."

Cody licked Kell's hand and wagged his tail in a sign of recognition. Not a Guardian or mortal, yet it still made Kell smile to be acknowledged. He scratched Cody behind the ear. The wolf made a contented sound and cocked his head in pleasure.

"There is a familiarity to his face," said Nigel.

"I still can't place him," said Wess.

"There are many soldiers and only a few commanders," said Chad.

"You can't remember how you came here from the Southern Forest?" asked Nigel.

"No, Highness. One day I was there and the next—outside Burleigh. Mistress Vivian found me and took me to her brother for treatment of my injuries."

"What were you doing in the Southern Forest?"

"Hunting, Highness." Movement caught Kell's attention. Armus moved beside Nigel. For the first time, Kell made eye contact with his lieutenant, comrade and friend since the beginning. Behind Armus' stoic expression, Kell saw pain. He feared he knew why, making the words of reply stick in his throat. However, when Armus' eyes narrowed with inspection, Kell forced himself to speak. "Is there something wrong with that, Highness?"

"A horrible incident occurred around the same time and we want to know if you saw anything unusual while hunting."

Kell understood what Nigel meant. It would not be wise to say so, especially the way Armus stared at him. By the familiar glare, Armus was watchful for danger. Lie or be evasive, and Armus would know. Avatar joined Armus in coming beside Nigel. Avatar stood braced, silver eyes direct and with a readiness and willingness to strike if Kell so much as twitched wrong. Oh, how he depended upon them over the centuries! Only, now, he became the object of their focused scrutiny. Ridge appeared thoughtful, Vidar and Wren wary while Kendrick and Virgil showed no expression. Not good when warriors were expressionless. The situation made him realize how intimidating Guardians appeared to mortals. The pause barely lasted a moment when Nigel asked:

"Well?"

"Come to think about it, I heard eerie howling sounds and stumbled upon usually large animal tracks."

"Natural or unnatural?"

Kell heaved an awkward shrug in trying to maintain his demeanor under the scrutinizing gaze of his former comrades and Nigel's questions. He didn't want to make them suspicious. He was already accused of being a thief. "Not like any natural sounds or tracks I recognize."

Vivian came to support Kell. "My brother said the attack came from behind before they cold-cocked him."

"The next thing I remember is waking up outside Burleigh." Kell followed Nigel's questioning glance to Armus. The Guardian's stoic expression remained unchanged. Again, what he saw in Armus' eyes troubled him and he fought to mask his disturbance from being visible.

"Well?" Nigel asked Armus but Mirit spoke.

"If they attacked him to keep from being discovered could whoever controlled the beasts have sent him here using dimension travel?"

"That is possible," said Ridge in consideration. "I did a thorough search and found no tracks or any objects in the vicinity of where Mistress Vivian found him."

"Is this the same attack you mentioned earlier?" asked Wess.

"Ay," said Nigel, grim in voice and face. "Part of the reason we're here is because of it. When returning from the first hunt of the season, Vidar and Wren sensed danger. Kell and Armus accompanied Vidar to discover what while Wren and Avatar informed us. It turned out to be *madah-dune.* By the time we arrived as reinforcement, the unthinkable happened. The beasts killed Kell."

Wess stared at Nigel, thunderstruck. "What?"

Kell flinched at hearing the dreaded announcement of his death, which confirmed his deepest fear. Everything within him wanted to scream *No, I'm alive* but a heavy restraint prevented him from speaking. His attempt to keep his reaction and struggle from being seen proved unsuccessful.

"Kelvin?" asked Vivian. She took his arm in support.

"I'm sorry. I got a sudden headache." He closed his eyes as if blinking back pain when in reality he couldn't look at anyone.

"He's not fully recovered, Highness," she said then sent a prompting glance to Wess.

"Take him to a guest room," he said.

Kell lowered his head and opened his eyes when Vivian steered him out of the room. He was grateful to leave and fought to contain his emotions as they went upstairs. Although caught off-guard at sight of them, Cody's greeting helped to allay his initial discomposure. The pain in Armus' eyes and Avatar's unflinching readiness brought his emotions to the surface, while hearing his death proclaimed was sheer agony! Worst of all, he couldn't do or say to ease their pain on his behalf.

Once in the room, Vivian's asked about his headache.

"I just want to be left alone. No tonic, nothing."

"At least let me help you to bed."

"No!" He shook off her attempt. "Just leave!" Despite the hurt on her face at his rudeness, she left.

Finally alone, he sat on the edge of the bed. Hearing of his death provided the most dreaded answer he ever experienced. His Guardian life was finished! The suppressed emotions overwhelmed him, and he bitterly wept. The question of *why* kept racing through in mind, nothing more, just a deep yearning to know why? Finally, physically and emotionally exhausted from heart-wrenching lament, he fell into a fitful sleep. The conversation with Nigel and the faces of his comrades invaded his dreams. He stirred to roll over and briefly opened his eyes. A figure flickered in the candlelight and he sat up in fright.

"Armus!"

"Ay," said the Guardian without any expression.

Kell took a deep breath to swallow back his shock. The room remained dark, save for the single candle now half the size of earlier. "What time is it?"

"Late."

In an attempt to recover, Kell ran a hand over his face. Mud from earlier had dried and caked, flaking off when he picked at it. He moved to a toilet stand with a mirror, basin, water-filled pitcher, bar of soap and a towel. He inspected his face and saw where his tears smeared some mud. He also noticed Armus' reflection, watching him. Kell tried to assume a casual attitude and poured water into the basin to wash his face.

"What are you doing here? Is something wrong? Nigel perhaps?"

"No, and why would you ask about the *prince*?" Armus placed emphasis on the word *prince*.

Kell balked at realizing his use of Nigel's name made Armus wary. He covered his miscue by wetting his face, paying particular attention to the dried areas of mud. "I'm a soldier. It is my duty to be concerned for the prince's welfare."

"Were you on leave while hunting?"

"Ay." In the mirror, Kell saw Armus cock his brow in a manner showing skepticism. "You don't believe me. Why?"

"You're not telling all you know."

Despite the truth of Armus' statement, and the fact he couldn't make anyone completely understand, there was only one way to allay a Guardian's suspicion. He put down the soap, turned to face Armus and spoke with all sincerity. "I don't remember much, only disjointed images I'm still trying to piece together. If I could, I would gladly tell you. I don't wish you, the prince, or anyone else harm."

After a brief moment of enduring Armus' intense regard, Kell noticed a subtle softening of expression.

"Now, I believe you," said Armus.

Relieved, Kell said, "Thank you."

"Finish washing and go back to sleep. You need to rest." He turned to leave.

"Armus," said Kell, drawing his friend's attention back to him. He wanted so much to offer comfort and encouragement. The restraint returned, while seeing the deep, suppressed grief in Armus' eyes, nothing seemed appropriate. Still, he needed to speak. "I'm sorry about the captain. I know he was your friend."

Armus nodded and left.

Vidar and the other Guardians stood watch in the hall while the mortals slept. He joined Armus when the lieutenant emerged from the room. Armus stared at the door so Vidar asked, "Something wrong with Kelvin?"

Armus shook his head. "I'm not sure."

"What do you mean?"

"Ridge is right. He's truthful about not remembering, yet I sense there is more to him."

"You think he's hiding something?"

"Not consciously." Armus drew Vidar away from the room to where the others gathered to continue his explanation. "According to Vivian, he suffered a head injury. Eldric explained how mortals suffering such injury often experience short and long term memory loss."

"Ah," said Vidar with understanding. "So he's not consciously hiding something while being truthful about what he can remember with certain gaps caused by memory loss. Is that your theory?"

"Ay. He may not be aware of it."

"Could casting suspicion on his behavior be detrimental to the regaining of his memory?" asked Kendrick.

"Eldric repeatedly warns about pushing a mortal too hard and too soon by citing the possibility of causing permanent mental and physical harm," said Avatar.

"He told you that to keep you from pestering Nigel when he first returned and was still crippled," said Wren in her wry teasing manner.

Armus' deep frown of disapproval made Avatar speak to divert the lieutenant's marked attention from Wren. "What did Kelvin say to make you think that?"

It worked. Armus turned to him to reply. "Not so much what he said," his focus changed to the door and kept speaking, "There is something oddly …"

"Familiar," said Ridge when Armus hesitated. The others looked at the ranger, both annoyed and curious. "Everyone's saying it. I thought so when he called me by name before we were introduced. How did he know me if we haven't met before? He claims to be a soldier only I can't place him."

"Then why hasn't one of these keen warriors recognized him?" asked Wren.

"Unload your bow, Wren! Now is not the time for your sarcasm," scolded Armus.

Visibly stung by the harsh rebuke, she started to speak when Avatar drew her back from Armus. He shook his head in warning to stop her. The others also grew cautious at Armus' usual display of anger.

Armus' jowls flexed with the strain of conflicting emotions. "I'm going to keep an eye on him for when he does remember." He spoke in a husky voice then moved to stand at the door to Kelvin's chamber.

"I didn't mean to upset him," she said in apology to Avatar.

"I know. Under normal circumstances he wouldn't have lost his temper. Just be more careful around him until he finishes grieving."

"You mean until you both finish grieving," said Kendrick.

"I'll be fine," chided Avatar in rough dispute.

"Really? Then why snap at me?" asked Kendrick in a benign tone.

Avatar sighed and admitted, "Well, perhaps before Armus."

"How long will it take for him?" asked Virgil.

Avatar answered in a somber voice. "Hard to say."

"Have you tried to engage him in conversation?"

"No. He'll speak when he is ready."

"Until then, you shield him like you did Kell when we thought Armus was dead," said Vidar.

Avatar's silver eyes narrowed in anger at the archer. "Do you expect me to do otherwise? He too was my mentor along with Kell."

"No, and don't get touchy with me. I too feel Kell's loss, and perhaps more deeply then you realize. There aren't many of us left from the beginning. I can only think of a handful, myself, Armus, Gulliver, Gresham, Barnum, Chase, Egan, Priscilla."

"Hard to imagine our elders dwindling to so few," said Virgil, the youngest present at almost twelve hundred years.

"If the rest of us someday are gone, it falls to the next eldest group to assume the full mantle of leadership." Vidar looked to Avatar and Wren, both in the group at over eighteen hundred years old.

"I need to apologize." She carefully approached Armus. Even in a jovial mood he was a formidable Guardian. Angry, upset or in battle, he was frightening. Just seeing his intense profile made her balk in step. He stared straight ahead seeming not to pay attention. Even when she stopped beside him, he stared across he hall. "Armus," she said, trying to keep the nervousness from voice.

"Ay," he said, still not looking at her.

"I'm sorry for my ill-timed humor. I didn't mean to upset you. I know this is difficult for you. It's difficult for all of us," she paused to gather her emotions. "I wanted you to know I'm sorry and it won't happen again."

He glanced at her to nod an acknowledgement then returned to staring straight ahead.

Timid, she withdrew and stood between Kendrick and Avatar. Kendrick's larger frame blocked her view of Armus. Her voice barely rose above a choked whisper, "I hope he recovers soon."

"We all do," said Avatar in sympathetic agreement.

<hr />

At the shack, Fitch appeared from the fading light of his arrival. Locan sat at the table, unfazed. Two mortal males jumped in fright. Both were in their early twenties, similar in facial features, obviously brothers. They were dingy and grungy in appearance with whisker stubble from lack of shaving.

"Why can't you tell us when you're coming and going?" one chided.

Locan shrugged with indifference. Fitch's expression and gestures showed excitement. "I gather you were unsuccessful cornering Kelvin."

Fitch continued his wild motions and pulled Locan to his feet.

"Leave off!" He brushed aside the shape-shifter only to aggravate Fitch, who seized him again. "What's wrong with you?"

Impatient and annoyed, Fitch waved at the brothers.

"I guess we're being dismissed," the youngest said in a huff.

"Come on. It's best we don't anger them." The elder steered his brother toward the room indicate. Fitch seized his shoulder whirled him about and placed a hand on his forehead. He fainted just as Fitch transformed into his appearance.

"Hey! What did you do to Preston?" He knelt beside his brother.

"He'll be fine," said Fitch/Preston. "Take him to the room and when we're done I'll wake him up. No harm done."

Locan nodded to the mortal. "Reilly, do as he says."

Reilly picked up Preston under the shoulders and dragged him into the room and shut the door.

"Now what is—"

He drew Locan a corner to speak privately. "He's here!"

"Who?"

"Him! *Kell*," said Fitch/Preston low and dreadful.

"Impossible. We saw him die."

"I tell you it is him."

"Can't be. No Guardian, even one as powerful as Kell, can come back to life when vanquished."

Irate, Fitch/Preston waved the torn piece of doublet in Locan's face. "I had him in my grasp, only I couldn't shape-shift."

"You mean Kelvin?"

"Ay! You know I must appear in my original form and touch their face or forehead in order to change. And I can only do so with mortals, not Guardians!"

"Ay, but what does Kelvin have to do with Kell?"

"The moment I touched him, something wasn't right. He grabbed my hand and wrestled it away from his face. When our gaze met, his *eyes* altered in appearance to brilliant gold. With power and authority he declared his identity. That's why I couldn't shape-shift. In physical appearance he is mortal, but in spirit and essence it is Kell!"

Locan became guarded during the explanation. "Why would he assume the appearance of a mortal?"

"I don't know! Maybe he's undercover. Assuming a mortal's identity to thwart us." Agitated, he kept pulling at the torn cloth.

"By faking his own death? It doesn't make sense."

"I tell, you, it is Kell!" Again he waved the piece of cloth at Locan.

89

"All right, then answer me this—how did he know we were here to facilitate such an elaborate disguise?"

"He's Jor'el's captain! He knows everything."

"He's not omniscient. He only knows what Jor'el tells him."

Fitch/Preston wasn't listening, his fear beyond reason as he paced. "We've gone too far this time. Our end is near."

Locan seized Fitch/Preston to get his attention. "You said he is in mortal form, which means he is more vulnerable."

"I have Guardian strength and faculties in mortal form, so he should."

"Did he recognize you as Spaulding?"

Fitch/Preston thought for a moment. "I don't think so. No."

"You said elite Guardians can detect you in mortal form, and you still possess your all your Guardian attributes. But Kell, the captain, couldn't sense you in his mortal state?" When Fitch/Preston began to smile, Locan continued. "We may have a chance to prevent him from exposing us if we catch him unaware and strike before he can respond."

In command of his emotions, Fitch/Preston began to think out loud. "We have to find a way to isolate him."

Locan motioned toward the room. "What do you think they're for? Besides, you already put *Kelvin* under suspicion. Unlikely he will endanger mortals to get at us."

Fitch/Preston slapped the cloth in Locan's hand. "Keep this. It may come in handy to deal with him. This time when Kell dies, no one will mourn him."

Chapter 6

THE FOLLOWING MORNING, FITCH JUST ARRIVED AT THE constable's office in Burleigh to continue his role as Spaulding when unexpected visitors arrived: Wess, Nigel, Fraser, Chad, Ridge, Avatar, Armus and Kendrick.

"My lord." He tossed Wess a hasty bow. His eyes shifted to the others, though he avoided direct eye contact with the Guardians.

"Sheriff. I don't think you had the pleasure of meeting his royal highness Prince Nigel, the King's Champion, and Prince Fraser."

"No. Your Highness," he said to Nigel and then to Fraser.

Nigel continued the introductions. "This is Sir Chad of the North Plains, Lieutenant Armus, second-in-command of the Guardians, Commander Avatar of the Jor'ellian Guard and Kendrick. You already know Ridge."

Fitch/Spaulding flashed a forced toothy grin of acknowledgement. "Indeed. To what do I owe this visit?"

Wess replied, "Two reasons. First to inform you Kelvin is no longer with Doctor Lester—"

"I ordered him to remain!"

"He is at Burleigh Castle under my supervision."

Maintaining the mortal's known combative façade, Fitch/Spaulding stiffened with insult. "You interfere in my jurisdiction, my lord?"

"The safety and administration of the *entire* South Plains is *my* jurisdiction."

"I am well aware of that fact, my lord."

"Then how is it you keep overstepping your bounds, and using bullying and threats to do so?"

When Fitch/Spaulding snarled with intense anger, Nigel spoke, rough and loud. "Gentlemen! It is the king's business to maintain law and order in any province experiencing trouble it cannot resolve on its own. Which is why we are here, on the *king's* business. The second reason for this morning's visit, Sheriff Spaulding."

"My apologies, Highness," said Wess.

Fitch/Spaulding didn't reply, rather made a curt nod to Nigel.

Having made his point, Nigel spoke in a calmer voice. "What have you discovered about Master Kelvin? Did your men find stolen items?"

"Not yet, Highness," answered Fitch/Spaulding in a begrudging manner. "But they will. The connection is too obvious to ignore."

"Or manufactured," said Wess.

Fitch/Spaulding again became angry. "You accuse me of impropriety, my lord?"

"Without proof, you accuse my friend of harboring a fugitive. Can you not accept such questioning it when it happens to you?"

"And Master Kelvin," added Chad. "If no evidence is found, you have wrongly labeled him a thief."

"*Yet*, my lord, no evidence yet," stressed Fitch/Spaulding.

"Be careful, Sheriff. The king's justice will not suffer being misused," said Nigel in heavy warning.

Fitch/Spaulding proudly squared his shoulders. "In all my years of service under Sir Gareth I have never wavered in fulfilling my duty, Highness."

"You haven't been very cooperative in joint matters," refuted Ridge.

Fitch/Spaulding gave the Guardian ranger a dismissive wave with an expression showing clear disdain.

Nigel stepped toward Fitch/Spaulding. "Gareth's administration was never looked upon favorably by either my father, King Ellis, or now by King Tyrone, and ended in disgrace and shame. The new administration is held in favor, both mortal and Guardian," he indicated Wess and Ridge while speaking. "A wise man would understand the difference and act accordingly, not bandy about false accusations or employ former detestable strong-arm tactics. Do I make myself clear, Sheriff?"

"Very clear, Highness. Yet would you have me cheapen the king's justice by not following every lead during an investigation?"

The continuing hostility brought Avatar to stand beside Nigel. The silver eyes appeared leery and watchful in their focus. Fitch/Spaulding shied away from meeting Avatar's stare. He assumed a less threatening posture to stop from further inciting the Guardian commander.

Nigel's gaze never left Fitch/Spaulding. "Tread carefully, Sheriff. Since learning of Master Kelvin, you've had four days to find evidence to support your accusations against him. Instead of producing confirmation of your theory, you cast suspicion on Doctor Lester. Heed this—you have three more days, for the total of one week, to obtain legitimate results. If not, you will leave these men alone and turn your attention elsewhere to put down the rash of crime plaguing the area."

Fitch/Spaulding pursed his lips with annoyed consideration. He flashed a cautious glance to Avatar, who still watched him. Thus far Armus had not moved or reacted, and it would be unwise to arouse him. Avatar's interest was enough to contend with, thus he replied in a more controlled tone. "How long will you be in Burleigh, Highness?"

"For as long as necessary."

Fitch/Spaulding inclined his head in agreement. "I understand."

"Good," said Wess in smiling triumph. "We hoped to reach an amiable agreement."

Fitch/Spaulding tried to smile, and only managed a toothy sneer. "My lord. Your Highness."

Nigel departed first with the rest following. Avatar lingered a moment, with long steady look at Fitch/Spaulding before exiting.

Fitch/Spaulding sat at the desk contemplating the visit. Guardian presence was a bit unnerving. If successful, he could mask his true identity even from their prying eyes. Avatar was prying. Fortunately it was just in the way of warning to Sheriff Spaulding. If Avatar suspected something more, his would have employed his heavenly senses. Since Avatar didn't become suspicious, Armus remained an observer. If roused, Fitch/Spaulding knew he would have difficulty hiding his identity from Kell's lieutenant.

Although he knew his inevitable end, he wasn't ready to be sent into oblivion. Not while Kell lived. The venerable captain left him maimed and trapped with Dagar for centuries. Despite the blunder with the *madah-dune* attack, he savored the initial thought of Kell's death. Discovering him masquerading as a mortal changed everything. The arrival of Nigel, Armus, Avatar and the others pointed to a clever plan to capture him and Locan. Kell faked his own death and took on mortal form to fool them. It nearly worked, until he attempted to shape-shift into Kelvin and unmasked Kell. However, this visit proved curious since the others played their parts rather convincingly of being unaware of Kelvin's true identity.

What if they don't know? He dismissed the thought of Kell withholding such information from Armus and Avatar. The mortals perhaps he left unaware, but purposely leaving his counter-part and aide ignorant? Unlikely. Their presence warranted moving with caution. Still, if he could make Kell suffer while in mortal form, perhaps he could enjoy some revenge. The evidence he *discovered* must be fast and enough to satisfy and convince them to leave the South Plains. Only after succeeding, would he and Locan be free to wreak more havoc.

<hr />

At the castle, Mirit, Ellis, and Valery occupied themselves in the drawing room. Vidar, Virgil, and Wren stood by while Cody stretched out on the floor sleeping. Nigel, Wess and the others returned.

"What happened?" asked Mirit.

"Uncle threw the fear of Father into Spaulding," snickered Fraser.

Nigel grinned and jerked his thumb at Avatar. "Actually, Avatar provided the visual motivation. I just spoke the words."

"At least someone could," groused Wess. "Spaulding's disregard is growing tiresome."

"Ay," groused Ridge.

"Hasn't most of the trouble centered around Hawthorn and Oakley?" Armus asked Ridge.

"Ay."

"But Mistress Vivian found Kelvin injured outside of Burleigh. How far are those towns from here?"

"Oakley is a five hour ride east into the foothills. Hawthorn, an hour further."

"Spaulding thinks there is a connection at such a distance?" asked Avatar.

The ranger snorted, harsh and sarcastic. "Spaulding has his own way of thinking and dealing with matters that often defies logic."

Wess chuckled an agreement to the assessment.

"Sounds more like self-advancement and importance. Perhaps hoping to widen his scope of influence," said Chad.

"Oh, ay. If nothing else, Spaulding is ambitious," said Wess.

"May I inquire why you haven't replaced him?" asked Ellis.

"I can't replace everyone Gareth appointed all at once and maintain a semblance of order. The more troublesome ones I discharged immediately. Although Spaulding is an annoying, dislikable bully, I haven't found falsehood in his work, and he keeps law and order in his jurisdiction."

"We'll see what he does under pressure," said Nigel.

"Three days isn't a lot of time for investigation," said Chad.

"It is if we split up. I want you, Fraser, Ellis, Valery, Avatar, Kendrick and Wren to go to Hawthorn and Oakley. Learn what you can about Kelvin, this crime spree, and if there is a connection. The rest of us will make inquires around here."

"I think it would be good to keep Kelvin with us," said Armus.

"Why? He's the object of our investigation."

"Despite the fact I believe he is telling the truth about his lack of memory, there is a mystery regarding him I can't quiet discern. Like Spaulding, I want to see what he does under pressure."

"Very well. Have any of you see him this morning?" Nigel asked those who remained at Burleigh.

"Mistress Vivian went to his room," said Valery.

"Oh?" asked Wess in a decidedly protective tone.

Valery corrected herself at his reaction. "She carried towels and bandages. He is still recovering."

Wess' expression turned to determined when he spoke to Nigel. "I'll order the horses ready and inform Kelvin of his good fortune." He left.

"Somehow I don't think that will go well," said Mirit.

"Which is why I intend to join him." Nigel then spoke to Chad. "Return in three days." He tossed a prompting nod for Armus to accompany him.

Kell sat in a chair at the table where the basin and pitcher were easy access for Vivian to tend his wounds. He was stripped to the waist and she put salve on his shoulder injuries. The door opened, no knock, just opened. Wess arrived, and not pleased.

"Had a relapse?" His tone matched his stern features.

"No." Kell moved from Vivian to fetch his shirt and put it on. "The wounds are where I can't reach them."

"He's doing much better. This is probably the last time he'll need salve," she said.

"Which you had to administer?" chided Wess.

"He is in my care," she insisted.

"Ah, up and about I see," said Nigel in a friendly tone. He moved from the threshold and smiled at everyone. Wess scowled; Vivian appeared relieved and Kell formal in his reply.

"Ay, Highness." He partially bowed before closing his doublet.

"I hope you are well enough to aid our investigation into your misfortune."

"I thought Sheriff Spaulding was tending to that?"

"He is. A man who claims he is being falsely accused, usually wants to discover the truth for himself."

Nigel stared at him, studious and with a hint of prompting. Kell realized the opportunity being presented. Armus still showed no emotion, continuing to size up the situation and how he fit into. Whether for good or ill, he would have to trust his lieutenant's judgment. Something he did many times over two thousand years, only never under such unique circumstances. It was a brief moment for the consideration and his response.

"Of course I do, Highness. I just don't want to annoy the sheriff any more than I have already; place the doctor under further false suspicion, exhaust the general's patience or presume upon your generosity."

Nigel grinned with approval. "Well, said." He glanced up and down at Kell. "I noticed you came unarmed. You will be properly outfitted before we leave. Including a new doublet, yours is ripped." He pointed to the collar.

Kell felt the collar. "I hadn't noticed. Must have been caught on a thorn bush when I was nearly run down."

"You'll have a new one." Nigel turned to leave and Kell fell in step behind him.

"Do you think this is wise?" asked Wess.

Nigel paused in departure long enough to reply. "If he can disarm and frustrate a general by a single look, I'd like to see what he can do with a sword."

Nigel didn't notice Wess' smoldering irritation due to leaving. Kell did. Armus nudged him to leave with Nigel.

"Wess, why can't you trust me?" asked Vivian.

"I do. I don't trust him and I want him to know it."

"You aim your volley at him, he volleys back, and I get caught in the crossfire. If it's not you acting jealous without cause, Kelvin mistakes my nursing for affection with a kiss," she spoke in high frustration.

"What?" He snarled and began to leave.

She stepped in front of him to physically stop his departure. "I told him there could not be anything between us so don't reload for another round. I can't take any more!" she said the last sentence with a quiver in her voice.

He held her hand. "I won't let him presume upon you again."

"Not him, it's you!" she said in exasperation. "Your constant defensiveness on my behalf with warnings to others, but never stated directly to me. Your desire to protect but not to possess. A woman can only take so much attention from a man who won't speak the obvious or even acknowledge it!" Seeing his reticence, she continued. "Oh, Wess, will you ever say you have feelings for me? Kelvin realized my feelings for you when I rebuffed him."

He lips jowls flexed to contain his emotions. He sent a glare toward the door.

"Wess." She gently touched his face to get his attention.

97

The tenderness and compassion in her eyes drained his anger. He held her hand against his chest. "I never meant to treat you with contempt."

"No, not contempt …"

"I have treated you wrongly," he insisted. "I guess I'm thickheaded at times."

She was mildly confused. "Then you didn't realize how I felt?"

"No. I mean moving beyond my grief." He kissed her hand. He smiled, a hint of the rogue coming through. "You don't think I asked Lester to move here solely for his company, do you?"

She laughed in relief. "I hoped there was another reason."

He went to kiss her on the lips when …

"My lord."

The address and appearance of Cameron stopped him. "Ay," he said with sarcastic annoyance.

"The others have left and His Highness is waiting."

Wess chuckled and spoke under his breath, "Nigel, you have lousy timing." He spoke aloud to Cameron, "Tell him, I'm coming." He didn't wait for Cameron to leave and finished what he intended by kissing her. "I'm sorry I waited so long."

She smiled and took his arm to make their way to the courtyard. "You will try to be objective about Kelvin during the investigation, won't you? If not, it could aversely affect Lester."

"I would do nothing to harm Lester. Besides, I may finally be able to deal with Spaulding. I've been so busy that he's had free rein." He gave her a thoughtful side-glance. "I want you to accompany us."

"To keep you in line?" she teased.

"No," he chuckled. "I promise to behave. Aside from enjoying your company, you can show us where you found Kelvin then I'll take you home."

In the courtyard, Nigel, Mirit, and Kell were mounted. Ridge, Armus, Vidar and Virgil stood beside the horses. Kell wore a sword and dagger, and a livery doublet of Burleigh castle.

Wess mounted and spoke to Nigel. "We'll start by having Vivian show us where she found Kelvin. Then we can take her back to the farm." He reached down for Vivian to mount behind him, when Armus lifted her onto the horse. "Where to?"

"The bend in the road past the farm when it veers off toward to the lake."

Wess nodded and said to Nigel. "The quickest way would be cross country, avoiding the road and town."

"Lead on."

Once away from the castle, Wess turned into an open field instead of following the main road. Vivian held onto him when he kicked the horse into a canter. Nigel followed with Mirit then came Kell. Guardians could out run horses, so they had no problem keeping pace. All the same, Kell occasionally glanced at Armus during the journey cross-country. Again there were things he wanted to say, he just couldn't do so without causing suspicion or being misunderstood. He was accused of something totally impossible, or at least very improbable. Under the circumstances, he began to rethink the word *impossible*. In his mind everything that happened since the *madah-dune* attack he once considered impossible. Now, he hoped and prayed it didn't get any worse.

A few minutes later, they reached the road leading to Lester's farm. Being mid-morning they encountered traffic and slowed the horses from a canter to walking pace. They passed the short path turning off to Lester's farm and kept going.

"I found Kelvin near where those men are," she said.

Half a dozen men wandered about the area. A wagon pulled by two horses waited nearby.

Wess cocked a dry-witted grin. "Appears the sheriff is making good on the allotted time."

"Let's see if they found anything," said Nigel.

The exchanged banter wasn't what Kell wanted to hear, nor seeing such a diligent search for evidence against him. Not that he feared anything being found; simply annoyed by how others responded to the accusations against him. Reactions ran the gamut from serious threats, skepticism and uncertainty to dry humor. Most of it from people who knew him! He tried to take consolation in the thought that if the same accusations were made against Kell rather than Kelvin, there would be no doubt, no cynicism, and no uncertainty on anyone's part. Of course, to them Kell was dead and Kelvin a stranger. The warring feelings and reasoning did little to ease the dismay at each innocent comment.

The truth of his situation deepened when he caught Armus' piercing gaze upon arriving at the search area. This opportunity went beyond convincing anyone of his innocence to being under heavy scrutiny from Armus. His new life as a mortal hung in the balance. First he dealt with his transformation, coming to terms with the change, being accused of thievery then hearing of his death. Now his whole existence as a mortal hung by a thread. Any misstep could doom him to prison or worse. Wess' voice drew attention.

"Deputy Crawford!" he called to the leader of the group.

"My lord." Crawford approached Wess.

"I'm assuming this is on Sheriff Spaulding's instructions?"

"Ay, my lord. He didn't want to disappoint the prince."

"At least he's speedy when prodded," said Nigel to Wess then to Crawford, "Show us what you've done so far." He dismounted; Mirit and Kell followed his lead. Ridge helped Vivian down before Wess dismounted.

Crawford led them to where the men worked. Some poked the ground with poles or used shovels to dig shallow holes.

"We're doing a search of the area, Highness. Testing the ground for any loose soil or objects then digging when we think we found something."

"You seem to be going about it in a rather haphazard manner, no method to the search."

"We weren't sure exactly where he was found, only somewhere in this vicinity," he made an awkward excuse.

Mirit wandered the search area. She noticed something half-hidden behind a log and squatted to discover a handsome satchel. Judging by the weight and shape, it contained items. She stood, holding the satchel. "Deputy. What's this?"

"Eh, those are items we found—"

"Impossible!" said Kell. "I had nothing when Mistress Vivian found me."

"Indeed, he wasn't even wearing clothes," said Vivian.

"We found these items. So don't tamper with the evidence, miss." Crawford grabbed the satchel from Mirit.

"Her *Royal Highness* to you, deputy," corrected Virgil.

The identification startled Crawford.

"My wife, Princess Mirit, the Queen's Champion. Notice the likeness of uniforms," said Nigel, not disguising his scolding.

"My apologies, Princess," said Crawford to Mirit.

"Highness, upon my word of honor, I had nothing when found, much less ever owing so fine a satchel," insisted Kell.

At the declaration, Nigel took the satchel from Crawford to examine it. "This is a handsome and expensive satchel. It also looks fairly new. No scuff marks or dirt of abuse."

Wess took from Nigel and did his own examination. "Nor a hole from a poking stick or nick of a shovel. You obviously didn't find this around here."

Crawford slightly paled. "I said we found items today. I didn't say what or where."

"Where else have you searched for evidence?"

"We stopped by Doctor Lester's farm—"

"You wouldn't have found such a satchel there," said Vivian, almost irate. "My brother's satchel is well worn from use in his practice."

"If you allow me to finish, miss. The satchel is mine. The items inside are what we found."

"You own this? On deputy's pay?" asked Nigel, skeptical.

"An inheritance from a wealthy relation, Highness."

"You have an answer for everything, Deputy Crawford."

"It is my duty to find and have answers, Highness."

"May I see the items?" asked Vivian.

Crawford intercepted the satchel when Wess went to hand it to Vivian. "Sorry, miss, evidence."

"I may recognize them since you claim to have found them at my home."

"Give her the satchel," Armus spoke for the first time.

The Guardian's brightened chestnut eyes caused a moment of indecision before Crawford yielded the satchel to Vivian.

She sat on the log and pulled out the items: an older round pewter-serving platter, a set of small pewter cups, and finally a well-used set of forks and knives. She spoke in dispute to Crawford. "You could not have found these at my house."

"You recognize them?" asked Nigel.

"Ay. When we first arrived Lester treated a destitute elderly couple, Edna and Ben," she said to Wess. He nodded and she continued her explanation to Nigel. "He suffers from terrible gout and arthritis. She's not much better. Seeing they had nothing for eating and drinking, Lester gave these to them along with much needed medicine."

"They reported the items stolen," insisted Crawford.

"Who would steal from a destitute couple?" she challenged.

"I didn't steal from anyone," declared Kell.

"That's what we're going to find out." Crawford snatched the satchel from Vivian. He reached for the items when Wess stopped him.

"We will return these to Edna and Ben."

"They are evidence, my lord."

"Of what? Mistress Vivian identified them as gifts. Why would Doctor Lester steal back items he gave them?"

"I didn't say the doctor stole them."

Indignant toward Crawford, Vivian rose to confront him. "You said you found them at our house. Master Kelvin had nothing on when I discovered him and was too infirmed for days to leave the house. So how did they get there for you to find?"

The question stymied Crawford.

"Well? Where are your clever answers now?" asked Nigel

Crawford shied away. Armus stepped forward and lay hold of Crawford's shoulder, making the deputy look up. "The truth."

The deputy became uneasy while speaking. "I thought finding something would help the sheriff."

"Spaulding put you up to this?" asked Wess.

Crawford shook his head in shame "He doesn't know."

"You realize falsifying evidence is an affront to the king's justice and punishable by hanging?" chided Nigel.

Fearful, Crawford spoke in a weak voice. "I thought—he's a stranger, no one would know or care."

Kell snorted in annoyance. "If this is how you treat strangers around here I hate to think what you do to a friend who angered you."

"He's my cousin! I didn't want him to get into trouble and be replaced with someone else."

"Your misguided loyalty could have cost a man his life!" scolded Nigel.

"It still may if they find some other tainted evidence," chided Kell.

"Nothing's been found, real or otherwise." Crawford turned to Wess, his voice and face uneasy. "Pray, my lord, what will happen to me?"

"That's for the prince to decide."

"You!" Nigel motioned one of the men over. "Your name?"

"Devon, Highness."

"Take him to Sheriff Spaulding and properly report all that transpired here. And convey my orders he is to be flogged with twenty lashes, stripped of his office without future pension or present recompense."

Relief crossed Crawford's face. "Thank you for your mercy, Highness."

With unmistakable warning, Nigel confronted Crawford. "If I find anything more than misguided family loyalty, you won't escape the hangman again."

"Ay, Highness," he said in a forced, nervous voice.

Nigel motioned Devon to take charge of Crawford. Devon escorted Crawford to the wagon while ordering the other men to gather their equipment for departure. They all piled in the wagon.

Wess came alongside Nigel to watch the wagon drive away. "I don't know if leniency will affect Spaulding. You spare his kinsman while threatening him."

"We both know the cost of misguided family loyalty. I won't have the innocent suffer by inflicting the harshest penalty unless absolutely necessary." A brief pricked expression passed over Wess' face, so Nigel clapped him on the shoulder. "We have business to conduct." He turned Wess around and spoke to Vivian. "Is this the area?"

"A little further." She moved twenty yards south of where the men searched. "Here, is exactly where I found him. It was early and I was coming back from gathering medicinal plants when he popped up and startled me." She pointed in the direction she came from.

Mirit glanced over the short shrubbery. "Anyone would be startled by a naked man popping out of the bushes."

"Hoping to find another?" teased Virgil, catching her by surprise.

"No! I'm perfectly happy with the one I have."

"Naked or clothed?"

Embarrassed, she jabbed an elbow into Virgil's side.

Kell tried to hide his smile at the banter. It became a common occurrence between Virgil and Mirit since he became her Overseer. Wess grinned when Nigel rolled his eyes at the ribbing. Ridge and Vidar smiled. Armus appeared humorless, another disturbing sign of his affected demeanor. Often he teased Kell about a lack of humor even under serious circumstances. Occasional lightheartedness served as a release of tension and helped to keep a situation from getting out of hand. He suspected Armus didn't have much to be jovial about these days with believing him dead and assuming leadership of the Guardians.

"You sensed the area, correct?" Nigel asked Ridge.

"Of course, only I found nothing unusual."

"Let's see what Armus and Vidar can discover."

The lieutenant and archer moved from the group. Ridge accompanied them, telling of his experience and making a broad motion indicating the area. Despite Ridge's promotion to Trio Leader, everyone knew Armus to be the more highly skilled tracker while Vidar, the master hunter. If anyone could discover a sense of what happened, they could.

Armus got down on one knee, took a deep breath, placed a hand on the ground and closed his eyes. He focused his senses to search and probe. Vidar stopped ten yards from Armus and spoke in the Ancient language of the Guardians. While Armus came in contact with the ground, Vidar called upon the eyes and ears of nature to inform him of what they witnessed. The appearance and cries of two hawks circling above and the howling of wolves did not break Armus' concentration. Suddenly, the mighty warrior went flying backwards twenty feet. He landed flat, with the wind knocked from him upon impact.

"Armus!" Kell rushed forward and Nigel intercepted him. "I want to see if he's hurt."

"The Guardians know what they are doing."

Ridge helped Armus sit up to catch his breath. The lieutenant's face was pale. "What happened?"

Armus shook his head and made motion for Ridge to help him stand. He took several deep breaths of recovery before moving to rejoin the mortals.

Vidar gave a brief report, and grew concerned about Armus' pallor. "The animals saw nothing unusual, but you learned something."

Armus' eyes fixed upon Kell. "He was sent here by dimension travel."

"I should have sensed that," said Ridge, a bit perplexed.

Kell didn't recoiled from Armus, rather stared back, curious of the discovery. How he came to the South Plain was also a mystery to him.

"Not this travel. It took all my skill to discern it."

"That would account for his lack of memory," said Vidar.

"How?" asked Vivian.

"Dimensional travel is not meant for mortals. Your frail bodies can't take passing through time and space. When mortals travel at the hands of a Guardian they often faint and are always disoriented and confused."

"Also accounts for why no evidence was found. Objects don't travel well unless small enough to fit into a pocket," said Virgil.

"Or a satchel?" asked Wess.

"I had nothing with me," rebuffed Kell, briefly looking from Armus to Wess.

"Then clothes don't travel well either?" asked Vivian.

Ridge chuckled. "No, clothes remain on the mortal. Master Kelvin's nakedness is for another reason."

"So he was attacked, made naked and sent here by a dimension travel, why? Was a Guardian involved?" asked Mirit.

"I don't think a Guardian would strip a wounded man naked and send him across the country," said Nigel.

"The Dark Way then, since they used dimension travel."

"He did say he heard unnatural sounds while in the Southern Forest," said Vidar.

"May be they tried to hide a witness, hoping he wouldn't survive his wounds and the travel," said Ridge.

Kell turned from Armus, as his interested was drawn to the discussion. *Disposed as a witness to my own death?* he thought yet spoke aloud. "I was attacked, that much I remember. Why and by whom, isn't so clear."

Armus continued staring at Kell. "There is a strange familiarity surrounding the attack. However, I encountered an obscure image of someone. When I tried to push further to learn by whom or why, I was struck back."

Nigel thoughtfully pursed his lips. "Is there anything more here to discover and help provide answers?"

"No," said Armus. For the first time, he took his eyes off Kell to look at Nigel.

"This only deepens the mystery around Kelvin," said Mirit.

"Imagine how I feel, Princess. Suddenly transported across the country by a vague image, suffering great injury and not knowing why."

"Well, the next place Kelvin went is my home. I don't know if you'll find any more clues, but I can offer refreshment and a place to decide what to do next rather than standing in the open," said Vivian.

"A fine idea," said Wess.

The mortals mounted. Ridge lifted Vivian to sit behind Wess. Kell grew thoughtful on the short ride. Indeed, the mystery deepened and became a bit unnerving with Armus' interest after being thwarted by the powerful rebuff. Under such scrutiny, Kell fought to keep his composure and not burst forth with all manner of pent up emotion and knowledge. Not that Armus—or anyone else—would believe him.

A few moments later, they reached the farm. Vivian told Wess to steer around back. Lester, Donovan and Howey worked to finish repairs on the barn.

"Well, this is some entourage." Lester put down the hammer and wiped his hands. "Highness, I heard you were in Burleigh." He took hold of the horse's bridle for Nigel to dismount.

"Hello, Lester. How do you like retirement?"

"What retirement? With Wess it's always work."

Wess dismounted after Ridge helped Vivian off the horse. "Ah! I don't think you know what a holiday is, much less how to slow down."

"You see what I to put up with, Highness?" said Vivian to Nigel. She then spoke to Lester. "I brought them here for refreshment."

"Come inside." Lester escorted them the house. The Guardians paused at the door to wait outside while the mortals entered. "You can come in also," said Lester.

Virgil smirked at observing the small kitchen. "I don't think we'd fit."

Lester laughed and went to tend to his guests. Vivian, Howey and Drusilla passed out cups for cider and placed trays of bread, cheese and small cakes on the table. Donovan fetched two more chairs.

"What brings you here, Highness?" asked Lester.

Nigel swallowed some cider before replying. "Kelvin."

"You heard about him at Waldron?"

"No, we came to call on Wess and learned about him."

"They bring bad news," began Wess soberly. "Kell is dead."

Shocked, Lester paused in taking a seat at the table. "What?"

To hide his discomfort, Kell took a long drink, though they continued speaking about his demise without taking notice of him.

"A sudden and unexpected event to say the least. We were on a hunting trip when Vidar sensed something wrong. It turned out to be *madah-dune*."

"I thought all were killed."

Nigel nodded since he drank again. "So did we. Anyway, we came to tell Wess since someone of the Dark Way must control the creatures of infrinn."

"Along with trouble in the South Plains," said Mirit.

In guarded curiosity, Wess looked to Nigel for clarification.

"Tyrone surmised from your reports that more trouble has been occurring in the South Plains than any other providence."

Wess grew visibly annoyed. "You neglected to tell me this, why?"

"It's a not a question of your administration, Wess, merely an observation. Remember, Gareth was deeply involved with Ellan and Hueil."

Wess' irate glance found Lester. "You sent word behind my back."

"No!"

The accusation brought Vivian her brother's side. "Lester didn't, so don't be angry at him."

"Indeed not," said Nigel. "The Dark Way killed Kell. Now we learn of Kelvin's arrival here by dimension travel, possibly sent by the vague image Armus encountered and repulsed him."

"You think there is a connection?" asked Lester.

Nigel shrugged since he took a bite of the cake Dursilla served them. "Too soon to tell, but there are many unanswered questions."

"Spaulding accused Kelvin of being a thief and me of harboring a criminal. Where does that come in?"

Nigel washed down the cake with a drink. "As I said, there are more unanswered questions."

"The sheriff's men found the items you gave Edna and Ben and claimed they were stolen," said Vivian.

"Stolen? Who would steal from them?" Lester barely finished when he paled in pain and rubbed his eyes. "Is Spaulding saying I stole them back?"

Vivian comforted him. "No, and Wess would not tolerate the suggestion when Crawford made it. In fact, Crawford admitted to falsifying evidence to help Spaulding."

"Lester, are you all right?" asked Mirit.

"A headache, Highness. I've been working too hard."

"I'm the cause of that." Kell took his cup of cider and left out the back door.

"Kelvin," said Vivian, but he ignored her.

"He won't go far," said Wess

In Kell's mind, the farther away the better so he could find some solitude to try and figure everything out. He couldn't leave, not with the Guardians close by, so he went and sat on the bench under the oak tree. He stared at the cider in the cup and pondered the situation. Some of the theory from earlier made sense, at least with there being a connection between the attack and his arrival in the South Plains. Did the connection include his chance encounter with Fitch? Madah-dune must be controlled. Did Fitch have anything to do with them? If aligned with the Dark Way, it was possible he had the ability.

And did it give him the power to change me into a mortal? He first wanted to dismiss such a notion, but could that be the explanation? Dagar found ways to manipulate and crossbred natural animals with the creatures of infrinn to produce others like the madah-dune. So could Dagar have discovered a way to change a Guardian into a mortal and somehow passed along that knowledge? It was a frightening thought that only led to more questions and no solid answers.

A shadow cast over the cup and Kell looked up. This time he wasn't surprised by Armus' arrival. Actually, in his present state of mind, he became annoyed.

"What do you want; to inspect me more?"

"Do you have any connection to the Dark Way?"

"No!" refuted Kell, sitting upright and boldly looking at Armus. "It is an abhorrent effrontery to Jor'el."

"Do you know why someone would dimension travel you here?"

"No," groused Kell in frustration. "And I've been racking my brain to figure out why and how Fitch fits into it."

"Fitch?" echoed Armus. He sat beside Kell, his interest piqued as told by his change in tone and grabbing Kell's arm. "You said you have no connection to the Dark Way so how do you know him?"

Kell tried not to grimace at the miscue and hastily replied. "I've heard his name. He escaped the battle, along with Locan. All soldiers are on alert to watch for any suspicious Dark Way activity. I'd say my being dimension traveled cross-country qualifies." By the last statement, he sounded more resolute.

Armus released his hold. "Ay. Yet why do I continue to get contradictory feelings about you?"

Kell heaved an awkward shrug and took a drink to stall for an answer. At Armus' unwavering interest, he tried to deflect the question by using dry wit. "When you figure it out tell me and then we'll both know." He started to take another drink, but at Armus' growing skepticism, he slammed the cup down on the bench and stood. "I don't even know what I'm doing here so can I answer you?"

Armus rose, his chestnut eyes steady upon Kell.

This time Kell noticed confusion behind the probing and silently prayed, *Please, Jor'el, let him see something of my true essence.* The hope faded when Armus made an audible sigh of frustration. "Armus," he began in earnest entreaty. "I wish I could say something to allay your doubt and convince you to trust me."

"So do I. The question is—do I dare trust you?"

That stung, deep and painful, making Kell recoil. For the first time in over two thousand years, Armus doubted him. *No, he doubts Kelvin,* he tried to soothe his reaction.

"Time to leave!" called Nigel. He and the others filed out of the house.

Armus nudged Kell, and they joined the others. "Where to, Highness?" he asked.

"Back to the castle for now." Nigel mounted.

Wess kissed Vivian and she hugged him before he mounted.

First Kell felt the sting of Armus' uncertainty now a prick to his heart at the sight of the shared affection. What he suspected become vivid reality, and the reaction caught him by surprise. He set his jaw against the disturbance and vaulted into the saddle.

Following the same route back to Burleigh Castle, they rode in silence, which suited Kell. The incident showed him the true danger of his situation while the strong sense of jealousy aroused anger against Wess and Vivian. This was unacceptable. He knew Wess since he was a boy. Vivian was a gentle, caring person to whom he owed his recovery. Granted he knew her and Lester due to their involvement with the royal army, but more familiar with Lester, than Vivian. However, this constant dealing with unexpected and strong mortal emotions became tiresome. Just when he thought he had a grip on his new existence, something else came along to challenge him.

When they dismounted in the castle courtyard, and Kell caught Wess' staying motion. While the others went inside, he remained for the inevitable confrontation.

"I saw the way you looked at Vivian earlier. She is spoken for. You would do best to stow your anger. Better yet, if you want to vent it, do so on me. Steel to steel, if that will satisfy."

"It might satisfy me, but not Vivian. For her sake, I will let you live."

Wess couldn't help an ironic chuckle at the retort. "You are a brash one to speak so to a general." He turned on his heels and went inside.

"Don't push me anymore, Wess," muttered Kell to himself. He glanced skyward. "Pray, don't let him push me any more." He entered the main hose and went to the drawing room.

Unfortunately, the pushing would come in the form of Fitch/Spaulding, who immediately accosted Kell upon arrival.

"I bet you thought you managed to elude me."

"I haven't tried to elude anyone. You notice I'm still here."

"Not for long." Fitch/Spaulding turned to Nigel. "I am grieved by my cousin's action, Highness. However, I have uncovered evidence connecting *Master* Kelvin," he said the name with high mockery, "to the robberies in Hawthorn and Oakley."

"Impossible!" Kell moved to stand toe-to-toe with Fitch/Spaulding. "Who helped you falsify evidence this time? Another relative?"

Armus pulled Kell back from Fitch/Spaulding.

"Kelvin, let us handle this. You saw I have little tolerance for any compromise to the king's justice," said Nigel.

"No compromise this time, Highness," began Fitch/Spaulding. "Stolen goods were discovered in the woods off the main road between here and Oakley. I also received a description of the thief from Deputy March of Oakley that matches you exactly." He sent a toothy predatory smile to Kell.

Kell returned the edgy smile. "I've not been to Oakley and they can confirm it. Especially him." He jerked his thumb at Armus. "Care to dispute a Guardian?"

Fitch/Spaulding sneered, and he barely looking Armus. "Troublesome creatures. Never took much stock in them."

Armus stiffened with insult. Ridge, Vidar and Virgil also became offended.

"Now you've made them angry, and me!" declared Kell. For a moment he and Fitch/Spaulding locked eyes, neither backing down. Kell grew curious at a momentary flinch but no further reaction as Fitch/Spaulding looked away at hearing Nigel's stern voice.

"Enough! Kelvin's manner may be bold and blatant, but he speaks the truth. Our investigating shows he came here directly from the Southern Forest."

"March says the witness in Oakley is willing to identify him."

"I'm not going to Oakley."

"You will if you don't hold your tongue!" snapped Nigel.

Realizing he pushed too far, Kell bowed in submission to the rebuke.

Nigel spoke to Fitch/Spaulding. "Have the witness come here."

"He is too infirmed to move. That is how *Kelvin* made off with the goods. He preys upon the helpless and infirmed."

Armus seized Kell to prevent a reaction, and Kell barely managed to hold his tongue.

"Then I will send word and have my people interview him."

"Your people?" asked Fitch/Spaulding, suspicious.

"I sent some to Oakley for further investigation. I told you we were remaining."

Fitch/Spaulding visibly fought to contain his temper then winced in pain. "That you did. I'll send for him," he spoke in a strained voice, made a hasty bow and withdrew.

"Rather abrupt. Come spewing fire and make a quick exit," said Mirit.

"He's up to something," said Wess.

"Ay! Making certain I have a date with the hangman." Kell jerked away from Armus, rather the Guardian let him pull away.

"Virgil, find Chad and tell him to speak to Deputy March about interviewing this witness," said Nigel.

Virgil saluted and vanished in the white light of dimension travel.

"You must learn to hold your tongue," Nigel scolded Kell.

"I'm sorry, Highness, but the whole situation is taxing. I don't mean to be rude or disruptive. I appreciate your investigation on my behalf —"

Nigel put up a hand to stop Kell. "This investigation is to aid Count Wess and ensure the king's justice is done, not for you personally."

Kell flushed. "I misspoke, Highness. I realize that, only it is hard not to be personal when my reputation, and perhaps my life, are in question."

"We understand." Mirit moved beside Nigel to take his arm.

To her words and actions, Nigel's features and posture softened. "Indeed. Until we hear back from the others, Armus will escort you to your room so you can rest."

Kell bowed and left. For several uncomfortable moments of silence they made their way upstairs. Once in the room, Kell finally spoke. "I suppose you're going to scold me too."

"I think the prince said enough. However, I will ask a question. Why did you became angry and defensive when he insulted Guardians?"

Again Kell had to be coy with his answer. "From my experience you are noble creatures and I felt offended for you."

Armus made a curt shake of his head. "What I sensed from you was a deep seeded resentment to his scorn that went beyond any mortal I've been closely associated with over the centuries. It felt personally protective of me, of us."

"I would protect you. To the death if needed," affirmed Kell in all sincerity. "Just like I would protect Avatar, the prince, princess and the others. You can trust me, Armus." He thought he noticed a smile, though Armus responded in a neutral tone.

"Get some rest. I'll be outside if you need anything." Armus left.

Fitch/Spaulding urged his horse at breakneck speed from the castle while wincing in constant pain. He steered the horse off the main road and into a patch of wood. With a great outcry of agony he jerked back the reins. The horse skidded and reared in protest, throwing him to the ground. He no sooner hit the ground than he changed back into Fitch.

For several moments he lay stunned and waited for the pain in his head to subside. Carefully he sat up then reached to touch the back of his head. He hissed at feeling a large gash and discovered blood on his hand. Not good. He had to find Locan. He wobbled in rising to his feet and couldn't move fast, rather staggered deeper into the forest.

Chapter 7

THREE HOURS PASSED SINCE THE GROUP DEPARTED BURLEIGH, so Virgil reasoned the others didn't have time to reach Oakley. He reappeared on the main road half the distance between the destinations and began running with the intention of catching them en route. This far out into the country, he encountered little traffic so spotting them wouldn't be too difficult. Sure enough, after ten minutes, he noticed the group a half-a-mile ahead. Cody started barking, which alerted them to his arrival. They halted to wait for him.

"What news? Is something wrong?" asked Fraser.

"Your uncle sent me with instructions. Sheriff Spaulding received word from Deputy March of Oakley concerning a witness who can identify the thief, possibly as Kelvin. He wants you to speak to the deputy about interviewing the witness."

"Why can't the witness go to Burleigh?"

"We're already on our way to Oakley, so why bother?" said Ellis.

"According to the sheriff, the witness is infirmed and can't travel. However, from our investigation, there is reason to believe Kelvin may not be involved. In fact, we caught the sheriff's cousin attempting to plant evidence against him. He did it without the sheriff's knowledge."

Fraser was both incredulous and curious. "What did Uncle do?"

"Ordered the man flogged and stripped of his office without pay. He also warned the man that if he learns this was more than just an effort to help his cousin, he would face the hangman."

"Rather lenient for someone fabricating evidence," said Chad.

"Nigel is suspicious of the claim, especially after what happened to Armus."

Wren and Kendrick braced for more bad news. Avatar reacted sharply by jerking Virgil around to face him. "What happened to him?"

"Easy! He became repulsed by a strong force that sent him off his feet. No injury. Well, maybe his pride—" he checked his humor at Avatar's full-throated interruption.

"How?"

"During his attempt to track how Kelvin arrived here from the Southern Forest. He learned it was by an unusual dimension travel that involved some vague image. When he tried to press further to discover the source, a repulsing force sent him flying twenty feet."

"I thought you said he wasn't injured?"

"Just winded. It took several moments for him to catch his breath and be able to speak."

"Must be a powerful force to knock him around," said Kendrick.

"Indeed," agreed Avatar, grim and thoughtful. "We must proceed with caution."

"Naturally, but at least we now have a place to start," said Chad. He kicked for his horse to move again and they continued.

Oakley was a quaint town of two thousand people nestled high in the foothills. Tall birch trees and brush dominated the lower elevations with oak and evergreens in the higher elevations. Oakley stood near the peak on a nice open, grassy plateau. The steep inclines around the town were suitable for grazing. Small herds of cattle, goats and sheep climbed the hills on the outskirts of town. Many of the town inhabitants were merchants.

They learned Deputy March lived behind the mercantile he owned. A nice courtyard garden of herbs and flowers separated the business from the house. By the appearance of the store, house and décor, March was a man of a good income. Prosperous merchants of a small town tended to serve as town officers. They waited in the front living room for March to arrive. He was a pleasant looking fellow of thirty. He halted in surprise at seeing Cody.

"He won't hurt you," said Valery.

"It's a wolf."

Cody made what sounded like a moan of frustration and sat beside Valery. She patted Cody's head.

"He is friendly and only to be feared by enemies."

"If you say so, miss." He flashed an uncertain smile. His gaze swept over the group. "You asked to speak to me?"

"Deputy March, I am Sir Chad of the North Plains, and I have the pleasure to acquaint you with his highness, Prince Fraser. Count Ellis of the Meadowlands and his wife, Countess Valery. Commander Avatar of the Jor'ellian Guards, Virgil, Kendrick and Wren."

Impressed, March said in awe, "My lord. Your Highness, Count, Countess, Commander." He gave the other Guardians a smile and nod. His gaze shifted between Chad and Valery, observing their red hair and facial coloring. "Forgive me, but are you two related?"

Chad chuckled and Valery smiled. "No," he said. "But it is a common mistake."

"To what to do I own the honor as to be visited by his highness and members of the Council?"

"We have been sent by the king to investigate trouble plaguing the South Plains the past six months. We first stopped at Burleigh, where Prince Nigel is presently aiding Count Wess in this matter. Circumstances made us widen the investigation."

"Ah, I see. Actually, I was hoping for some more help. Mind you, the general, Count Wess," he corrected himself, "is a fine man and very diligent in his efforts. However, the malcontents are persistent and elusive, even for one of his vast experience."

"We'll take that in the manner you meant and not as an insult to the count," said Fraser.

"Oh, by no means, Highness! I think very highly of the general … count." He again corrected himself.

"You seem familiar. Have we met?" asked Chad.

March smiled. "Indeed, my lord, when you first came to the Jor'ellians."

"I remembered you as soon I heard your name," said Avatar. "He served as a Fortress Guard for years before his father died and he returned to take over the family business."

"Ay, Commander."

Chad smiled in recollection. "You stood watch on the dawn shift."

"Ay. My life has changed since then."

"For the better," commented Ellis.

"Comfort wise and monetarily perhaps, but I did enjoy my time at the Fortress. Now, how can I help your investigation?"

"You wrote Sheriff Spaulding concerning a witness," said Chad.

"Ay. Squire Morley."

"We'd like to speak to him."

"It won't be easy. He's become a recluse since returning from Tunlund."

"Tunlund?" asked Fraser.

"Ay, he fought with your father and suffered near fatal wounds from stygian arrows. He's not been right since." March motioned to his head while speaking.

Avatar scowled in an effort to contain his ire.

"Is something wrong, Commander?"

Chad intervened to divert March's attention from Avatar. "Regardless, we'd like to talk to him."

"As you wish. I'll fetch my horse and join you on the street to take you to him." He bowed to them and they left.

"You seemed disturbed when he mentioned Tunlund, why? Didn't you, Prince Nigel and Sir Chad rescue Titus?" Valery asked Avatar as they returned to their horses.

"Ay," said the Guardian in a tone suggesting he didn't want to discuss the topic.

"Stygian metal," said Chad then added at Avatar's displeasure, "She has a right to know since it deals with this investigation."

Avatar pursed his lips in annoyance but didn't argue so Chad continued the explanation.

"Hueil fashioned tribal badges out of stygian metal, which can be harmless to mortals but dangerous and potentially lethal to Guardians.

Nigel, Avatar and myself, each wore a badge as part of our disguise, and totally unaware of the true nature of the metal. Hueil incorporated just enough to escape immediate detection upon touch. However, over time, it weakened Avatar's strength and ability." He paused in telling the tale for mounting. "At one point Avatar became so weak, mortal guards overpowered him and dealt him near fatal wounds. His stubborn persistence exposed Hueil."

"But mortals can't kill Guardians," said Fraser, a bit confused.

"Under normal circumstances, no. My condition wasn't normal, rather affected by the Dark Way," chided Avatar.

Wren added clarification to Avatar's curt response. "Without proper treatment, we can bleed to death."

"How did you survive?" asked Ellis.

Avatar grew reflective before answering. "By an act of Jor'el. At the lowest point of my ebbing life force I sensed death near, and fearful Nigel, Mirit and Chad would suffer for my failure. I pleaded not to let that happen. Unknown at the time, Jor'el sent Vidar to aid me. By his intervention, Jor'el restored me."

"Chad said stygian metal is harmless to mortals, so how can Morley be suffering from it?" asked Valery.

"It's harmless to the touch," began Wren. "Any wound can inflict suffering. For example, a kelpie bite is very dangerous or lethal to mortals depending upon the severity. Such a bite is only a nuisance to Guardians. For Guardians, exposure to stygian metal, say used as shackles or a badge, causes illness while a wound from a stygian arrow can kill."

"So since he claims near fatal wounds, he could be suffering from the effects."

"Possibly."

"My lords. Highness." March arrived mounted upon a bay gelding. "If you'll follow me, I'll take to where Morley is living."

"How far?" asked Fraser.

"About an hour's ride into the forest."

⟡

Inside the old shack in the foothills, Preston sat at the table to take inventory of the stolen items. Squire Morley sat in one of the two rocking chairs before the hearth and smoking his pipe. Morley appeared around fifty years of age with long, stringy gray hair and grizzled whiskers serving as a beard. The morning fire was now ebbing with occasional small flames among the red embers. Being a nice spring day is why the fire was allowed to die and the windows opened. Tattered curtains ruffled in the light breeze.

The door burst open and Reilly rushed in. "March is coming! And he's not alone. A whole group is with him including Guardians."

Preston rushed to scoop the items into a large sack. Reilly helped and they dashed into one of the back rooms.

Morley gave them a passing snarl of disapproval. "Young scamps. Afraid of your own shadows!"

Only five minutes passed before a hailing shout and knock at the door.

"Squire Morley. It's Deputy March."

"Unless you brought food, go away."

"No, I have brought visitors who want to speak to you."

"Did they bring food?"

"No, just good wishes from the king," added Chad.

"If those wishes can be cooked and eaten I'll take them."

"How does boar sound?" asked Wren.

"Like an over grown hog!" Morley made obnoxious pig noises.

"I mean to eat."

"I thought you didn't bring food?"

"If you let the others come and talk to you, I'll snag a boar, clean and cook it by the time you're done."

"Ha! That would be worth the pain of listening to babble. Come in."

March entered first and followed by Chad, Fraser, Ellis, Valery and Avatar. Kendrick and Virgil remained by the opened door.

Morley sneered at Avatar, yet avoided direct eye contact. He chided March. "A Guardian. What's he doing here?"

"A Guardian is fetching you boar," said Avatar.

"Well, I suppose your kind is good for something," he groused. "Now, what do you want to talk about?" he asked March.

"Tell them about the thief you saw."

"Why? Is the king finally taking interest in the common folk?"

"My father is always interested in the common folk," said Fraser.

"Father?" Morley snorted as he glanced up and down at the young man.

"I am Prince Fraser."

"Squire Morley at your service, *Highness.*" He spoke the title in obvious mockery, and made an elaborate bowing gesture while remaining seated. "Oh, you don't mind me remaining in my rocker? Some people think I'm off it."

March grimaced at Morley's theatrics.

Unfazed by the rudeness, Fraser responded. "I don't mind. In fact, I'll join you." He sat in the other rocker opposite Morley.

The beginnings of a small sarcastic smile crossed Morley's lips. "Smoke?" He offered Fraser the pipe by leaning forward. This brought Cody to Fraser's chair, growling at Morley. Kendrick stepped further into the cabin to come up behind Fraser. Morley sat back, cautious of the wolf. He only gave Kendrick a passing glance.

"They thought you were a threat." Fraser patted Cody's head. "Now, can we begin the discussion in a more civilized manner, *Squire?*"

Morley put the pipe between his teeth and started laughing. "Ay, Your Highness," he said in polite formality.

"What can you tell us about the thief's identity?"

Morley made an affected thoughtful expression. "Well, I'll have to see what I can recall."

"Will fresh boar jog your memory?" asked Chad.

"It might, although awfully dry by itself."

Avatar fetched a tankard off the sideboard. "*Leanntan oir pathdh.*" Ale filled the tankard to the brim with some foam running down the side. "Will this wet your lips and help your tongue?"

Morley's eyes grew wide with pleasure. He set the pipe on the floor to take the tankard from Avatar. Again, he avoided eye contact with the Guardian. After a long drink, he sighed with enjoyment. "Ay, that will do just fine."

"Now, what about the thief?" asked Fraser.

"Young, but not like you." He glanced at Chad. "Maybe his age."

"Height, hair coloring?"

Morley laughed. "Not his carrot top. Too easy to spot."

Chad frowned. "My hair is a sunset color not a carrot."

"Would you prefer flaming red?"

Avatar stopped a piqued Chad from answer and spoke instead. "So he isn't a redhead and in his middle-twenties. How tall?"

Morley took another satisfied drink before answering. "Average height."

"Anything more you can tell us about him?" asked Fraser.

Morley showed more interest in drinking than answering questions. He shrugged. "I'll know him if I see him again."

Wren entered. "Anyone hungry?"

"Done already?" asked Morley in surprise.

"I'm a Guardian hunter," she said with a proud grin. "Have you a platter for the meat?"

"On the sideboard." Morley jerked a thumb for pointing. He went back to his ale, and frowned at seeing the tankard empty.

Avatar gave the platter to Wren. He had an empty tankard shoved in his hands when Morley passed him on his way to the table.

"More to wash down the boar."

Avatar cocked a curious brow in watching Morley move with no limp or halt to his step. The others also noticed. Chad pointed to the tankard and made a motion toward Morley. Avatar spoke the Ancient to refill the ale. He placed it on the table and tried to catch Morley's eye. The mortal still avoided him by focusing on drinking.

Wren entered with a platter of meat and set it in front of Morley. He didn't appear pleased. "Is that all of?"

"No, the rest is on the spit."

"Don't you need a knife and fork?" asked Valery.

Morley grabbed a leg to begin eating.

She wrinkled her nose at the lack of table manners. "I guess not."

"Anything more about the thief?" asked Chad.

His mouth being full didn't stop him from answering. "I told you I'll know him when I see him. Now get out and let me eat in peace!"

"Will you come to Burleigh to identify him?" asked Fraser.

"Are you as deaf as he is?" He used the boar leg to motion at Chad. "I said I'll know him when I see him. I said nothing about going anywhere."

Irate at the insult, Ellis rebuffed Morley. "Rude behavior to the prince is not a way to show gratitude for the boar and ale."

Morley waved the leg like one waves a finger. "You're the ones who invaded my home uninvited, and asking personal questions, *my lord.*" Cody again growled at him. "And take your mangy wolf with you," he said, although a bit nervous.

"At least he has better manners!" Valery called Cody and departed.

"Leave the meat!" shouted Morley when the rest filed out. He ate some more, watching the door and listening for their departure. After a couple of moments he crossed to the threshold to see them ride off with the Guardians following on foot. It took a few more moments before they were a mile down the hill and out of sight. He shut the door. "You can come out now, boys."

Preston and Reilly rushed from the room. "Fresh boar!" Reilly grabbed a fist full of meat and began eating.

Preston shoved some meat into this mouth. "This is good," he slurred his words.

"Better than what those two provide," complained Morley.

"You're lucky to be alive after what your incompetent sons did!" Locan's frame filled the threshold, and his face appeared very lethal.

Reilly had difficultly swallowing to speak. "We didn't mean it!"

"Ay, it just happened," said Preston.

"I told you all they're only good for is stealing, not anything requiring brains," chided Morley.

Locan slammed the door. "What did March and the Guardians want?"

"For me to identify the thief. Although I'd hardly turn in my own flesh, despite being tempted." He sneered at his sons.

Alert, Locan whirled about ready to confront danger a second before the door flew open. To everyone's momentary relief, Fitch, in his real form, stumbled in. He seized Locan to keep from collapsing. Upon sight of the head wound, Locan helped him sit in a chair.

"I was afraid of this," he said.

Fitch grunted in frustration for an answer.

"Spaulding's dead. That's why you lost your shape-shift."

Fitch nodded he understood and gestured with the motion of *why?*

"They killed him." Locan jerked his thumb at Preston and Reilly. "Claimed he was trying to escape.

Angry, Fitch stood. He swayed and Locan caught him to keep him from falling.

"How did he get injured?" asked Reilly.

"In mortal form he suffers whatever the mortal does, up to the point of death. He can only remain in the form of a mortal while the mortal is alive. By killing Spaulding you compromised him," said Locan.

Again Fitch lurched forward toward the boys. They dodged out of his way.

"Oh, no! One time of you being me is enough," said Preston.

The movement made Fitch unsteady and Locan held him up.

"We'll find someone else for a shape-shift," said Locan.

"I like him quiet," said Reilly, grinning.

Incited, Fitch bared his teeth. He was incapable of anything more.

"I'll take you to the creek and tend your wound. We'll figure out what to do."

Locan helped Fitch to a large creek a half-mile from the shack. Spaulding's body lay where it fell, face down in the creek bed with a large bloody gash on the back of his head where something heavy smashed his skull.

Fitch stumbled in taking a seat on a rock. Locan tore off the hem of Spaulding's uniform to use as a cleaning cloth. He wet it and approached Fitch. The shape-shifter flinched away when Locan began cleansing the wound. He seized Locan's arm to stop more treatment, adamant in his gestures toward Spaulding.

"I don't know how he got away. The ties are still on his wrists with the rope cut in-between. He must have managed to get something sharp to make his escape."

Fitch made a prompting for further explanation.

"It happened when I went to town." Locan seized Fitch's shoulder to keep him from rising in obvious anger and frustration. "I wanted to learn of any new developments we could use to implicate Kell. You're not the only one who wants revenge. I told you I'm tired of waiting. Now, sit still and let me tend your wound and tell you what I discovered." Fitch complied, and he continued. "One of the princes is here along with others and several Guardians, including *Avatar*," he said with an emphasis to stress the name. "Apparently, *Sheriff Spaulding*," he again made an emphasis, "told them about a witness."

Fitch rolled his eyes and nodded.

"You sent them straight to us."

Fitch shook his head in dispute.

"All right, the information did. Either way, they are nosing around. And Avatar's interest is more troubling than a meddlesome ranger. We're just lucky he didn't discover the body."

Fitch made an expression of agreement. His eyes darted to Spaulding as Locan continued to cleanse the gash. He smiled then flinched in pain. He stopped Locan again, only now with a pleased expression and a motion to Spaulding.

"You have an idea of what to do with him?"

Fitch's smile grew devious. The warrior backed away, leery of the implication. "You're not going to do *know by the mind communication*, are you?"

Fitch nodded.

"Oh, no! I didn't like it when Hueil used it. It hurt. I take back what I said about wishing for a silent parent. Speaking is easier, okay?"

Fitch jerked Locan down to meet at eye level. With great concentration, he focused on the warrior. Locan grimaced, but his eyes never left Fitch until finally he hissed in pain and pulled away. When the pain subsided, Locan smiled in wicked pleasure.

"Good idea. We'll wait until nightfall."

Chapter 8

B Y THE TIME THEY RETURNED TO OAKLEY THEY HAD BEEN IN the saddle for seven hours; five on their journey to the town and two hours for the trip to interview Morley. Add to that, an hour-long stop for a noonday meal and to refresh the horses, for a total of eight hours since leaving Burleigh. Even for an experienced officer, riding so long made Chad stiff when dismounting at March's mercantile.

"I'm afraid my wife's family is visiting and I don't have spare rooms for the night," said March with regret.

"An inn will do," said Chad.

March still appeared regretful. "The inn is hardly adequate for his highness or distinguished Council Members."

"As long as the beds are passable." Chad tossed a smile and wink at Fraser while tilting his head toward Ellis and Valery.

Fraser smiled, impish and wide.

"Joby keeps a respectable establishment, my lord," insisted March.

"I was joking."

"At my expense," quipped Ellis.

"You mean mine," said Valery.

"Our."

"Newlyweds," said Chad.

The deputy grinned. "I understand. The Oakley Inn is two streets down, and turn to the left. Better yet, I'll escort you." He went to mount when Chad stopped him.

"We'll walk."

March left his horse tied to a post in front of the store to escort them.

"Where can we stable the horses?" asked Ellis.

"The livery is directly across from the inn, my lord."

"We'll take care of the horses," said Kendrick of himself and Wren.

Being dinnertime, the inn teemed with customers. The sight of royal and Jor'ellian uniforms, along with Guardians, caught the patrons' attention.

A middle age burly man weaved his way through the tables. "Deputy March."

"Joby. I brought you guests for the night. Felicia's family," he said.

Joby nodded with understanding. "Unfortunately, I only have two rooms left."

"That'll be fine. Sir Chad and I can share while the count and countess take the other," said Fraser.

In guarded surprise, Joby looked at March.

"His highness Prince Fraser, Sir Chad of the North Plains and Count Ellis of the Meadowland, his wife, Commander Avatar of the Jor'ellian Guards and," he paused when realizing he didn't know Virgil's name.

"Virgil," said the Guardian.

Startled, Joby took a step back when Cody entered and stood beside Valery.

March took Joby's arm to stop his retreat. "The countess' friend. He's temperamental. Doesn't like being called a wolf," he added in low warning.

Some of the other patrons also reacted wary or negative to the wolf.

"He's friendly. There is no need to fear," said Avatar in addressing the patrons.

A few remained skeptical, though no one disputed the Guardian commander and returned to eating or conversation.

"Will you and your Guardian companion require a room, Commander?"

"No. We do not require sleep like mortals."

"Would you care to eat before going to your rooms, Highness?"

"Sounds good."

"Smells good too," said Ellis.

Joby widely grinned. "This way, please." He led them to one of the three vacant tables capable of seating four or five. "I can pull another table for your Guardian friends."

"That's not necessary," said Avatar.

"Please, Commander, if I can't house you allow me the honor to feed you."

"Very well, and we require two more seats for our companions tending to the horses."

Joby called to a male servant. They put together the tables and chairs to seat the group. He then sent the man to fetch drinks.

"The food will be out soon. With a plate of bones and meat for your wol—friend, my lady," he corrected himself at Cody's low growl.

Valery leaned down to Cody. "You must stop intimidating everyone to get what you want." He whimpered and laid his head on her lap. "You act like a spoiled child." He licked her hand. "And I fall for it. Now, lie down and behave." Cody curled up behind her chair.

"Amazing," said Joby and left to fetch the food.

Ellis chuckled into his tankard while taking a drink.

"You treat him the same as I do," she said, smiling.

"I won't dare do otherwise if I want to get into bed."

"Don't tell me he sleeps in bed with you?" asked Fraser, suppressing a smile.

Ellis nodded since he continued to drink.

"He probably uses a bone to coax him down," said Chad, to which Fraser chuckled.

Ellis joined the banter. "Heaven forbid I get up at night, he takes my place and we start the coaxing all over again."

She slapped his arm. "Since when is our bed a topic for discussion?"

Fraser and Chad desperately tried not to laugh. The effort didn't last long and the men enjoyed a good chuckle.

Avatar spoke. "Since the hunt, my lady. Newlywed mortals seem to be objects for base humor."

Ellis avoided her gaze by taking another drink.

"Him I expect base humor from," she scolded Ellis while motioning to Fraser. "But the hunt included the king, Prince Nigel, and the duke."

"And Titus and Eli," added Fraser, a chortle escaping despite his best effort to refrain.

She huffed and glared at Ellis.

"I don't think he'll get in bed tonight," said Chad to Fraser. The prince grabbed his mouth and turn aside to avoid laughing out loud.

Wren and Kendrick arrived. "The horses are being well-cared for," said Kendrick. He took a seat beside Virgil.

Wren sat next to Avatar, which was across from Valery. The young lady appeared very displeased. "Something wrong?"

"Mortal banter of a relationship nature," said Avatar. He poured a cup of ale for Wren and added when giving her the cup, "Like the hunt."

She rolled her eyes. "Typical male bragging at the expense of females."

"Infuriating, isn't it?" chided Valery.

"Ay, only we have our ways of getting back at them." She smiled, and sent a side-glance to Avatar.

"Why is it that when you load for a shot, I'm your target?"

Her smile remained as she shrugged. "Always best to practice on a straw target before going after the real prey."

"Or sharpen a sword on a stone before going into battle."

"Meaning he's fodder and she's dense," Virgil explained the exchange to Valery.

Chad tried to calm his laughter to speak. "As amusing as this relationship topic is, we came to Oakley for a reason." He paused when Joby and several servants brought a hearty amount of food, plates and utensils. Joby set a tray of bones and large fatty pieces of meat on the floor for Cody.

They waited for the servants to leave before saying the blessing and continuing the conversation while eating.

"With night falling, there isn't much more we can do today," said Fraser.

"Not exactly, Highness. Since thieves tend to work under the cover of darkness, I can make reconnaissance of the town tonight," said Wren.

"Two will make reconnaissance," corrected Avatar.

"Not through being a straw target?" quipped Virgil.

Avatar smirked. "I meant you going with her. You need to sharpen your sword."

"Cody can accompany you," said Valery.

Wren shook her head. "Not wise for a wolf to wander around town. Virgil and I will do fine. You and others rest for the night."

"We might want to speak to March in the morning and see what else he knows. Then proceed from there," said Chad.

"He didn't say much more than about Morley," said Fraser.

"We only have tomorrow before heading back to Burleigh and he's the best one for information."

Light conversation dominated the rest of the meal. After eating, Wren and Virgil left the inn. Joby took the others upstairs.

"We don't get many visitors to Oakley. Those who do come, usually stay with family. This room can be for your highness and Sir Chad. The next one for the count and countess." He opened the door for Fraser and Chad.

From the threshold they viewed a clean, adequate room with a decent size bed, large enough to accommodate two people. Along one wall stood a chest of drawers, side table with a basin and pitcher with hanging mirror. There was also a freestanding rack with towel and blankets draped over it and small stove in one corner. A single window opened for air and light, but no other door.

"Where's the privy?" asked Valery.

Joby heaved an embarrassed shrug. "As I said, my lady, we don't get many visitors, so I never installed one upstairs. The outdoor privy is complete with a tub, basin, three stalls, inside water pump, and stove if you want the water heated."

"Outside?" she said with a measure of disapproval.

"Does your family and guests from the tavern use that privy also?" asked Ellis.

"No. My family has a small modest one, and I built a few stalls for the tavern patrons just last year. But I lock the tavern around eleven so you couldn't use it. That door leads to the outside stairs. The privy is just a few feet away." He indicated the stairway door at the end of the hall.

"It's only for one night," said Chad to the young couple.

"Ay, we can make due with the accommodations," said Fraser. "Besides, the food was very good."

"Thank you, Highness," said Joby in relief. "Maybe next time you come I'll have an upstairs privy. For now, I'll have my boy bring up water for evening care then warm water in the morning."

Fraser kindly smiled. "Thank you. Good night," he said to Valery and Ellis before entering the room with Chad.

In their room, Valery pointed to the bed. "Cody." The wolf jumped on the bed and laid down.

Ellis chuckled. "Valery, we were only joking."

She didn't reply and began to undress for the night.

He took her in his arms. "In no way was there demeaning or scorn, just simple, playful teasing of newlyweds." He laughed. "I can't wait to tease Titus."

"Jillian is your sister. Will you compromise her like you allow your wife be compromised in an effort to get back at him?"

"That's not fair. They didn't compromise you and I wouldn't tolerate it if I thought they were. Besides, Titus has gone out of his way to be kind and put the past tension behind." He lifted her chin when she looked away in annoyance. "In two weeks, he will be your brother-in-law. And you know how dearly he loves his sister. He loves his entire family."

"Ay." She hugged him. "I'm sorry I'm so touchy about the subject. It's hard not to think about the way my father treated my mother with ridicule and scorn."

The statement stunned him. "Oh, no, my dearest Valery! If that is what troubles you, I won't let it happen again."

"I realize it is not the same. I never experienced good-natured bantering in my family. Although I have since witnessed it between you and Titus, Fraser and even the king." She smiled. "I remember when the queen and Mirit told me about the king's humor. I found it hard to believe so strong and honorably a man could be so jovial, but he is. I'm still trying to grow accustomed to it all."

He stroked her cheek. "From now on, I will try to be more sensitive to your feelings in the matter."

"And I'll try to not be so sensitive, especially having Titus for my brother-in-law."

Cody loudly yawned and stretched his body across the entire bed. With pleading eyes, Ellis gazed at Valery. She laughed. "Cody. Time to get down." The wolf snorted as if snoring. "Cody," she said more sternly. He got down and nudged Ellis' hand.

"Sorry, no bone. We're not at home."

Cody did a grunting sneeze and lay down near the empty stove.

Later, Ellis tossed and turned in bed. He grimaced and held his abdomen.

Sleepy, Valery asked, "What is it? Something wrong?"

"The last slice of kidney pie isn't sitting well on my stomach."

"I told you it was too rich for your digestion."

"Ay." He tossed aside the covers and sat up. He wore only his breeches and socks to bed. "I think I'll make use of the privy."

"That bad?"

He nodded, due to swallowing back the bile. He pulled on his boots then stood to put his doublet over his bear chest, not closing it.

"Want Cody to go with you?"

He paused at the door to smirk at her. "I'd rather do this myself." In the hall he met Avatar and Kendrick. The Guardians stood watch outside the rooms.

"Problem, my lord?" asked Avatar.

"Upset stomach. I'm going to the privy."

"I can mix you a soothing elixir."

"I might take you up on the offer if I don't feel better afterwards."

Ellis made his way down the outside stairs. To the right was a door upon which hung a sign saying *no admittance*. He reckoned it led to the family residence. He noticed a lantern fixed to the wall of a building about fifty feet from the door. Hardly a few feet like Joby said. Fortunately, the privy was nicer than expected with enough light to see clearly. When finished, he felt better and left.

Ellis barely stepped outside the privy when something was thrown over his head and someone tackled him to the ground. He squirmed to get free and call out. A hand grabbed his face through the sack, almost smothering him. A blow to the head rendered him unconscious.

"Hurry, before someone hears," said Preston.

Reilly took a rope and bound Ellis' hands then he and Preston wrapped the rope around Ellis' torso to secure the sack over his head and shoulders. They carried him from the inn.

Before they moved two blocks, they ducked into the shadow of a building at seeing movement up ahead. They waited and listened while holding Ellis between them. By the fringe light of a street lamp, Wren made her way through an intersection. When she left, they proceeded to carry Ellis out of town.

Upstairs Cody whimpered and scratched at the door to be let out.

Valery lazily stirred. "Oh, no," she groaned. "Did the bones disagree with you?"

Cody proved persistent in his efforts. She got up and opened the door. He ran to the stairway door and scratched at it. "Going to join Ellis," she told Kendrick and Avatar.

Kendrick opened the outer door and Cody bolted down the stairs. "I'll let him in if he doesn't return with Lord Ellis."

She stifled a yawn to say, "Hopefully they'll both feel better."

"I don't know if my stomach remedy will work on a wolf," quipped Avatar with wry smile.

She snorted a weary chuckle, closed the door and crawled back into bed.

In a hollow about a quarter mile from town, Preston and Reilly met with Fitch.

"I told you we'd get someone," said Preston.

Fitch shrugged the sign for *whom?*

"We don't know, a guest at the inn."

"Ay, he was on his way back from the privy," snickered Reilly.

Fitch rolled his eyes. He undid the rope holding the sack over Ellis' head and jerked it off. Ellis moaned at the violent movement. Fitch knelt to get a closer look.

"Will he do?" asked Preston, curious of Fitch's inspection.

Fitch grinned with pleasure. When Ellis began waking up, Fitch acted. His large hand covered Ellis' face and forehead. Ellis struggled against his hold. Fitch shaped-shifted into Ellis, and Ellis fainted. Fitch/Ellis stood.

"This time, be more careful with him. And tell Locan to move to phase two."

"Ay."

Fitch/Ellis made his way to the inn and around back to the privy. He proceeded upstairs where he paused just inside the door at seeing Avatar and Kendrick.

"Are you feeling better, my lord?" asked Avatar.

"Eh ... I think so," replied Fitch/Ellis.

"Do you want me to make the elixir?"

"No, that won't be necessary."

"What about Cody?" asked Kendrick.

"What about him?"

"He went scurrying after you. Also feeling just as ill."

"Well, you can hardly blame him."

"You didn't see him?"

"No, I was otherwise occupied." Fitch/Ellis went to the wrong door.

"My lord, it's this room," said Avatar.

"Ah. Hard to tell the difference at night."

Avatar grinned.

Inside Fitch/Ellis heard and saw movement in the bed. Lying beside a mortal female was not what he wanted to do, however his cover required doing so. He took off the doublet and boots before carefully slipping under the covers in an effort not to disturb her. He settled down. For a moment believed he succeeded, until she rolled over and snuggled up to him.

"Feeling better?" she sleepily asked.

"Ay."

"Cody?"

"I didn't see him."

"Well, Kendrick will let him when he comes back." She snuggled closer.

Fitch/Ellis never fell asleep, being uncomfortable about sharing a bed with a female. She eventually let loose and turned over. The one consolation is she wasn't in an amorous mood. At first light, he rose and began to dress. His movement woke Valery.

"Morning, already?" she asked.

"Ay."

She stretched, yawned and sat up. She only wore her loosened shirt to bed and her hair down in a long single braid. "Where is Cody?"

"I don't know." He shrugged and closed his doublet.

"Why are you dressing yourself?" she asked in a playful manner.

"Isn't that what one does first thing in the morning?"

"Silly. Just because we're not home doesn't mean I can't dress you." She crawled out of bed on his side, smiled and slid up to him.

Fitch/Ellis smiled with uncertainty. "Well, as you can see, I'm almost finished." He caught her arms about his neck. "When we get back home." He moved to sit in a chair and pull on the boots.

"At least give me a good morning kiss." She approached, placed both hands on the arms of the chair and leaned over him for a kiss.

He slipped away by ducking under her arm. "I think I hear Cody in the hall."

"What is wrong with you this morning? Are you still not feeling well?"

"Ay, and I don't want you to get sick."

"An upset stomach isn't contagious."

"I'm still feeling unsettled and I don't want to do anything to make me sick again."

"Are you saying kissing me will make you sick?" she rebuffed in offense.

"No. The thought of —"

"The thought!"

"Of food," he added and snatched her hand. He had to act fast and keep her from getting too upset. "The thought of food, not you." He kissed her hand and smiled.

She pouted and hugged him. "I can understand you not wanting to eat breakfast, but why did you dress yourself?"

He fought to keep the frustration from his face and voice. "I'm sorry. I won't do it again. Now, get dressed and I'll meet you downstairs."

She looked somewhat hurt. "You're not going to dress me?"

He smiled, a bit mischievously. "I'll save that for undressing when I feel better." When she closed her eyes expecting a kiss on the lips, he kissed her forehead. "A token." He winked and left the room.

Avatar was alone in the hall. "Kendrick accompanied his highness and Sir Chad down to breakfast."

Before Fitch/Ellis replied, Wren and Virgil arrived.

"Sleep well, my lord?" asked Virgil with a teasing smile.

"Unfortunately, no. Upset stomach."

"Did the countess provide you with a remedy?"

Wren gave him a sharp, warning poke in the ribs.

"What?"

Fitch/Ellis did not answer. His disapproving frown said enough as he passed the Guardians to go down to the tavern.

"Doesn't sound as if you got the chance to sharpen your sword last night," said Avatar.

Wren answered, merry and smiling. "He makes a better straw target than you."

Avatar laughed at Virgil's scowl.

Valery emerged from the room. "Have any of you seen Cody?"

"Not since Kendrick let him out to be sick," said Avatar.

Wren and Virgil exchange conferring glances. "No," she said.

"Strange he hasn't come back. I hope he's all right. He acted very agitated."

"Don't worry. Wolves tend to wander off from time to time. If he became ill from all the gristle, he may have gone into the woods to recover. If he doesn't return by mid-day I'll call for him," said Wren.

"The rest are down at breakfast," said Avatar.

***

In the hollow, Ellis stirred and woke. He felt groggy and it took a moment to realize he lay on the ground with his hands bound. The sky appeared lighter, perhaps dawn. Although his hands were bound, his feet remained loose. Voices came from nearby and he carefully moved his head for a better view. Preston and Reilly sat on a log. They must be the ones responsible for his condition. They had not yet noticed he was awake. Bushes ringed the area, about twenty feet from where he lay. If quiet and careful, he could crawl away unseen into the bushes before getting to his feet and fleeing.

"We could take him to the cave," said Preston.

"Ay," began Reilly—when, "Hey! He's trying to escape."

Ellis scrambled to his feet and began running. Preston and Reilly tackled him. He struggled, kicking at Preston while Reilly attempted to pin him to the ground. "Leave off, varlets!" he ordered. With his hands bound and unarmed, they easily subdued him.

"Get the sack!" said Preston.

"Why?"

"So he can't see where we're taking him."

Reilly left to follow instructions, leaving only Preston to hold him. Again, Ellis struggled again to break free. "You would be wise to let me go!" He grunted in anger.

"No, it wouldn't be wise at all!"

Ellis increased his efforts to escape. He kicked Preston aside and scrambled to his feet only to be tackled again. "Release me! Or the king will hear about it."

"Like the king would care."

"I am Count Ellis of the Meadowlands and Member of the Council of Twelve. The king will care!"

Reilly became distressed by Ellis' identification. "We should do as he says."

"We have to kill him."

At the statement, Ellis grew more vigorous in his resistance.

"No, remember what happened last time," argued Reilly. Preston didn't listen as he continued to wrestle with Ellis. "They'll kill us if we do!" he insisted.

"We're dead if the king finds out. Remember what happened to our family. Now, hold him!"

When Reilly took hold of Ellis, Preston reached for his knife. He raised his blade to strike. A vicious growl came a split second before Cody's jaw clamped down on Preston's arm. He dropped the knife and tied to fight off the wolf by hitting him on the snout. Cody released him and leapt at Preston's face and neck, taking him down. Reilly drew his dagger with the intention of rescuing Preston. Ellis kicked Reilly's legs out from under him and he fell hard onto his back.

Ellis scrambled to his knees and shouted, "Cody!" The wolf released Preston and assumed a protective position in front of Ellis.

Reilly rose to his knees with dagger in hand. Sight of Cody, snarling and blood on his muzzle made him pause in striking out.

"I stopped him from killing, but I won't do so again if you make another move toward me!" said Ellis.

To add emphasis, Cody snapped at Reilly.

Reilly lowered the dagger. Hearing Preston groan, his eyes darted to his brother. Severe, bloody wounds covered Preston's face and neck. To get to him, Reilly had to pass the wolf.

Ellis' eyes shifted from Reilly to Preston then back again. "You two are part of the group responsible for the crime spree. Why kidnap me?"

"It's what we do. Take people for ransom."

"You mentioned others. Who are they?"

"No one you would want to mess with, even if you are on the Council."

Preston groaned, this time in great pain. Reilly tried to move toward him but stopped when Cody growled. "If he dies, the wolf won't stop me from killing you!"

"Why should I care if he dies, you kidnapped me?"

Another moan, then stillness.

"Preston!" Reilly became concerned at no response or movement. "I'll make a bargain. I'll cut you loose and let you go if you call off the wolf and let me tend to him."

"Why should I trust you? You can just as soon use the knife to kill me."

"He's my brother! I don't want him to die!"

During a brief hesitation, Ellis glanced to Preston. "Very well. Cody, be still and watchful."

Reilly moved toward Ellis. Cody stepped aside, growling with keen eyes watching. Reilly warily shifted his attention between Cody and cutting the rope. Once free, Ellis shook his wrists to get the circulation going. Cody snapped at Reilly, who backed away and moved to Preston.

"Cody." Ellis summoned the wolf and they ran from the hollow.

March just opened the mercantile for the day when the group arrived. "Good morning, Highness. I hope the accommodations were satisfactory?"

"Aside from the lack of a proper privy, Master Joby's inn is very satisfactory. We came to inquire if there is anything else you can tell us about this thief in connection to the crime spree," replied Fraser.

"Not much since I've been unable to catch any of them. Morley is the only witness, and you saw how difficult he is."

"No one else reported anything suspicious?" asked Chad.

"No, my lord."

"What about stolen items turning up in unexpected places?"

"Nothing yet. Morley is the first real lead. If he identifies the person, I maybe able to get catch the culprits. Until then, there's nothing more I can do."

Fitch/Ellis saw Reilly rush into the apothecary a couple of streets down. "Maybe we can ask around."

"You can, but I doubt if anyone will tell you different," said March.

"I'll start down the street." Fitch/Ellis added at seeing Fraser's quizzical regard, "It can't hurt to ask. We only have today." Without further delay, he left.

"Ellis," called Valery, only to be ignored.

"Is he all right? He acted rather subdued at breakfast," said Fraser.

"He says it's his stomach," she groused in disbelief.

"You're not sure?" asked Chad.

She shook her head. "He's behaving rather odd this morning. He didn't even give me a good morning kiss." She lashed out to stop a reaction from Fraser that never came. "Don't start teasing! I'm serious. He avoided me, claiming my kiss would make him sick."

"I believe you. I said I thought he acted subdued at breakfast. I'm not so coarse as to tease when something is wrong." He took hold of her hand and spoke in earnest. "I promise, cousin, I'll find out what is troubling him. In the meantime, let's go ask some questions." He steered her in the opposite direction Ellis went.

She took a deep breath to calm down. "I told Ellis I'll try not to be so sensitive since he says you're not trying to be mean or vindictive in your teasing."

"Oh, no," he said then grew a bit sheepish. "Although we tend to go overboard at times. It's all meant in merriment never in spite."

"Titus used to do so whenever he and I met. And you weren't too friendly for awhile."

Fraser cocked a wry grin. "Titus used to do many things differently. I assure you, his attitude has changed towards you." He squeezed her hand. "Again I apologize for my rough behavior. I feel like a different Fraser after what happened, and know I have much to redress."

She smiled, soft and reassuring. "I think we both learned much since then." She paused in step and glanced back in the direction Ellis/Fitch left. "Before Ellis came along, only with Grandfather Allard could I laugh and be unguarded. My father constantly criticized and scorned mother and I. That's why I became combative with Titus, to keep him off balance and protect myself.

"Hopefully now, you know how important family is to us. I needed a refresher."

She nodded and they continued their trek. "Your part of the family is closer than mine ever was. You not only share humor and good-natured banter but love and forgiveness. Being with Ellis has shown me not all men are abusive or mean-spirited. As such, I can tolerate a younger, impish cousin."

Fraser laughed. "I promise to be more discerning in the future." He stopped in front of two shops side-by-side, one a bakery, the other a creamery. "Which one?"

"I'll take the creamery."

Reilly left the apothecary and headed down an alley. Fitch/Ellis caught him by the arm and jerked him into a secluded part of the alley.

"What are you doing, you idiot? You're supposed to be watching him."

"A wolf attacked Preston. I came to get medicine for his wounds."

The news was alarming. "What about ... is he still safe?"

Reilly hemmed and hawed before answering. "He escaped when the wolf attacked. I'll find him as soon as I get this to Preston." He indicated the jar he carried.

Fitch/Ellis' grip tightened on Reilly, his face and voice low and angry "You will find him before he reaches town or both you and your poor excuse for a brother will die." He shoved Reilly in the direction he was heading. "Be quick! I'll take care of the girl."

Valery moved from the creamery to a peddler's cart where she spoke to a woman selling flowers. Someone called to her. She barely turned around when Ellis embraced her. Cody stood up on his hind legs to join in the greeting.

"What a night, you wouldn't believe," he said.

"You're right, I don't believe it." She pushed him off.

He became baffled at her anger. "What's wrong?"

"What's wrong? How can you ask that?"

"Because I just got back. Didn't you miss me?"

Her hands went to her hips as she spoke in disbelief. "From where, the apothecary? Please. Did they give you an elixir that settled your stomach and suddenly you're amorous?"

"What?" he asked utterly confused.

She glared at him and noticed he wore only his open doublet and no shirt. "Where's your shirt? Why are you suddenly half undressed in the middle of the street? Is it supposed to inspire me? I thought my kiss made you sick!" She stormed off, leaving him dumbfounded.

Cody whimpered in a confused noise at Valery's departure. Ellis went to pursue her when he heard his name.

"Ellis! Have you learned anything yet?" asked Fraser.

Frustrated, he waved in the direction Valery left. "That my wife is angry with me and I don't know why."

"You can't blame her considering your odd behavior."

Ellis stared incredulously at Fraser. "What are you talking about? I just got back. Can't you see I'm half dressed and covered in forest soot?" He made an exaggerated gesture at himself.

Fraser glanced in guarded curiosity at Ellis. "You are acting strange this morning. Why did you alter your appearance? Are you sure it's only your stomach troubling you?"

Ellis was almost beside himself in exasperation. "Not if you call being kidnapped at the privy and spending most of the night in the woods with my captors acting odd! Cody rescued me. I come back, hoping to be warmly greeted, only to find my wife angry, you annoyed and both unconcerned about my welfare despite my obvious marred appearance. If you don't believe me, ask Cody!" He motioned to the wolf.

During the passionate reply, Fraser became concerned. "This can mean only one thing. Let's find Wren." He took Ellis' arm and moved to search for the Guardian huntress.

Agitated by the encounter, Valery walked fast in weaving her way in and out of the growing crowd of people emerging for the day's chores.

"Valery."

She rolled her eyes when Fitch/Ellis joined her. "What now?"

"I came to apologize. I have not been myself this morning."

"That's an understatement!"

"If you want, we can go back to the inn." He smiled.

She stopped and glared at him. "We have a task."

"I just thought making up would be better sooner than later." He took her hand and drew her into a nearby alcove and kissed her.

She balked and drew away.

"Something wrong? I thought you like my kisses."

She put a quick hand to stop him from kissing her again and noticed he was fully dressed. "How did you clean up so fast?"

"Valery! Valery, where are you?" a very familiar voice called.

"Ellis?" she said in confusion then gasped in fright when the face of the Ellis holding her turned fierce and deadly.

Fitch/Ellis whipped out his dagger. Before she could act, Cody bit his hand. Valery broke free and stumbled backward to the street. Fitch/Ellis used his strength to knock Cody away. In dealing with the wolf, he saw the entire group coming towards him. Wren loosed a bolt. He barely avoided being impaled by the arrow that grazed his left shoulder. In a flash of white light he vanished.

Ellis dropped to his knees beside Valery. "Are you hurt?"

Stunned, she stared at him a moment before replying. "What happened?"

"Fitch"

"Fitch?" she said in disturbance.

141

"He shape-shifted into me after I was kidnapped at the privy."

Her hand covered her mouth and she turned sickly pale.

He held her by the shoulders, greatly concerned. "What did he do to you?"

She shook her head. "Nothing past a kiss. That's when I knew something was wrong." She threw her arms about his neck and sobbed.

He held her close and grinned in relief. "Nice to know he couldn't match me in everything."

"Fitch being here changes things," said Chad.

"Ay," groused Fraser. "I wish Wren had done more than wing him, because I would love to get my hands on him."

"Keep your wits. Revenge can be an ugly thing," said Kendrick.

"Uglier than him almost destroying my family using my persona?"

"No. Still, there is a difference between personal revenge and justice according to the Jor'ellian code." He gently tugged on Fraser's uniform.

Fraser pursed his lips and nodded. "Uncle will want to know."

"So will Armus," said Avatar.

"We better start now. It's a long ride back," said Ellis.

Chad shook his head. "No. With this news, we'll take the Guardian way. It'll be safer and faster."

142

Chapter 9

VIVIAN TOOK HER DAILY EARLY MORNING WALK FOR GATHERING medicinal plants when she spotted Spaulding's horse grazing near the spot where she found Kell. The horse was fully saddled, only no sign of Spaulding. She moved off the road to investigate and became startled at seeing Spaulding lying face down. Upon closer inspection, she noticed a large bloody gash on the back of his head. Perhaps from being thrown from his horse.

She knelt beside him. "Sheriff?" she cautiously asked. "Sheriff Spaulding, can you hear me?" It took some effort in turning him onto his back. To her shock and horror, face was an ashen blue and vacant eyes opened. All signs of death. She bolted to her feet. A hand covered her mouth in an effort to swallow back the bile. She ran to the house.

In tears of fright and upset, Vivian entered the kitchen. Lester, Howey and Donovan ate breakfast with Drusilla serving the men. Despite the flush on her cheeks from the exertion of running, her expression showed terror and tears.

Lester rose from the table. "Viv? What's wrong?" She couldn't speak so he helped her to sit. "Howey, wine, quick."

Howey complied and Lester gave the cup to her. Her hands shook so fiercely he held the cup for her to drink.

"Slowly. Find your voice and tell us what happened."

"In the field, at the turn. A horse … his horse. The sheriff—dead!" She wept.

"I'll have a look," said Donovan.

"Howey, go with him. Drusilla, fetch my bag." Lester knelt beside Vivian. "I'll give you something to calm down, but can you tell me anything more?" She shook her head still weeping. He held her. "It's all right."

Drusilla returned with the medical bag. Lester found what he needed and mixed some poppy juice into the wine. "I used just enough juice to help you calm down not to sleep. If it is as you say, Wess will need to ask you questions."

She drank. "I've seen death before, but what this could mean—"

"Easy. You must calm down." He tapped the cup for her to drink.

Nothing more was said as she kept drinking, or rather he made silent motions and expressions to encourage her. She just finished the wine when Donovan returned; his face flushed and labored breathing from running.

"Spaulding all right. Dead some time by the look of him, and not natural."

Lester stared at his son, mindful of the implication. "Are you certain?"

"Ay."

"Go to the castle and inform Wess."

"Howey is saddling the horse so he can go. I should stay."

"No, go back and make certain no one disturbs the body until Wess arrives."

In a gesture of tender support, Donovan touched his aunt's cheek before leaving.

<hr>

At Burleigh castle, Wess, Nigel, Mirit and Kell sat at the table finishing breakfast. Although Guardians didn't require food, Armus, Ridge and Vidar joined them. Armus sat beside Kell.

Wess pursed his lips in consideration. "Since we turned up nothing where Kelvin appeared, let's hope the others are having more success finding answers in Oakley."

"There won't be any answers to find since I am not involved," insisted Kell.

"A rash of crimes in the area are unsolved. Not to mention your appearance is a bit of a mystery."

"Who says they are connected?"

"Who says they're not?"

Kell shrugged. "I don't know. But I do know, I'm not a thief."

"Until we have the answers, it is best you stay here."

"Under house arrest?"

Wess cocked a sly grin. "If you're not a thief then why under arrest?"

"Under suspicion then."

"Under protection," said Armus.

Kell snorted an ironic chuckle. "By you? Despite what you say, I know you don't believe I'm innocent anymore than the mortals do. Don't deny it! Your stoic expression and lack of defense on my behalf is a give away. I can read you like a book."

Curious, Armus' questioning gaze found Vidar. The archer regarded Kell, who turned away in anger. Vidar responded to Armus by heaving a shrug of indecision.

Further conversation halted when the door opened. Chad, Fraser, Ellis, Valery, Avatar, Wren, Virgil, Kendrick and Cody entered.

"What are you doing back so soon? Have you found something?" asked Nigel.

"Disturbing news to report," replied Chad.

"Fitch was in Oakley," said Fraser, his face fixed and angry.

Indeed, the news proved disturbing. All knew how Fitch used Fraser's persona to set the Fortress of Jor'cl on fire. He also led most of royal family into a trap in an effort to help Ellan and Hueil during their coup attempt. The family barely escaped alive, and for a while, suspicion was cast upon Fraser, which caused a great rift.

"Fitch?" echoed Ridge in annoyance. "Again I couldn't sense him," he said in defense to Armus.

"It's not your fault. Considering the effort I needed to discover this particular dimension travel, something of the Dark Way must be acting as a shield."

"How did you learn this?" asked Nigel the others.

"Fitch assumed my identity," chided Ellis.

Nigel motioned for them to take seats at the table. "Start from the beginning and leave nothing out."

"I was kidnapped late last night on my way back from an outdoor privy. I don't recall Fitch, but with Cody's help I escaped my kidnappers. When I returned to town I tried to speak to Valery, only she was angry at me and I didn't know why."

She took up the explanation. "The result of an annoying conversation I had with—well, Fitch. I thought he was Ellis since nothing seemed unusual when he returned to bed last night."

"He didn't—I mean Fitch didn't?" Nigel tried to be delicate in his questioning.

"No!" she insisted, a blush immediately rising to her cheeks. "He did kiss me in the morning, and I felt something wasn't right."

"I got the brunt of anger for something I didn't say," complained Ellis.

Chad knowingly grinned. "Happens to all husbands."

Nigel and Wess both chuckled. They stopped when Ellis continued in a voice of annoyance.

"Anyway. She walked off in a huff. I went to follow, when Fraser accosted me about acting strange and I lost my temper. Being kidnapped, partially dressed, covered in forest soot, I was not in the mood to endure rebuking and told him so—along with the events of my kidnapping."

"The prince brought Count Ellis to me. From listening to him and speaking to Cody, I confirmed his story to be genuine," said Wren.

"I knew of only one explanation, and wanted Wren to verify my suspicion," said Fraser.

"We hurried to find Lady Valery. She was with Fitch and we secured her before harm could be done," said Avatar.

"I winged him as he vanished in dimension travel," said Wren.

"Did you track where he went?" asked Nigel.

"No. We came here directly."

146

"Having Fitch around would explain some things," said Wess to Ridge. The ranger nodded, though visibly irritated.

"Not everything." Armus sent a thoughtful, prompting look to Kell.

"I told you I have no dealings with the Dark Way."

"He may have something to do with you."

"You mean using a shape-shift of Kelvin?" asked Ridge in piqued interest. "Could be why I didn't discern the travel."

"Impossible. When I—" Kell stopped, as he realized what he was about to say.

"When what?" pressed Armus.

Since he couldn't explain Fitch's inability to shape-shift into him, Kell searched for a quick reply. "When I arrived, Mistress Vivian was the first person I met, then the doctor, Donovan and the servants. Since then I've either been at the farm or here."

"You were unconscious. Fitch could have acted then."

"I was asleep when he changed into me," groused Fraser.

Kell adamantly shook his head. "Not possible."

"Along with shielding Kelvin's travel, could Fitch be the vague image you encountered?" asked Mirit.

"Fitch strong enough to repel Armus?" asked Virgil, doubtful.

"If he's been enhanced by the Dark Way, perhaps," admitted Armus, howbeit with skepticism.

For a moment, Kell pondered the probability. Could that be it? Did Fitch dimension travel him from the Southern Forest to the South Plains? Was he the one controlling the *madah-dune* at the ambush? "What about Locan?" he blurted out.

"Locan? He's here too? I think I'll turn in my quarterstaff," Ridge groused to no one in particular.

"Armus and I didn't sense him either," said Vidar to the ranger.

Armus ignored his fellow Guardians to inquired of Kell. "How do you know about Locan?"

Kell shrugged at the reactions to his impulsive miscue. "I told you, all soldiers are ordered to be on the lookout for anything unusual since they escaped the battle and were reported to be working together."

"Those were the orders I gave when the forces disbanded to return to their provinces," said Wess.

"Did you get to speak to the witness?" asked Mirit.

"Ay, and he wasn't infirmed as reported," replied Chad.

"I'm not surprised," groused Kell.

"Did he identity Kelvin?" asked Nigel.

"Highness, I said I'm not a thief."

"But you are impertinent and it grows tiresome!"

Kell made a defiant rebuttal. "Try constantly being accused of something you know you didn't do and no matter what you say, no one believes you."

Nigel leaned forward on the table to give a counter argument. "I've been in a more dire situation. Try being so altered in appearance no one recognizes you from who you once were."

"I'm that way now! No one who knows me would recognize me or understand what is happening. So since we have something in common, maybe you can give me the benefit of the doubt."

Nigel sat back to studious regard Kell. This made for a momentary pause in replying. "In all honesty, I would like to. And if the witness failed to identity you, maybe I can." He looked to Chad for an answer.

"Well, Squire Morley, the witness, wasn't very cooperative even when Wren fed him fresh boar and Avatar gave him ale."

"Squire Morley? Why does that name sound familiar?" asked Wess.

"I told you about him. He's the unstable war veteran who's taken to living as a cantankerous recluse in the hills above Oakley." Ridge pointed to his head when saying *unstable.*

"That's putting it mildly," complained Fraser.

"Did he give you a description?" asked Mirit.

"Only that he's not a redhead and is of average height," said Chad.

"Oh, well," began Kell with great sarcasm, "based upon such a wonderful description from a lunatic, I can understand why Spaulding claimed it to be me."

"He said he would know him when saw him again," said Valery.

"Fine, let's go to Oakley so he can secure the noose around my neck!"

"Kelvin, enough!" snapped Nigel.

Kell fought to contain his temper to reply. "With all due respect, Highness, they had to prod him with boar and ale for a universally vague description. We already found planted evidence. So What makes you think for a handful for coins from Spaulding, this Squire Morley won't indentify me just for spite?"

Nigel questioned Avatar. "Did you sense any deception?"

"Hard to tell since he avoided direct eye contact, and verbally combative."

"He ordered us to leave after receiving the boar and accused us of invading his home to ask personal questions," said Ellis.

"Doesn't sound like a reliable witness," said Armus.

"That's the first thing we agree on," said Kell.

Nigel tugged on his lower lip for a moment of pondering. His gaze shifted from Kell and Armus to the returned group. "Did March provide any other information?"

"No," replied Chad.

"He said if Morley can identify the thief, he may be able to catch those committing the crimes," said Fraser.

"Then we go to Oakley," said Wess.

Kell visibly reacted, yet managed to keep his tongue. Or rather, Armus' heavy grip on his shoulder kept him from speaking.

Nigel noticed the restraint, yet told Wess, "Order the horses ready."

"Eh, we left our horses in Oakley," began Chad. "With such news, I thought it safer to return the Guardian way than give Fitch another opportunity."

"I have enough," said Wess.

Cameron entered, and escorted a fretful Howey. "My lord, this man insists upon seeing you. He claims there is horrible news to report."

"Howey. Is something wrong at the farm?"

"Not at the farm exactly, my lord, though it does involve Mistress Vivian and Sheriff Spaulding."

"Why can't he leave them alone?" complained Kell.

"He won't be troubling anyone any more," began Howey in a dreadful voice, then turned from Kell to Wess and announced, "He's dead. Mistress Vivian found his body off the road near the bend when she went out this morning. Master Donovan and I went to confirm it is the sheriff then I came here to tell you."

"How horrible for her," said Valery.

"She is quite shaken."

"How did he die?" asked Wess.

149

"I don't believe it happened due to falling off his horse by the look of his smashed head. If you take my meaning."

"Foul play?" Wess' level glance shifted from Howey to Kell.

"Why are you looking at me? I've been here – with him as my jailer." Kell jerked his thumb at Armus.

Wess spoke to Nigel. "I think we'll change our destination."

<hr>

Vivian regained her composure and ate a light breakfast at Drusilla's insistence. They heard sounds of arrival in the back yard. Lester kept Vivian from leaving the table. The door opened. He and Wess barely exchanged greetings, Wess' focus searching for Vivian. She rose at first sight of him and for a moment, she held onto him as she fought back emotions. Kell waited near the door; his jowl's tightening to contain his agitation at watching the tender meeting.

"What can you tell us?" Nigel asked Lester.

"Not much. I've been helping Vivian recover from the shock. I sent Donovan to watch over him," he said, a cautious eye at his sister.

"I can handle it now," she said as she clenched Wess' hand.

"I wanted to make sure of your well-being before seeing Spaulding for myself," he said.

"I'll take you to him."

"No!" said Kell before Wess could object.

At Wess' piqued reaction, Armus jerked Kell outside while saying, "You must learn to hold your tongue."

"I'm really well enough to face it," she insisted to Wess. "It was just the initial shock. I'm over it now. I have seen death before."

"Very well. However, at first sign of distress you leave." Once outside, he spoke instructions. "Virgil, Wren, keep Kelvin here."

"Why?" demanded Kell.

Wess ignored Kell to mount. Ridge lifted Vivian onto the horse behind Wess.

"I said, why?" insisted Kell.

"Isn't it obvious? You're too volatile," said Virgil.

"I can help!"

"Wren, shoot him if he tries to leave," ordered Wess.

"Wess!" objected Vivian.

"Just enough to stop him, not to kill," he amended the order.

"To avoid causing Mistress Vivian more distress, I'll stay," said Kell.

Wess abruptly turned the horse to leave. The rest followed his lead.

"Armus is right. You need to learn to hold your tongue," said Virgil.

"I'm concerned for Vivian."

"Wess will take care of her." Lester laid hold of Kell. He signaled for Virgil and Wren to remain. "I want to speak to him privately." He took Kell to the oak tree bench and made him sit.

"What do you want to talk about?" asked Kell.

"You recall our conversation about my hopes for Wess and Vivian?"

"Ay. You also wondered if I was the answer to your prayer."

"Well, I don't think that any more. Too much trouble has accompanied you."

"I told you, Wess, the prince and everyone else, I'm not a thief."

"A little too loudly perhaps."

"What do you mean?"

"Your continuing insistence of innocence is growing annoying and a bit suspicious. Why keep claiming it rather than let the circumstances prove it? If you are truly innocent."

For a moment, Kell allowed the words to sink in. Indeed, he had been more vocal than was common for him, and with unusual sarcasm. Over the centuries, Armus counseled him about being too serious. He tried to moderate his tendency, especially during more peaceful and quiet times. Now sarcasm seemed to be all he was capable of. Rather he made knee-jerk reactions instead of his usual thoughtful approach to problems and situations.

"You're right and I'm sorry," he said at length. "The last thing I want is for my verbosity to harm you or Vivian. I'll try to keep my temper and my tongue while letting things take their course."

"I'm sure Nigel and Armus will be glad to hear that," said Virgil.

Lester and Kell noticed the Guardians moved closer.

"We're supposed to be watching him," said the warrior.

"You can watch, only I'm not going anywhere. And you won't have to shoot. I wouldn't get five yards before you strike me down."

Wren's green gaze regarded him. "You say that with absolute certainty. When have you seen me shoot?"

Kell boldly met her stare. "Many times, Wren, and always with deadly accuracy." He held her gaze for a moment before she shied and took a few awkward steps back.

Virgil watched with great interest. When she retreated, he took up a protective position to accost Kell. "What did you do to her?"

"Nothing. I have no power to do anything."

Virgil wasn't convinced. "Move, and you won't even get those five yards before I act!" He gently drew Wren away to speak privately.

The conversation was easy for Kell to overhear, though the Guardians spoke in confidential voices and in the Ancient. He pretended not to be interested. Lester appeared curious, since he didn't understand.

"What happened?" asked Virgil.

Her expression showed she searched for words to reply. "Like Armus said, there is a striking familiarity about him." She shook her head in befuddlement. "I don't recall ever seeing him before."

"What did he do to make you retreat?"

"No power, no evil, rather a strong sense of confirmation in my spirit that he *does* know me. I've not felt such keen recognition from a mortal before. That is why I retreated, bewildered by the sensation." She spoke the last part in a lowered voice.

"Wren, are you all right?" asked Lester.

She flashed her usual wry smile, her voice returning to dry wit. "I'm fine. We're just discussing what to do if Kelvin does decide to attempt an escape."

Kell laughed with a contrary shake of his head. He did refrain from making eye contact with the Guardians.

Silence fell. Lester and Kell remained on the bench beneath the oak with Virgil and Wren nearby. There really wasn't anything more to say. In fact, Kell already said more than was prudent. First he made Armus suspicious with the question about Locan, and now Wren and Virgil. True, he desperately wanted to be recognized by his companions, but not at the risk of causing them discomfort or trouble.

Jor'el, give me peace of mind and in my spirit to act as Lester suggests. Provide the means to prove my innocence in this mortal's death, that I'm not a thief. It is so difficult to be this close to my comrades and not be known. If possible, please, show me the reason this has happened to me, and the purpose it serves.

Armus again touched the ground near Spaulding's body. Vidar called upon the creatures. Ridge closed his eyes, stretched out his senses and clenched his quarterstaff to act as his connection to the trees and nature. Nigel and Wess examined Spaulding. Mirit and Valery stood to one side with Vivian. Despite her insistence, Vivian exhibited signs of being troubled by the sight of Spaulding.

"Seeing death in battle and coming upon someone who may have been murdered are different," said Mirit in an attempt to encourage Vivian.

"I've never felt such repulsion before. The hideous look on his face."

Valery's hand on her arm drew Vivian's focus from the investigation to her. "I'll take you back."

"No. For all concerned, I must stay."

"All? Don't you mean Wess and Kelvin?" asked Mirit directly.

Vivian's look grew sharp. "Wess more specifically."

"Then you're not concerned how this will affect Kelvin?"

"This shouldn't affect him. He was at the castle." She lowered her voice to continue in discretion, "Now Wess—some people talk unfavorably about him assuming Sir Gareth's position. I believe a few of those malcontents are behind the rash of crimes, hoping to either disgrace him or at least cast doubt upon his ability to govern."

"You wouldn't want that to happen, would you?"

"No."

"Because of an understanding between you and Wess?" Mirit posed the question in a manner that told she knew the answer.

"You already know my reason so why ask?"

Mirit grinned. "Wess is well regarded by my husband."

"I'm acquainted with their history. Shortly after Wess became King Ellis' squire, he and Lester met. I was a girl of six when we arrived at Waldron for Lester to begin his studies with Doctor Charlton. Being teenage boys, they struck up a friendship that has lasted all these years. Wess requested we to move to the South Plains and help him establish his new administration. I don't want to see anything or anyone threaten that."

Mirit grinned during the explanation. "Nigel won't let it happen."

153

Nigel and Wess were too preoccupied to hear the exchange. Wess steadied Spaulding's body on its side so they could view the wound. "This didn't happen from falling off his horse. Nothing around for him to strike his head on."

"Whoever struck him was strong," said Nigel

"Or the object real heavy." Wess lowered the body.

"The blood has drained from his face and he looks like a ghost. There is no pool of blood on the ground. This suggests he was brought here and died someplace else."

Chad arrived and knelt opposite Nigel. "No sign of disturbance nearby just his horse." He pointed to where the Guardians conducted their investigation.

"This may provide a clue." Wess removed a piece of cloth from Spaulding's clenched left fist and held it up. "Look familiar?"

"Somewhat." Nigel took the cloth for closer examination. "Looks like part of coat or doublet."

"Ay, and it's been torn. Kelvin's doublet was torn and dirty, *and* made of a similar fabric."

"You think this is from his doublet?" asked Nigel, guarded.

"Why not? Spaulding threatened him. There are signs of struggle and injury on his wrists"

"Don't get carried away, Wess. Kelvin's been at the castle with us."

"Then how did the torn piece get here?"

"I don't know. Nor are we sure of a match."

"I intend to find out." Wess snatched the remnant from Nigel.

Nigel seized Wess' hand. "If anyone is going to confront Kelvin, I will." He went to take back the cloth only Wess wouldn't yield it.

"With all due respect, this is my jurisdiction and my sheriff is dead."

Nigel sent a quick glance to where the women stood. "There is enough animosity between you and Kelvin for another reason. *If* he is involved, then it would be better coming from a neutral party. Understand?"

"Ay. Vivian's safety and feelings are very important to me." He yielded the cloth.

Nigel grinned and stuffed the piece in his pocket. "As if I couldn't tell." He stood and called for the Guardians to return. "Anything?" he asked once they gathered.

"He was brought here on horseback by another individual, no dimension travel," said Armus.

"The lack of blood confirms he was killed someplace else. The question is who and why?"

Armus shook his head. "Those answers can't be discovered here."

"Either way, he must be properly treated," said Wess. "Donovan, have Howey help you take the body to Bennett with instructions on proper burial. Tell him I'm investigating, and he is acting sheriff until another is appointed."

"Is this Bennett one of Spaulding's deputies?" asked Chad.

"Ay. A good man, a little slow at times, but dependable."

"Let's return to the house," said Nigel.

At the farm the group drew rein near the oak tree where Kell and Lester sat under the supervision of Virgil and Wren. Armus lifted Vivian down from the horse before Wess dismounted.

"Find anything?" asked Kell in a neutral tone.

"That you are still here and in one piece," retorted Wess.

"Can't say I'm sorry to disappoint you."

Nigel gave Wess a warning nudge before speaking. "Spaulding was killed with a severe blow to the back of the head. He showed signs of a struggle, and we found this clenched in one hand." He held up the torn cloth for them to see.

Lester took the piece to examine it. "It looks like it came from one of my doublets."

"Perhaps the one you gave Kelvin to wear." Nigel motioned to his own collar. "I noticed a tear."

"I didn't scuffle with Spaulding. It happened —" Kell began in defense and stopped as the implication struck him. So did the fact he couldn't mention anything more about Fitch. He opted for denial in a more controlled voice of objection. "I didn't kill him."

"Then how did this get ripped?" Nigel took the cloth from Lester.

Continuing to heed Lester's advice, Kell rose from bench and spoke with an even tone of conviction and determination. "On my way to Burleigh Castle to meet the Sheriff Spaulding's at his request, I was nearly run over by a wagon and fell among thickets to avoid the carriage. You saw my soiled state when I arrived, Highness." He turned over his hands to show some scratches on the knuckles.

"You know," began Wess, skeptical, "for a man who vehemently objects to being called a thief, you're taking a man's death very calmly."

Despite Wess' accusing tone, Kell maintained his composure. "What difference does my demeanor make when no one believes me?"

"It can make a great deal of difference."

"I have no reason to kill Spaulding."

"He had a witness who could identify you."

"Who turns out to be suspicious, as reported by Sir Chad and the others." Kell's eyes briefly left Wess to indicate Chad.

"Only by sight can that be confirmed."

"General, you're forgetting one important factor," began Fraser. "And one from whom I've suffered personal injustice. Fitch is here and on the loose."

"And shape-shifting into me," added Ellis.

"Not to mention the thieves responsible for the rash of crimes," said Mirit. "Like Crawford, they may have planted evidence to divert attention and suspicion."

"Maybe one of them attacked Kelvin," said Valery.

Kell turned to Armus. "How was Spaulding brought here?"

"On horseback."

"So Fitch and the obscure image you encountered may not be connected to Spaulding?"

"Possible."

"Wess, there are too many scenarios to eliminate before declaring who is responsible," said Nigel.

"I say we start eliminating them by calling upon Squire Morley."

"Kelvin, are you willing to face the squire and possibly identification?"

Kell squared his shoulder. "Highness, I told you before I am not a thief, nor a murderer. However, if confronting this witness will prove it, and perhaps lead to identifying the person who killed Sheriff Spaulding, so be it. No one wants the king's justice, or Jor'el's justice, more properly administered than I in this matter."

"Very well. Lester, do you have a spare horse for Master Kelvin?"

156

"No, I only have the two Donovan and I use to tend to the sick."

"He and Howey will be using them for the wagon to take Spaulding's body to town." Wess motioned to the barn where they the two were finishing with the harness.

"To Bennett?" asked Lester.

"Ay. With instructions I'm conducting the investigation, and until I appoint a new sheriff, he'll be acting in that capacity."

"We'll stop at a livery in town. In the meantime, Kelvin, you will ride double with Chad," said Nigel.

"I'd like to go also, Highness," said Vivian.

"Why?" asked Wess.

She continued to speak to Nigel. "Kelvin is still in my charge until my brother declares him fit and recovered."

Wess poked Lester, who said, "I haven't examined him to say either way," much to Wess' chagrin.

"I'm fine," said Kell.

However, Vivian kept up her argument to Nigel. "You saw at the castle his wounds still need tending."

"I did."

"Avatar is good with medicine," said Kell.

The declaration drew a skewed expression from Avatar.

"He's a Guardian not a physician or assistant," she rebuffed. "Highness?"

Mirit fought a small smile and nodded at Nigel. By his return grin, he understood and spoke. "Very well. We'll be getting two horses."

"One. She'll ride with me," said Wess.

"For a five hour journey? No, too uncomfortable," said Mirit.

"We'll get two horse," insisted Nigel.

Wess went to disagree when Vivian took his arm to steer him to his horse. "I'll ride with you into town."

Once the mortals were situated in the saddle, Ridge took the lead. Armus and Avatar joined the ranger. Wess, with Vivian, followed the Guardians, Nigel and Mirit behind them. Next came Chad with Kell riding beside Fraser. Ellis and Valery came last. Cody trotted alongside her horse. Kendrick and Virgil flanked the mortals with Vidar and Wren serving as the rear guards.

Again Wess glanced back and Vivian sighed. "Wess, you have nothing to fear where Kelvin is concerned. At least not on my behalf."

"You're coming along on his behalf.

"No, I'm coming for *you*. I used Kelvin as an excuse so the prince would agree and still your objections."

His brows leveled in vexation. "I'm not sure how to feel about that."

"You respond to Kelvin based upon his reactions to you, not facts. I feel for him like any other patient I've treated and made that *fact* clear to him. I've loved you for years. Even when you married Glenda."

The admission surprised him. "Why didn't you say anything then?"

"I'm not of royal blood like you, nor of noble heritage. I'm of the common people. Your Uncle Iain determined to find you a suitable wife, and rightly so. Glenda fit his ideals." Her voice trailed off.

Wess took a moment to consider her admission before he replied. "Was that why you agreed to marry Slater, because I married Glenda?" When she hesitated to answer, he insisted. "Vivian, was that the reason?"

"Ay," she said, demure and low.

"I wish I had known," he said with regret.

"It would not have changed anything. Your uncle made a proper marriage for you."

"In his opinion."

"Not yours?"

"No. I acted in obedience to him and," he continued, holding her hand tightly, "believing you were happier with Slater than me."

"Oh, no, Wess! I didn't want to bring you shame or ridicule for marrying beneath your station. When Meredith died and Lester left alone with the boys, it gave me a reason not to follow through and marry a man I didn't love," her voice quivered.

"All these years of not confessing our true feelings. If I listened to you sooner and not wallowed in grief—I feel like a complete idiot. Forgive me." His kissed her hand.

She tightened her hold on him. "There is nothing to forgive since I made the choice. I too regret not speaking sooner, yet I don't regret helping Lester and the boys."

He grinned. "Often he spoke of gratitude for your sacrifice, yet bemoaned it also. He wants you to have a life. Well, that will change. We'll marry when this is over. No waiting, no more wasted time."

"Ay." She hugged him again. After a moment she asked, "So does this mean you will be more tolerant of Kelvin?"

He heartily laughed. "That's stretching things a bit."

"Wess," she playfully scolded.

"He's an irritant."

"No, he's an incorrigible, just like you, which is why I'm coming. To keep you from acting irrationally." She took a handful of his doublet and tweaked his side.

"Ouch!" He flinched and chuckled. "I'll try. Seriously, I would rather have you out of harm's way with Fitch and Locan involved."

"Circumstances have shown that even at the farm I'm just an incident away from being involved again. Besides, this is the safest place." She leaned against him.

He smiled. "You'll get no argument from me."

She grunted and squirmed. "Still, I'm glad the princess made objection. Five hours without a saddle would not be very comfortable."

He laughed. "You'll have your own mount soon."

A short distance ahead, Avatar and Armus walked with Ridge. Avatar tossed a third glance back at Kell, who rode double with Chad.

"Is there a problem?" asked Armus.

"How does he know I'm good with medicine? Did you tell him?"

"No. Perhaps the same way he claims, he can read me *like a book*."

"What?"

"He told me at breakfast he knew I didn't believe him because he could see it in my face and behavior," Armus spoke with some dismay.

"That troubles you?"

"He sounded like Kell. Even had the same facial expression when he would take me to task on something."

Avatar gave a hearty, supportive clap on Armus' shoulder. "We all miss Kell."

"Ay, but you can't see him in places he isn't. No mortal will ever replace him," said Ridge.

Armus spoke in refute. "Kelvin is unique in a way I can't figure out."

"Some mortals are gifted with heavenly insight. Maybe Kelvin is one of them."

"No! I tell you there is something different about him."

Avatar shook his head in warning at Ridge, to which Armus frowned. "Now I know how Kelvin feels at his words being doubted."

"I didn't mean it as doubt rather concern for you," said Avatar.

"Ay. You practically snapped Wren's head off when all she did was speak with her normal dry wit," said Ridge.

Armus tightly pressed his lips in an obvious gesture of restraining his temper. "I accepted her apology."

"Even now you are still too sensitive to acknowledge she did nothing wrong and you lost your temper."

This time Avatar verbalized his warning. "Ridge!"

"Look, everyone knows he and Kell were created to function together as captain and lieutenant. Now, the bond is broken. It can't be ignored or avoided."

"I was Kell's aide, and apprentice to both he and Armus! So heed me when I tell you to mind your words and stand down."

This time Armus intervened with a gentle word in the Ancient. "*Soirbhe, Avatar.*"

"He doesn't want anything to upset you," said Ridge.

Avatar stiffened, which made a small grin appear on Armus' face. "So you protect me against injury until you think I can handle myself again?"

"Like he did with Kell when everyone thought you were dead—" Ridge dodged out of the way when Avatar reached to seize him.

Armus caught Avatar's arm. "*Fois, mo caraid, fois.* Ridge means no harm." His hand went from Avatar's arm to a warm, friendly clasp around the neck. "The same personal protectiveness you exhibit for me is what I sensed from Kelvin when he defended us to Spaulding."

In recollection, Avatar regarded Armus. "I felt it also, along with a sense of familiarity. I haven't given it much thought since."

"Your mind is focused on *other* things," said Ridge with discretion.

"My mind can best a ranger any day regardless of personal feelings."

"And *my* mind is still active in considering everything about this situation, despite how I may appear on the outside," said Armus, quelling further exchange between Avatar and Ridge. "What I sense from Kelvin goes deeper than any mortal I've met in all my years of existence. When we went upstairs, I asked him about the personal nature of his defense.

He didn't shy away in saying he would defend any of us to the death. Again, he looked and sounded like Kell."

"Now that I think about it, there are striking physical similarities between them." Avatar took a careful glance back to Kell. Ridge's voice brought his attention forward.

"That doesn't change the present situation."

"If I can identify the vague image then I would know," said Armus.

"I thought you believed it was Fitch?"

"I said, possibly." His expression grew reflective. "When Kelvin declared he had no dealings with the Dark Way he spoke with undeniable authority."

"You thought you saw Kell again," said Ridge. This time to Armus' annoyance prompted him to add, "Could his mannerism be akin to Tyrone?"

"You think Kelvin is part Guardian?" asked Avatar.

"Too small. I'm only trying to account for the familiar you *both* claim to sense."

"Whatever the reason, I intend to keep a very close eye on him," said Armus.

"As if you haven't been already," said Ridge with a sarcastic snicker.

Avatar threw up his hand. "I'm done with him. He's all yours, Lieutenant."

Ridge recoiled slightly at the invoking of rank.

"I hope this witness will put an end to any reservations," said Armus.

"Don't count on it from Morley," groused the ranger.

"I agree." Avatar leaned closer to speak confidentially. "I didn't want to say this in front of Kelvin, rather watch his reaction to the confrontation. Spaulding misrepresent Morley's physical status, and I sensed nothing to support the claim of the lingering effects from stygian arrows."

"Could Spaulding have intimated him to use as a ruse?" asked Armus.

"Maybe. With a such disagreeable personality, Morley didn't follow through by exaggerating or inventing his infirmities to fool us."

"Morley and Spaulding are contentious mortals. Morley would only help Spaulding if it were to his advantage," said Ridge.

"Still leaves the question of why?" said Armus.

Avatar scowled. "I wasn't there long enough or able to make eye contact to sense past what I've told you. He is personally disagreeable, physically mobile, and totally ill mannered. The reasons *why* are up for scrutiny."

"They have been since he arrived," said Ridge. "Until a few months ago Oakley remained one of the few quiet places in the province. I never investigated him or those living in hills. Since I started, I haven't been able to discover anything other than the cantankerous mortal he is."

"Nigel and Wess should be told before the interview," said Armus

"Nigel, ay. I'm not sure about Wess. There seems to be a part of him that wants Kelvin to be proven guilty," said Avatar.

"Because of Vivian."

Avatar scowled with perplexity. "Even after watching mortals for over eighteen centuries, I still have difficulty understanding what makes them react so irrational when relationships are involved. Why males are possessive and territorial and females jealous and vindictive. Or better yet, why some males and females constantly exchange sharp banter and insults when it's obvious how they feel?"

"Really?" asked Ridge, a large gin appearing.

"Ay. Nigel and Mirit did so in Tunlund," he answered before seeing amusement.

"Just *mortal* males and females?"

"Ha, ha," he mimicked. "Wren and I have been at odds since our creation. It's part of our natural charm and personality."

"Did I hear my name?"

Her appearance caught Avatar off guard. He tried to cover it by asking, "Something wrong?"

"No," she said, smiling. "We are in town. I guess the topic of discussion was so interesting it made you oblivious."

"No, we knew. At least Armus and I did," said Ridge.

"I need to speak to Nigel." Avatar left.

On his way, Avatar met Kell, who was now on foot. For a moment, no words were spoken, as they regarded each other. Avatar's silver eyes grew intense, as he searched for the familiar. Kell flashed a smile to which Avatar nodded. He continued his trek, yet paused and almost turned back to Kell. Hearing Nigel speaking to Wess prompted him to proceed.

Across the street, Reilly ducked into the shadow of a building to avoid being spotted when the group arrived at the livery. He ran until he reached the far side of town in a rather lower class neighborhood. He slipped inside a boarded up mill. He took a few gulps of air to catch his breath, before calling, cautious and weary.

"Locan? Are you still here?"

"What do you want?"

He jumped from fright when the Guardian appeared behind him "They're here. At the livery stable."

"Who?"

"The ones who came to the shack to speak with the squire."

"I wonder if they found the unfortunate sheriff yet?"

"Ay. That's what I was coming to report when I saw them. A wagon arrived at the jail bringing the sheriff's body."

Locan grinned with pleasure. "You did well on your own."

"I'm not totally inept, despite what fath—the squire says."

Locan scoffed in ridicule. "You can't even call him *father*, only refer to him by his former title."

"That's beside the point. I can do things without his interference or having Preston around." He became melancholy. "I hope he's better when we return."

"Fitch will see he's cared for."

"Only to be used again by him."

"Would you rather that I tell Deputy March about your little enterprise?"

"No, of course not. The squire would be furious," he stammered.

"I thought you could stand up on your own? Pitiful mortal." Locan sneered and shoved Reilly back so hard that the mortal hit the floor with a hard thud.

Reilly scowled in painful anger. "You relied on this pitiful mortal to take the sheriff and his horse to the field because you, a mighty Guardian warrior, are afraid to be seen in the open."

Locan seized Reilly by the doublet and hoisted him off the ground where he dangled in the air. "Speak to me like that again and it'll be the last words you ever say."

Reilly nodded, unable to reply because of Locan's choking hold.

"Find out why they're at the livery." He roughly released Reilly. The young man stumbled yet he landed on his feet.

By the time Reilly returned to his surveillance point, the group left riding east. He followed at a safe distance since they were easy to spot and he could duck away if any one of them happened to turn. No one seemed interested. He stopped near the edge of town and watched them turn northeast on the road leading toward Oakley. With a satisfied smile he went back into town.

Chapter 10

IN THE SHACK'S FRONT ROOM, FITCH, STILL IN THE SHAPE-SHIFT OF Ellis, rinsed out bloody cloths. Morley sat in his rocking chair smoking his pipe. His expression was far from passive or combative rather concerned.

"I'm doing what I can," said Fitch.

Morley chopped down on his pipe and started rocking. He paused when a flash of light filled the room. Locan appeared.

"They found Spaulding and brought the body back to Burleigh," said the warrior.

"Excellent. What do they plan to do with Kelvin?" asked Fitch/Ellis.

"They're heading for Oakley. Probably to bring him for identification."

Morley snorted, kept rocking and staring at the hearth. "How will my identification convict him of Spaulding's death?"

"We've taken care of the physical evidence. You just need to be convincing."

They heard low moaning from one of the back rooms.

"And you need to see to my boy. It's your fault he's injured!"

"Mind yourself, mortal," warned Locan.

"Or what? You'll kill me? I'm the way I am because of your kind."

"You're the way you are by your own choice!"

They heard more moaning, and Morley became anxious. "Whatever the reason for my state, doesn't change the fact Preston was attacked because he brought another victim for him to use." In an angry gesture, he used his pipe to indicate Fitch/Ellis.

The shape-shifter motioned Locan not to respond. Fitch/Ellis gathered the freshly washed cloths, a jar of salve and went into the room.

Locan moved closer to Morley, and spoke low and deadly. "Fitch may still have a soft spot for mortals, but I don't."

For the first time, fear crossed Morley's face. "I'll do my best."

Locan cocked a sneering smile before joining Fitch/Ellis. The shape-shifter tied off the bandage around Preston's neck and shoulders. The mortal lay unconscious and barely moved. "Will he live?"

Fitch/Ellis soberly shook his head. "I don't know. The wolf nicked the artery. I've kept him from bleeding to death but he needs a surgeon. I never could heal a mortal properly." He felt Preston's forehead. "He's developed a fever. Perhaps infection is setting in."

"Then he dies."

The response was sharp. "Morley's right, I would be responsible. What about you healing him? Have you done that before, healed a mortal?"

"Whether I have or haven't is immaterial. Our presence here is risky enough with Kell, Armus and the others coming. Don't go soft now."

He straightened in offended determination. "I want Kell dead more than you for leaving me injured and trapped."

"Then don't concern yourself with the mortal's fate and find a place to hide. They can't see you like that again. Unless you'll become a silent partner."

Fitch/Ellis scowled. "How did Mannix ever put up with you as his Trio Mate for so long?" Before he could react, Locan pinned him against the wall with a dagger to his throat. Locan's blade pressed so hard he didn't dare breathe, speak or swallow.

"Twice you have tried my patience and twice you insulted Mannix. Do it a third time, and you'll be in oblivion before you realize it."

Fitch/Ellis carefully nodded and Locan released him. His voice sounded unsteady in recovery. "What will you do while I'm in hiding?"

"Mask our presence and watch them. Unlike a shape-shifter, a warrior can move with stealth and avoid being seen. Now, hide while I take up surveillance."

Without further argument, Fitch/Ellis vanished in dimension travel.

Locan went to the front room. "Remember, you must be convincing and *I'll* be watching." He vanished with a flare that temporarily blinded Morley.

<hr />

Stopping to refresh the mortals and horses added time, thus the trip took almost seven hours to reach the hills surrounding Oakley. Since Ridge accompanied them, they didn't stop to fetch March. Wess eventually wanted to tell him of Spaulding's death.

Like the first time, they rode single file up the narrow and winding road to the shack. Ridge took the lead with Wren, Virgil behind them and the mortals following.

"Think we should bring boar again?" asked Virgil.

"There should be plenty left. He could not eat it all in one day," she spoke over her shoulder.

Cautious, Ridge studied the surroundings. "Something uneasy stirs the trees."

"I don't sense anything," she said.

The ranger sarcastically snorted. "I didn't sense what Armus and Vidar did about Kelvin's arrival."

"No need to act touchy, like Armus. I wasn't disputing, only making an observation."

"I was directing the sarcasm at myself. I'm disappointed at not sensing what they did. This is now my province."

"All of us need to be less sensitive to each other and more attuned to the surroundings," said Armus. He came up behind Wren and startled her.

"I didn't hear your approach."

His smile grew humorous, showing a lighter side not seen of late. "I know how to move without being seen or heard, even by the best Guardian huntress."

Her return smile appeared guarded.

167

"Wren, it's my turn to apologize. I let my emotions get in the away and overreacted when there was no cause."

Her guardedness turned to sympathy. "I understand. I too miss Kell."

"We all do," said Virgil.

"I realize that. As I said, I let my emotions get the better of me," he said over his shoulder to Virgil, then turned forward to continue speaking in Ridge's direction, "Being told I have yet to acknowledge my error, it's time I did. Grieving for Kell is one thing, but dishonoring his memory by taking my temper out on my comrades is unacceptable."

Ridge turned around while continuing to walk backwards. He smiled. "Welcome back to the South Plain, Armus."

The lieutenant laughed.

Wren smiled in genuine relief. "It's good to hear you laugh again."

"It feels good."

"You scared the birds," quipped Ridge, at hearing the flapping of wings. "Morley knows we're coming now." He turned forward.

Arriving at the shack, the mortals dismounted. Wess helped Vivian down from her horse since the terrain was uneven.

"It's been a long time since I've ridden that far all at once," she said.

"I'll see you get more practice after we're wed," he teased.

"Wed? When did this happen?" asked Nigel.

"He proposed after we left the farm," said Vivian.

Nigel smiled and clapped Wess' arm. "You deserve some happiness. I look forward to celebrating the wedding."

"Indeed," agreed Mirit.

"However, business before pleasure." Nigel headed to the shack.

Wess caught Kell's pricked expression. In a protective gesture, Wess took Vivian's arm to escort her to the shack.

"Don't cause trouble between them," said Armus.

Rather than respond, Kell headed for the shack. Armus stopped him. "I'll bring you in at the appropriate time."

Kell took a deep breath to calm his agitation. "What can I do to get you to trust me?"

"For starters, no matter what happens with the interview and identification, curb your temper and hold your tongue."

He knew there was more Armus want to say. "And?" he pressed.

168

"As I said, don't cause any more trouble for Wess and Vivian. Their relationship has taken years to finally come to pass. If you truly meant what you said about not wanting to cause any harm, then leave them alone."

Although painful to see Vivian favor Wess, he knew Armus spoke the truth. For years he witnessed their relationship from the time Vivian and Lester arrived at Waldron, through Wess' marriage until the present. Because of personal knowledge, it surprised him that in mortal form he felt such a strong attraction to Vivian. It was just a brief pause before he replied. "Consider it done."

Armus and Kell joined Kendrick and Vidar at the bottom of the steps. There wasn't enough room on the porch. Virgil and Wren stood beside the door. Ellis, Valery and Vivian sat on the only porch bench, Cody next to them.

Wess, Nigel, Mirit, Fraser, Chad, Ridge and Avatar entered the shack. Morley sat in his rocker with a pipe clenched between his teeth. He stared at the hearth, pretending to ignore their arrival. Chad stood in front of Morley. He barely received an acknowledgement before Morley returned to staring at the hearth.

"So, you brought more visitors. I don't have enough boar to feed this many." His actually sounded a bit sheepish.

"Wren can accommodate you again if needed," said Chad.

"I was told you could identify one of the thieves plaguing the area. We brought a man for you to look at."

Morley flashed a glance at Wess, not completely looking at him. "Who are you?"

"Count Wess, the new lord of the South Plains."

Morley grumbled a sarcastic laugh. "So Gareth has finally been replaced."

"Stop pretending you are unaware of the change," said Ridge.

Morley again showed signs of uneasiness in avoiding eye contact with the ranger. This made Ridge suspicious.

"What's wrong? You're acting unusually nervous."

"Nothing," said Morley in haste and changed back to surliness. "I'm not used to having so many uninvited guests." He waved. "Fetch him and get this over with and leave me in peace!" He clenched the pipe between his teeth and assumed the posture of ignoring them by staring into the hearth.

Fraser went to the door. "Armus."

A long tense moment passed before Armus entered with Kell. The squire didn't move and Kell studied him in profile. This was the man who could change his entire new existence by a single word. He wanted to remember his face, expression and tone.

"Well?" asked Nigel with impatience. "Is this him?"

Slow and reluctant, Morley's turned and lifted his head. The moment their eyes met, Kell's gaze narrowed in anger and recognition. Morley abruptly turned away.

"Do you recognize him?" demanded Nigel.

Morley further shied away in an unwillingness to answer.

"If he doesn't, I do!" declared Kell.

"You recognize him?" asked Nigel in confusion.

"Ay, Highness, and so should you."

Morley's quick, anxious glance of Kell passed to Nigel. He turned back to the hearth trying to shield his face by fiddling with his pipe.

Nigel stepped in front of Morley. "Look at me."

Morley turned further away in avoidance. Kell passed Nigel and jerked Morley by the arm. "The prince said look at him, knave!" When Morley resisted, Kell moved around the rocker and jerked Morley's head back so Nigel could clearly see him.

"Kelvin!" protested Wess.

"His name isn't Morley." Kell nodded to Armus and Avatar.

The warriors stepped forward and flanked Nigel to take a good look at Morley.

"Look them in the eye!" Kell commanded and Morley complied.

The Guardians showed recognition with Armus the first to speak.

"Indeed. Although he is aged past his years."

"Ay," agreed Avatar with an angry sneer. "Enduring Zebulon and Gareth's brow-beating aged him physically, but not in the eyes. Now I know why you didn't look at me last time. To avoid being discovered."

Stunned, Nigel turned from the Guardians to—"Ayers?"

"Ay," said Kell in disgust and roughly released the man. "Lord Ayers."

"How did you know?"

"Kelvin said he fought in Tunlund," said Wess.

"I did. And aware of the duplicity involved in Prince Titus' kidnapping."

"He was involved?" said Mirit in surprise. She moved to get a better look of Ayers. "The voice and signet ring I identified belonged to Loren not him."

"You mean it wasn't Sir Gareth's son who was responsible?" asked Fraser in confusion.

"No, he was responsible," affirmed Avatar.

"Ayers is married to Zebulon's daughter," said Nigel.

"Loren was my best friend," said Ayers with difficulty then his abrasiveness returned. "His treason and execution ruined my life!" His bitter face and voice found Mirit. "When Zebulon went into his self-imposed exile, he forced my family to go with him. I lost everything I owned then my wife, a daughter and became reduced to this!" He motioned to the shack while speaking. "Assuming the identity of dead man to survive!"

Mirit seized Nigel's arm, her face paled with disturbance. He gripped her hand in support and gently said, "You are not to blame." He scolded Ayers, "The princess is not responsible for what happened to you!"

Ayers offered stubborn resistance to Nigel's rebuke. Kell stepped into the line of sight to draw Ayers' attention from Mirit. "That doesn't explain why you claim to be able to identify me as a thief."

Before Ayers answered, a great painful groaning came from a back room. Wess, Chad and Fraser were closest to the room and became alert.

"Who's in there?" demanded Wess.

Ayers grew anxious but he didn't immediately respond. When Chad and Fraser drew their swords, Ayers bolted up, fearful. "No! He's my son. He's dying."

Chad sheathed his sword to open the door while Fraser remained armed. "There is someone in bed and he looks badly injured."

"Please, I'll answer any questions if someone will help him," he pleaded to Nigel.

After a brief pause for thought, Nigel nodded to Wess, who went to summon Vivian. She entered with Ellis and Valery.

"We discovered an injured man." Wess took Vivian into the room.

Preston stirred on the bed, groaning. She felt his forehead. "He burns with fever and the bandages are soaked with blood."

Ellis stepped inside the room for a better view. "He is the kidnapper Cody attacked to free me."

"Accounts for severity of the wounds."

Wess, Avatar, Kell, Ridge and Nigel gathered at the door to watch Vivian continue her examination of Preston.

Fretful, she shook her head. "Whoever tried to medicine him did a poor job and I don't have any supplies."

"Ridge, find what plants Mistress Vivian needs for fever and wounds. Lord Ellis, please step aside to let Avatar help her." Kell said to Ellis.

Although neither Guardian questioned the instructions, by their visual exchange they were curious about the commanding influence.

"Kelvin, find some cloth for bandages, a bowl and basin," she said.

"Excuse me, my lord," he said to Wess, who blocked the exit.

Nigel nudged Wess out. "Not enough room for all of us."

Kell inquired of Ayers for the items Vivian requested. Not having much, there were only a few items for him to gather. When he returned to the front room again he said, "Mistress Vivian and Avatar are tending him."

"Thank you," said Ayers.

"Now, why did your son kidnap Count Ellis?" asked Nigel.

"For the Guardian to use."

"Fitch."

"Ay. Preston and Reilly went to town to find another person for him since Spaulding is dead."

"How did Fitch become Spaulding if he was dead?" said Wess.

"That's why he needed another person, and my sons went to town to get him one."

At the mortals' befuddlement, Armus explained. "A shape-shifter can only maintain the form of a mortal while the mortal is alive. Once dead they can no long sustain the form."

"So Spaulding was the original one kidnapped for Fitch?" asked Nigel.

"Ay," said Ayers. "We kept him here, but when he managed to get free, my boys stopped him the only way they knew. We didn't know what it did to the Guardian until he came back injured."

"Injured?" asked Mirit.

Armus answered, "A shape-shifter experiences whatever happens to the mortal they are using. So Fitch would have had a head wound."

"Ay, and was very angry. The warrior took him out before he attacked the boys," said Ayers.

"Locan?" asked Nigel, to which Ayers nodded.

"Is this where my kidnapping comes in?" asked Ellis.

"Ay. Reilly said they snatched the first person they came across. Although Fitch was pleased since Reilly said he recognized you."

"I don't know whether to be angry or flattered."

"Considering you were returning from the privy and he got into bed with your wife—" Fraser stopped at Ellis' annoyance.

Nigel ignored the side humor to ask, "Where is Reilly now?"

"He went with Locan to take Spaulding's body someplace and hasn't returned."

"Where is Fitch?" asked Armus.

Ayers shook his head. "I don't know. Everyone left after Locan reported Spaulding's body had been discovered. Fitch went to hide since he still looks like him," he jerked his thumb at Ellis, "Locan for surveillance. If he learns I betrayed them—" he couldn't finish for fear.

Nigel heaved an inconsequential shrug. "You chose to join them."

"No, the boys! Living like this, their ways have grown wild."

"Leading to thievery and murder," chided Wess.

Ayers sighed with admission, "Ay."

Ridge returned. "I couldn't find enough. These will have to do." He spoke about the plants he carried before passing into the back room.

"This will be a long night. Kendrick and I will secure a campsite since not everyone can fit inside," said Virgil.

"We'll take care of dinner," said Vidar of himself and Wren.

"Highness. What will happen to us?" asked Ayers.

"You confessed to being an accessory to thievery and murder, so neither the king nor Jor'el's justice will go unpunished. If Preston survives, he too will face justice."

"He'll face the ultimate justice if he dies," said Armus.

"Reilly will be found and dealt with," said Wess.

Both statements disturbed Ayers. "Then I pray Reilly is not found until he can do I what I did not," he said with great remorse.

"What is that?" asked Fraser.

Ayers looked direct at Fraser. "To make amends for my sins."

Fraser took a reeling step backward and turned from the others. Kell lent an arm of support about the young prince's waist.

"You already made amends," he said in low, encouraging voice.

"The thought struck me of what my fate would have been if I had not."

"Don't dwell on it."

Fraser felt another hand. Mirit appeared concerned. "I'm all right, Aunt. Merely a momentary lapse."

"All the same, let's help Kendrick and Virgil." She turned him toward the door and motioned for Ellis and Valery to accompany them

In watching them leave, Kell caught Armus' eye. The Guardian wore a distinct expression of approval. A definite shift in attitude, which gave him some relief. However, there were questions to be answered so he directed his attention to Ayers. "You still haven't clarified how I fit into this?"

The forlorn man shrugged. "I don't know exactly. Spaulding needed someone to take the blame and I wanted to protect my boys. He said he'd fine someone for me to identify."

"Why?"

"Maybe he was Fitch at the time. It's hard to tell the difference. Before the Guardians arrived, Spaulding knew about my boys and wanted part of the profits for his silence. Only his portion kept increasing. When we refused further payment, he began arresting those helping us."

"This went beyond you and your sons?" said Wess.

"Ay, three friends of the boys."

"Interesting little enterprise," commented Chad.

"How did Locan and Fitch find you?" asked Armus.

"By chance, from what Reilly said. He and Preston were caught in the act of stealing by a merchant when the Guardians helped them escape. Soon after we discovered they had their own agenda." He heaved a hapless shrug. "There wasn't much we could do to be rid of them."

"They blackmailed you also," said Nigel, and Ayers nodded.

"Are you saying I just happened to be the person Spaulding chose to use to protect his interest?" said Kell in summation.

"Ay. He said you were a stranger in these parts."

"Fitch and Locan tried to capitalize on that after Spaulding marked you," said Armus.

"They nearly succeeded." Kell tossed a skewed glance to Wess. The response surprised him.

"For that, I sincerely apologize. I let other concerns taint my judgment."

Kell flashed a gracious smile. "Apology accepted, my lord."

Nigel appeared pleased. He noticed the dimming light out the window. "Since we'll be staying the night, posting of guards will be necessary."

"Avatar and Ridge will be inside with Mistress Vivian. The rest of us will be positioned around the shack and campsite," said Armus.

"I'll take the first watch of Lord Ayers," said Chad

"Ellis will relieve you at midnight," said Nigel. He then spoke to Ayers. "Don't try anything foolish or justice will be immediate."

"I know, Highness. In all honesty, I would rather face you or the king than those Guardians."

Before following Nigel out, Wess said, "I want to speak to Vivian first." He gave Kell a quick, parting smile before heading to the back room. "How is he?"

"Very bad. He's lost a lot of blood and I don't have the proper instruments to cauterize the wound," she replied with sobriety.

"What about heating a dagger on the fire?"

"We thought of that, only there is so much damage it may do little good and cause more injury. Ridge and Avatar are attempting to make a poultice to serve as both a cauterizing agent and healing ointment." She moved closer and said privately, "He may not survive the night."

In sympathetic consideration, Wess regarded Preston. "Armus said he would face divine justice for his crimes."

"Indeed," said Avatar. He handed the bowl containing the ointment to Ridge for him to begin the application. "Still, we will do what we can to help him."

"Death for thievery?" asked Vivian, disturbed.

"Murder," said Wess. "According to Ayers, he and his brother are the ones who killed Spaulding and helped Fitch and Locan to shift the blame to Kelvin."

"Then Kelvin is innocent of all crimes," she said in relief.

"Ay, and I apologized to him for my behavior."

She tenderly smiled. "Your heart was in the right place."

"To bad my head didn't follow."

Avatar chuckled under his breath. "A common malady among mortals."

"Something I know you repeatedly told to Nigel." Wess then spoke to Vivian. "Ridge and Avatar will remain with you. Chad will guard Ayers until midnight then Ellis. The rest of us will be camped outside. Unless, of course you want me to stay."

"Always," she said with a laugh. "But it is a little cramped in here."

He kissed her cheek and left.

Outside, Virgil stood guard at the bottom of the porch steps. About thirty feet from the shack, Nigel, Kell, Mirit, Ellis, Fraser and Valery gathered around a campfire eating venison. The carcass hung on a spit to one side of a fire. Wren served them. Wess sat beside Kell.

"Smells good."

"Did you expect differently?" Wren handed Wess a portion of venison on what appeared to be a flat stone. "Sorry, no plates."

"What do we do for cups, clench our fists?"

She held up a flask. He accepted it and took a drink. He immediately started choking. Kell took the stone from Wess to keep him from dropping the meat while he recovered. He and the others laughed.

"That's not water. What is it?" Wess could barely speak.

"Liquid refreshment from a still out back." Wren smiled and took back the flask.

Nigel thumped Wess on the back. "She played the trick on me also."

"We knew about it." Mirit indicated Ellis, Fraser and Valery.

"Knew? The joke was your idea, Aunt."

"What?" Nigel asked in amused disbelief.

Mirit's smile grew impish, only the merriment didn't reach her eyes. "There is so much tension, something needed to break it."

Wess leaned toward Nigel and spoke sideways. "I'll need your help to keep her away from Vivian and influencing her."

"Unfortunately, I can't do the same with Valery," said Ellis.

176

"Who said I haven't already employed a trick or two I've learned?" Valery mimicked Mirit's grin at her husband.

"Are you sure you want to get married again, Wess?" asked Nigel.

Since he ate, Wess nodded before replying. "I look forward to it."

"Well, I suppose at your age you need to keep your reflexes sharp."

"They've always been sharp enough to deal with a pesky prince." He swallowed hard. "Now, is there really anything to drink?"

Mirit reached behind the log upon which she sat. She retrieved a flask and held it out to Wess. He arched an eyebrow of skepticism. "No, really. I hid it for playing the joke."

Kell took the flask, removed the cork and took a whiff, "Water."

"Let me see you take a drink," said Wess.

He did so. After no reaction, Wess took the flask and drank.

Nigel grinned and wiped his hands, having finished his venison. "Mirit, you, Valery, Fraser and Ellis get some sleep. We'll keep watch." He indicated himself, Wess and Kell. "At midnight I'll wake Ellis to relieve Chad in guarding Ayers."

Armus arrived. "No need, Highness. There are enough of us to keep watch." He tapped Wren on the shoulder. She readied her crossbow. "Wren will go east and I'll remain here."

"Where are Kendrick and Vidar?"

"Vidar is a hundred yards down the trail and Kendrick behind the shack." He pointed in the various directions.

"All the same, we'll stay awake."

177

Chapter 11

THE MAJORITY OF THE NIGHT PASSED QUIETLY FOR THOSE OUTSIDE. Inside, Vivian, Ridge and Avatar diligently tended to Preston. Ridge frowned while watching Vivian examine the bandages and discover fresh blood.

"I couldn't find any more betony and only a few sprigs of clover wart," he said.

"What about hind's gaze?" she asked.

"I hadn't thought of that."

"It grows all around Burleigh, so we may find some nearby."

"I don't recall hearing of hind's gaze," said Avatar.

"A regional plant found only in the southern part of the province. Stay with him while we look for some." Ridge escorted Vivian into the front room.

Ayers slept in his rocker. Ellis sat in the opposite rocker, awake. Cody lay on the floor beside him. Valery sat at the table with her head down, sleeping. Ridge paused to quietly tell Ellis where they were going. Outside, he also told Virgil before going around to the rear of the shack.

"We forgot a light," she said.

He smiled and took his quarterstaff from the sling on his back. "*Alasdh,*" he said in the Ancient and tapped the bottom end of his staff on the ground. The top of the staff glowed. "Avatar is *he of the lightning sword*, I am Ridge of the *lightning rod*."

She just looked at him. "I don't understand."

He scowled at his humor not being understood and explained. "Avatar's special power is his ability to call forth deadly lightning form his sword. I can summon blinding and debilitating light from my staff. Not as lethal, but effective. Wren and Vidar communicate with animals. I communicate with the tress and plants through the staff. They are living organisms with voices that mortals can't hear."

"The ability to move quickly and unseen can be both lethal and effective," said a new voice.

Ridge whirled about with his quarterstaff ready to meet the threat. He grunted in annoyance. "Kendrick."

The warrior grinned. "What are you two doing?"

"We need to find hind's gaze for my patient," said Vivian.

"Try not to go too far."

"We won't." Again Ridge took Vivian's arm and they walked another hundred yards. "This is where I found the clover wart. Hind's gaze is usually near by. I'll increase the light so we can both search." He spoke the Ancient and raised his hand at the same time. The glowing increased to expose about a fifty-foot radius.

Vivian kept her eyes on the ground and used the toe of her shoe to scrap aside the surface debris for better viewing. "I'm not seeing any."

"Keep looking until the edge of the light in that direction. I'll look this way."

She did as instructed.

At the campsite, Kell sat up and craned his neck to see the house. Virgil stood guard, but something didn't feel right.

Wess sat on the ground leaning against the log in an attempt to rest. He noticed Kell's interest. "Something wrong?"

"I felt a chill," was the best way to describe his uneasiness.

Nigel also stretched out on the ground with his shoulders and head propped up by the log. A dozing Mirit lay on the ground with her back to him. "The wind. It gets chilly in the hills at night."

"Maybe."

179

"If there's something stirring, we will know," said Armus.

"Still, I'll check on Vivian and the others." Kell stood.

Wess scrambled to his feet and stepped in front of Kell. "I'll go."

"You apologized but still don't trust me."

"No, I need to stretch my back from sitting against a log."

"Cold making the old bones ache?" asked Nigel.

"You tell me when you get up," retorted Wess. He headed for the shack.

Nigel grabbed Kell's pant leg to keep him for leaving. "She is his responsibility."

Kell watched Wess enter the shack, and in doing so caught Armus' regard. Recalling their conversation, he sat down. All the same, he wondered why he sensed something amiss when Armus didn't appear concerned. Could it be his Guardian senses returning? Only when encountering Fitch, did he feel the return of his old power, strength and authority. Why this unsettled feeling in the pit of his being?

Despite the uneasiness, he no longer possessed his former Guardian senses so he couldn't reach out to convey his disturbance to Armus. Nor did he have the ability to determine the cause. Mortals called this type of disturbance *intuition*. Just like what he heard from them in the past, this proved frustrating to not discern what caused the uneasiness. Perhaps he'll learn overtime how to interpret those feeling. Now was not the time. He became startled at a jostling of his arm. Wess sat beside him.

"According to Virgil, she and Ridge went to collect some plant for Preston."

"And you're not concerned?" asked Kell.

"She's with Ridge."

"As opposed to me?"

"I already apologized for my behavior, so why are you continuing to press me? Vivian is now my betrothed and you would do well to remember that."

Angry, Kell turned aside. Armus moved a step closer and he saw the Guardian's stern scowl. He immediately changed his tone. "You're right, my lord. I have overstepped my bounds. Forgive me. This whole situation has placed me on edge. I normally have more command of my emotions."

"As do I."

Nigel pressed his mouth shut to contain a laugh. A tittering escaped.

"Oh, hush. You're not immune to lapses in temperament," chided Mirit, though her eyes remained closed.

Nigel became curious at her scolding, but Wess' speech drew his attention.

"I'm going to look for them."

"Wess," said Nigel.

He put up a hand and smiled. "Teasing aside, I'm going."

"Take Virgil."

Wess waved an acknowledgement and left.

Nigel turned and leaned down to speak a private word to Mirit. "I know Ayers upset you."

Her eyes opened only she didn't look at him. "I am tired."

The tone was not convincing, yet he knew better than to press her. "All right. Rest." He kissed her cheek and settled back in his previous position. Fraser raised his head. Nigel smiled at his nephew and made the motion for sleep. Fraser lied down.

The search brought them farther than Ridge anticipated. He paused to look in the direction they came. "We should go back."

"We haven't found any hind's gaze and it is badly needed," she insisted.

"All right, five more minutes. If we're not back in a reasonable amount of time the others will come looking for us."

"That's why I'm not worried." She waved for him to keep looking. A moment later, "I found some!"

Ridge knelt beside her. He put his quarterstaff down and took out his dagger to cut the plant near the root. He handed her the plant.

She showed displeasure in examining the scrawny plant. "This may not be enough."

"I found some when I heard you call." He used his dagger to point.

She glanced around for the direction to go. "Is that the camp?" she said about a light in the distance.

"Ay. We went further than we should."

"Get more plants and I'll start back."

"Not alone."

"The firelight will guide me. Besides, how long should it take you?"

"Only a moment."

"Then do so. We're going to need more. I'll start with this." She headed in the direction he indicated.

Ridge moved to where he searched and squatted down near a clump of hind's gaze. He laid his quarterstaff on the ground to deal with the plants when a foot kicked him under the chin and sent him back ten feet. His head hit the ground when he landed flat on his back. Dazed, he couldn't react when a hand seized him, lifted him off the ground and threw him against a large oak. Despite the pain, he fell to one side to avoid being grabbed again. He spied his quarterstaff and lunged for it. A foot came crashing down on the staff. He got to his knees and briefly looked up before something struck him from behind and rendered him unconscious.

Locan remained in the attack position with his right hand stiff from a chopping motion. Satisfied, he grinned at Fitch, whose foot remained on the staff.

"That should keep him for quite awhile." He relaxed off the stance.

Reilly arrived. "Is he another Guardian?"

"Ay. A ranger."

"Vivian?" called Wess from a different direction.

"They're coming," said Reilly, agitated.

"Vivian!" Wess called again.

Pleased, Fitch smiled at Locan.

"I thought the voice sounded like him," said the warrior. "I'll cause a distraction in case he isn't alone. You, stay with Fitch," he said to Reilly and rushed off.

Fitch pulled Reilly in the opposite direction of Locan.

Wess trailed ten paces behind Virgil. "Are you sure they went this way?"

"Ay. Kendrick confirmed it." Suddenly alert, Virgil stopped and reached for his sword. "Danger. Go back to camp."

"Not without Vivian." He moved forward. "Viv—!" Virgil clapped a hand over Wess' mouth. He shoved the hand away. "Let's see what it is," he spoke in a whisper. He stealthily made his way toward the sound.

Virgil began to follow when movement from another direction captured his attention. "General," he called in warning. Wess didn't respond. He vacillated on whether to follow Wess, or head in the direction of another possible threat. Seeing more movement, he went in the other direction.

Wess drew his sword when the noise grew louder. He couldn't tell whether it was a person or animal. "Vivian? Ridge?" he called in a cautious voice.

From the corner of his eye, he caught a glimpse of something swinging at him. He managed to parry it with his sword using an off balance blow. A whack in the back of the knees made him fall hard to the ground. A smack from a club or branch knocked the sword from his hand. Someone tackled him from behind and he struggled against the attacker. He was easily overcome and turned on his back. He recognized Fitch a moment before the Guardian's hand covered his face and he fainted.

After shape shifting into Wess, Fitch stood. "Bind him well and keep him hidden," he ordered Reilly.

The young man knelt to carry out the instructions.

Locan arrived and smiled at seeing Fitch/Wess. "This should be interesting."

"Make sure he is kept alive this time!"

"The boy or the general?"

At Reilly's fearful reaction, Fitch/Wess sternly replied, "Both." He snatched up Wess' sword and left.

Vivian became startled at hearing someone approach. "Ridge?"

"No, Virgil. What are you doing out here by yourself? Where is Ridge?"

"Fetching more hind's gaze. I went ahead with what we found to start the ointment. I thought you were him."

"I haven't seen him, only you walking alone."

"Vivian!" Fitch/Wess hurried over. "Are you all right? You know you shouldn't have gone off like that?"

"Ridge went with me."

"Oh?" Fitch/Wess pretended to look around.

"He's close behind gathering more plants."

"Well, Ridge can take care of himself. Let's get back to camp." He took her arm and began walking. "Come along, Virgil."

"It's not like Ridge to leave a charge," said the warrior.

"Like one Guardian abandoning another?"

"What is that supposed to mean?"

He waved the comment aside and kept walking. "Before your time."

"General?"

"Don't be so touchy. Or have you been around Avatar too long?"

Virgil hesitated in following. He cast a curious glance up the hill looking for any sign of Ridge.

"Virgil!" called Wess.

The warrior hastened after them.

Kell rose at seeing the trio return.

Nigel once again seized Kell's leg. "No."

"I'm not going to interfere, rather offer to help."

"You can help by staying put." Nigel sat up. "Look, I appreciate your feelings in the matter. Vivian helped you when injured and you feel indebted. Wess has been defensive, while you have been antagonistic. Good intentions aside, under the circumstances it is best you stay out of his way."

Kell sat to continue the discussion. "Granted, I appreciate *your* feelings since you are indebted to him and are defensive on his behalf. Your good intentions aside, I have proclaimed my desire to help from the beginning. And, where the rivalry between myself and the general may have been cause for some concern and misunderstanding, I still intend to help those who have wrongly accused me."

Nigel spoke with a sarcastic smirk. "You are an impertinent and brash man."

"Highness," began Kell with weary sigh, "I am physically tired and emotionally taxed. Brashness is the best I can manage right now."

Nigel laughed. "Considering the circumstance and your attitude, I don't understand why, but I like you."

Kell smiled. "Thank you."

"Could you have waited until a descent hour to like him?" groused Mirit.

"Ay. Uncle's laughter could wake the dead," grumbled Fraser.

"I think it did. Chad stirs."

Chad sat up, yawned and stretched. He noticed the way they regarded him, curious and rueful. "What? It's morning."

Nigel chuckled. "I'm going to see how they're getting on with Preston."

"I'll start breakfast," said Wren.

Inside, Valery remained at the table still sleeping. Ayers slept in one rocker. Cody stretched out on the floor beside Ellis' rocker. The young man exhibited signs of fatigue. He became alert upon sight of Nigel.

"Any word yet?" asked Nigel in a whisper.

"No, although Vivian returned with some plant."

Nigel entered the back room, and greeted by grim faces from Avatar and Vivian. Fitch/Wess looked impassive.

"I was too late," she droned.

"He died a short time before she returned," said Avatar.

"Where is Ridge? Didn't he go with you?" asked Nigel.

"He found some more of the hind's gaze, the plant we were searching for. He said he was right behind me," she replied, now a bit concerned.

"From my experience, Ridge tends to come and go on his own schedule. I don't believe there is anything to worry about," said Fitch/Wess.

"Really? As a Trio Leader he would be more diligent," said Avatar.

Fitch/Wess appeared indifferent. "He says a ranger is called by the wild within. Whatever that means. We're done here." He took Vivian's arm to draw her from the room. He shook the rocker to wake Ayers. "You son is dead," he flatly said.

"Wess," she said in surprise. "Where's your sympathy?"

"He was a thief and a murderer. I save my sympathy for the victims."

Stunned mute, Ayers turned to Nigel for conformation. When the prince nodded, he wept.

"I'm sorry. We did what we could," said Vivian with compassionate.

"Come. You can shed your tears on the way to Deputy March." Fitch/Wess pulled Ayers to his feet.

Nigel intervened. "Give him a moment, Wess." He took Ayers from Fitch/Wess and helped the distraught man to sit. He spoke to Ellis and Avatar. "Stay with him until we're ready to leave." He motioned for Fitch/Wess and Vivian to leave. Once at the bottom of the porch steps, he confronted Fitch/Wess. "What was that about?"

"He and his sons have caused a lot of trouble and grief since I arrived. Besides, you're the one who said the king and Jor'el's justice will not go unpunished. Well, one criminal has been taken care of."

"Ay," said Nigel, a thoughtfully steady gaze at Fitch/Wess. "Vivian, tell the rest we're leaving." He detained Fitch/Wess. "I can't recall you acting so heartless."

"Not heartless. It's my responsibility to restore order here. I can't always do that with only compassion as my guide. And I saw the way you looked upon discovering his true identity. Where was your compassion? Since it wasn't in reserve for those who nearly cost the life of your nephew and then future wife?"

The rebuffed briefly stymied Nigel. "Very well. We'll take him to March and he'll stand trial."

"After which, I intend to hunt down Reilly and put an end to this crime wave." Fitch/Wess briskly walked toward the horses.

Armus, Mirit and Chad joined Nigel. She appeared fretful so he knew Vivian told them about Preston. Indeed this visit upset her. He knew better than to press her in public, thus he spoke to Armus.

"Other than Vivian and Ridge leaving to fetch some plants, did anything unusual happen last night?"

"No. Why?"

He shook his head, perplexed. "I'm not sure. Wess is out of sorts."

"Perhaps for the same reasons Kelvin is out of sorts," said Mirit.

"Kelvin I don't know very well. Wess I do, and some of his comments are uncharacteristic."

"Neither I, nor the others, sensed anything wrong last night," said Armus.

"What about Ridge? He's not back," said Chad.

"Wess thinks Ridge is answering the call of the wild, and says he tends to come and go on his own schedule," said Nigel, apparently unconvinced.

"That doesn't sound right," said Armus.

"Agreed. Avatar questioned Wess but he passed it off. Speaking of, tell Avatar and Ellis to bring Ayers, we're taking him to March," he instructed Chad. He looked to where the others saddled their horses. Fitch/Wess focused his attention on Vivian, while Kelvin kept his distance, staring at Fitch/Wess. Nigel spoke to Armus. "Have Virgil discreetly stay behind and make contact with Ridge."

"You really think something is wrong?" asked Mirit.

"Let's just say, I want to make sure all is well. Also see Preston is buried," he added to Armus. He noticed Mirit shiver. He took her arm to lead her to the horses and privately said to her, "Please, love, don't take this to heart."

She squared her shoulders in attempted resolve and mounted her horse.

Armus conducted a quick burial by speaking the Ancient and using his sword to carve out a gravesite fifty yards from the shack. Another phrase in the Ancient, and burial clothes wrapped Preston's body. After placing the body in the ground, he spoke and used his sword to replace the dirt and cover the grave.

Avatar waited a few paces away, keeping an eye out on all fronts: Armus, the mortals, the shack and hills.

"Any sign of Ridge yet?" asked Armus.

"No, and something isn't right." He sent a studious glance toward Fitch/Wess.

"Nigel feels Wess is acting out of character. Mirit attributes his behavior to Vivian and the situation with Kelvin."

Avatar snorted a chuckle. "Possible. Mortal males do act unusual in respect to female relationships. However, that doesn't answer the question about Ridge's absence."

"Which is why Nigel wants Virgil to remain behind to make contact with Ridge and determine if there is problem."

"Armus," called Nigel.

He acknowledged Nigel then instructed Avatar, "You and Wren take the lead."

On the way back to the group, Avatar called to Wren and they moved forward.

Armus explained to Nigel. "They will lead; you and Mirit follow. Vidar and Kendrick with walk between you and Kelvin and Fraser, then Vivian and Wess. Virgil and I will watch the rear."

Fitch/Wess heard and asked, "Why?"

"Precaution."

When the others were down the path, Armus spoke to Virgil. "Nigel wants you to look for Ridge. He believes something isn't right about the excuse of his absence."

"He's not the only one. I thought Ridge leaving her alone was strange."

"Did you sense anything?"

"I didn't think so at first, then I heard strange multiple noises, which caused us to separate."

"Any sense of evil?"

"No, but I'll make sure. Now, you better catch up to them." He nudged Armus toward the trail before racing off behind the shack.

Chapter 12

WHEN RIDGE WOKE, HE NOTICED THE DAYLIGHT. HE COULDN'T move his limbs and felt no sensation from the neck down. Out of the corners of his eyes, he realized he lay on the ground. Images of what happened came to mind. First being kicked backward, thrown into an oak tree followed by a severe blow from behind. A nerve-blocking blow or had his neck been broken? The force was powerful. He recognized Fitch before being knocked out, which meant Locan came at him from behind. That didn't bode well from the others. He tried to speak and call for help, yet only managed a feeble grunt. Now what? Neither his voice nor body worked. At least his mind remained alert. He closed his eyes, and stretched out his senses in a search for any Guardians nearby. He winced at touching an essence along with the pain and fatigue brought on by the effort. The contact was not long enough to determine identity. He hoped the individual proved friendly—if not …

"Ridge?"

His eyes snapped open in anticipation. Virgil knelt beside him.

"What happened?"

Ridge unsuccessfully tried to reply. His face screwed up in pain.

"Easy. Did you see who did this?"

Again, Ridge tried to move in with an affirmative nod, and ended up whimpering in pain.

"I'm going to feel if your neck is broken." Virgil carefully placed his hands on both sides of Ridge's neck. "Ready?"

After a grunt from the ranger, Virgil began probing. Ridge screwed his eyes shut against the pain. A groan escaped during the examination.

Virgil sat back on his heels. "I'm sorry that hurt. The good news is it hurts because it's not broken. The bad news is I'm going to have strike again to unblock the nerve blow."

Ridge haplessly groaned.

"The alternative is to remain as you are."

The ranger rolled his eyes to the contrary.

Virgil grinned. "I didn't think so. I'll have to sit you up so I can get at your neck. Understand, the blow will be hard. I hope I don't break your neck in the process."

Ridge looked at Virgil, pain changing to determination accompanied by an agreeing grunt. Virgil lifted him to a sitting position. Ridge tried to withstand the pain then gasped when his head fell forward on its own.

"I pray this works. Forgive me if doesn't. By your will, Jor'el!" Virgil brought a stiff hand chop down on Ridge's neck. The force of the blow sent the ranger face first to the ground. Virgil anxiously watched. For a long, tense moment, the ranger didn't move or make a sound. "Ridge?"

"That hurt!" he said in low gravelly voice.

Virgil chuckled in relief. "It loosened your tongue. What about the rest of you?"

Ridge gingerly moved onto his back. "Give me a couple of minutes to assess if anything is broken or not working."

"Do you know who did this?"

The ranger sneered. "Fitch! At least he's the one who stepped on my staff when I tried to make defense. The nerve-blocking blow came from behind."

"Locan."

"That would be my guess."

"I'm surprised they didn't kill you."

"You and me both. I didn't sense any presence thus at their mercy when attacked. I hardly think they'd incapacitate me for fun and exercise. What about Vivian and the others?"

"Wess and I found her safe and unharmed. Preston died and they're taking Ayers to Deputy March."

Motioning for help, Ridge sat up. With curiosity he regarded Virgil. "Nothing else happened?"

"Nothing unusual. Armus wanted me to look for you since you hadn't returned and no one accepted the excuse of you answering the *call of the wild*."

He rubbed his neck and rotated his shoulders. "Who gave that excuse?"

"Wess."

"I never saw him, so why would he say something like that?"

"I questioned him when we found Vivian. He said something about Guardians abandoning each other, which didn't sound right either."

"Guardians abandoning each other?" Ridge repeated, more to himself than as a question. Again he pressed Virgil. "Are you sure nothing unusual happened?"

"None but I what I told you about Wess."

"Were you with him the whole time during the search?"

"No, there were several distractions," he paused with annoyed understanding. "It would be bold of Fitch to become the general."

"He became a prince and a sheriff. And it would explain such a lame excuse to cover my supposed absence."

"Then the real Wess is in danger. They killed Spaulding when he tried to escape. Can you move?"

Ridge reached for Virgil to help him stand. The ranger wobbled, unsteady at first before finding his balance. He released Virgil to stand on his own. "How much time has passed since I left with Vivian and you came looking for me?"

"Less than a hour. I'll warn the others, you look for Wess."

Ridge stopped Virgil from leaving. "No, Wess is in immediate danger. I maybe a Trio Leader, but Locan is a warrior, who turned and possibly enhanced by the Dark Way. He may be holding Wess so Fitch can act. Securing Wess will help unmask them." He retrieved his quarterstaff, which remained near where he fell.

"They could dimension travel him someplace, like Kelvin."

Ridge scowled and his golden eyes flared with determination. "I'll find them."

"Which way?"

Ridge clenched his quarterstaff in both hands, closed his eyes and for a moment reached out to the trees. His eyes opened and he grinned with an unmistakable confidence. "This way." He headed away from the shack and into the hills.

Regaining his senses, Wess discovered he was bound and gagged with his hands tied behind his back. He took stock of his surroundings. He was alone, and appeared to be inside an earthen tunnel or hollow. He heard water, steady and close. He saw no one. Surely they wouldn't leave him unattended? He waited a moment to see if someone would appear.

He fought against the restraints on his wrists. In moving, he discovered a large root embedded in the hollow's bank encircled his waist. That's why he was alone. Securely bound with his hands inaccessible, confined by a branch and relieved of his sword and dagger. He tried flexing his face and lips to loosen the gag to call for help. Didn't work. He ceased his efforts to consider the situation. He remembered being attacked, disarmed then briefly seeing Fitch, which means the crafty shape-shifter probably assumed his form.

Why else keep me alive and hidden? Perhaps one of the Guardians will notice something wrong. If they haven't already. What could Fitch gain by becoming me?

The thought sparked fear of Fitch meaning lethal harm to Nigel, Fraser, Vivian or any of the others. Again, he tried to get free. Not until near exhaustion and failing to get free did he stop. He had to think. Killing Vivian would accomplish nothing other than bring him more personal grief. Nigel and Fraser's deaths would devastate the royal family and he would be blamed. There had to be something more, but what?

Fitch became Spaulding to cast suspicion onto Kelvin. True it was to hide Spaulding's connection to Ayers and his gang. Was Kelvin really a random choice? According to Ayers, it was. He also said Fitch and Locan had their own agenda. What could that be? Fitch shape-shifting into him gave the Guardian the upper hand by putting him in command of the South Plains. Another thought struck Wess hard.

In disguise, Fitch could influence the Council and even get close to the king! Heaven forbid anything happened to Tyrone. With Kell gone, who would be able ferret him out from among the mortals? Armus was strong, dependable and undoubtedly dedicated, being second-in-command. Does he have Kell's familiarity and personal relationship to all Guardians to sense Fitch?

Over the years Wess inquired of Kell, curious about the captain's ability to know each Guardian by name. He tried to employ the same example of leadership by becoming acquainted with his men to establish a personal connection. This is why Kelvin proved perplexing since he couldn't place him. Over time it became clear Kelvin served as a soldier in key battles. Recognizing Ayers proved beyond doubt his claim of innocence.

Approaching footsteps interrupted Wess' pondering. Curious and wary, he watched the hollow opening. He drew back in fear when a large male boar appeared. The animal snorted and pawed the ground. This must have been its den and he had no means of defense if it charged. A sudden shout and something struck the boar. The animal bolted away. A young man's head poked into the hollow opening.

"You don't look any worse," he said.

Wess tried to speak, and only managed a muted grunt and growl.

The young man grinned. "You won't get away so stop struggling and enjoy the view." He laughed in mockery and left.

Wess shouted. Although muffled, his outcry drew the young man back. He titled his head back indicating thirst.

"The last time I gave someone a drink, it ended badly. You'll just have to wait."

Last time? Spaulding. He's Reilly. He snarled in vexation and began to think some more.

⚜

Ridge put up a hand to stop and take cover. He and Virgil knelt behind a small outcropping. "Someone's up ahead, by the stream."

"Mortal or Guardian?"

"Reilly." He stopped Virgil from drawing his sword. "I have a better idea." He took his quarterstaff in hand and spoke in the Ancient. *"Craobhan, gu Jor'el's laogh et beir e aobhare ansfois."*

A creaking and low moaning echoed all around followed by the rustling of leaves. Baffled by the strange noise, Reilly jumped off the rock where he sat to search for the source of the noise. Several branches of a nearby tree ensnared him and lifted him ten feet off the ground. He gasped in fear and struggled to get free.

Ridge and Virgil arrived. "Well, what have we here?" said the ranger.

"Who are you? What is the meaning of this?" demanded Reilly.

Ridge leaned on his staff. "Why, Reilly, I'm disappointed you don't recognize me."

Reilly scowled. "The devil Guardian who roams the hills."

"Devil? He can't mean you, can he?" said Virgil in mock outrage.

"Apparently. I consider myself one of the good guys."

"He must have you confused with another." Virgil's teasing changed when he drew his sword and pointed it at Reilly. "You didn't mean Ridge, now did you?"

The young man's eyes grew wide with fear. "No," he stammered.

"Fitch perhaps? Even Locan?"

Reilly swallowed back his fright when the blade moved closer. "Ay. Those are the devil Guardians."

"Where are they?"

He trembled, apprehensive of the sword. "I don't know. They left."

"Leaving you alone in the wilderness?" Ridge made a sarcastic motion in spreading his arms wide. "Where I can easily find you?"

Virgil's face grew harsh. He slapped Reilly's leg with the flat of his sword. "What trap is laid?"

"No trap. I swear! They left. Fitch now looking like—" Reilly clamped his mouth shut.

"Count Wess?"

"Ay."

"Locan?"

Reilly shook his head, the lethal look of Virgil unnerving to the point of affecting his voice. "He told me to make sure the count didn't leave or he'd kill me."

"Where is Wess?"

Careful, he nodded to the right. "Not far. Up stream in a hollow."

Virgil headed in the direction indicated.

"He better be unharmed or it won't go well for you," said Ridge.

"He's not hurt. I even scared off a boar that found him."

The hollow stood a hundred yards from where Reilly hung ensnared. Virgil slid down the slippery embankment to the opening. He stooped down to peer inside and kept his sword ready for trouble. Wess appeared apprehensive at first, then relieved at seeing him. Though the words were muffled, Wess obviously wanted to be freed. Virgil crawled inside the hollow, which was cramped for his large Guardian frame. He placed his sword down to remove the gag. Wess sighed and flexed his jaw.

"You don't appear harmed."

"If you call being caught by Fitch, bound, gagged and held by a smelly root unharmed."

Virgil chuckled and untied Wess' hands.

"Fitch has taken my place."

"We figured that after I found Ridge paralyzed by a nerve-blocking blow and learned of his encountered with Fitch and Locan. Reilly confirmed it."

Wess rubbed his freed wrists. "What of the others? Do they know?"

"No. After what happened to Spaulding, we came to find you first. Ridge is watching Reilly." He inspected the root around Wess' waist. "I'll have to cut it." Since the hollow was too small for him to stand and use his sword, he removed his dagger and hacked at the root. Another root shot out from the earth and smacked the Guardian in the face, sending him sideways.

Startled, Wess flinched to one side. "What was that?"

Virgil rubbed his jaw. "I don't think it wants to let go." He got to his knees in an anticipatory move. The root struck out at him again. He ducked aside.

Wess tried to avoid the swinging root while still ensnared. "Do something before we're both trapped!"

The attacking root forced Virgil out of the hollow. "Ridge!"

The tree to which the root belonged took a swipe at him using one of its low branches. In his avoidance of the root, Virgil left his sword in the hollow. This left him armed only with his dagger for defense against the tree. A second branch knocked him into the stream.

Ridge arrived and used his quarterstaff to block another blow at Virgil. "*Bi furasda!*" he commanded in the Ancient. The tree didn't respond. This forced Ridge to use his staff to deflect the root trying to ensnare his legs.

"Can't you stop it?" Virgil scrambled to his feet and readied his dagger for another attack.

"Something made it angry."

"Help!" called Wess from the hollow, gasping as if being choked.

Virgil dodged toward the hollow. He tried to avoid the whip-like motion of the attacking root and ended up falling face first into the bank. "I'll anger it more if Wess is harmed!"

When the root tried to smash down at him, Virgil rolled away. He ended up at the hollow opening. Wess labored in distress, near fainting for lack of air. Virgil's sword lay between Wess and the opening. The swaying root moved back and forth over the blade. If he timed it right.... He drove for his sword when the root passed over it and away from Wess. Virgil snatched the hilt. From on his back, he aimed at the swaying root and spoke in the Ancient.

"*Na bunan gu deigh!*"

Immediately a stream of ice flew from the edge of his sword and encased the root. Using his foot, Virgil kicked and broke the frozen root into pieces. He pointed his sword at the root ensnaring Wess, again speaking "*Root to ice.*" An ice stream leapt from his sword to freeze the root. He used his fist to smash it to pieces and free Wess. The mortal gasped for air. For a moment Virgil waited for Wess to recover. "Better?"

Wess nodded and reached for Virgil to help him sit up.

"Virgil! What did you do?" came an angry shout from Ridge.

He peeked out to see Ridge engage three branches. Another root emanated from the bank to attack the ranger. Virgil scrambled out of the hollow and into the shallow water He aimed his sword at the attacking tree. "*Craobha gu deigh!*"

This time the stream of ice continued from the tip of the blade until the entire tree, branches and root where encased in ice. Virgil used his flat of his blade to shatter the root wrapped around Ridge's left leg up to the hip. The ranger glared mercilessly at him.

"It wasn't listening to you. I had to do something before it choked Wess to death and you were overtaken."

Wess emerged from the hollow and stared at the frozen tree. "What happened?"

"I'm not sure. Something made it angry," said Ridge.

"The root hit Virgil after he tried to cut me free. It held me trapped around the waist and I couldn't move."

"Why did you do that?" demanded the ranger.

"I told you, it was choking Wess so I freed him."

"You should have called me."

"I did!"

Ridge asked Wess. "How did the root trap you?"

"I don't know exactly. I briefly woke to see Locan and heard him speak something in the Ancient. Then I blacked out again. When next I woke, I was alone, bound, gagged and held by the root."

"Locan?" From the melting broken ice, Ridge picked up a piece of the shattered root. Closing his eyes he stretched out his senses. In a hiss of pain, his eyes sprang open. He dropped the root and shook his hand as if stung or burned.

"Ridge?" asked Virgil.

The ranger's eyes narrowed with intense fury. "It wasn't you. Locan used the Dark Way to corrupt the tree."

Taking his quarterstaff in hand, Ridge climbed the bank to the frozen tree. He spoke the Ancient and struck the trunk with his quarterstaff. A burst of light engulfed the tree followed by a thunderous crack. The ice shattered, making pellets rain down from the top branches. Ridge ignored the pieces of ice. He spoke, and struck the tree again with another burst of light. The branches and roots withered into a stump then exploded into nothingness.

Virgil and Wess climbed the bank to join Ridge.

"I'm sorry. I know it is not easy for you to destroy one in your care," said Virgil with sobriety.

Ridge's jowls flexed in fighting back emotion. "It had to be done, to keep the infection from spreading."

"Where is Reilly? He was guarding me?"

Ridge led him back to the tree where Reilly dangled.

Wess looked askew at the ranger. "Your doing?"

Ridge nodded, his face still grim.

"What do you have to say?" Wess asked Reilly.

"Get me down?" came the sheepish reply.

"I don't think Ridge wants to do that."

"Especially not after being called a *devil*," added Virgil sternly.

Wess didn't look pleased at hearing the remark and scolded Reilly. "You are bold! You are also unfortunate to have become entangled with the real devils, Fitch and Locan. It already cost your brother his life and your father is to face justice."

The news struck Reilly hard. "Preston is dead?"

"He died last night from his wounds. Now, where did Locan go?"

Reilly started crying.

Wess snatched Ridge's staff and smacked Reilly's leg to get the young man's attention. "Where did he go?"

"Easy." Virgil drew Wess back from Reilly. "Ridge can find Locan. We need to tell the others so we can deal with Fitch." He took the staff and gave it back to Ridge.

"He's not to go anywhere!" Wess pointed at Reilly.

"He won't." Ridge spoke the Ancient to the tree. It made a creaking noise in reply. The branches holding Reilly rose and placed the young man in a cleft of the trunk about twenty feet in the air. "If you know what's good for you, don't climb down."

"How long will I be up here?"

"Until I send my men to fetch you!" snapped Wess.

Ridge took the lead in departing.

"Wait! What if Locan comes back before then?" called Reilly, only to be ignored.

Chapter 13

ON THE RIDE DOWN FROM THE SHACK, KELL SENSED THE SAME disturbance he did earlier. He turned to check if Vidar or Kendrick showed signs of uneasiness. Riding single file, the Guardians walked behind him. They seemed unfazed. Armus and Virgil were somewhere in the rear and he had to crane his head to see past Vidar and Kendrick. Visibility proved difficult due to the trees and winding path. He caught glimpses of Vivian, Fraser then Fitch/Wess through the landscape. He didn't see Virgil and Armus.

"We haven't lost them," said Vidar at seeing the interest.

Kell didn't reply, rather turned further for a clearer view. "Where is Armus? I don't see him or Virgil."

The archer tossed an unconcerned glance to Kendrick. The warrior grinned. "Trust us. They're back there."

Kell faced forward. Did he trust their word or his gut instinct of something wrong? *Gut instinct,* another term the mortals called such feelings. As captain, he often sensed trouble before others yet able to determine the reason. Now? No term of identification gave him much comfort without understanding the cause

Fitch/Wess noticed Kell's interest. He didn't see Armus or Virgil either, but for him, that was good. Turning his attention forward, he changed his focus to the rear legs of Vivian's horse. He spoke the Ancient under his breath, trying to use as little power as possible to avoid detection. After several strides the horse began limping and favoring its right hind leg. None of the Guardians seemed to notice. Good.

"Vivian. There is some thing wrong with your horse," he said.

She looked back to the horse's rump. "I thought I felt something unusual."

"Pull up and dismount before it becomes lame." She followed his instruction while he also dismounted. Up ahead, Fraser stopped his horse, thus Fitch/Wess said, "Her horse is lame."

"Kendrick! Vivian's horse is lame," Fraser shouted.

Kendrick spoke a word to Vidar and dropped back. Fitch/Wess examined the horse's hind leg when the Guardian arrived.

"He must have pulled something since I can't see a burr or lost shoe. The leg is definitely tender." Upon straightening, Fitch/Wess noticed the lead group had stopped. "Lame horse. Go on. She'll ride double with me and we'll catch up. Ayers must be taken to March."

Fraser nod and relayed the message.

Fitch/Wess handed the reins to Kendrick. "Lead him at his pace." He waved the Guardian to move. He mounted and reached to help Vivian climb up behind him.

"I'll stay with you," said Kendrick.

"No need. Armus and Virgil are close behind. Now, go."

Kendrick caught a glimpse of Armus through the tress about ten yards up the incline. He led the horse forward.

By the time Fitch/Wess moved his horse again, the distance between the groups had grown, just like he wanted. He noticed Kell's interest again. A few times, he met Fraser's curious regard. Taking Wess' place might have been a good strategic move under the circumstances. However, with Kell and Fraser's presence among the group, he must be careful. Kell might be in mortal form, but still the Guardian captain. Once a mortal is used by a shape-shifter, they develop sensitivity to the Guardian's presence. To avoid detection, he usually disposed of the mortals. Unfortunately he wasn't able to do so with Fraser while Spaulding's death was premature, and Wess' death inevitable.

Although risky to use even a small amount of power to make Vivian's horse lame, he needed a shield to deter both Kell and Fraser from any hasty actions. Kell's interest may indicate he sensed Fitch, but neither Armus nor Avatar became alert or showed any concern. This act of assuming Wess' identity confirmed what he suspected earlier—none of the other Guardians were aware of Kell's new form.

He wondered about the possibility when they called upon him at the jail believing he was Spaulding. He originally thought it all part of a clever plan to unmask him and Locan. He got a sense of the others being unaware when he became Ellis, only had difficulty accepting Armus and Avatar not knowing. Why would Kell keep his closest confidant and aide ignorant? Whatever the reason, armed with such intelligence, he held the upper hand and would utilize it to the fullest. Vivian diverted his attention when she squirmed and grabbed onto him.

"Not Comfortable?"

"No. It was one thing riding double from the farm on flat terrain. But a horse's movement going down hill isn't very comfortable." She gasped in momentary fright at losing her balance and seized him to keep from falling.

"Oww! Not so tight."

"I didn't want to fall."

"Well, I can't steer the horse and keep us both from falling if you're constantly grabbing onto me."

"It was your idea to ride double. And I thought you liked me being close?"

"Ay, only so not painful."

She huffed and tried holding onto the saddle. However, that proved awkward and not good for balance. She was forced to hold onto his waist, making him flinch.

"Careful," he chided. "We're near the bottom. The ride will be smoother soon."

"Unlike your tongue."

"Would you prefer to ride with Kel … vin?"

"He may be better company."

"Oh, so you do prefer him?"

"I didn't say so. Why are you in such an ugly mood?"

Fitch/Wess scowled at dealing with another female and chose not to answer. His annoyance soon turned into a small, pleased smile when he looked to his left at sensing a presence. The trail ended at the bottom of the hill and in a meadow and he drew his horse to a halt.

Armus arrived in a rush, alert and drew his sword. Before he could speak a warning, another voice shouted in the Ancient. A tremendous, deafening noise filled the meadow. The exceedingly painful sound agitated the horses. The mortals fought to bring the beasts under control. Cody whimpered in pain and ran across the meadow to escape the noise. Mirit and Valery both slipped off their horses. Mirit fell to her knees and covered her ears. Valery swooned. Ellis clumsily dismounted to get to Valery. Nigel's horse threw him. Chad struggled to get his horse under control while using his shoulder to shield one ear. Fraser clung to his horse's neck, teeth clenched and eyes screwed shut. Vivian clung to Firth/Wess and buried her head into his back.

Kell faired only slightly better than the others in containing his horse and withstanding the noise. The Guardians fell to their knees, overwhelmed by the noise. The horse Kendrick led, broke free and ran off. Wren appeared on the verge of fainting. Armus' face showed the strain of effort to rise from his knees to stand. He used his sword to aid his attempt only unsuccessful.

"Hold on! I'll get you out of here," Fitch/Wess forced the words, as the noise affected him also. He kicked the horse into gallop and headed in the opposite direction from the group.

"Wess, stop! It's Locan," called Kell. Either Wess ignored him or didn't hear him over the noise, either way Kell urged his horse to pursue.

"Kelvin, no!" Nigel struggled to get to his knees only to fall back onto all fours due to the debilitating noise.

"Ayers is escaping!" said Ellis.

Ayers urged the protesting animal to move across the meadow.

Nigel snarled in anger. "Wren! Vidar! Bring him down! Shoot to kill if necessary!"

Vidar pulled Wren to her feet and they staggered in pursuit of Ayers.

"No!" Mirit reached for Nigel, but ended up placing her hands back over her ears.

"I'll get Kelvin!" Fraser kicked his horse to pursue Kell.

"Fraser, wait!" Again, Nigel tried to stand. When Kell and Fraser disappeared around the trees out of sight, Nigel stumbled to his knees and covered his ears in pain.

Kendrick managed a few steps in pursuit of Fraser before falling, on the verge of being overcome by the noise. Avatar struggled to reach an unconscious Valery. To shield her from further harm, he held her head against his chest with his arms wrapped to protect her ears.

Breathing heavy in his determined resistance, Armus watched the effects on his fellow Guardians and mortals. A small trickle of blood flowed from Avatar's ears; his eyes screwed shut as he held Valery. Ayers' horse was now at a full gallop with Wren and Vidar in dogged pursuit. Armus braced his feet and with a mighty shout bellowed, "*Locan! A sgur!*"

The noise ceased. For a moment, Armus waited. His eyes scanned the hillside in an effort to catch a glimpse of Locan. Nothing. At least the sound stopped and he could move. Nigel was the closest, so he helped the prince to stand. "Are you hurt?"

Nigel carefully touched his head. "No, I just hope the ringing in my ears stops soon." He aided Mirit to her feet. She appeared pale.

"Why did you order them to kill him?" she chided.

"He's escaping."

"His son is dead! Isn't that enough?" She jerked away from him and moved to Valery, Ellis and Avatar. Nigel followed.

Avatar yielded Valery to Ellis' care. The Guardian then sat back on his heels, lowered his head and rubbed his ears.

Mirit knelt beside him. "Avatar, are you all right? Your ears are bleeding."

"Eh?" He held up his hand to stop her repeating her question. "Give me moment to hear again."

"Valery?" asked Ellis when she stirred. He encouraged her to wake.

He eyes blinked then opened. "What was that?"

"I don't know, but Avatar protected you." Ellis indicated the Guardian. "Thank you," he said.

Avatar wasn't paying attention rather concentrated on recovering.

"The noise came from Locan," said Armus. He and the others arrived. He knelt on the other side of Avatar, opposite Mirit.

"How?" she asked.

Armus spoke while examining Avatar. "His special ability is to paralyze and immobilize the enemy using sound. Joined with Mannix's blinding speed by which to kill, they were a formidable force within the Trio."

"Who was the third member?" asked Ellis.

"Valmar, Guardian of the Highlands. He died in the battle against Dagar."

"Father spoke about Valmar. He said he was part of the Contest to test his worthiness to be king," said Nigel.

"Ay," said Armus, a touch of fond remembrance in his voice. "For centuries he believed Locan and Mannix were killed in the Great Battle. After the coronation, Mahon found them along with some others deep in the bowels of the nether dimension when he and his team did reconnaissance. Then Kell sealed it, for the first time."

Avatar waved off Armus' examination to stand. He swayed.

Armus steadied him. "You shouldn't move so fast."

Avatar flexed his jaw open and shut in an effort to pop the pressure in his ears.

Kendrick and Chad arrived. "Avatar, are you all right?" asked Chad.

"No need to shout, I can hear now."

"I wasn't shouting."

"Ear damage," said Armus. He wiped off some blood from Avatar's ear to show Chad. "It'll take time for his hearing to even out volume."

"I can hear! Oh, I spoke too loud." He held his ears.

"I'm sorry you were injured on my behalf," said Valery.

Avatar flashed a casual smile rather than speak again.

"Highness, should we go after Ayers or the others?" asked Ellis.

"Vidar and Wren will take care of Ayers. Gather the horses so we can find Wess, Vivian and Kelvin." Nigel caught Mirit's glare at him when she left to fetch her horse. At first opportunity he had to make her speak.

<hr />

Wess stopped at hearing a powerful, painful noise followed by an explosion. It came from some distance behind them. "What was that?"

Ridge snarled in fierce anger. "Locan." He started to return when Virgil intervened.

"You said Fitch went this way." Virgil pointed in the direction they were heading.

The ranger's lethal gaze shifted between the options.

At the indecision, Virgil added, "We need to stop Fitch." He motioned to Wess.

"Ay. Wouldn't do to have another of me running around the province causing havoc," said Wess on cue.

Without answering, Ridge continued on their course.

<hr/>

Fitch/Wess saw Kell following. Fraser came a short distance behind Kell. He didn't see anyone else. Good. The lure worked. Even in a mortal persona, he possessed his Guardian strength. Recalling his earlier encounter with Kell, he hoped the same could not be said of the captain. He would kill Fraser. Better yet, make it appear *Kelvin* killed Fraser in front of witnesses.

"Kelvin and the young prince. We should stop to let them catch up," said Vivian.

"We'll stop all right." Fitch/Wess pressed the horse for more speed. They rode along the base of the hill where the shack was located. Ahead, lay a sharp bend.

"Wess, what are you doing?" she asked.

Around the bend, he violently reined the horse then turned it around in the direction they came. At the same time he shoved her off. She fell hard to the ground, winded and in pain from impact. He drew his sword, ready to charge the first person coming around the bend.

Kell barely ducked in time to avoid the swinging blade aimed at his head. He drew his sword in time to parry the second attack. On the third attack, the swords came together and their eyes met. "Fitch!" He shoved the blade aside.

"This time, I'll make sure you don't survive!"

The attack caused Kell to lean too far back. He did an awkward somersault off the horse, landed hard on his stomach and briefly winded.

"Has the captain lost his strength after being reduced to a mortal? Well I haven't!" He hacked down at Kell with all his might.

Kell rose to his knees and lifted his sword in both hands to make defense. The might of Fitch/Wess' blow sent Kell flying fifteen feet. Another hard landing sent jarring pain through is body.

"Kelvin!" called Fraser.

"See how you fare when I kill him and you get blamed!" Fitch/Wess said to Kell before charging Fraser.

The younger prince dodged to one side and barely avoided the blade. Fitch/Wess turned for a second charge. Fraser drew his sword and parried the next attack. Another strong swing by Fitch/Wess and another attempted parry. Fraser became disarmed and seized the saddlebow to stay mounted.

"Fitch!" Kell snatched his fallen sword and raced to intervene.

Fitch/Wess did a backward swing to stay the advance. This time Kell didn't budge. When Fitch/Wess turned his horse to trample Kell. Fraser leapt from the saddle at Fitch/Wess. Both tumbled hard to the ground with Fitch/Wess ending on top.

"Haven't had enough of me, boy?"

Fraser didn't reply, rather flashed a triumphant smile. He drove his dagger hilt deep into Fitch/Wess' side. In loud growl of pain and anger, Fitch/Wess pulled out the dagger, and raised it to strike down at Fraser.

"Wess!" Nigel and the others pushed their horses in a gallop toward them.

The momentary distraction gave Kell the time he needed. His blade sliced deep across Fitch/Wess' back, sending him off Fraser and crying out in angry pain.

Vivian screamed in terror and Nigel shouted, "No!" He jumped from the saddle and reached for his sword, intent on rushing Kell.

Fraser intercepted him. "No, Uncle! It's Fitch."

"What?"

"Nigel!" Wess, Ridge and Virgil raced down a nearby incline. "That's Fitch, not me!"

Kendrick and Avatar seized the seriously injured Fitch/Wess when he started to rise. He clumsily fell to his knees in pain.

"Wess!" Vivian swayed with emotion. He caught her about the waist for support. "I thought it was you!" She wept.

Nigel approached, though wary with curiosity. "How?"

"Fitch took my place when I left to find Vivian and Ridge. They found me in a river hollow where Locan put me so Fitch could act."

Kell joined them and inquired of Vivian. "Did Fitch hurt you?"

She shook her head and wiped her eyes. "No, other than being sore from falling off the horse." Her smile quivered with emotion. "Thank you."

Kell kindly smiled. "Thank the prince also. It was a joint effort."

All the while Wess stared at Kell. "How did you know it wasn't me?"

"Ay. How did you know?" asked Nigel.

Kell replied in attempted humor. "You mean aside from the fact he ambushed me?" They didn't accept his humor so amended his demeanor. "After your kind apology I didn't think you would be so base as to attack me, nor do it in front of Vivian."

"Indeed not," said Wess.

"I suspected something wrong at the shack," said Fraser.

"How?" asked Nigel.

"I don't know," said the teenager with a shrug. "Something didn't feel right. My uneasiness became confirmed when he attacked me, and I looked in his eyes. Then I knew it was Fitch. I will never forget those eyes as long as I live."

"A mortal who experiences a shape-shift becomes keenly aware of the Guardian's spiritual essence," explained Armus.

Nigel turned to Fitch/Wess. Avatar and Kendrick held him, though he remained on his knees in obvious distress from his wounds. He appeared too weak to be of much threat. "What do you suggest doing with him?"

Armus closed his eyes. After a brief moment, Vidar and Wren appeared. "Any word on Ayers?"

"In Deputy March's custody," said Vidar.

"Fitch." Armus pointed to the wounded shape-shifter.

"Consider him imprisoned." Vidar pulled Fitch/Wess to his feet.

"It doesn't matter what you do to me, Kell will not survive," said Fitch in painful vehemence.

Armus' bright chestnut eyes flared in anger. "What do you mean?"

Despite his serious condition, the caustic grin and glance shifted to Kell then back Armus. "Ask Kelvin."

Baffled, Armus looked to Kell. Visibly distressed, a mute Kell heaved a hapless shrug.

By this exchange, Fitch had his revenge. A last act of cruelty confirming this was no planned action. What a satisfying reality to watch Kell unable to say or do anything. His satisfaction proved short lived when Armus seized him by the throat. The lieutenant's fierce face inches from his.

"What trickery is this? What do you know of Kell? Speak, or I'll destroy you here and now!"

A sadistic smile of triumphant appeared on the shape-shifter's face. "I know he is someplace you will never find him."

Enraged, Armus' grip tightened to the point that Fitch gasped for breath. "You controlled the *madah-dune*!"

Avatar seized Armus to stop him from choking Fitch. "No!" He attempted to loose Fitch, but Armus wouldn't yield. In fact, both of Armus' hands were now around Fitch's throat. Avatar increased his effort, and the strain of wrestling with Armus showed on his face, along with anxiety. "Killing him like this is dangerous. For your own sake, release him! Please, Armus! I don't want to lose you too!"

Vidar added his urging. "Listen to Avatar!"

In painful turmoil at the scene, Kell fought to speak but the words wouldn't come.

"*Armus! Umhal! Leig-rach!*" ordered Nigel.

Stunned by the command then dumbfounded at seeing his hands around Fitch's throat, Armus let go. Fitch collapsed to his knees, gulping for air. Avatar coaxed Armus away, which was a lot easier than stopping his earlier efforts.

"Get him out of here," said Nigel in quiet haste to Vidar.

In a flash of white light, Vidar and Fitch vanished.

"Where did they go?" asked Vivian.

"Vidar is Jor'el's Defender of Justice. More than likely he is taking Fitch to a Guardian prison," said Kendrick.

For a moment, Kell watched Avatar speak to Armus. Although Avatar spoke low and in the Ancient, his expression altered between angst, worry and compassion. Armus' features showed befuddlement bordering on utter shame. Nigel's speech diverted Kell's attention back to the others.

"I'm glad you found him," said Nigel to Virgil concerning Wess. "Was Ridge looking for him?"

"No, he became immobilized by Locan to cover for Fitch's charade. After I undid the nerve-blocking blow, we searched for the general. We thought finding him would help to unmask Fitch."

"Speaking of Locan. He's somewhere nearby," warned Ridge. His eyes narrowed in scanning the hillside.

"We mustn't forget Reilly," said Virgil.

"You found him too?" asked Mirit, sounding somewhat relieved.

"And left him hanging."

Wess chuckled at Mirit's confused annoyance. "Ridge used his power to have Reilly held up in a tree while Virgil employed his power to free me from an angry tree."

"That doesn't clarify anything."

"He'll explain as we fetch Reilly," said Nigel. "You and Vivian can use Fitch's horse," he said to Wess

"Highness. I have a suggestion I strongly urge you to consider." Kendrick spoke in a manner everyone knew wasn't a suggestion, rather a politely worded order. "Let Ridge and Virgil fetch Reilly and bring him to town. With Locan on the loose, there is no need to place everyone in further peril today by going back into hills. Return to Oakley, speak to Deputy March and recover."

"A fine idea." Mirit's discreet gaze shifted to Wess and Vivian.

Nigel fought a smile at her indication. "Then we shall. The Guardian way would be most efficient in retrieval."

"Consider it done, Highness." Virgil and Ridge vanished.

The others went to collect their horses. Kell approached Armus, who remained with Avatar and still tried to regain his composure. Not often did Armus lose his temper in blind fury. Oh, he was more passionate in nature than Kell, but losing his temper beyond reason rarely happened. For a brief moment their eyes met. Indeed, Fitch's taunting deeply pricked Armus. Kell spoke in all sincerity.

"I wish I could tell you what he meant when he singled me out."

"So do I."

Avatar held Armus by the shoulder. "He aimed the blow at both. You, because of your relationship to Kell, and Kelvin because he wounded him, and became the object of their enterprise."

"Avatar's right. A well placed shot, striking multiple targets at once," said Kell.

Armus nodded. "I'll fetch your horse." He moved off.

"Don't let his mood fool you. He appreciates your sympathy, as do I," said Avatar.

"I wish I could do more than offer sympathy."

"You have, by dealing with Fitch. Especially discovering he was responsible for the attack which killed our captain."

Kell shied from Avatar's steady silver gaze to survey the hillside. Oh, how he wished to heaven he could tell them! Sensing Avatar's interest he said, "Locan is still on the loose."

"Be assured, we *will* deal with Locan," said Avatar in deadly certainty.

Kell focused on the hillside yet shivered at Avatar's merciless declaration. Whereas Armus tended to speak his mind to release tension, Avatar turned his passion inward, and especially in respect to those he deeply cared about. *Please, not you too! I can't bear to watch both of you lose control on my behalf,* he thought. Avatar misunderstood his reaction.

"Dealing with Locan will be more difficult. Fitch is a shape-shifter in mortal form. Locan is a warrior and very formidable" He touched Kell's arm to draw his attention from the hillside. "You are no match for him."

Kell began to grin. "Who said I was?"

Armus returned with the horse. Once Kell mounted, they joined the others.

Reappearing at the tree where they left Reilly, Virgil and Ridge became thunderstruck by what they discovered. The tree had been brutalized. Only a scarred trunk remained with ashes and debris scattered around the base.

Ridge's initial surprised turned to grief and outrage. "Locan!" he bellowed. His voice echoed through the trees and startled birds.

Virgil seized Ridge's arm. "The tree wasn't his only victim." He indicated the charred bones. "We should bury the remains."

Ridge stopped Virgil from taking out his sword to dig in the dirt. He spoke the Ancient and tapped the end of his staff on the ground beside the bones. The earth opened and swallowed Reilly's bones. "No creature will disturb him."

"Let's return to the others." Virgil and Ridge vanished and reappeared on the road in front of the group.

Nigel drew everyone to a halt. "That was quick."

"Sad news to report, Highness. Locan found Reilly before we could secure him. He and the tree were destroyed," said Virgil.

"How?" Mirit asked with distress.

"A focused concentration of Locan's power. Not only can it immobilize, but when focused, can kill living things or destroy objects, like walls or fences. The force first incapacitated Reilly then ignited the tree. Only a stump and bones remained. Ridge buried the bones."

"Both sons within a day," she muttered as if speaking to herself.

"I want to search for Locan before he gets too far," said Ridge.

Kell voiced his dispute. "No need. He won't go anywhere."

"What makes so sure?"

"Two reasons. The first is to take revenge on me for Fitch. Remember, their aim was to make me their scapegoat. Second, he eliminated Reilly, so Ayers is the next logical target."

"Ayers is safe with March. Vidar and I brought him there," said Wren.

"How safe is a mortal prison from a determined Guardian?"

"March served as a Fortress Guard before returning home after his father died," said Chad.

"How long ago was that?"

"Five years."

Kell looked directly at Chad. "His father died six years ago."

Befuddled, Chad turned to Avatar.

The Guardian commander focused curious eyes on Kell. "How do you know?"

"Because I served with him back then."

"Are you saying you suspect March is also involved?" asked Wess.

"I'm saying, Ayers may be Locan's next target, and being in March's custody doesn't guarantee his safety."

"Ayers didn't mention March when speaking about others who helped them."

"No, but neither did March," said Chad in sudden recollection.

211

"What do you mean?" asked Nigel.

"Ayers said that when they refused to give into Spaulding's blackmail he began arresting others who helped them."

"March didn't mention any others when we asked him for more information," said Fraser.

"Ay," agreed Ellis. "He said Morley—Ayers—was his only lead, and until he identified the person, nothing could be done. The deputy made no mention of arrests and surely he would have known of any."

Nigel and Wess exchanged quick conferring glances before putting their horses into a gallop. They all headed for Oakley.

Chapter 14

UNFORTUNATELY, THE MIDDAY TRAFFIC IN OAKLEY CAUSED the group to slow. Kendrick and Avatar cleared the way for passage to the mercantile. Upon arrival, most dismounted without trouble. Kell grunted in discomfort from his fall off the horse and fight with Fitch. In mortal form, he found the constant fatigue and soreness due to physical exertion frustrating, and the need to rest and eat for recovery an inconvenience. The only time a Guardian experienced fatigue, pain or soreness happened when wounded. Otherwise the expenditure of strength, power and energy weren't taxing. Rest came in the form of meditation, not true sleep. Eating was totally unnecessary.

Serving as rear guards, Wren and Virgil noticed Kell wince. "Are you hurt?" she asked.

"Sore. I'll be fine." He waved them off to go inside.

The deputy waited upon customers and was surprised by the large group's arrival. Nigel and Wess confronted March.

"Where is Ayers?" demanded Nigel.

"Secure in a cell, Champion," said March, using Nigel's Jor'ellian title.

Nigel studied the deputy's face. "You're name was unfamiliar at first. Seeing you in person, I recognize you from the Fortress."

"I served under Captain Madden, and stood the midnight watch. I saw you and Princess Mirit come and go in the morning when relieved. It was an honor just being at the Fortress with you, Champion."

Nigel pursed his lips in momentary regard of March. He motioned to Kendrick and Virgil then indicated the patrons. The Guardians ushered the people from the mercantile. Some muttered in annoyance, others willingly left, apprehensive of what was happening. Once clear of customers, Kendrick and Virgil stood by the door to stop anyone from entering.

"Champion, is something wrong?" asked March.

"We have a few questions for you and you are to answer truthfully or I will know." As he spoke, Armus and Avatar flanked him, their gaze directed upon March.

The deputy didn't balk or flinch at their movement. In fact, he spoke willingly. "Of course, Champion."

"What do you know of Ayers' gang?"

"Gang?"

"I said answer truthfully."

"I swear, Champion, I know nothing about a gang." His glance passed to the Guardians.

Nigel nodded toward Fraser and Chad. "You told my nephew and Sir Chad that Ayers was your only lead, and you depended upon his identification to help solve the rash of crimes."

"Ay, Champion. He hasn't said a word since Wren and Vidar brought him. He just sits staring into space, sometimes weeping."

"Ayers told us Spaulding arrested three others who helped them," said Wess.

"I have no knowledge of any arrests, my lord."

"How is that possible?" asked Fraser.

March grew sheepish in reply. "I don't want to speak ill of the dead, but Sheriff Spaulding and I did not agree on how to administer justice. I tried keeping the peace by working with people, employing what I learned from serving at the Fortress and not intimidation. That was the sheriff's method. Many times he acted without letting me know. I very often dealt with angry or upset victims, who came to me complaining and seeking a remedy to his meddling."

"Did you know of Spaulding's involvement with Ayers for profit?" asked Nigel.

"No," scoffed March. "Nor am I surprised. He was a harsh, ambitious man."

"What about your father's death? You told me you left the Fortress after he died, only he died a year earlier," said Chad.

March grew somber. "I wanted to come home when it happened only my mother insisted she could manage until my time of service ended in two years. When she fell ill and suffered a stroke due to a high fever, I told the Vicar the whole story and he released me from service."

"Where is your mother now?" asked Nigel.

March's face became stricken with fearful concern. "She is almost totally confined to the house. My wife divides her time between the store and caring for her. Please, Champion, if you wish to verify my story, speak to the Vicar. My mother is not well enough to endure questioning."

At the genuine plea, Nigel spoke with compassion. "I won't trouble your mother."

"Thank you," he said in relief. "Are there any more question, Champion?"

Nigel glanced to the others to determine if they were satisfied. No one spoke. Finally he asked Avatar, "Well?"

"He answered everything truthfully."

"I would not do otherwise, Commander."

"Take us to Ayers," said Nigel.

"The jail is just a few buildings down." March gestured to the door in deference. "After you, Champion." Outside, he took the lead.

Three doors down, they entered a very sturdy brick building. Two men sat at a table near the entrance to a narrow hallway. Prison cells of iron bars line either side of the hall. The men came to attention when March entered with Nigel and the others.

"Is all secure?"

"Ay, Deputy."

"The King's Champion wants to speak to Ayers."

The men bowed when Nigel and Wess passed in accompanying March to the cells. Mirit bit her lower lip in apprehension then hurried after them.

215

Only one other cell was occupied. The man sneered at them before turning over on his cot, his back to them. They stopped in front of the Ayers' cell. Nigel gave Mirit a side-glance when she joined them. Although she focused on Ayers, Nigel noticed an expression of disturbed determination. When he turned his attention to Ayers, he saw what March described concerning the man's state of despondency. With red-rimmed eyes from weeping, and his face pale and distraught, Ayers sat on the cot staring at nothing.

"Ayers," said Wess in a clam and non-threatening voice.

He didn't respond.

"We bring you news of Reilly."

To this, Ayers flashed a glance at them. His face showed no emotion.

"It's not good news. Locan got to him before Ridge could."

He returned to staring into space, yet tears swelled in his eyes.

"Ayers," said Nigel. "We need to know if there is anything else you can tell us."

Again, he didn't respond.

"Ayers."

"Don't push him," chided Mirit.

Nigel's level gaze at her defensive manner passed to Wess, who said, "I don't think we'll get much from him."

Mirit's distress appeared to intensify, so Nigel took by her the arm and escorted her to the front room. He shook his head at the others. "Grief and regret have made him almost beyond reaching."

"Did you tell him about Reilly?" asked Fraser.

"Ay. The news barely got a reaction."

"What now?"

Nigel shrugged. "Justice must have it way. He'll face trial."

"He's too grief-stricken to comprehend," said Mirit in dispute.

"He will be treated fairly, Princess. Nothing will be done until he understands. I give you my word," said March.

The reassurance didn't satisfy her but the conversation continued when Wess spoke to March.

"There is something else. Locan is still on the loose. After killing Reilly, he may come for Ayers."

"I can double the guard."

"They wouldn't stand a chance against a Guardian warrior," said Armus.

"Highness, can I make suggestion?" asked Kell.

"What?"

Kell grew sympathetic as he continued. "This may sound a bit crass, but Ayers being used as a target may not be a bad idea."

"What? No!" exclaimed Mirit, her temper flaring.

Nigel waved her silent and asked Kell, "Meaning?"

"To draw Locan out. I know Ridge can find him, but why not bring him to us?"

"I don't like the idea of using any individual as bait."

"I understand. However, as long as Locan is free, Lord Ayers and everyone else in the area, is in danger not knowing when or where he will strike."

"He could leave the province," said Wess.

Kell shook his head. "Not if I'm involved in the escort."

Stunned, Vivian said, "You're volunteering to be...?"

"Bait. Ay," he said when she couldn't finish.

"Nigel," said Mirit only to be waved silent again as he continued speaking to Kell.

"You realize what you're proposing is extremely risky?"

"My life has been at risk since I arrived."

Nigel couldn't help a low agreeing chuckle. "True. Whereas I might consider your offer, I don't want to force the issue with Ayers. He barely acknowledged us."

"Let me speak to him."

"Your offer is unacceptable!" said Mirit in rebuff.

Nigel's restraining grip on her arm got her attention. "Let me handle this." She clamped her mouth shut with an expression showing her reluctance at doing so. He spoke to Kell. "If you can get him to understand and agree, I will consider your suggestion."

"Nigel, no!" She received a rebuking glare for her protest. She jerked away from him, crossed to the other side of the room and turned her back to him.

"Leave this to me, Highness," Kell said quietly.

Nigel, Wess, Avatar and Armus followed to watch Kell approach the cell and speak to Ayers.

"Lord Ayers," said Kell in a voice of serene authority.

Unlike with Nigel or Wess, Ayers gave Kell his immediate and full attention.

"If you had an opportunity to cooperate with the law and help to capture Locan, would you be willing?"

There was the barest pause before Ayers answered, "Ay."

"No matter the risk?"

"Ay."

Curious and bit concerned, Nigel joined Kell to make inquiry of Ayers. "Are you sure? It would mean becoming vulnerable to possible injury and death if it fails."

Although his face remained stoic, he replied in a strong voice. "He killed Reilly. What more can he do to me? I have nothing left in this world."

After a brief moment of thought, Nigel spoke again. "Very well. We'll let you know when the time comes." He drew Kell away from the cell, through the front room and out to the street. The others followed.

Nigel didn't speak again he found a place away from traffic at the corner of the building near an alley. "How did you get him to respond and agree when we couldn't get an answer out of him?"

"Oh, no," murmured Mirit in annoyed distress, only to be ignored.

"I simply stated the facts in laying the option before him. When one has nothing to lose, what harm is there in agreeing?"

"You could both lose your life. That's hardly nothing!" chided Mirit.

A touched smile crossed Kell's lips. "Princess, I already lost a part of my life I thought impossible to lose." The smile faded as he continued. "My deepest regret, is I will never be able to tell those I care most about why it happened."

"Maybe we can tell them for you." Nigel's clap Kell on the back of the shoulder, which made him flinch in pain. "Are you hurt again?"

"Same injury only sore." He grunted and rotated his shoulder.

"He was knocked off his horse by Fitch's attack," said Vivian.

"Actually, I did a controlled fall."

"It didn't look controlled."

He chuckled. "Granted the landing wasn't what I intended, but I avoided a worse fate."

"If you're going to serve as escort you'll need to rest and recover. The situation with Ayers can wait until morning," said Wess.

"Ay," agreed Nigel. "Kendrick and Virgil will stand guard at the jail."

"I'll go to the apothecary for a salve and pain elixir," said Vivian.

"I'll go with you," said Avatar.

"Meet us at the inn for supper and staying the night."

"Oh, no, please, Champion, I would extend my hospitality," said March.

"I thought your in-laws were in town?" said Chad.

"I'll make arrangements for them to stay at the inn and free up the extra rooms. I don't want the count or the young prince to be inconvenienced again," he said with smile to Ellis and Fraser.

"We'll accept your offer for rooms, but not food. It would be too much trouble for your wife to feed us all," said Nigel.

"You're very kind, Champion. I'll see all is made ready." He bowed and left.

"You'll find the food at Joby's Inn quite good, Uncle."

"As long as he doesn't have to use the privy," quipped Chad.

Ellis smirked in response to the dig.

At the inn, Joby widely smiled in greeting Fraser, Ellis, Valery and Chad again. "Highness, wonderful to see you again so soon."

"Joby," said Fraser with a friendly smile. "This is my uncle and aunt, the King and Queen's Champion."

"Oh, this is a double honor!"

Fraser continued the introduction. "Lieutenant Armus of the Guardian High Trio."

"First the pleasure of serving the Commander, and now you, Lieutenant." He inclined his head in acknowledgement. "My lord count," he greeted Wess with a smile. Cody poked his way through. "And you, my canine friend. I'll have a special plate prepared for you."

Cody barked and wagged his tail in agreement.

"Not too much gristle this time, please," said Valery.

"No, bones and fine meat, my lady." He led them to the inn's largest table, easily able to accommodate everyone. Being mid-morning the inn wasn't crowded. He ordered his servants to bring drink. "Today we have a treat. My son downed a buck yesterday and freshly dressed it last night."

"I knew I smelt venison." Wess turned to Nigel. "Joby dresses a fine venison. I've not tasted its equal. Even Tyrone would be impressed."

"My lord, you do me honor."

The servants brought ale, several loves of bread and a large hunk of semi-soft cheese on a platter.

Wess slightly frowned. "No wine?"

"My finest with the meal, my lord. In the meantime enjoy some fresh bread and my wife's special herb cheese."

"Herb cheese?" Armus took a slice and sniffed it. "Interesting." He placed the slice on the bread and ate. "Goes well together."

Joby smiled at the assessment. "Supper will be ready shortly. If you need anything else before than, just ask."

"Cody is interested in the cheese," said Chad when the wolf sniffed the table.

"It smells good." Valery took a small piece and held it out to Cody. The wolf sniffed it and suddenly sneezed. He shook his head, sneezed again and went to lie down behind her chair. Everyone laugh. "I'll think he'll wait for the venison."

"Probably the garlic," said Armus. He placed another piece a slice of bread and ate. "It is good."

Kell sat beside Armus. He winced when reaching for the bread then gingerly sat back to eat.

"Controlled fall, eh?" said Armus dryly, and a merry tilt in his smile.

The humor caught Kell off guard; being the first trace of Armus' wit he heard since before the attack by the *madah-dune*. He grinned. "Falling off a horse is not as easy as it used to be."

"You mean because of your age?" teased Fraser.

"And leaping to take someone off a horse is easier at your age?"

"I'm not sore." Fraser flashed a toothy grin of triumph, to which Kell laughed.

"That brings up a question," began Wess to Armus. "While in the form of Spaulding, Fitch suffered injury when Spaulding was killed, yet I'm unscathed even though Fraser and Kelvin wounded Fitch while he was me. How is that possible?"

"Ay," said Ellis. "Wren wounded Fitch when he was me, and I'm unscathed."

"Shape-shifters were created to mingle among mortals in a less threatening form, since some mortals aren't agreeable to Guardians."

"And for military reconnaissance," added Avatar. He and Vivian joined the group. By the look of the small bag she carried, they were successful at the apothecary.

"Ay," agreed Armus. "It was never intended for them to impersonate any particular mortal. That was a corruption of their power devised by Dagar during his rebellion. As judgment for the deviation, Jor'el imposed a curse for the shape-shifter to suffer whatever happened to the mortal while in their persona."

"Short of death. Since a mortal can't kill a Guardian," said Avatar.

Armus continued, "To protect mortals, Jor'el ordained they would not suffer if injury happened to the shape-shifter during the impersonation since they bore no responsibility for the actions committed."

"Good." Wess tossed a roguish smile at Fraser, "because I don't think my older bones could take being knocked off a horse in reality or vicariously."

Fraser returned the humor. "If I knew it was *really* you, I wouldn't dare. I'd answer to my uncle for it."

"Only after Wess gave you a thorough thrashing," said Nigel with a snicker.

Fraser still smiled. "I know my limitations. Going up against either you or Wess isn't something I'd want to do at any age."

Nigel laughed. Mirit sat beside him and didn't crack a smile at the exchange. He gave her hand a gentle squeeze and smiled. Her small return smile was plaintive and not reflected in her eyes. He leaned over further than necessary in reaching for the bread to whisper in her ear. "We'll talk tonight. I love you." This time her smile was genuine.

Joby and his servants brought the meal, which included potatoes, vegetables, sweetmeats, gravy pudding, more bread, wine and venison. He placed a plate of venison and bones on the floor for Cody.

Sitting made Kell's muscles grow stiff and sore. He fought displaying discomfort to satisfy his appetite. Still Avatar noticed and commented.

"The elixir will help your muscles relax and for you to sleep, while the salve will ease the pain."

"Sounds good."

"If by the morning, you are not capable of escorting Ayers, we'll think of something else," said Nigel.

Kell shook his head and swallowed before answering. "We can't wait too long and give Locan time act."

"I wouldn't place you or Ayers at any more risk then necessary. You'll need all your strength."

"I'm certain after a good night's sleep, I'll be ready."

"What are we going to do, Uncle?"

"We'll discuss that in a more private place."

They turned their attention to finishing a fine meal with fresh berry tarts. During dessert they saw March, a couple and two boys enter the inn. March spoke to Joby. The boys watched the group with great interest.

"Deputy March." Nigel beckoned them over.

The in-laws were surprised at the summons and the boys eager in approaching the table.

"Would you do the honor of introductions?"

"Champion, these are my wife's parents and her younger brothers."

"Champion," said the husband, bowing. The wife curtsied and urged the boys to pay their respects.

"I hope we have not inconvenienced you too much," said Nigel.

"Oh, no. We are pleased to be of service," said the husband.

"I hope to someday be a Jor'ellian," said the eldest boy.

Nigel smiled. "How old are you?"

"Twelve, Champion," he said, raising a proud chin.

"Have you begun training?"

"Ay, Champion."

"Ben has good skills with a sword. I've been teaching him," said March.

"Then he should be ready to enlist as a cadet when he is fourteen. Perhaps I'll see you at the Fortress."

"I look forward to it, Champion."

March signaled for the in-laws and boys to leave with one of Joby's servants. He remained. "All is ready at the house, Champion."

"Then we'll be along shortly."

They left with compliments to Joby's for his excellent supper and extra coins in his pocket.

At the house, March led them up to the bedchambers. "There are three rooms." He indicated the doors. "One for you and her highness, the other for the count and his wife and the third is the largest and has two beds."

"There is no place for Mistress Vivian," began Mirit. "So the women will take this room and the men divide others." She moved to stand by the first door indicated

"As you wish, Princess."

"Chad, Ellis, Fraser." Nigel pointed to one room. "Wess, Kelvin and I will take the other."

"What of the Guardians?" asked March.

"We don't require sleep, but thank you for your consideration." Armus ushered March toward the stairs.

"If anything is required—"

"We'll call you." Armus smiled and nudged the deputy on his way.

They waited until March left before Nigel led them to the largest room, the one he selected for himself, Wess and Kell.

"You didn't want March to know our plans?" asked Ellis.

"I'll tell him once we *have* a plan. All we know is Kelvin has volunteered to act as escort, not how it will be implemented."

"He can't go by himself that would be too obvious," said Armus.

They stopped talking when light filled the room. Vidar appeared. "Fitch is secure until this is over and Jor'el determines what is to be done with him."

"We were just discussing a plan to draw out Locan," said Nigel.

"Using Kelvin as bait."

"How do you know?"

Vidar just smiled.

"He went to the jail first," said Wren.

"Not afraid of giving away trade secrets?" asked Avatar in his dry wit.

"Consider it a free lesson to improve your tracking skills."

"As I was saying," continued Armus. "Locan is no fool. If he sees only Kelvin accompanying Ayers, he will know something is wrong."

"If he sees us all he might not risk an attack," said Fraser.

"I didn't say all. We not only need the word to get out that Ayers is being moved, we need a decoy for him."

"Meaning we split up again," said Ellis.

"While I take Ayers," said Kell.

"I'll go with you. There must be some Guardian presence," said Ridge.

"As will I," said Chad.

"I don't want to risk any more lives," said Kell.

"I'm a soldier."

"You're also a member of the Council."

"So is Ellis and so am I. You're going to be stuck with one of us," said Wess.

"What about me?" asked Vivian.

"No!" said Wess and Kell in unison.

"I didn't mean to go, I meant what am I to do? I'm the only one not a soldier, member of the Council or trained in arms."

"Dress my wounds," said Kell with a rakish smile.

"I'm spoken for. Avatar will take care of you," she bantered and took Wess' hand.

"Indeed, you are *betrothed* and unskilled," said Nigel. "Whereas we appreciate what you've done, there is no need to risk your life. Ridge will take you home now."

She was a bit taken back at the abruptness. Wess made her face him. "The safest place for you is home. For my sake." He kissed her cheek and she hugged him. "Don't fret. Old soldiers know how to survive." He handed her to Ridge. The ranger took her a couple of steps from the group and vanished.

"Thank you," said Wess to Nigel.

"This means we can sleep with our husbands," said Mirit

"Without fear of waking up beside an impostor," said Valery.

Chad, Fraser, Nigel and Wess laughed when Ellis scowled.

"You all laugh, but I need to make up for things I didn't do."

Valery took his arm. "Just knowing it is you beside me is enough. The thought of Fitch is still disturbing."

"At least there is an indoor privy," teased Fraser.

Although smiling, Nigel waved the humor aside. "We still need to decide on a decoy for Ayers."

Avatar's sly glance found Wren. "By using an old hunter's trick."

"Vidar is better suited for that," she refuted.

"I'm too large," said Vidar to Avatar's pleasure and Wren's chagrin.

"Ay," she said in resigned agreement.

"Now that all is settled, I'll tell March to put out the word that after breakfast Ayers will be moved to the provincial prison. In the meantime, Avatar will tend your wounds then get some rest." Nigel spoke the last sentence to Kell.

Wess lingered while the others left.

"Undress while I prepare the elixir," said Avatar to Kell.

Wess sat on one of the beds and watched Kell strip to the waist. "Why did you volunteer?"

"You heard what I told the prince."

"Is there nothing else? Some other reason you risk your life?"

"Here, drink this while I apply the salve." Avatar handed Kell a cup of elixir.

He didn't answer Wess to drink and then grimaced upon finishing. "That was awful."

Avatar smiled. "I never said it would taste good only relax the muscles and help you sleep." Kell flinched when he applied the salve. "Does that hurt?"

"It's cold."

Avatar chuckled. "First you can't stand the taste, now the cold."

Wess grinned at the humor and said, "You haven't answered my question."

"The reason should be obvious after what I've been through."

"I just want to be sure of the reason."

Since applying the salve made him squirm, Kell took hold of Avatar to stop so he could reply to Wess. "We didn't start off on the best of terms and I bear some of the blame. Vivian has made her choice. I must admit, she chose wisely. I can't come close to giving her what you can. Still, my volunteering is to clear my name *not* to impress her. Jor'el willing and I survive, perhaps someday I will be blessed with such a fine

225

woman." Suddenly feeling embarrassed and timid, he released Avatar and motioned for him to continue applying the salve.

Wess moved to stand in front of Kell to get his attention. "If you survive, I will request the king appoint you as my new sheriff."

"Me? Sheriff?"

"I too must admit I badly misjudged you. Through all this, you have proven to be a man of integrity, intelligence and honor. I can't think of anyone I would trust more to look out for the welfare of the people of my province."

Made momentarily speechless by the admission, Kell managed to say, "I would be honored, my lord."

Wess grinned. "Take good care of him, Avatar."

The Guardian paused to acknowledge Wess' departure. When the closed door, he continued treating Kell. "I've known Wess since he was a boy. He doesn't give such compliments lightly. Hardship forged his character, yet once his loyalty and respect is earned you can depend upon him, and usually for life."

Sobriety filling Kell's face and voice. "I witnessed his character during Tyrone's brief abdication. He struggled with remaining general because of his brother's decision yet chose to support Nigel."

"He and Nigel share a unique bond since Nigel's infancy."

"You mean when he and Bosley saved him from Sir Owain's coup."

"How do you know? You're not old enough to remember something that happened forty years ago."

Kell chuckled. "I heard the story. You were also involved."

Avatar grinned. "Three days prior to Owain seizing Waldron, I received my appointment as Nigel's Overseer. Even at two months old he was stubborn. It served him well, helping to survive days of fleeing into the wilderness in the dead of winter. Finished. How does that feel?"

Kell moved his shoulders. "Better. Not as sore."

"I told you it would help." He wiped his hands on a towel then replaced the lid on the jar of salve. "You should be experiencing the effects of the elixir soon."

"Come to think of it, I am drowsy." By the light coming in the window, it was early afternoon. "Seems too early to retire."

"Not for one recovering from injury. I noticed signs of the old bruising along with a few new marks of irritation from your *controlled fall*."

Kell paused in pulling down the cover of a bed upon hearing Avatar's sarcastic inflection on the words *controlled fall*. In profile, he noticed the way Avatar's goatee wrinkled in a familiar expression he seen many times over the centuries when Avatar employed his dry-witted humor. "Did Armus tell you to say that? A conspiracy of humor at my expense?" he offered in a good-natured challenge.

Avatar tilted his head with mild curiosity. "What makes you ask?"

"He teased me while eating and use the same tone when saying *'controlled fall'*," he said in perfect imitation of Armus' voice and facial mannerism.

The mimicking increased Avatar's interest. "He teased you?"

"Ay, before you and Vivian returned. The way your goatee wrinkles when smirking is a dead give away of your wry humor."

Avatar became intrigued and offered his own challenge. "Are you claiming you can read me like a book too?"

Kell was taken back by the reference then smiled. "Consider it knowledge gained by observation; same as with Armus. Those were the first civil words from him since this whole thing started."

Avatar smiled. "I'm glad to hear about his humor. I wondered when, or if ever, his lighthearted jesting would return." His tone droned at the end.

"You mean because of the captain?" asked Kell. His words came a bit halting since he knew the answer.

Avatar made a somber nod. "Perhaps what happened with Fitch proved cathartic. A release of his anger and grief."

Kell grew uneasy. "I thought he would kill Fitch."

"That is why we intervened. For a Guardian to kill under such circumstances as blind fury is dangerous, and can bring horrible, eternal consequences. I'm grateful Nigel's command stopped him. It's been difficult enough losing Kell, I couldn't imagine anything happening to Armus—again." His face showed the rising inner conflict and his attempt to suppress those emotions.

"Again," said Kell, more to himself since he understood the reference.

Avatar heard and mistook it for a question. "During Ellan's first coup attempt, Kell and Armus were reported killed. This left me alone and in command of the Guardians. Not something I wanted." He paused for moment when pain crept into his voice. Upon seeing the sympathetic regard, he continued. "We—Kell, Armus and I—form the High Trio over all Guardians. You must have been a teenager during the first coup, but probably heard about it. Fortunately, those reports proved untrue. Now is different, at least where Kell is concerned." His jowls tightened in another attempt to quell his emotions.

"I'm sorry. I didn't mean to upset you."

"I guess I've been so focused on Armus and this situation, I didn't realized my own feelings of loss. Kell was not just my captain; but also my mentor from the time I was created through the first few centuries of my existence. Actually, he and Armus both served in that capacity. Afterwards, I became his aide. Most of all, he was a very dear friend."

Moved by Avatar's confession, Kell said, "Again, I'm sorry."

Avatar tried to smile, but it was a half-hearted attempt. "Nothing to apologize for. I needed to acknowledge it. My release, I suppose. Anyway, I see the elixir is making you drowsy. I'll leave you to sleep."

Kell nodded, unable to watch Avatar's departure. After the door closed, he slipped under the covers. He lay on his side, facing away from the door. Silent tears fell. To hear Avatar admit suppressed grief, added to his misery on behalf of his closest comrades. He knew Avatar acted with Armus the same as with him when they believed Armus killed.

Kell swallowed back pain at recalling how close Armus came to committing the most unthinkable act, killing another Guardian in cold blood. When Fitch used his death to provoke Armus, he fought the heavy restraint to intervene. At Avatar's inability to stop Armus, everything within Kell wanted to shout a command. He opened his mouth to say something only nothing came. Finally Nigel spoke the Ancient words he couldn't. Oh, the stunned and confounded look on Armus' face in realization!

Kell blinked away tears, as the earlier scene continued to unfold in his mind now in connection with Avatar. First came Avatar's physical effort to stop Armus, the vocal plea of *I don't want to lose you too* then the hushed and emotional speech to Armus. How often he and Armus depended upon Avatar's unwavering loyalty and dedication to duty. Then and now, Avatar suppressed his emotions to lend stalwart and unconditional support in a time of deep personal grief and crisis. At least back then, he could send word that he and Armus survived. At present, all he could offer was a feeble excuse and not the comfort he longed to give.

"Why won't you let me speak, Jor'el? Why must I watch them suffer? Please, somehow grant them comfort and peace concerning me."

Although too early to retire, Nigel took advantage of the time by escorting Mirit to the room they would share. She appeared guarded and frustrated. Since the meadow something troubled her. She reacted and acted like she did early in their relationship, sharp tongued and combative. The behavior grew infrequent over the years and disagreements became rare. He didn't like rebuking her at the jail.

"I said we'd talk. Now is a good time. What is troubling you?"

"Are you sure about using Kelvin and Ayers as bait?"

"Ay. Why? Are you concerned about the plan?" he asked with some confusion. This was not a question he expected.

She appeared vexed and sat on the bed. "I'm not sure. At first I was surprised at discovering his true identity, but now, it troubles me."

He sat beside her. "I know, which is why I said you are not to blame." He watched her grow timid and avoid eye contact: another unusual sign. He took her hand to make her look at him. "Mirit, we have moved beyond withdrawing from each so don't do it now. Talk to me. Why can't you let this go?"

She took a deep breath and slowly exhaled. "You speak of the past, and it is in connection to the present which disturbs me."

"Identifying Loran doesn't make you responsible for what happened to Ayers. Loran acted on his own when he arranged Titus' kidnapping. His actions even surprised Gareth and Zebulon."

"But I too was involved! Granted I was duped, but I knew of an Allonian traitor."

"You didn't know about Lanzo. He fooled everyone by making us believe he wanted to help when all along he facilitated the plan to use Titus and start a war."

"True," she agreed, howbeit reluctant. "Perhaps if I had been more diligent in identifying the conspirators none of this would have happened." She grew upset again.

He tried to comfort her. "You couldn't anticipate that."

"Don't you understand what I'm saying about how the past affects the present?"

He shook his head. "Not unless you tell me."

She grew hesitant again and he knew she was coming to the heart of the matter.

"Ayers' speech deeply affected Fraser, and I feel responsible for allowing it to happen! Each incident adds to my failure to protect him."

"Oh, no," he said in complete understanding. He held her as she wept. "Ayers said that on purpose. You didn't fail, and Fraser would never believe that. I told him you suggested he join the Jor'ellians."

"Really?" she asked somewhat shyly.

"Ay." He wiped the tears from her face. "He knows you love him and want the best for his future. More than once you have shown love for all our nieces and nephews. And they love you. Ayers and his sons are reaping the consequences of their actions, not anything you did or didn't do in the past or present. Don't let his attempt to shift blame take root."

"I still wish the situation was different and Fraser not hurt, and Ayers' sons still alive. When you ordered them to shoot—"

"Shhh, easy." He again held her close when she wept anew.

A brief knock came on the door before Fraser and Avatar entered.

"Uncle," said Fraser. He grew concerned at her weeping. "Aunt Mirit? What's wrong?"

"Seeing you upset by Ayers upset her."

"I wasn't upset by him," he began then amended his statement at her annoyance. "What he said about making up for sins struck me because of allowing myself to be duped into helping Ellan and Hueil. Then Fitch using my persona to nearly kill my family."

"Everything turned out well for you," said Nigel.

"Thank Jor'el. I don't care a wit about Ayers or his sons! In fact, maybe some good can finally come from that cursed family."

Avatar placed a hand of on Fraser's shoulder at hearing the scornfulness. Understanding the warning gesture, Fraser got down on one knee in front of Mirit, and took hold of her hands.

"I'm sorry you are upset on my account. Please, don't be. I'm fine."

She flashed a touched smile and wiped her eyes.

"I told you he doesn't hold you responsible," said Nigel.

"Responsible?" echoed Fraser, to which Nigel nodded. "No. Responsibility for my past stupidity lies with me. Ayers and his sons are responsible for their actions. Dear Aunt, you had no hand in any of it."

"I know you're both right. I just let it get to me."

"Because you care," said Nigel.

Fraser smiled and squeezed her hand. "Uncle's right. Please don't cry any more. I feel bad for causing you tears." He embraced her and kissed her cheek. "Will you be all right now?"

"Ay," she said in a voice sounding more resolute.

Fraser smiled. "Good." His focus changed to Nigel, and with specific intent. "Wess says March has a few suggestions of those who can aid our plan."

"Did he explain the risk?"

"Ay, but Wess thinks it's best if you also speak to them, which is what I came to call."

Nigel held Mirit's hand. "Will you join us or wait here?"

She tilted her head with determination. "My selfish spasm is over, but our situation isn't, so I'll come."

"That's my girl." Nigel smiled and kissed her hand.

<hr />

Locan beat a hasty retreat after Armus commanded him to stop. He successfully completed his task in creating the distraction for Fitch. When he stumbled upon Reilly, the mortal blabbered on about everything connected to the situation. However, mentioning Ridge put him up in the tree and told him not to climb down, made Locan destroy them. He meant it as a bold message that he was to be reckoned with and would not go tamely like Fitch.

A mile and a half up the hillside overlooking Oakley, he watched and considered. At that distance, his presence would not be sensed while from this vantage point, he could see the entire town. A Guardian's eyesight exceeded mortals. He could make out individuals among the crowd from up to two miles away with a clear line of sight. Earlier he witnessed Ayers' escape from the meadow along with Vidar and Wren's pursuit. He had no doubt the hunters secured Ayers. He followed the group at a safe distance and witnessed Fitch's wounding by Kell, his

231

capture and departure with Vidar. When Kell appeared to sense him, Locan withdrew to Oakley.

By the group's activity, and the fact Vidar and Wren rejoined them, Ayes must be in March's custody. Confirmation came when Virgil and Kendrick entered the jail and the rest went to the inn. He reckoned they would stay the night.

Despite being in mortal form Kell remained a formidable opponent. If not physically, he would do so in logic and planning an offensive against him. He must be careful in considering his next move. The option to simply leave the South Plains was available, but no. For all the aggravation of dealing with him, Fitch served a vital purpose in their enterprise. Kell needed to be disposed of, to avenge both Fitch and Mannix. Thus he watched and considered.

Of course he could use his power to immobilize Virgil and Kendrick and dispose of Ayers. However, guarding him showed they anticipated an attempt on the mortal's life. They might move him to the provincial prison by way of one of the two roads leading out of Oakley. Or dimension travel him to the prison. Locan grinned.

"No. Kell wants me."

The roads were visible from his vantage point. One road entered a grove of trees and other one wound its way down the foothills. To cover both routes required a little surprise of his own, thus he waited until nightfall to make his move.

Chapter 15

THE ELIXIR DID HELP KELL TO SLEEP. ONLY THE NEEDED REST turned into a fitful night of dreams. The scenes ran the gamut of replaying recent events to the possibility of being reunited with his comrades, to the disappointment and dismay at their rejection of him now being mortal. Through it all, an obscure presence held him back. He fought the strong grip, struggling to understand and be understood. In his dream, he heard his name called by a familiar yet distant voice. "Kell … Kel … Kelvin." Someone seized him and he jerked awake.

"Chad?" he said, surprised at who sat beside him and held his arm. Chad wore only his breeches and looked like he just woke up.

"Are you all right? You sounded like you were having a nightmare."

Kell realized he lay in the same bed where he fell asleep. "I think so."

"You fooled me," grumbled Wess. He yawned and stretched. He lay in the other bed. "You woke us, which sent Fraser to the chair." He motioned to where Fraser slept in a cushioned chair in the corner of the room. "When you got too loud, Chad tried to keep you from waking the whole house."

"I'm sorry. What time is it?"

"Dawn."

Kell noticed light filtered into the room and he heard a distant rooster. "I thought you usually woke an hour before dawn?"

Wess turned on his side and propped himself on his elbow. "How would you know? Wait! I know. Some place, sometime you were my orderly, right? Well, I've been trying to break the habit since I retired."

Chad leaned closer to Kell, yet spoke loud enough to be heard. "It'll be easier once he's married. Then he won't want to get out of bed." A pillow struck him in the head.

"Better Vivian than you. You snore," quipped Wess.

"Magan has never complained."

"She probably has her own way of shutting you up."

Kell laughed. A pillow smacked his face, also tossed by Wess.

"That's for encouraging him."

Chad crossed to the chair and slapped Fraser's leg, which startled the teenager. "He's awake and all is well. Just a nightmare."

"Oh, good." Fraser squirmed in the chair to sit up.

"I'm sorry for disturbing you, Highness."

"That's all right. I'm not used to sharing a bed anyway. I hadn't fallen asleep until I got in the chair."

"I'll go to the privy and fetch us water." Chad grabbed the pitcher on his way out.

"Seriously, was I too disruptive?"

"Not until this morning. In fact you were sleeping soundly when we retired," said Wess.

Kell held his head and grunted. "Avatar was right about the elixir helping me sleep, but I wonder if he made it too potent. I normally don't dream."

"Possible. Guardian medicine is powerful. I've seen it have ill effects on some mortals, though it is mostly well tolerated."

Chad returned with Nigel and Avatar accompanying him. Nigel wore his breeches, shirt and boots and more awake then the rest in the room.

"Kelvin. How are you feeling this morning?"

"Avatar poisoned him," said Wess, and winked at Kell.

"What?" the Guardian asked in a tone of skepticism.

"I told you he is in a grumpy mood," said Chad concerning Wess. He finished pouring water into the basin.

"A little lingering grogginess is all," said Kell.

"How is your back?" Avatar examined Kell's shoulders. "Looks better."

"No soreness. I'm fine, just like I said."

"All right," said Nigel, a smile growing. "I needed to be sure since I don't want Wess to be out another sheriff before you can take office."

"I didn't know anything was official."

"I will add my recommendation to Wess' nomination. The king will not decline."

"Thank you, Highness."

"Now, when everyone is ready, we'll go to Joby's for breakfast."

"I'm assuming Ridge has returned," said Kell.

"He did so after seeing Vivian safely home. And we made arrangements for others to help in assuming identities so as not to signal our intentions prematurely." Nigel and Avatar left.

Joby just opened for the day when the group arrived. Again the generous and jovial innkeeper lavished them with a hearty and satisfying meal.

"Indeed, Joby and his family feed their patrons well," said Nigel as they made their way back to the mercantile.

"I've not found many inns with such quality food," said Wess.

"He just needs an indoor privy," teased Fraser.

"Will I ever live that down?" chided Ellis.

"No," said Chad, Fraser and Valery in unison.

Ellis frowned, which brought Nigel's hand to his shoulder and the prince to say, "Consider this as consolation. Angus, Tyrone and Titus weren't here to witness it."

"Their absence hasn't stopped them from teasing you on matters they didn't witness."

"You're right, it is no consolation." He patted Ellis' shoulder.

They entered the mercantile through the back door. The front door remained shuttered and closed to patrons. Inside, four local men dressed like Kell, Chad, Ridge and Wren waited. Two were the tallest found in Oakley for impersonating Guardians. Both stood near six and half feet, making a six-inch height difference for Wren and a foot for Ridge. The one posing for Wren was an older teen, thin, lanky and wearing a long brunette wig to help convince any casual passer by he was a woman. At a distance, they hoped to fool Locan since the mortals would be riding, thus lessening the obvious height differential. With Armus, Avatar, Virgil and Kendrick being warriors there was already a natural height advantage from other Guardians. There would be enough separation from the imposters so as not to detect contrast.

"When you four exit by the back door, we'll leave out the front to draw attention," Nigel instructed the real Kell, Ridge, Chad and Wren. He looked steadily at Kell. "Take no unnecessary risks."

"No one wants this to work out more than me."

"Try to keep them safe," said Nigel to Ridge. He then patted Chad on the arm in a show of encouragement and signal for departure.

The assigned group quickly exited the back. Wren and Ridge turned to the left while Kell and Chad went to the right. All kept to the shadows and out of sight. Nigel and the others left by way of the front door and headed for the jail.

March waited outside along with one of his deputies. Both held the reins of the group's horses. "All is ready for your departure, Champion."

"Not *all* is ready," said Avatar in a distinct tone of satisfaction. "Deputy?"

"On the back porch of the jail as you instructed."

"We'll be back shortly." Avatar took the reins of a horse and went down the alley.

Nigel smiled. "He's enjoying this too much."

"Wren will get back at him," said Vidar.

Being early in the morning, the rear porch of the jail remained in shadows and away from prying eyes. Wren now wore Ayers' clothes with an old cloak placed in such a way as to hide her crossbow but accessible if needed. She tucked her hair under the ratty torn hat. Kendrick and Virgil waited with her, and both amused compared to her impatience. Hearing an approaching horse, she stepped off the porch. Avatar widely smiled.

"Don't start!" she warned.

"Me? No, I rather savor the moment in silence." His silver eyes were merry in surveying her appearance.

Kendrick and Virgil chuckled. She vaulted into the saddle.

"Easy! You're supposed to be an infirmed mortal male," said Avatar.

She placed her feet in the stirrups and found her legs severely bent at the knees. "How do you expect me to ride like this?"

"You can't have your legs dangling. In fact, I may have to shorten the stirrups if the cloak doesn't cover your legs enough."

"Oh, no!" She tried to slap his hands away only he persisted in his efforts. She tolerated him fixing the cloak for her legs to appear a normal length. "Seriously, do you think this will fool him?"

"Let's hope so." Avatar placed a hand on the saddle horn to look at her. The teasing was gone from his eyes and voice. "We won't let anything happen to you."

She gave him a confident grin. "I know." She squirmed in discomfort. "My legs are already cramping."

He chuckled, and took the reins in preparation to lead the horse. "Slouch and look infirmed."

"Is this good enough?" she complained and crouched down.

"No talking. Once we're on the road we don't want him to hear you."

"Then I'll just kick you when I want to get your attention."

"Don't move so he can see you," said Virgil.

"Come here so I can kick you."

"Seeing you still and quiet is best done from afar."

Avatar smiled at Wren. "His sword is getting sharper." He avoided her attempt to kick him. "I hope that relieved your leg cramp. Now put your foot back, we're leaving."

Avatar led the horse from rear of the jail to the front street. Kendrick and Virgil followed at a safe distance. When they arrived, the mortals were mounted and waiting.

"*Now*, we're ready," announced Avatar, trying not to smile.

Nigel spoke loud enough to be heard by any passer-by. "Deputy, make certain all is well after we leave with the prisoner."

"Ay, Champion."

Nigel waved at the man dressed as a ranger. "Ridge, take the lead."

March waited until they were out of sight before going inside the jail. He rushed to the cell hallway. The real Ridge waited at the door to Ayers' cell, the latter wore different clothes. The other prisoner was nowhere to be seen.

"They're away," said March.

"Time to join the others." Ridge turned his hand in a flicking manner and the cell unlocked. When Ayers stepped out, the ranger took hold of him and they disappeared in a flash of white light. They reappeared at the livery to join Kell and Chad. Ayers fainted and Ridge tapped the mortal's face to rouse him. "Wake up."

Ayers blinked and shook his head in an effort to regain his senses. "I don't think I've ever done that before."

Kell took Ayers' arm to get the man's full attention. "Are you sure you can do this? If not, speak now, for many lives are at risk."

"I can and will do this."

Satisfied, Kell nodded. "Mount."

Being infirmed made it difficult, so Ridge lifted Ayers into the saddle.

"We'll meet you a half-mile outside of town," said Kell to Ridge.

The ranger nodded and vanished. They rode from the livery stable to take the second road from town; the one that wound down the hillside to the plains.

The men posing as Ridge and Wren lead the group. Vidar hung back to escort Nigel, Wess and Mirit. About ten feet behind them, Avatar held onto the bridle of Wren's horse. She tried to appear as small and feeble as possible. Virgil followed with Ellis and Valery behind him. Cody trotted beside Valery's horse. Fraser rode with those posing as Chad and Kell. Kendrick and Armus guarded the rear.

"We've travelled over a mile with no sign of Locan," said Wess.

"I didn't expect anything the first mile since Guardians can sense another's presence over that distance. From here on, we need to be more alert," said Nigel.

"I understand the precautions since last time we weren't prepared. But what can he do against all of us now that we are ready?" asked Ellis.

"Don't under estimate Locan," warned Virgil. "He placed a curse on a tree that ensnared the general and attacked us. Ridge had to destroy it to keep the curse from spreading."

Ellis seemed confused by the answer, so Avatar explained. "All Guardians can speak commands to influence or manipulate nature if needed. Curses come only from the Dark Way. Locan now freely employs such means to aid his capabilities."

Wary, Ellis looked at the grove of trees they approached. "Maybe it would be better if the ranger was here," he spoke with discretion.

Avatar felt Wren prod him with her foot. "Vidar can sense any uneasiness in nature." At a second, harder kick, he winced. "And another," he gruffly added.

"Ay, Cody," said Valery in a light, teasing voice.

Avatar received a third kick from Wren. He glared over his shoulder at Valery for receiving the consequences of her statement. She sweetly smiled at him.

Upon entering the grove, all conversation stopped to keep a watchful eye on the trees for signs of movement. Wren started to look around and Avatar poked her leg.

"Be still," he said in a harsh commanding whisper.

Vidar stopped to raise a warning only a second before it happened.

"*Ionnsaigh! Marbh!*" a deep unnatural voice came from an old oak tree.

Branches reached down toward them and roots sprang up from the ground trying to wrap around the horses' legs. The frightened animals attempted to avoid being ensnared. Those armed with swords, drew their weapons to hack and slice at the branches and roots.

A branch knocked Valery off her horse. A root shot up to trap her and she rolled away. It lashed the ground where she had been with a whipping sound. Cody snatched the root between his teeth. It lifted him off the ground and flung him across the road. She scrambled to her feet and used her sword to cleave the root in half.

"Cody?"

Unharmed, the wolf rejoined her. Once more they were on the defensive against the attack.

Ellis' horse reared when a root sprang from the ground. He managed to stay in the saddle and hack off the root tip. Wounded, the root retreated into the ground. He turned his horse to help Valery. A branch grabbed him from the saddle and held him aloft about twenty feet.

"Ellis!" Valery raced to the tree holding him and sliced at the trunk.

The tree creaked in anger and Ellis cried out in pain. His sword fell to the ground as he struggled against the crushing grip.

"You just made it mad!" said Fraser. He moved his horse near the tree, stood in the saddle and jumped onto a lower branch. The tree began shaking in an effort to dislodge him. "Valery! Distract it!"

She heeded his instruction and began taking swipes at the tree. She dodged the branch and root trying to drive her away.

"What are you doing? Get down before it snares you!" said Ellis. He grimaced in trying to withstand the pain of entrapment.

"Not before I free you." The tree did another more violent shake to dislodge him. Fraser withdrew his dagger and plunged it into the trunk to maintain his balance. Again the tree creaked at the wounding.

"Ah!" exclaimed Ellis at more crushing. He fainted and hung limp in the tree's grasp.

"Ellis!" shouted Valery.

Twang! Twang! Vidar's shots impaled the branch behind and in front of Ellis. Wounded, the tree released him and he began falling.

"No!" cried Valery.

Kendrick heard her shout. Being too far away, he pointed his sword at Ellis and commanded in the Ancient, "Stop!" Instantly, Ellis hung in midair. "Slow and gently." Kendrick lowered his sword and Ellis floated to the ground, still unconscious.

Anxious, Valery knelt. "Ellis?"

He groaned and blinked his eyes. He woke at her touch on his face. A root sprung up beside Ellis. Kendrick pulled them aside to avoid it.

"Root to ice!" shouted Virgil. Ice shot from his sword and encased the root.

"Kendrick!" called Fraser. The tree's violent reaction to the wounding by Vidar caused him to slip. He dangled from the tree by holding onto the hilt of his dagger buried in the trunk.

Kendrick left Valery and Ellis and positioned himself beneath Fraser. "Let go."

Fraser struggled to look down. One hand slipped and he seized the dagger harder. "Are you serious?"

"Trust me and let go."

Fraser closed his eyes. With a face screwed up in fear, he let go. Instead of floating, his eyes snapped open at being caught.

"You were just out of my arms' reach." Kendrick set Fraser on his feet.

Nigel, Mirit and Wess fought from horseback in defense of the townsmen. The men were terrified and uncertain of what to do against Dark Way enchanted trees.

A branch picked up Ridge's double and flung him like a slingshot into another tree. He collapsed in a heap on the ground. The men posing for Chad and Kell managed to free their horses and retreated from the grove the way they came. The teenager dressed like Wren knew how to handle a crossbow. He made several decent shots before a branch knocked him unconscious.

A branch of an oak tree ensnared Nigel and his horse. Nigel's sword arm was free. The angle made it difficult to hack his way loose.

Armus called upon his special power of added strength of twenty Guardians. He used his sword to chop at the base of the tree. With such might, it only took four swings to slice through thick trunk. The branch released Nigel and the horse before toppling over. The animal hit the ground hard. Nigel rolled away to avoid the flying hooves. The tree fell into another tree, starting a wave that took down four of the attacking trees. Armus breathed heavy in recovery and flinched in pain from the effort to utilize his power. He then helped Nigel to stand.

"Are you hurt?"

Nigel took brief stock of his state. "I don't think so. Let's see if the horse is injured."

Due to fright and agitation, the animal began to bolt at their approach. Armus seized the reins and spoke calming words in the Ancient. The horse responded by standing still, although breathing heavy and chomping at the bit.

Nigel examined the horse. "She appears sound."

Wren fought to steady the frightened horse when a root shot up from the ground to grab the animal. Avatar chopped off the root before it reached the horse. Another root came from the base of a tree toward him. Wren brought out her crossbow loaded and ready.

"Avatar! Down!"

He ducked. Her shot whizzed over his head and pinned the root to its tree. The distraction gave enough time for the other root to reach up and wrap spindling twig-like fingers around the horse's neck. The animal reared in an attempt to break free, throwing Wren backwards. Avatar dodged the frightened horse to reach Wren in time to hack off another branch before it ensnared her. A larger, thicker branch smacked him in the chest and sent him across the road.

Vidar pulled Wren to her feet. "We have to end this!"

They held hands and spoke in unison. "Nature, hear your creator's voice and give no heed to darkness sway. By Jor'el's will, we chase the curse away!" Twice they repeated the phrase. Soon the attacking roots withered back into the ground, the branches returned to their places and the trees became still.

Avatar rose. He rubbed his chest where the branch smacked him, and took a careful breath to gauge any injury. Pain, yet nothing felt broken. In measured steps, he joined the others. All stood alert and watchful to make certain the attack had ended. No further movement.

"Are you hurt?" asked Wren.

Avatar stopped rubbing his chest. "No."

"Good. Here's your sword." Virgil accidentally on purpose hit Avatar hard in the chest with the hilt. Avatar flinched with a muffled gasp. "Sorry." Virgil's apology sounded far from sincere.

"He can hit straws targets too." Wren chuckled.

Avatar shoved Virgil toward the side of the road. "Reconnaissance!"

Virgil joined Armus and Vidar in examining the trees.

"Truly, is anything broken?" asked Wren.

"No, just bruised. Let's help the others."

Nigel moved to Ridge's double. By the pale features, angle of his head and lack of a pulse, the man died of a broken neck. He said a prayer and closed the man's eyes. Nearby, Wess help the teenage archer sit up. "How is he?"

"Dazed, otherwise unharmed," answered Wess.

"The others fled," said Kendrick.

"Can't blame them for that," said Ellis.

"Are you all right?" asked Mirit.

"I may have a few bruised or cracked ribs." He rubbed his left side, ginger and flinching.

"You and Avatar. A branch smacked him across the road."

"The tree seemed bent on killing Ellis, not just knocking him around," said Valery.

"I think they meant to kill us all. Vidar and I were able to counter the attack. So it was of the Dark Way," said Wren.

"Locan?" asked Nigel.

"A logical guess. We won't know for certain until reconnaissance is completed," said Avatar. He tried not to show too much discomfort.

Wess joined them. "I told Fenton when he's ready, to take his friend back to town. I also gave him some money to treat his injury and for a proper burial."

"Fenton," said Nigel.

"Ay, Champion."

"Did your friend have any family?"

"His parents, and he was supposed to marry next month."

Nigel sighed in lament. "Tell his parents and betrothed, the king expresses his condolences and gratitude for his courage. As a token, they are exempt from this year's taxes. I know it doesn't replace their loss, but hopefully it will ease some burden."

"I will tell them, Champion."

Armus, Virgil and Vidar returned. All wore grim expression. Vidar made the report. "Locan infected the trees for a predetermined attack."

"That means he knew we were coming this way," said Wess.

"Not necessarily. He could have set a trap on one road and lies in wait on the other in order to cover both routes," said Armus.

"They won't survive a direct attack, we barely escaped a trap," said Mirit in urgency.

"Find them!" Nigel ordered Armus and Vidar before mounting.

243

Chapter 16

RIDGE LED THE GROUP. AYERS RODE BETWEEN KELL AND CHAD. They rounded the second bend about a mile and a half from town.

"I hope the others are all right," said Chad.

"We've come further than I thought without trouble," said Kell.

"If he fell for the deception, the others are having trouble," said Ridge. His eyes shifted about. "I sense uneasiness among the trees."

The loud cawing and cry of birds made them look back in the direction they came. Ridge reached for his quarterstaff. A loud command in the Ancient sent him flying across the road and into a tree. His neck snapped back, striking his head against the trunk. He fell to the ground, dazed and fighting unconsciousness.

Armed with his sword, Locan appeared on the road in front of Kell, Chad and Ayers. "Trouble stands before you."

Chad and Kell reached for their swords but Locan moved quicker in attacking them. Kell jerked his horse out of the way. The animal stumbled and he did an awkward dismount to avoid another controlled fall. Locan's blade slashed the neck of Chad's horse, killing the animal. It fell to the ground, pinning Chad's left leg underneath it. He lay on top of his sword with the hilt poked into his side.

While Locan concentrated on Chad and Kell, Ayers turned his horse around in retreat. It didn't last long. Locan threw his dagger. The force of impact buried it hilt deep at the base of Ayers neck. He fell from the horse, dead.

Kell sneered in anger at Ayers' demise. He hurried to help Chad before Locan attacked again. He pushed with all his strength and the carcass slightly moved. He tried again. His arms failed and the horse fell, making Chad cry out in pain.

"Sorry. I'll try something else."

"No! It's dead and I can't move," said Chad through gritted teeth.

Locan advanced and raised his sword to strike at them. Suddenly, he lurched forward when a blow from behind sent him to his knees. Unsteady and blinking, Ridge grimaced against the pain his effort cost him. Still, he moved to strike Locan again. The warrior bolted up, whirled around, caught the quarterstaff and thrust his sword through Ridge's body. The ranger grew wide-eyed in surprise. He released his staff and staggered to the side of the road where he collapsed. He didn't disappear.

"Ridge!" shouted Kell. With the ranger seriously wounded and Chad helplessly pinned, he had to confront Locan. He drew his sword.

"Kelvin, don't!" Chad tried to snatch Kell's leg and missed. Desperate, he focused on trying to free himself. Despite the difficulty, he took out his dagger then pulled himself up on the saddle. He attempted to cut the girth and loosen the saddle. At that angle, it hurt to hold himself up.

Fifty feet from Chad, and across the road, Kell attacked Locan. The warrior easily turned him aside. Kell assumed the Jor'ellian first position.

Locan scornfully chuckle. "That won't help and you know it, *Kell.*"

"So Fitch told you."

He heaved a nonchalant shrug. "Call it destiny or fate, that you, the mightiest of all should come to so pitiful an end—as a *mortal.* You're only chance of survival is to run."

Kell knew Locan spoke the truth about the inevitable end of such a mismatch in power and strength. He had been responsible for the demise of mortals, those who turned to evil. He wouldn't yield, he couldn't. "I have never run from a fight and I won't start now, especially from a traitor!" He launched at Locan, and once more, was easily turned aside.

"Traitor? Who was changed into a mortal?"

"You and Fitch did this to me when the *madah-dune* attacked. What Dark Way trickery did you use?" demanded Kell. He again struck out at Locan. "Tell me!"

Locan exchanges a few blows with Kell before shoving him back. "We didn't do it. Not that hasn't been amusing to watch," he said with a hearty laugh. "Oh, you must have really angered Jor'el for him to demote and debase *his captain*."

That stung! Kell again attacked. Locan humored him with a few more exchanges before using his a stiff arm to send Kell off his feet.

"Enough! Run and live out your pitiful mortal years in shame and disgrace. It will be more amusing and satisfying to watch than killing you outright."

With a growl of outrage, Kell pushed himself to his feet to rush Locan. The warrior waved his hand and sent Kell flying and smashing into a tree. The impact broke Kell's left shoulder. In terrible pain, he fell hard to his knees.

"I gave you a chance." Locan advanced.

Kell use his sword to stand. With only the use of one arm, he couldn't successfully deflect the attack. Locan disarmed him, and the warrior's sword plunged completely through his chest. Stupefied by the lethal stroke, Kell stumbled and fell into a ditch at the side of the road.

"So much for the once mighty captain." Locan spat on ground.

Exhausted from the effort of trying to cut the saddle girth, Chad fell back on his elbows in time to witness the fatal blow. "Kelvin!" His call drew Locan's attention. The warrior advanced on him. This was not the way for a soldier to die. Chad readied his dagger in defense.

Locan came within a couple of yards when a booming voice shouted, "Traitor!"

Chad strained his neck to Armus racing to intervene.

Locan faced the full fury and might of Armus in an exchange of sword clashes. At one point Locan wandered too close, and Armus sent him off his feet by a vicious backhand. Locan rose to his knees to block another attack. For the brief moment the swords hung together. Locan seized his dagger and swiped at Armus' leg. Armus leapt aside to avoid the dagger. Locan rose to his feet and began to summon his power in the Ancient when …

"An dealanach siuthad de namh!"

Locan's head snapped around in time to see Avatar point his sword. A bolt of lightning shot out from the tip of the blade. Locan tried to dive out of the way, when the explosion of the bolt on the ground sent him hurling through the air. Another command, and another bolt sent Locan again diving to avoid being struck. Locan scrambled to his feet to watch Avatar ready for a third strike. A quarterstaff caught him under the chin and he staggering backwards. He managed to catch his balance, when Wren and Vidar simultaneously fired. Two crossbow darts impacted Locan in the chest. He vanished in the grey light of demise.

Ridge swayed and leaned heavy on his quarterstaff to remain standing. He felt support about the waist. Virgil. Ridge shook his head. "You can't help me this time," he murmured before losing consciousness. Blood stained the entire front of his tunic.

"I'm taking him to Eldric!" Virgil lifted Ridge in his arms and vanished in the white light of dimension travel.

Wess, Nigel, Mirit and Fraser reined their horses to a stop. Nigel leapt from the saddle beside Chad. Mirit and Fraser hurried to dismount.

"I'm pinned." Chad grunted in frustrated and shoved at the saddle.

"Is your leg broken?" she asked.

"Maybe. I can't tell for certain, the horse is heavy."

"Avatar! Lift the beast so Fraser and I can drag him out." Nigel and Fraser got into position behind Chad and held him under the arms.

Avatar went around to the other side of the horse and grabbed either end of the saddle. "Ready?"

"Ay," said Nigel.

Avatar pulled on the saddle and lifted the horse to a near standing position. Nigel and Fraser drug Chad free just in time. The girth broke, leaving the saddle in Avatar's hands when the horse fell back to the ground.

"I tried to cut the girth to free myself." Chad rubbed his left leg.

Avatar tossed aside the saddle to examine Chad's leg.

"Where is Kelvin?" asked Wess.

"Dead," said Chad. He flinched at the examination. "He tried to protect me and Ridge, but no match for Locan." He motioned toward the other side of the road.

Wess struggled with anger and sorrow. "Find his body!"

Armus, Wren, Vidar and Kendrick searched the area on foot. Ellis and Valery carefully maneuvered their horses to make a search.

Cody sniffed the ground then bolted down the road to the ditch. He sniffed a small pool of blood and pawed at the hilt of a sword. He whimpered then let out a mournful howl.

All heard Cody. Being the closest, Armus reached the ditch first. Cody yipped when the Guardian knelt. Armus placed a hand on the ground next to the bloody spot. He quickly withdrew his hand and lowered his head to whisper a prayer. Cody nudged Armus. He responded by patting the wolf's head. He picked up the sword and stood. Wess, Ellis, Vidar, Wren and Valery arrived.

"This is where Kelvin fell," he said.

"So, where is he?" asked Wess.

"Gone."

"Mortals don't just vanish!"

"Under normal circumstances, no. Upon inspection, I got a similar sense to how he arrived in the South Plains. Locan must have used some Dark Way power and sent Kelvin where we won't find him."

"Why would he do that?" asked Ellis.

Armus shrugged. "Any number of reasons—anger, irritation. We won't know unless Kelvin survives and is able to return."

"Do you believe he survived?" asked Wess.

Armus sighed. "Sadly, no. Not many mortals survive a Guardian encounter."

The answer was unacceptable, and Wess argued. "Nigel did! And he fought a Shadow Warrior."

"His survival was added by the arrival of Kell and myself," said Vidar.

Wess' jowls flexed and his expression shifted between regret and determination. "Though our acquaintance was brief, I owe him much. Give me his sword. I'll keep it in case he returns." Armus yielded it, and Wess stuck the sword in the saddle sheath. He returned to where Nigel, Mirit, Fraser and Avatar helped Chad. "How is he?"

248

"His leg isn't broken, just badly bruised in a number of places and the ankle swollen," said Avatar. "He'll need to stay off it for at least a week, two would be better."

"Can he ride?" asked Nigel.

"He shouldn't."

"Take him home."

"I can make it," said Chad.

"No. Our task here is done. Return as soon as you can," Nigel spoke the last sentence to Avatar.

The Guardian lifted Chad in his arms and vanished.

Ayers' body lay on the road with Kendrick examining him.

"What about Ayers?" asked Nigel.

"Dead."

Nigel gave Mirit a quick look. She appeared to be holding up well so he said to Kendrick, "See he's properly buried before we return to Oakley." He then asked her, "How are you doing?"

"About Ayers? I'm dealing with it. I feel more sorry about Kelvin."

"We all do. Yet, along with sorrow is also gratitude." His eyes darted toward Wess, which made her smile.

"Not to mention finally dealing with Fitch," said Fraser. He had fetched the horses and held out the reins to her horse.

She mounted. "Your father will be pleased by how you handled yourself when confronting him."

Nigel mounted and moved his horse beside Wess. "I hope Kelvin does survive. If not, the debt goes beyond you personally."

"I still have to tell Vivian. Although she assures me she has no feelings of affection for him, this will hit her hard."

"We'll tell her together. Then," he smiled "plan a wedding. Focus on that, for both your sakes."

Wess grinned in agreement. "He would have made a good sheriff."

"So would March," said Fraser.

Wess regarded the younger prince. "I think you're right."

"Come. Kendrick will join us when he's done." Nigel turned his horse for Oakley.

Nigel insisted upon stopping at Burleigh castle to rest from the events of Oakley before continuing to the farmhouse. They appeared cleaned and refreshed when arriving. Unfortunately, that didn't help Wess in telling Vivian about Kelvin. She sat at the kitchen table in shock. Lester didn't appear much better. Donovan quietly told Drusilla to fetch wine for recovery.

Wess sat beside Vivian and held her hand. "I'm truly sorry. I wish there was an easy way to tell you."

She shook her head. "There is no easy way when speaking of . . . death." She wept and he held her.

"It is more than his death," said Lester in vexation. "After enduring our suspicions and ridicule, he placed everything aside to help, and it cost his life."

Wess fought a pricked frown to reply. "Know that he and I made amends. In fact, I wanted to recommend he become my new sheriff."

"With my endorsement," said Nigel.

"I suppose that is some consolation," groused Lester.

"More than a consolation, it is a proper reward. He exposed Locan and Fitch, identified those responsible for the rash of crimes, and saved the lives of Ridge and Chad. For that, I will always be grateful." A brief look of melancholy overcame Nigel.

"Chad will recover. Magan will make sure," said Avatar.

Lester gave a feeble wave, as his vexation turned to regret. "I wish more could have been done while he lived to make up for how badly we treated him."

"He held no bitterness or resentment when he and the count spoke in Oakley," said Avatar.

"Ayers held deep seeded bitterness and acted on it," said Nigel.

"Ayers," snorted Lester in annoyance. He accepted the cup of wine from Donovan. "I don't think either Gareth or Zebulon believed he had it in him. To them he was an incompetent whipped puppy."

"I don't think any of us thought him capable," said Mirit.

"Lunch is ready, sir," said Drusilla demurely.

"Is there enough for guests?"

"Ay, sir."

"We won't disturb you further," said Nigel.

"No, please. We can use the company."

As the mortals arranged themselves at the table to eat, Armus slipped out the back door. Avatar said a private word to the other Guardians before he and Vidar left. Armus stood at the oak tree staring at the bench.

"What troubles you?" asked Avatar.

Armus' focus remained on at the bench. "I never discovered the mystery surrounding Kelvin. I can't recall a time I was unable to discern an enigma about a mortal."

"Sometimes we don't know the answer, but we can't let failure stop us from doing our duty, and you didn't," said Vidar.

"Not failure! I was prevented by the vague image I kept encountering."

"Fitch and Locan."

"No! They weren't powerful enough in the Dark Way to cloud my thinking or repulse me like in the field. I swear it had a direct link to Kelvin."

Vidar's expression grew confused and he reasoned out loud. "You said Kelvin proved he had no connection to the Dark Way. So if Fitch and Locan weren't strong enough to thwart you how could Kelvin?"

"No, no!" chided Armus in angry frustration and sat on the bench.

Avatar sat beside him. "You felt a similar sense on the road where he died like in the field where he appeared, didn't you?"

Armus' look was sharp and direct. "I accept you disputing my reasoning and opinion, but not my sensing! No one can tell me otherwise."

Avatar replied with calm compassion. "I speak in sympathy not accusation. I've been too concerned for you and others to bother about myself. However, in Oakley, when I treated Kelvin, we spoke about Kell. I felt compelled to admit my feelings of loss and grief. I don't mind telling you, it hurt. I miss Kell more than I can say." He paused for a deep breath before continuing. "Of course Kelvin expressed sympathy, believing he upset me. I told him it was my catharsis, similar to yours with Fitch."

"Less violent, I hope."

Avatar flashed an impulsive smile. "Ay. Yet during our conversation, I got the same sense you did concerning him."

"What is that?" asked Vidar.

Avatar looked up the archer. "A striking familiarity of mannerisms reminiscent of Kell. Even the likeness of his features and coloring were hard to miss." His brows grew level in recollection. "He precisely mimicked Armus' voice, speech pattern and facial expression in teasing about his *controlled fall*. I thought I *was* talking to Kell."

"Did he also claim to read you like a book?" asked Armus.

"Not in those exact word. He said the way my goatee wrinkles when I smirk is a dead giveaway of my wit. The sense of familiarity intensified, for who else knows us so well?"

Vidar questioned Armus. "You sensed this earlier?"

"Ay, during several conversations he and I had in which his tone, look and inflection were eerily similar to Kell. When he defended us to Spaulding, I experienced a deep personal empathy in my spirit I found surprising. I questioned him, and he declared he would die to protect us. Ultimately he did so in defense of Ridge."

"And Chad," said Avatar.

"Strange the rest of us didn't sense a similarity," mused Vidar.

"You weren't created Kell's counterpart!"

Avatar laid a restraining hand upon Armus' shoulder for calm, and spoke to Vidar. "At first I thought his sense was brought on by grief. Oakley showed me differently."

"I tried to determine the source before making a full disclosure, but you and Ridge pressed me," Armus reminded Avatar.

"We were trying to comfort and encourage you, not press you. Same as Vidar and I are attempting to do now."

"Have you felt anything since Kelvin's death?" asked Vidar.

Armus shook his head, his voice and expression rueful. "Although, when inspecting the ground, I experienced the same intense chill as when Kell vanished. I never felt that for a mortal before. The frustrating part is I may never know why I had such conflicting feelings about him or how it fits into helping unmask Fitch and Locan."

"The answers may come in time," said Vidar. A small smile began as his eyes shifted from Armus to Avatar then back again. "Perhaps after you become captain."

"Oh, no! This has shown me I don't have the skill or perception to be captain."

"You said you were prevented."

Armus again shook his head. "That wouldn't have stopped Kell from discovering the mystery I did not."

"With the Palace about to be rebuilt, we need a captain, and there is no one better suited or qualified than you to fill the void."

Armus grew apprehensive. "Kell and I were created to compliment each other in command. I don't want to act alone. Nor can I imagine him not being present for the rebuilding." He struggled as new emotions surfaced. He felt Avatar's supporting hand on his shoulder.

Vidar's gaze shifted to Avatar. "Who said you would act alone? There are still two remaining of the High Trio."

Avatar snorted a laugh at the implication. Vidar kept staring at him. "You can't be serious," he said to Vidar then to Armus, "He can't be serious."

"You were created to be the captain's aide. There is no one better suited or qualified to be my lieutenant."

"Suddenly feeling inadequate?" asked Vidar.

"Humbled."

"Now you understand what I mean at the initial suggestion of me being captain," said Armus. "But we talk ahead of ourselves since Jor'el has said nothing. For the time being," he stood and drew Avatar to his feet, "we must see the mortals through whatever comes their way. We start by returning to Waldron and reporting all to the king."

Chapter 17

H E THOUGHT SOMEONE TOUCHED HIM AND SAID HIS NAME, only his mind dazed and uncertain. He then remembered being involved in a battle with Locan and became alert. He sprang to his feet in anticipation of attack. His eyes squinted at the brightness surrounding him. It took a moment to comprehend that he was no longer on the ground and saw no trees. In fact, a bright grayish expanse stretched as far as endlessly in every direction with a view of the distant world beneath his feet. *The Fringe!*

Thunderstruck, he felt for his wound. He still wore mortal clothes with a hole in the fabric where Locan's sword ran him through. "I'm dead!" he said in horrid realization. His whole existence, both as a mortal and immortal was ended. Overcome, he dropped to his knees.

In desperation he cried up to heaven. "Why? What did I do wrong? Please, Jor'el, tell what I did that you so punished me! That you inflict despair upon my comrades, who mourn my death!" He waited in anxious dread for the answer. When met with silence, he hung his head and bitterly wept.

After several agonizing moments of heart wrenching sobbing, he heard a voice speak his name, "Kell." The voice echoed from all around before a hazy figure stood in front of him. The opalescent eyes were kind and tender in regard of him.

"Kell," said an indulgent voice coming from the haze. "I did not inflict sorrow upon anyone. Grief is natural due to their deep attachment to you."

"But I couldn't comfort them! Why? How did I displease you that you changed me into a mortal and let me die? Or allow them to suffer grief a second time?"

"They did not know Kelvin like they do Kell."

"Why? For pity's sake, please, tell me what I did to anger you. Do not leave me ignorant or my friends comfortless."

"You did not displease or anger me, yet there were personal reasons along with divine justice that needed to be addressed."

The answer confused him. He wiped the tears from his eyes to clear his vision. "If I didn't anger you, what could those reasons be?"

"The first reason was to draw out Locan and Fitch. They could have kept up their charade for years, and already survived too long for their crimes. I permitted the *madah-dune* to overcome you to facilitate your change."

"Why as a mortal? I could have assumed an identity to fool them."

"Your *death* provided the motivation for Tyrone, Nigel and your fellow Guardians to pursue the matter and deal with the last remaining traitors of the coup. Granted, I understood their need to grieve, to rest and recover, but the time had come for action. Once Fitch discovered you in mortal form, you became their focal point."

"So I led him and Locan into the open for the others to find, the same as Avatar exposed Hueil in Tunlund?"

"Ay."

This didn't provide much clarification. "I could have done so in disguise, not fully mortal."

"Now, for the personal reasons."

Voices came from all around, as he heard a replay of his exchange with Armus, Wren, Vidar and Avatar en route from the hunt.

"In our position we're supposed to be above such feelings and maintain a calm objective to better serve them," he rebuffed.

"Oh, really? You've been able to do that?" challenged Armus.

"As captain, it is my duty."

"You fooled me, especially when Shannan was in danger. I thought you'd take on Dagar and his forces single-handed."

"Or when you ordered me to destroy Morrell for killing her," said Vidar.

"You both sound as bad as the mortals," he chided.

Kell winced at his own pompous condescension. The replay continued with Avatar speaking.

"Kell, despite our station and duty, we can't deny there are times we are affected by our feelings."

"I'm not denying them. I just control them better when they flare up."

That stung, as Kell recalled his difficulty dealing with self-control as a mortal. He experienced a temper, sarcasm and impulsive sensation toward Vivian, which resulted in jealousy toward Wess. All were emotions he considered weaknesses in mortals, despite some of their more endearing qualities. Wren's voice and comment drove home the point of his insensitivity.

"I thought we moved beyond such male arrogance after what happened with the Sorens. Next he'll say all females are emotional."

"If he does, will you shoot him?" asked Avatar.

Kell now wished she had shot him in listening to his callous response.

"This isn't about arrogance or denial, it's about duty and controlling one's emotions and not acting fickle like mortals."

He heard Armus' response to his rebuff. *"Any louder and they will hear you. Then try explaining your unfeeling reasoning to them."*

He bowed his head in regret and shame. He couldn't look up when Jor'el spoke.

"You boasted with pride about your knowledge of mortals while denying your own weakness. Mortals, who look to you for help, and consider you their friend. In that conversation, you scorned them without sympathy or the understanding only experience can bring. Tell me, Kell, what did it feel like to have your affection rejected?"

He swallowed back his emotion to glance up and reply. "It hurt my heart. Unlike anything I have ever known."

"To be wrongly accused, mocked and unable to convince anyone you were telling the truth? To feel pain and experience sorrow and not be comforted or give comfort?"

Kell whimpered and bowed his head again. "Utter agony! Oh, I'm sorry I let my pride become an obstacle! I swear," he said, looking up with new tears upon his cheeks, "as you know my heart, I would never turn my back on you, my comrades or the mortals you allowed me to serve and protect for so long."

"I know. Still, a strong lesson was needed to prevent such pride from taking root. The same pride and arrogance led to *Dagar's* fall. He refused to learn when I gave him the opportunity, and instead, caused rebellion. So with you, my captain and first created, I took more drastic steps. Especially with the time of my return drawing near."

Kell winced in distress that Jor'el compared his action and speech to Dagar. Because of Dagar's rebellion the Dark Way infected Allon and caused so much misery, tragedy and suffering. Things he fought hard against, along with his fellow Guardians, with some vanquished. Good and faithful mortals also fought and died along side Guardians. He couldn't imagine ever being so evil or causing such sorrow and affliction.

"Painful though it was, I can accept your divine instruction. For I would rather be dead than become like Dagar." He looked up. "My deepest regret is I will never be able to reassure my friends and comrades. Or to see your Palace rebuilt and the restoration of Guardian rule." His voice faltered with emotion then he became gripped by a sudden panic. "What about Vivian, Wess and Lester? I don't want them to suffer because of my foolishness."

Jor'el's eyes smiled. "They will be fine. Wess needed some prodding. Providing a rival gave him the prompting to act, thus answering Lester's prayer to grant Vivian a long-loved companion."

Kell impulsively smiled, which vanished with another question. "Will Lester lose his sight?"

"Not until all is settled with his family. He will be well cared for."

"So my death proved good for them. At least I could do one last service," he droned and wiped the tears from his face.

"*Kelvin's* death," stressed Jor'el.

Kell shrugged, discomposed and confused. "There's a difference?"

"Ay." A hand appeared from out of the haze and drew Kell to his feet. "Behold the difference!"

Light engulfed Kell and surged in brightness. With a flare, the light vanished to reveal Kell restored to his former station complete with new uniform and sword. For a moment, he marveled then smiled at the renewed power and strength coursing through his body. He drew his sword and his golden eyes brightened with authority. It felt good to hold the blade again. Regarding the sword, a symbol of his station, he became concerned.

"But I, Kell, am believed dead. How will I explain my return? And what of Kelvin?"

"Only to the comrades with you in the South Plains will you tell of your time as Kelvin. That way, your prayer for comfort and peace on their behalf will be granted. Once done, it will be to the mortals and the rest of the Guardians that Kell never died, rather returned to the heavenlies after the *madah-dune* attack and issuing orders about Locan and Fitch. You will return for the wedding and cornerstone ceremony. The mortals will remember Kelvin for what he did during his short time among them. The lessons for you and your comrades will remain, and hopefully all the more wiser and compassionate."

Kell turned the point of his sword down to the ground. He held the quillon, knelt and bowed his head until it touched the hilt. "Great One, upon the life you have restored to me, I swear, I will never again act so unworthy toward you or scorn those in my charge."

"Arise to your duty, *my* captain."

In the heart of Midessex stood Arundine, Council Hall of the Guardians. It was a six-sided domed shrine constructed of white marble, similar to the Temple of Providence. Being well past midnight, bright light filled the entire area in front of Arundine. Armus, Avatar, Wren, Vidar, Kendrick, Virgil and Ridge arrived. Virgil steadied a swaying Ridge.

The ranger's face was pale. "That was hard," he complained.

"You're not recovered enough to dimension travel. However, our fearless leader insisted." Virgil jerked a thumb at Armus.

"I'm simply following Jor'el's instructions. If you have objections take it up with him."

Virgil raised his hand in mock surrender. "Whatever you said, Lieutenant."

Armus cocked a wry grin and led them inside.

Six pillars held up the interior dome. Twelve marble chairs were arranged in a semi-circle and the high chair on an elevated platform. The colored marble of the floor created a map of Allon, naming each province in front of the respective chair. Two lamp stands flanked the front door and kept lit. Moonlight filtered through the six stained glass windows. No one else was there.

"Looks like we're the first to arrive," said Virgil. He aided Ridge to sit in the South Plains chair.

"Did Jor'el give any indication of what this is about?" asked Kendrick.

"No, only to bring all of you to a meeting."

Vidar clapped Armus' shoulder. "Maybe he's decided upon a new captain. We'll need one with the Palace being rebuilt."

"I'm not ready for that. Besides, I assume he would summon all the Trio Leaders for such an announcement, and not just us."

"Might as well get comfortable while we wait for the others and the big decision." Wren sat in her chair of the Southern Forest, nearest to the high chair.

"There won't be any others," spoke a voice from a dark corner near the high chair. He stepped out of the shadows into the moonlight.

Wren rose from her seat, and her eyes grew wide in surprise. She could barely speak his name, "Kell?" Upon her pronouncement, all the lamps sprang to life, illuminating Arundine to reveal Kell. She threw her arms about his neck. "You're alive!"

Avatar, Vidar, Virgil, Kendrick and Ridge were also enthusiastic in greeting Kell. Armus shoved his way through them to engulf Kell in a bear hug, lifting him off his feet.

"Armus!" grunted Kell while trying to catch his breath.

He loosened his tight hold, yet didn't release Kell. "By the heavenlies! What manner of miracle is this? I saw you die!" He battled to contain his emotions.

"I didn't die, at least not then. I had a mission. Upon completion, I was restored."

"What mission? And why wasn't I told? Why scare me out of half my existence?" He punched Kell's shoulder.

259

Kell chuckled and rubbed his shoulder. "I wasn't told about it until after."

"What nonsense are you babbling about? How could you not know?"

"It's a long story so make yourselves comfortable." He motioned to the chairs. "Understand this, once I have completed my tale the memory of what happened to me will be gone from among the mortals and our comrades, yet Kelvin will remain. Only we here will know the truth and the lessons to be learned."

"You *were* Kelvin!" declared Avatar.

"He shape-shifted?" asked Kendrick in confusion.

"Not during battle. I saw him struck down and vanish," said Armus.

"I didn't shape-shift," said Kell.

They ignored him and kept speaking to each other.

"That's how he knew things about us and the mortals," said Vidar.

"And why I kept getting conflicting feelings," said Armus.

"*We* kept sensing an uncanny familiarity," said Avatar.

"How come the rest of us couldn't sense him?" asked Wren.

"Because I was restrained in declaring my identity!" Kell spoke loud enough to get attention.

"Why?" Ridge's simple question silenced the others, and they waited in anticipation of the answer.

Kell took a deep contemplating breath before replying. "Jor'el. During my mission I was fully mortal. As such, I experienced all the emotions, foibles and fragilities we Guardians tend to negate or scorn. The difficulty came when Jor'el restrained me from telling anyone." He grew remorseful. "Imagine hearing reports and personal stories of my death and being unable to say anything to change the situation or bring comfort. I stood helplessly mute."

"Oh, Kell, how awful," said Wren in great sympathy.

He swallowed back his emotion to continue. "Stripped of my powers, yet aware of who I was, and no one recognized me except Fitch and Cody."

"Fitch?" asked Virgil.

"The torn collar happened when I encountered Fitch on the way to the castle. He tried to shape-shift into Kelvin, but couldn't. Despite being a mortal in form, I remained in essence me—Kell. Only when I came face-to-face with evil, could I declare who I was with authority and power. He used the piece of fabric to link me to Spaulding's death."

"That's why you were certain Locan wouldn't leave Oakley, because Fitch told him about you," said Avatar.

"Ay. As a mortal I was vulnerable, yet hoped if Locan and I met, the surge of power I experienced in confronting Fitch would return. It didn't, and that is when I truly died."

"All part of the plan, right?" asked Wren in distress.

Kell shrugged in uncertainty. "I didn't know how or why anything happened until I went as a mortal to be with Jor'el and he told me." His eyes grew misty and he couldn't look at any of them as he continued, "He said I began to display the pride that lead to Dagar's fall. To prevent it from taking root, he resorted to more drastic measures to teach me a lesson, along with answering prayer."

A heavy silence followed the explanation, as each considered the confession and the dire implications. All fought against Dagar, his progeny or machinations, with some suffering great personal pain. Kell managed a glance at Vidar. The archer spent centuries enduring torture and torment in Dagar's nether prison. Vidar stared with intense distress at the floor, and every muscle of his face and body rigid.

"Vidar," began Kell with sober conviction. "You know I would never turn against my comrades."

Pain reflected in the archer's copper eyes along with a hint of hesitation in his answer. "I want to say I know."

Armus bolted to his feet. "You do! We all do." He moved beside the high chair.

Avatar joined Armus. "Indeed! Even as Kelvin he proved himself by defending us to Spaulding and ultimately dying to protect Chad and Ridge."

Kell held Vidar's gaze. The captain's golden eyes filled with unwavering sincerity. "I would rather Jor'el left me as a dead mortal than return if there was the slightly possibility I would betray him, you or any of my comrades."

"Kell being restored shows Jor'el knows there is *no* possibility," said Armus.

Vidar's entire body relaxed and a small smile appeared. "Welcome back, Kell."

He grinned in relief and nudged Armus and Avatar to resume their seats. "I must admit, my time as a mortal was the most difficult, challenging and enlightening experience I've even had. I'm not sure which affected me more profoundly, being transformed into a mortal or dying as one."

"You also mentioned answering a prayer. How?" asked Kendrick.

"Again by way of me." His answer baffled them and he grinned, sheepish. "Having feelings for Vivian and causing friction with Wess was in response to Lester's prayer for their happiness."

"You had feelings for a mortal female?" asked Wren in astonishment.

Abashed, Kell scratched the back of his neck. "I *was* mortal and not always in complete command of my emotions."

Virgil quipped to Wren, "You can say that again."

Avatar laughed. Kendrick and Ridge snickered. Even Armus fought to contain his amusement.

Kell chose to ignore their reactions and continued. "I gained tremendous insight into the complexities of mortal passions and responses."

"How did friction cause happiness?" asked Kendrick.

"Simple," began Avatar in his usual humor. "Male and female mortals who often clash and cause friction end up with married to each other."

Kell laughed. "Oh, do you have a lot to learn about mortal relationships."

"And you did?" asked Wren in merry skepticism.

"Although they tend to clash or even repel, something can be said for kissing."

Thunderstruck, she asked, "What? You experienced a kiss?"

Avatar laughed so hard he could barely catch his breath. Armus, Kendrick, Vidar, Virgil and Ridge also laughed.

This time Kell didn't ignore their amusement. "I'm glad you find humor at my expense, *Lieutenant Avatar.* The feelings of love and companionship compelling mortals are most powerful."

"I'm not laughing at you, *my captain,* rather Wren. She looks so hapless and confused. It's wonderful!"

"Ha, ha," she scoffed.

"How did your feelings help Wess and Vivian?" asked Ridge.

"Wess viewed Kelvin—me—as a rival, which prompted him to confess his long-held feeling for Vivian. Joined with my personal lesson, and after drawing out and disposing of Fitch and Locan, my mission was complete. Or rather the mortal phase."

"So you, Kelvin, died to facilitate you, Kell's return," said Vidar.

"Ay. Like any mortal, I was unaware of the time, place or manner of death. Whereas that ignorance is welcomed, I learned it is important to live with the knowledge that life is fragile and not neglect telling those closest to you how you truly feel. When the time comes and you can't speak, it is agonizing! We hear the mortals say it all time, and usually give them a condescending smile to maintain our façade of aloofness. Oh, we grieve when we lose comrades, but do we tell them while they are among us that we care? That and their welfare is of great personal concern?"

"We know as captain you care for every Guardian," said Ridge.

"Not solely as captain to subordinate. I mean as Kell to Ridge, to Vidar, Virgil, Wren, Kendrick, Avatar and Armus." He looked to each when he spoke their name.

"We care about you too, Kell," said Wren.

"Then take to heart what I've told you and learn from my experience. The time of restoration to our station of governing Allon is near. This is why Jor'el allowed me to speak to all of you. I know I will not see things the same way again when dealing with mortals."

"What about Tyrone? He is our king. What will become of him when we resume our positions of authority?" asked Vidar.

"Tyrone will remain king for as long as he lives. His reign will serve for a transition. The House of Tristan shall take on a different role afterwards."

"I can't see Nigel giving up his position as First Jor'ellian during his lifetime," said Avatar, with a wry grin.

"He won't have too. He is highly favored, and will also play a key role in transition." Kell then spoke to Virgil. "Take Ridge back to Melwynn. He needs rest. Vidar, you, Wren and Kendrick return to Nigel and continue to Waldron. Armus and Avatar will join you shortly while I'll meet you all at Waldron upon arrival."

Nothing was said until the others departed. When alone, Kell wasn't certain of what to say especially the way Armus regarded him, expectant and attentive. "I can't tell you how many I wanted to say something, anything to get you to recognize me! To believe me, trust me. Due to Jor'el's restraint, I couldn't!"

"The vague image you kept encountering," said Avatar.

Armus nodded. "I assumed that earlier when he spoke of restraint. Did you encounter any hindrance during the discussion in Oakley?"

"No, just the sense of uncanny familiarity of Kelvin felt very strong. I didn't push to discover why. Voicing my feelings was hard enough."

"Fortunately, you expressed yourself less violently than I."

Kell gripped Armus' shoulder. "Being helpless to intervene gnawed at me when you confronted Fitch. It's also when I experienced the heaviest hand of restraint. Throughout the ordeal Jor'el kept me from revealing myself, and either of you from discerning the truth of what you sensed. Even if you had, would you believe that I became mortal?"

"Stranger things have happened," said Avatar with a snicker.

Kell looked askew. "Name one?"

Avatar began clicking off incidents on his fingers. "Dagar produced off-spring with a mortal female, not to mention Tyrone's Guardian heritage. Mirit's life restored in Tunlund, Hueil went undetected for centuries masquerading as god; Ellan, a mortal, escaped the nether dimension prison. Need I continue?"

Thwarted, Kell scowled a partial smile. "You made your point, as did Jor'el. I admit it was the strangest and most disconcerting event of my existence."

"Because it was personal, not an unusual occurrence."

"Avatar's right. It's the reason we were prevented from fully discovering the truth about you being Kelvin, and not lack of belief. The whole situation would have changed if we had."

"Ay. If it were me—Kell—there would be no doubt to my veracity or questions of character. All of you were reacting to a stranger. However, understanding the situation didn't make it any easier watching and listening to personal stories about me or expressions of grief." He smiled in relief. "In the end, Jor'el answered my prayer to bring comfort to all of you on my behalf."

Avatar chuckled. "Good, because I didn't want to be second-in-command again. Once with you was enough."

Kell's questioning glance found Armus, who smiled with slight embarrassment.

"Some suggested this meeting was to appoint me as the new captain. A logical choice, though I feel inadequate. I needed a lieutenant and Avatar was my choice."

Kell laughed. In fact, he laughed so hard he sat.

Avatar frowned. "I didn't think my appointment was that funny."

Kell tried calm down enough to speak. "No, I laugh in relief. You shielded Armus the same you did me when we thought him dead. Your actions confirmed what I believed, and relieved a great burden by giving me peace of mind. Now, if my time truly does come, the Guardians will not be without good, strong leadership. Armus is my natural successor, and I always thought of you as his second-in-command, but he had to make the choice with no influence or suggestion from me."

"Oh," said Avatar, humbled by the answer. "I don't know what to say."

"Don't say anything; to the others. This is between the three of us."

"What about Vidar? He made the suggestion."

Kell smiled. "I'll speak to him in private. I'm sure he can keep a confidence. Let the others remain blissfully ignorant."

"Oh, I enjoy keeping Wren off balance," said Avatar with a mischievous smile.

"Not through being a straw target?"

"Those days are gone with what I have in mind."

Kell threw up his hands in mock surrender. "Don't tell me or in my position I might be forced to do something about it beforehand."

"Don't worry, *Captain*," he emphasized the rank, "this is something even you will appreciate, especially after your recent adventure."

Kell cocked a grin. "Good to hear the title again."

"Let's keep it that way. I don't want to go through this again," said Armus.

He laughed. "You and me both. Rejoin Nigel and the others. I'll meet you at Waldron in a few days."

Chapter 18

FOR HALF-A-MILE, TALL STREET LAMPS WITH FIVE OIL VESSELS LINED the wide road leading to Waldron. Mirit, Nigel and Fraser rode side-by-side in approaching the castle.

"Are you going to say anything to Tristine about Ayers?" asked Mirit.

Nigel cocked his head in consideration. "I've been wondering about that. We haven't discussed the matter in years. Tyrone told me how Gareth and Zebulon's involvement with Ellan stirred up bad memories. So much so, she wouldn't even talk to him about it."

"You can hardly blame her. Titus kidnapped, you, Chad and Avatar missing and Tyrone drawn into war. All happened while pregnant with Mikaela. You saw how it affected me, and at the time Titus wasn't my nephew. I felt I had to make up for the trouble I caused. Identifying the traitor was the best way."

"Don't upset yourself again."

"I'm not. I'm concerned for Tristine. If you don't know her heart and mind in the matter, perhaps it's best to err on the side of caution and not mention his identity to her."

"I agree, Uncle. Father and Titus will certainly want to know, but let Mother believe his name was Squire Morley."

"That means everyone in the group must keep the secret."

"We can," said Ellis of himself and Valery. They rode behind the others.

"Guardians are the souls of discretion," said Armus. He walked beside Nigel. "You know I would do nothing to harm to Tristine."

"Then you agree about keeping this from her?"

"Ay. I also advise keeping it from Necie. Daria was born the same night."

Nigel snorted an ironic chuckle. "As if I'd forget. I thought Angus would lose all self-control to get to her and ruin any chance of catching Loran by revealing our return before springing the trap."

"Mahon kept him shielded so it all worked out," said Avatar, grinning. He walked on the other side of the group.

"I remember," said Fraser in recollection.

"You were only five," said Nigel with some skepticism.

"I admit, I didn't know much since Kendrick and Skylar kept us safe. I recall Mother often being upset. Oh, she tried not to show it around us, still, I could tell. I knew Father and Titus were gone and you went off to do something. The whole time didn't feel right until everyone was back together."

"I think you have your answer," said Mirit

"I'll find a way to tell Tyrone, Titus and Angus privately."

"You'll have to write and inform Wess and Chad."

"Later. Right now, it's good to be home." Nigel smiled as they approached the gate.

Twilight faded and the lamplight in the royal garden grew stronger. The younger children played a game of chase and tag with Tyrone, Titus, Eli and Angus. Necie and Tristine sat on a bench trying to contain a squirming Mikaela. She wanted to participate.

When Arlen, Spencer and Galen managed to grab Tyrone's pant legs, Angus aided their effort in capturing him. All tumbled to the ground. Mikaela broke loose from her mother and ran to climb on top of the pile. She giggled in triumph.

"I yield!" said Tyrone, laughing. "Now let a man breathe." Angus and Titus lifted the boys off him. Eli went to take Mikaela, when she balked and held onto Tyrone. He waved off Eli then stood and picked her up.

Kell entered the garden.

"That was a short visit to the heavenlies. Is everything all right that you're back so quickly?"

"Ay, Sire."

"Titus' wedding is next week. Kell wouldn't miss it," said Angus.

Titus turned bright red with nervous excitement, which made Tyrone laugh.

Kell grinned at the exchange. "Also, Prince Nigel and the others have returned." He motioned to Nigel and his retinue at the garden entrance.

Cody trotted alongside Valery. Upon sight of Kell, the wolf ran and jumped up to place his front paws on Kell. Cody braked and wagged his tail in a most enthusiastic greeting.

Kell widely smiled and ruffled the wolf's head between his hands. "Good boy, Cody."

"Well, he's happy to see you," said Tyrone.

"Cody, down," said Valery, a bit abashed. "I'm sorry, Captain, he's usually not so energetic in greeting people. He didn't hurt you, did he?"

Kell chuckled. "No."

The focus went to the group and Tyrone inquired, "I take it all went well in the South Plains?"

"Indeed," said Nigel. "Locan and Fitch are finally dealt with per your instructions, Captain. Sorry you missed the fun."

Kell simply smiled.

"Ay, a merry chase at times. If it wasn't for Cody, Ellis might not be standing here," said Fraser. He tossed a smile and wink at Titus, to which Ellis frowned.

The reaction intrigued Titus. "How so?"

"Fitch temporary took his place."

"And tried to take liberties with my wife," said Ellis.

"What?" asked Tristine in surprise.

"Nothing happened, Majesty," said Valery in quick reassurance. "I knew it wasn't Ellis by his gruff manner." That didn't ease Tristine's concern, so she added, "I mean speech—nothing more."

"I jest about the liberties," said Ellis with color rising to his cheeks.

"You need practice on your humorous delivery," said Tyrone with a chuckle.

"I'm open to any suggestions you can offer, Sire."

Armus interrupted the banter. "Unfortunately, there is tragic news. Sheriff Spaulding was killed."

"How is that tragic? He was as bad as Gareth," said Angus.

"All death is tragic, no matter how the mortal lived." Armus snatched a glance at Kell. The captain listened with a cordial expression and made a short, private nod to Armus. No mortal noticed the brief exchange.

"And Kelvin. He died too," said Mirit.

"Who is Kelvin?" asked Tyrone.

"A unique man who became caught up in events when Fitch and Locan tried to use him as a scapegoat to cover their activities," replied Nigel. He flashed an ironic grin. "They had no idea they picked the wrong man to try and use."

"He is dead as a result?"

"He died saving Chad and Ridge from Locan."

"Where is Chad?" asked Tristine, anxiously looking among the group.

Avatar replied. "I took him home for recovery. His leg became pinned under a dead horse. It's badly bruised and a twisted ankle but nothing broken. He should be fine in time for the wedding."

"Dead horse? What about Ridge?" asked Tyrone, growing annoyed by the report.

"Ridge suffered a head injury and abdominal wound. I took him to Melwynn. Eldric says he'll recover," said Virgil.

"Sounds like this Kelvin did a great service," said Angus.

"He did," said Nigel.

"What about his family?" asked Tyrone.

"As far as we know, he had none."

"He did bring a couple together," said Mirit. She smiled at Nigel.

Tyrone became curious. "Did you two have a falling out?"

"When she tried to find a naked man behind a bush," Virgil spoke sideways to Mahon. The latter bit his lip to keep from laughing.

Tyrone overheard. "What?" he asked with a suppressed snicker.

"Ignore Virgil's base humor, Sire. He's been around Avatar too long," said Wren.

Virgil feigned a strike in the chest. "Two straw targets in one shot."

Avatar slyly smiled at Wren.

Nigel laughed and shook his head at Tyrone. "That's how Kelvin was originally found, injured after being attacked."

"Found by Mirit?" asked Tyrone.

"No, Vivian. You remember her—Doctor Lester's sister."

"Ellis and Valery must be the couple. Not enough rest," said Angus.

Valery blushed with embarrassment. "No, Your Grace."

Nigel again laughed. "No, Wess and Vivian. We stayed a couple of extra days to witness their wedding."

"Wess remarried?" said Tristine in pleasant surprise.

"Isn't that rather fast for a wedding?" asked Necie.

"Wess isn't getting any younger," said Nigel.

Tristine gave him a friendly slap on the arm. "You're mean to tease him in his absence."

"I said so to his face. He deserves some happiness. Besides, he and Vivian have known each other for years, so not a whirlwind romance."

"Age doesn't matter with *romance* in the air for another upcoming wedding." Angus winked at Titus.

Again, Titus flushed with embarrassment.

"Looks like you're getting a reprieve with the newlywed humor finding another target," said Nigel to Ellis.

Ellis laughed until Valery poked him in the ribs. He quickly amended his attitude. "On my sister's behalf, I shall refrain from partaking."

"I'll make up the difference with double doses of teasing, right, cousin?" Fraser smiled widely at Valery.

"Ay," she said, struggling not to laugh.

Tristine took pity on her eldest son and came to his aid. "We're glad all of you are back in time since we leave in two days for the Temple."

"We'd hardly miss it," said Nigel with a suppressed chuckle. At Tristine's glare of mild rebuke, his altered to a cordial yet decisive tone. "For now, you and Necie take the children to begin preparations for departure, we'll be along shortly." She looked a bit curious at his abrupt change, so he added with a kind smile, "Please, we won't be long."

"Of course. Jade," she called the female Guardian warrior.

Jade took Mikaela from Tyrone. Tristine and Neice, Skylar and Mahon, gathered the other children and headed for the main building.

Nigel sent a discreet signal to Angus, Titus and Eli to remain. He waited to speak until the others were inside. "I didn't want to say this in front of Tristine and Necie and possibly upset them."

The statement made Tyrone wary. "What?"

"Fitch and Locan caused trouble in the province to their advantage. However, the leader of the gang of thieves went by the alias Squire Morley. In actually, it was Ayers."

Tyrone first appeared stunned then concerned for Titus. His eldest looked dumbfounded yet managed to speak in the form of a question.

"Ayers? How is that possible?" asked Tyrone.

"He said Zebulon forced him and his family to join him in exile. As a result, he lost all his holdings and driven to poverty. His wife and daughter died, leaving him and his sons to fend for themselves. Disgraced, he assumed the name of Morley."

"He told you this?"

Nigel nodded. "In exchange for helping a son who was injured by Cody when freeing Ellis after being kidnapped for Fitch's use. Ayers confessed about Fitch, Locan and Spaulding."

"The sheriff?" asked Angus.

"Before Fitch and Locan arrived, Spaulding blackmailed Ayers for a share of the profit from his sons' thieving enterprise. When Ayers refused, Spaulding began arresting their accomplices to intimidate them into cooperating."

"He used Ellis to facilitate this?" asked Angus, a bit confused.

"No, Fitch became me after Spaulding was murdered and they tried to blame Kelvin," said Ellis.

"Murdered?" echoed Tyrone.

"The boys tried to protect their father when Spaulding escaped while Fitch was still impersonating the sheriff," said Valery.

"I recognized Loran's voice and signet ring as the instigator of the kidnapping, not Ayers," said Mirit with insistence to Tyrone.

"I know you did. However, this is getting confusing. Blackmail, murder, aliases." Tyrone confronted Nigel. "I thought you said all went well in the South Plains?"

"It did. All is resolved. Fitch and Locan are dealt with."

"What happened to Ayers and his sons?" asked Titus.

"The son wounded by Cody died. The other was killed by Locan."

"Ayers died while volunteering as bait," said Mirit, in a level voice.

"Bait? As in a trap?" asked Tyrone.

"A mutual one by us and Locan," said Nigel. At Tyrone's displeasure, he added, "Needless to say there are more details to be filled in."

"That's an understatement! You said he died voluntarily."

Armus intervened. "No, Sire. By his own confession, Ayers and his sons were responsible for murder and thievery. Murder carries a death sentence. His volunteering didn't change what they had done."

"It might have mitigated his punishment to life in prison."

"In the eyes of mortal law. However, Jor'el is the ultimate judge."

"Remember, Kell relayed Jor'el's instructions to stop Fitch and Locan," said Nigel. When Tyrone scowled at the counter argument, he gripped Tyrone's arm. "All is resolved, perhaps not to our satisfaction, but as Armus said, Jor'el is responsible for ultimate justice. The South Plains is finally calm and the last traitors dealt with."

"You suggested the hunt for rest and relaxation, Sire," said Kell.

For a moment, Tyrone regarded the captain. "I did at that."

"Then do as you propose, and leave everything in the past. There is a future to celebrate." Kell's glance passed to Titus.

"Ay," said Tyrone with a large smile. "I would have enjoyed seeing Wess remarry."

Nigel laughed. "Oh, it was enjoyable!"

"You mean teasing him," said Mirit. He rakishly smiled and she continued. "At least with Wess you have hopes of succeeding." She tossed a prompting side-glance at Tyrone and Angus.

"I think there's an amusing story we need to discover," said Angus.

Ellis huffed and rolled his eyes.

Titus smiled. "Somehow I don't think the story involves Uncle."

Nigel laughed. "I'm not involved at all." He tugged on Tyrone's arm to begin moving toward the main building. "Yet I will relish the telling." Angus, Titus and Eli came alongside as he started to speak. Valery and Fraser added a few details.

Chapter 19

THE SUN SHONE DOWN UPON THE TEMPLE, AS THE BRIGHT AND beautiful late spring day greeted all who gathered to celebrate Prince Titus and Lady Jillian's wedding. The white marble Temple shone with extra brilliance while the stained glass windows displayed a kaleidoscope of dazzling colors.

Dressed in his formal Guardian Captain's uniform, Kell stood beside the main gate of The Fortress observing the festivities. Tents and booths lined the Temple plain. All the pomp and circumstance of priests and nobility from each province was on vivid display. Royal weddings were always a cause for making merry. Now joined with the laying of the Great Cornerstone for Jor'el's Palace, brought an exuberance Kell had not experienced in centuries.

Had it really been six hundred years since the Great Battle? The last century passed in a flurry of activity. It began with Niles escaping a coup meant to destroy the House of Tristan. He saved Akilles and preserved the royal lineage. Then came the births of Ellis and Shannan, which signaled the coming battle to take back the kingdom for Jor'el and restore the Guardians to Allon. The victory against Dagar started the cleansing of the Dark Way, which only recently ended. Ellan's first coup attempt led to the discovery of the Great King as a half-breed blacksmith living in obscurity, and all that came since in Tunlund, Soren and Natan.

So many memories flooded Kell's mind, memories of adventures, trials, victories and tragedies from that fateful day of the Great Battle until now. Names and faces of Guardians and mortals connected to those events accompanied those memories. This is what everything led to, this day, and this final victory. A day he almost didn't live to see.

"But I have. Thank you, Jor'el," he spoke in heartfelt gratitude.

A wide, happy smile appeared as he looked toward the original site of Jor'el's Palace. Guardian warriors dressed in white uniforms and polished sliver breastplates stood watch around the area prepared for the cornerstone. Royal guards joined the Guardians at their posts. On a small platform built for it, two large pieces of stone block rested. Some faded Ancient writing was carved into the stone face, divided by the crack that created the two pieces. When placed together, the stone measured six feet long by four feet wide and three feet high. A hole was dug in the ground behind the stone block. The massive crowd waited for the arrival of the royal family and the Vicar.

From the battlement of The Fortress, trumpets sounded in clear unison, announcing the time for attention. The procession emerged from The Fortress, including the royal family, ranking Guardians, the Vicar and his attendants. No expense was spared in the finery of clothes and accessories. Regally adorned and crowned, Tyrone and Tristine walked in the lead with Armus as escort. Kell fell in step beside Uriah, who came directly behind the King and Queen. Uriah wore his finest high priestly robes. Behind them came Titus and his bride, Jillian, wearing her stunning wedding gown complete with veil. She would not reveal her face until after wedding. Egan accompanied his charge. Nigel, Mirit and Avatar followed the young couple, all arrayed in their ceremonial uniforms. The remainder of the royal family followed with the Guardians Mahon, Skylar, Jade, Virgil, Kendrick, and healed Ridge bringing up the rear of the procession.

The crowd greeted the stately parade with enthusiastic applause and cheers. The trumpets continued to sound until the entire procession reached the cornerstone area. When the trumpets ceased, Uriah raised his hands and summoned the crowd for silence and to give heed. When he had their attention, he spoke.

"This is the blessed day. A day long awaited, when the final subduing of the enemy has been achieved."

Rousing cheers interrupted the Vicar. He let them have a moment of jubilation before calling for attention.

"This day, we celebrate a time foretold in Prophecy with much rejoicing, yet also some sadness for those who gave the ultimate in sacrificing their lives for this end, both mortals and Guardians. Let us take a moment of silence to remember them."

The sober moment passed and Uriah continued.

"The pieces that were broken so long ago will now be rejoined, and it is fitting to be done so by Captain Kell."

Kell stepped up to the stone. He caught sight of Wess and Vivian in the crowd. He felt a twinge of regret and let his gaze swiftly pass from them. He held no lingering feelings for Vivian, rather regretted the fact that they would never know how grateful he was to them for what he learned during his time as a mortal. His brief pause went unnoticed, save for Armus and Avatar. To their curiosity, he simply smiled then started speaking to the crowd.

"Today brings a joy I cannot adequately express, for I saw the Palace when it was first built over two millennia ago then destroyed in the Great Battle, now to see it raise again." He paused due to emotions of the past. "I did not witness all this alone, thus I do not rejoin the stone alone. Jor'el created us to work together as the High Trio in defense of Allon, so now, we come together to repair the stone." He nodded to Armus and Avatar.

Armus and Avatar moved to stand on the opposite sides of the stone with Kell taking up position at the rear, leaving the front visible to the crowd. Drawing their swords, they held the tips on top of the stone. In unison, they spoke the Ancient. *"Dat Jor'el's cumhachd bi lesaich!"*

Immediately, lightning from heaven stuck each sword at the pommel, funneled down the blades and began fusing the stone together at the crack. The process continued for several moments and ended with a bright burst of light that startled the mortals. When the light faded, the stone was in one piece with no sign of a crack with the Ancient writing clearly visible. Excited applause erupted from the crowd.

Avatar widely smiled with great delight and satisfaction. Armus mirrored Avatar's joy. Kell briefly closed his eyes in grateful relief and also smiled.

Uriah raised his hand for silence. It took a moment before the applause ceased. "Now, the King will join in placing the cornerstone."

Tyrone stepped around to the front of the stone. The Guardians sheathed their swords and made ready to lift the stone. *"Bho neart gu neart!"* said Kell, Armus and Avatar together.

They bore the brunt of the weight, with Tyrone merely lending a hand in moving the stone from the platform to the prepared hole. Once the stone was in place, a royal guard handed Tyrone a golden shovel.

"Although I am the Great King of Prophecy, those who came before me, the Son of Tristan and the Daughter of Allon, are responsible for the restoration of the Guardians and defending the honor of Jor'el." He smiled in looking at his wife and her siblings. "It is only right that their children be the first to partake in the rebuilding." With one hand he beckoned them and with other, held out the shovel.

Nigel escorted his sisters forward. He took the shovel from Tyrone. "In honor of our parent's memory, we so partake." He used the shovel to pick up some dirt and placed it in the hole. He passed the shovel to Tristine, who mimicked his action. Tristine gave it to Necie. With tears in her eyes, Necie placed a shovel full of dirt in the hole.

Tyrone gave Necie a quick hug about the shoulders before he took the shovel and did his ceremonial shovel of dirt. "Each member of the Council will now have a turn, and once that done," he paused with large proud smile at Titus, "it is onto the wedding!"

When the laying of the cornerstone was completed, the crowd eagerly followed the royal family to the Temple. Once the King, Queen and family members positioned, the Guardians and royal soldiers allowed the nobility and others to fill the Temple. People crammed into every inch of space to view the wedding.

Beautiful in its simplicity, the ceremony proceeded. Normally self-assured, Titus couldn't hide his nervous excitement, nor could he take his eyes off Jillian. They spoke the words as instructed. When Uriah made the official pronouncement, Titus lifted the veil to reveal his bride and kissed her. The Temple erupted in cheering. The exuberance of the

SHAWN LAMB

crowd and family ushered the newlyweds from The Temple to The Fortress for a night of feasting.

The Guardians lingered while the mortals filed out of The Temple. Kell's gaze met that of Wess and Vivian as they departed. Earlier they had not made eye contact. Of course, neither mortal knew the truth, and it showed in their innocent smiles at him. He returned their smile with a nod of acknowledgement. They were among the last of the mortals to leave, so his gaze shifted to the altar.

Words seemed inadequate at that moment. Only a few days ago, he feared he would not see this day in his original state, as Captain of the Guardian. He thought to witness it as a mortal. Then came death, unexpected and final. How close he came to losing everything! The pain of that thought made Kell lower his head to gather his emotions. Startled, he flinched when a hand gripped his shoulder. Armus. He, Avatar, Ridge, Virgil, Vidar and Wren had moved closer.

"Are you upset at seeing Wess and Vivian again?" asked Armus.

"No, I was struck by the thought of almost missing this day. A day we all fought hard to bring about." He quickly quelled his discomfort to smile with genuine happiness. "As for Wess and Vivian, he can give her what *another* could not, complete and unhindered commitment. I'm very glad for them."

Wren leaned closer and spoke discreetly. "You admitted to kissing a female and liking it."

Kell gave her a large roguish smile then sent a side-glance to Avatar as moved from the altar and left The Temple.

She became wary in watching Kell leave and accosted Avatar. "Why did he look at me like that and then turn to you?"

Avatar wore one of his impish grins. "He knows what causes attraction between mortal males and females."

"Oh, and he told you?"

"Demure, quiet, not given to fits of physical temper."

She made a laughing scoff at the answer. "In other words, someone to stroke the male ego."

"Then again," Avatar's tone softened and he leaned towards her face. "Brashness and a quick wit can be very appealing." He kissed her on the lips, making her speechless and flushed. He straightened and heaved a

277

nonchalant shrug. "Then again, I'm not a mortal male and resistant to such feelings." He moved to leave.

"The straw target disarmed the archer!" said Virgil in smiling triumph to Wren. He, Vidar, Ridge and Armus laughed and they followed Avatar.

Incredulous with embarrassment, she lashed out. "See if I ever save your conceited hide again!"

Avatar partial turned to respond. "How? You're out of arrows for this target." He laughed and continued on his way.

Her scowl turned into a mischievous smile. "I'll find a new weapon." She vanished.

Explore the Kingdom of Allon

www.allonbooks.com

Featuring:

- Read excerpts of Allon books
- Original Character Art
- Interactive Map of Allon
- News and Events
- Photo and Video Gallery
- Links to:
  - o Facebook - The Kingdom of Allon Page
  - o Contact Shawn Lamb